Slipfinger Ni

About the Cover

As a young lad of five years, I stood there, transfixed, in the hallway of my grandmother's home in Newton, Massachusetts. The oil on canvas held me in its sticky grip, pulling me into its frothy seas, beckoning me to come aboard and feel the bellowing winds blow through my toe head curls. For my grandmother, the work of art was the result of her passion for creation; for me, it was a window into some other time, an adventure to be had.

Fast forward to fifty-five years later when, after years of my own passion had been poured out onto the page and I was searching for a proper cover that would not only be the final ribbon on the package, but something apropos and meaningful...alas! I was blasted backward through time and space to that hallway yet again, only this time it was in my own home. There it was, Dorothy M. Heath's 1927 painting of a vessel pitching on the high seas, gunning towards greatness, while barely outrunning the foreboding dark clouds of a secret, waiting to be discovered.

Slipfinger Nine

Jason Douglass

Aardvark Press

Jason Douglass

****

Copyright © 2009, 2015 Jason Douglass, Aardvark Publishing
All rights reserved.

ISBN-10: 0986384305
ISBN-13: 978-0-9863843-0-1

The characters, names, and events as well as all places, incidents, organizations, and dialog in this novel are either the products of the writer's imagination or are used fictitiously.

First Printing: 2015. The editorial arrangement, analysis, and professional commentary are subject to this copyright notice. No portion of this book may be copied, retransmitted, reposted, duplicated, or otherwise used without the express written approval of the author, except by reviewers who may quote brief excerpts in connection with a review.

United States laws and regulations are public domain and not subject to copyright. Any unauthorized copying, reproduction, translation, or distribution of any part of this material without permission by the author is prohibited and against the law.

To learn more about this and other works by the author, friend Jason Douglass on Facebook.

****

In Memory of

Nash Bradford Beever
01/11/97 – 01/28/14

You always believed.

Jason Douglass

Acknowledgements

    I would like to thank my wife and soul-mate for weathering the rough seas and never abandoning ship. You are my North Star.
    And I would like to blame my oldest son for getting me into this mess. Although to his credit, he did go a considerable way towards working off his debt, offering invaluable critique and moral support. His diligence and perseverance stayed the course throughout eight years of testy moments and loving conflicts, all bitter sweet.

    The story within all of us would offer limitless diversion from the ugly realities of current events that bombard the senses twenty-four-seven. If only our seemingly fathomless technological advances included a gadget that hotwired our mind's eye, your story already indelible and processed from beginning to end, and one could just flip a switch for download. If only it was that easy.
    Every one of us shares a commonality: What is my purpose? Why am I here? Where the heck is it that I'm going? Dreamers, schemers...pro-active, reactive...the journey we all take IS the thrill of the ride, although the destination somewhat anticlimactic. Skeleton closets,

demons and seraphs, bad luck and good fortune earned or just damn lucky, we are all held captive on the same rollercoaster: two minutes of exhilaration and fear that is seemingly endless. Return to the station, and just like life, as you grow older and reach those ten-year milestones...it's but a *blink of an eye.*

    I wish I could say a wise man's sage advice guided me through to this juncture, but rather the recommendations I most adhered to were courtesy of a baseball legend, whose malapropisms and zany nonsensical quotes do not quite fit the bill as 'wise'...I thank you Yogi Berra. "When you arrive at a fork in the road, take it." That pretty much sums up the playbook handed to me when self-imposed exile sent me packing off to the school of higher learning called LIFE in the real world. Such guidance was flawed when one fork led to another and then another, followed by even more options decided by a coin flip. I had not brought along enough twine to retrace my steps, but in retrospect the past is something better left where it belongs...yesteryear. The consummate explorer with a thirst for wanderlust, and taking full credit for my own actions, I more often than not would sink myself waste deep in the unmentionable...*how the heck did I come out smelling like a rose*...I give full credit to The Man, the unseen, which validates my faith. Luck? Fate? Perhaps. But if a cat has nine lives, I sit here recapping misadventures resulting in numerous potentially terminal outcomes: wicked bad accidents, illnesses which only ICU saved me from in order to live another day. *OMG, I'm living my eleventh!* Was it worth it, you bet it was! Not one day is taken for granted. Friends and family are cherished, for without them, I may very well not be sitting here jabbing at this damned keyboard.

Forty years (a lifetime) ago a twenty year old embarked on an impromptu, self-imposed odyssey in search for that elusive pot of gold. No, the quest was not seeking fame or fortune, but rather purpose and meaning...sanity in a life SO convoluted. The road traveled, with all its twists, turns, and dag-blasted **FORKS,** has after all these years led me to the mother of no-brainer conclusions: family, close friends, inner peace, and health is the chalice we all should endeavor to realize.

Peace to all. Enjoy the trip.

Jason Douglass

Slipfinger Nine

Jason Douglass

PROLOGUE

The Boogieman Cold War. Demonstrations. Riots. Vietnam. Civil Rights. Hippies. Long hair. Rock and Roll. Free love and communes. Bra burnings. A generation subjected to a cornucopia of drugs...call it "Manhattan Project II." Timothy Leary played Pied Piper. Fathers disowned sons; sons flicked-off fathers. Abbie Hoffman and the Chicago Seven. Bobby Seale, Black Panthers, and the SDS. Tricky Dick's demise, thanks to Plumbers gone awry at a place called Watergate. Chairman Mao and Che Guevara suitable as poster boys. Woodstock beyond imaginable. Hells Angels laying down the law at a Stones concert painted black juxtaposed against the idea that OUR generation had a "peace-love" exclusive. Experienced Jimi Hendrix checked-out prematurely as did the Lizard King, Jim Morrison. When Janis Joplin followed suit, I wondered if there was a conspiracy against Christian names beginning with the letter 'J'. To this day I regret a premature thought: *jeez who's next, John Lennon?* Only later on did I make the connection to the fact that I gave my firstborn a 'J-name'. Doing my part to replenish?

  I am struck by the ghostly image of Armstrong taking that one small step for the rest of us while The Beatles were kind enough to take us down to strawberry fields where nothing was real. And let us not forget The Who admonishing the older generation to just fa-fa-fade away cuz they don't dig what we all say. Watts rioted while Detroit burned in panic. Bobby Kennedy joined his older brother. Martin Luther had already entered the Kingdom.

The end of the sixties and dawn of the seventies was a period of sensory overload that changed a generation for better or worse. We were lab rats, volunteers who saddled up for one hell of a wild ride. We did it all and then wondered, wide-eyed, at what we did.

CHAPTER ONE

The slow, rhythmic creak and groan of stressed wood rocked in time to the piles' gentle sway as water lapped the hull. A soothing harmony was conducted by an unseen moon: deliberate cadence of tidal ebb and flow evidenced by the slip's water level rising and lowering marginally in unison. The sensation of motion was negated by the sheer size of the schooner, allowing those below to sleep unmoved, serenaded by the faint, unconscious lullaby.

An occasional thump, rattle of chain, and crank of a winch indicated the vessel was coming to life. Cacophonous screeches of distant seagulls and the sun pouring in over eastern bluffs of Long Bay inducted a new day in paradise not to be denied.

"Rise and shine lads!"

The rapid clangity-clang of ladle to cast iron pan was the old man's marquee wakeup call, and it never failed to provide a rude awakening from dreamy pleasures. Such impropriety was often a surefire way to start the day on an uneven keel. The aging curmudgeon admittedly enjoyed it...his recipients, not in the least. As quick as the incursion invaded their rest, it was gone again, all quiet, the retreat a response to a faint call for assistance up on deck.

The deadheads' stubborn return to slumber, vain attempts to revive fading dreams frustrated, was an insubordination that was short-lived. What seemed like an hour's reprieve was merely minutes of worn out patience. The problem would be resolved, as the 'rooster' returned, fortified, and not to be denied. The air horn's piercing blast was the decisive blow. No one needed further prodding.

"Gonna get up sometime today, ya stiff pricks?"

Even at eighteen, Stuart seemed to have a chip on his shoulder and a pole up his ass. Coffee in hand and leaning against the hatchway, his striking resemblance to the old man and the fact he was firstborn, gave the cocksure lad 'heir apparent' status and he flaunted it with reckless abandon.

Rick, on the other hand, the younger of the two Blaine boys only by a year, was a more steady and convivial character. Among his mates in training, he was regarded as levelheaded, reasonable, and a pleasure to be around; the brothers presented a stark contrast in disposition and in the way they asserted authority. Everyone preferred Rick to be the skipper in charge, everyone except Artimus, Stuart's right hand man. Loyal in friendship and a wingman with a diabolical mindset, his complement to the elder Blaine made for a Machiavellian duo subject to interpretation. Still, the five boys got along quite well and enjoyed the annual summer sailing trip together. It was a chance to bond with fathers and each other. In those weeks at sea each summer, they would hone their sailing skills to a sharp point and their sharp wit to a razor's edge. These were times of adventure and mystery, of challenge and testing boundaries, and over the course of a few short years, boys grew into young men.

"Just go in there man, she'll take REAL good care of you."

Slipfinger Nine

David suffered his friends' goading, working up the courage to enter the knocking house. The last holdout to innocence lost, it was high time he once and for all put to bed his peers' incessant innuendos regarding his manhood. Emerging from the shadows of the corner bar, the bumpy cobblestone street exacerbated his wobbly knees as he closed the distance to the unassuming row house. It was not fear that gripped him, but rather the anticipation of solving a great mystery that quivered his being.

The virgin was greeted at the door by Maria, a lovely, full figured woman who had initiated the other boys' rites-of-passage as well. Her reassuring smile and soft, supple breasts that were enticingly exposed and so alluring made it dreamlike to take her extended hand. As they ascended the steps, Maria shot a reassuring wink over her shoulder to the huddled boys across the street. Stuart nodded and raised his beer in return.

"He's gonna be just fine." Artimus was certain of it, as he inhaled deeply from the tightly rolled joint and then passed it off.

The receiver, a local, toked the offer down to a nub. The last gasp held long and dear, his teeth bore a grin from ear to ear. In the shadows, the contrast between his pearly whites and his dark complexion made for an amusing sight; a metamorphic animation partially induced. For the longest time, Rick stared at the smiley face waiting to see if it was real or plasticized, the matter becoming a waiting game to see which happened first: exhalation or facial twitch. It was a tie, as smoke billowed out of a relaxed mouth forming a lippy 'O'.

"Mon, you Americans crack me up. I juz really have so much fun with you...always sure 'nuff miss you guys."

Rick patted their friend on the shoulder and declared; "We shall return." MacArthur's pluralized quote did not register.

The friendship that had been founded years prior had become kindred and brotherly, and most recently took on an enterprising nature. The avant-garde opportunist had been chumming the waters with wild proposals of high risk and high reward. Lured to the bait, hook set, the Blaine Brothers were reeled in.

"Ah hell, what are we doing just standing around for? Let's have one more round while we wait. He'll probably be done and back before we get served up." Laughter enveloped Stuart as he led the way back into the bar and subsequent one-liners followed, all at David's expense.

The considerable length of the majestic ship sliced with purpose through the cool Atlantic waters on a northwest course, a constant strong wind spiriting them homeward bound. They were moving at a good clip and would be able to operate a skeleton crew throughout the night and still make splendid progress. The sinking, golden sun tried against hope to assert its warm rays on the bare backs of the crew as the day's activities winded down.

"Man that line!" A determined Captain Blaine called out from the helm. "These sails won't unfurl themselves!"

Up in years, the landlubber was slowing down noticeably, yet once on the water the old man's rejuvenation seemed to quantify something Ponce De Leon never realized. It was as if he drew up a life source out of the depths, infusing it directly into his mortal soul. He WAS the vessel riding the sea onward, unbounded. Confident in ship, confident in self, it was utmost respect for nature's final say that brought good fortune and never failed a safe return trip home.

The mighty ship dipped into a trough and then heaved forward over a crest, throwing a wall of seawater onboard, soaking everyone.

"Hah-ah!" The captain now stood taller, breathed deep, and panned around as if surveying all he owned.

The Blaine boys, drenched, looked at each other in disbelief having been nearly washed overboard.

Stuart turned his attention to the helm while addressing his brother, "Look at him. He's in his element."

"Pops hasn't shown such gusto in months", Rick agreed. "It's good to see him like this."

"Let's get the rest of these ropes tied off," Stuart focused.

Rick tied off the hitch without much thought, the memory of muscles in his hands doing the work. "You really think we're ready to command this ship ourselves?"

"We will be, when the time comes."

Night had fallen. The boys not on watch settled down with bedrolls on the foredeck as they often did when weather was agreeable; a quiet reward after another arduous shift. Recapping the day and forging rudimentary plans for a time that would one day come, they lay there taking in the brilliance of stars in the southern sky.

Stuart drifted off. The third mate was already in slumber leaving Artimus to whisper to the wind, "Clouds moving in." One by one he watched the stars fade to black...

*   *   *

1970. South Central New Hampshire....

    Life at Dysfunction Junction came to a dramatic close for the nineteen year-old college boy, well aware of Uncle Sam's keen interest in his services. Like so many of his peers, higher education meant nothing more than a stall tactic, a 'get out of war free' pass. A dozen years of trying to guide a ship through turbulent waters, his parents, each consumed by alcoholic demons, had long since ceased to be the captains of their family's fate. They were on a ship with no rudder, caught in a vortex whirlpool and the only thing oldest son and younger brother and sister could do was to don the life preservers and declare it was every man for themselves.

    Will's meltdown with his twisted, abusive father reached the boiling point that Friday afternoon. Once again the old man came home from a week on the road, drunk and ready to do battle with his already plastered wife. Sister, brother, and mother froze in timeless incredulity as Will, mesmerized, turned from the kitchen drawer and moved in on his father. Brandishing a ten-inch butcher knife, he backed the monster up against the dining room wall and stuck the tip of the blade just below the sternum.

A small patch of blood began to streak down the white dress shirt.

"Leave right now or I'll gut you on the spot."

They were inches from each other's faces. The crazed, yet unflinching madness in Will's eyes was such that even though the King was inebriated, he knew his time had come.

Without packing or saying a word, he allowed Will to escort him out the door, his son's hand on his shoulder and the cold steel prodding the middle of his back.

The look on Will's face as he kissed his sister and brother goodbye was of someone desperately trying to suppress a grin. Will's thoughts turned to the fairy tale sitcoms of Leave It To Beaver, My Three Sons, and the Ozzie and Harriet Show. *What the hell was supposed to be normal?*, he thought as he exited the house into the early winter's bite.

"Get me the hell outta' here Johnny. I don't think I'll be making this trip much anymore," sighed the disheveled and thoroughly pissed off young man. "I've got to get some wheels soon, this bumming rides up and down the interstate is getting old fast."

Pulling his 1968 Volkswagen Van out of the neighborhood for the ten-mile drive to interstate 93, John looked over at his childhood friend and wondered to himself what kind of ugly situation went down this time, precipitating yet another hasty retreat to the safe confines of college in the north woods.

Jason Douglass

"Hey man, you okay? I'd give you a ride to Concord, but dude, I'm behind schedule and need to get back to the U myself."

UNH was in Durham, in southeastern New Hampshire, their schools located at opposite sides of the state.

There was no response. A deliberate, hardening, far away gaze had set in on his old friend. John took this as a cue to crank up the radio to Chicago's "25 or 6 To 4". Without missing a beat, air-drum his steering wheel nearly through the dash.

Up ahead, the exit ramp came into view and John shifted down while his shotgun pal unceremoniously gathered his knapsack, put on his shades, and zipped up his fatigues parka. He lit up the smoke before the van came to a halt, the passenger door ajar with one foot ready for touch down.

"See ya, Johnny. I'll look you up after semester finals." With a quick handshake he was out the door, the van never having come to a complete stop.

Will Bradford inhaled deeply, crisp air filtering through the gray and crimson slate of winter's woods. The wind, a bitter reminder of an inevitable onslaught, was actually a blessed relief. It seemed to blow his mind free from the continuous replay of the touching moment where father and son bonded for the last time. Adjusting his pack, he gazed down the steep grade of the entry ramp trying to regain some sort of perspective after the maddening episode back home. His eyes followed I-93 north up the gradual incline that sixty miles later would put him well into White Mountain National Forest. Needing only the saving grace of a single, benevolent motorist, refuge would be found at the quaint state college of Plymouth. A blast of north wind kicked up road sand and rudely etched his face. Pivoting his back to the wind, he cupped a Marlboro and kept the Zippo lit until he could feel his hands. He glanced back over his shoulder at the ominous storm clouds approaching in the distance. "Thanks a lot, Canada." The sound of a rumbling freightliner turned him around just in time to avoid another sand-blasting facial.

He made his way down the ramp, surveying the situation. Five hours of daylight to negotiate a one-hour drive. *Damn. I sure hope there's some sympathy on the freeway today.*

There are certain rules and etiquette concerning the art of thumbing a ride. One is to present a sign showing your destination. It is somewhat less intimidating to travelers when they can see a stranger's intent. Will struck out on that one, considering the fact that his departure was more of an emergency evacuation than a planned retreat. Second was to always keep on the move, preferably walking backwards so the driver can see your face. Seeing that you are at least making an effort to get from point A to point B sometimes strikes a chord of pity, especially when the weather is not cooperating. Third, and most important, never turn your back on Volkswagens! They almost always save the day.

Anyone portraying the look of a longhaired, noble-faired hippie can pretty much count on receiving a vast array of responses from prospective rides. Case in point: a Dodge station wagon with a family of four approached. Mom glared a repugnant glance, as dad ceremoniously shot a bird. Will almost reciprocated, but the two boys flashing

Jason Douglass

peace signs out the rear window brought a conciliatory nod.

It was not looking very promising: countless rigs, your standard fare of Olds and Buicks, even a half dozen Volkswagens, and no takers. Will had walked a mile up the turnpike, his frustration mounting with the biting wind. *Come on people! What happened to humanity?*

Numb thumb out, walking backwards into the stiff breeze, salvation was sensed when he eyed the light blue Ford Falcon far down the road in the fast lane. Seasoned hitchers, who are at the mercy of the mobile public, have a sixth sense when it comes to potential rides. The Falcon whipped in behind a flatbed carrying concrete culvert pipe. Using the massive load as a drafting tool, the driver swerved into the next lane, a car coming up fast honked in disapproval. He managed the slow lane, had to have been doing seventy, and passed right by Will. Kicking up gravel, his ride came to a stop way down the road. Will shouldered his pack and sprinted through the hundred yards in a dash.

"Thanks for the lift, mister." He tossed his gear on the floorboard, knocking a half-emptied pint of Jim Beam off the seat. Perry Como, or was it Frank Sinatra, swooned on the radio.

Will fought against his disdain. The boozing salesman, insufferable music, and the same damn car his father drove, all hauntingly nostalgic of earlier times accompanying his father on day-long sales calls to ski resorts.

"Where ya headed, bubb?" asked the slightly bloodshot-eyed salesman.

Will was adept in masking his emotions. "Getting a bit blustery out there...trying to get to Plymouth." Unzipping his coat, he settled back to get comfortable, suddenly overcome by mental exhaustion.

"The name's Ellis, and yours?"

"Will, pleased to meet you. What are you smoking?"

"Cavendish, in a cherry wood pipe, can't beat it." Seeing his opening, he merged back on the road. "This must be your lucky day. I'm headed to Laconia so just sit back and enjoy the ride."

Glad to have an outlet for conversation, the salesman asked Will what he was majoring in at college. There was no response. The lad was out like a light.

CHAPTER TWO

"Wake up call, college boy!"

The car came to an abrupt halt at exit 26. Startled, Will's foot jammed into the floorboard. He tried to reel in his senses, as the view outside gave him solace. *Home at last.* The wasted sojourner collected his gear, offered his father's twin a conciliatory goodbye, and stepped out into the noticeably colder air that was somewhat tempered by the absence of wind. A smattering of nickel-sized snowflakes floated in the air. Heaving his pack, he set out on the mile-long hump to campus.

The trek took him past the newly built field house, over the bridge spanning Baker River, and into the peaceful little town. Population eight thousand, half of which were students and faculty, this cozy corner of the planet had become his surrogate home. Consisting of two gas stations, a couple greasy spoons, college bookstore, hardware store, a movie theater, a very small but adequate grocery store, an unfrequented barbershop, and a half dozen fraternity houses...and not much else more...Main Street was typical of a sleepy New England settlement. Highlighting the square was the proverbial bandstand gazebo. The only thing missing was the flimflamming Music Man, Robert Preston, spinning his magic on the townsfolk.

The remote serenity of this college town, cradled in a valley gateway between two ridges funneling towards ascension, was safe sanctuary to Will. He made his way up

Slipfinger Nine

the steep hill towards his dormitory at Grafton Hall, acknowledging friends drifting towards destinations that, being Saturday afternoon, probably entailed some sort of mischief and mayhem. The only curricula being offered on the weekends were drinking, debauchery, and drugs.

Will entered the dorm, briefly scanning the game room lounge. Two combatants at the ping pong table either really sucked or were very stoned. The tops of a couple heads on the couch were watching Syracuse take Boston College to the woodshed in hoop. The pool table was racked and ready for play.

The elevator door opened. Will's purposeful entrance split the quick exodus of flustered lovebirds. His eyes closed, the blind jab illuminated number seven as he backed into the corner and floated to the top.

Room 714 was keyed. A familiar smell greeted him along with the melodious sound of The Band bemoaning the shape they were in.

"Hey, Frenchy. What's going on, man?"

"Aw, you know, getting right for tonight." Jean Ricard put the finishing touch on a finely rolled joint while "Man, you look a bit tattered. Here, try some of this".

Will fired up the stout blunt. Inhaling deeply, he considered his bunkmate. *Sure changed since their senior year in high school.* Coarse, long black hair tied in a ponytail, mustache and goatee, his trademark tweed jacket.

French studied his friend, thinking the same thing. Gone was the straight laced hockey jock of yesteryear. Silky-brown shoulder length hair and a Fu Manchu mustache accentuated a handsome, albeit noticeably gaunt, face. "Mellow weekend?"

"Mellow dramatic, for sure. Damn, it's good to be back."

Will's melancholic demeanor told Jean that any further attempt at conversation would be forced. *Best leave him alone for a while.* "Going to check out the ladies at Blair Hall, shoot a little on their virgin tables. If you feel up to it, I'll oblige kicking your ass."

Will leaned back in the chair, his feet resting on the sill of the opened window and a Miller Highlife in hand. Their small fridge was always stocked, courtesy of an upper-classman who lived off campus in a fraternal attic.

Frenchy saw his distant friend somewhere out the window. "Hey man, did ya hear what I said?"

"What? Ah, yeah. I'll catch up with you in a bit; need to shower off the road dust."

"Right. See you when I see you then."

Gazing north, deep into the White Mountain range, Cannon, Loon, and Wildcat ski areas beckoned his call. *Haven't skied in a year.* He wondered how it had all gotten so crazy, so fast. It seemed like just yesterday, when in reality it was a year and a half ago, that he caught his little sister smoking a joint. He may as well have been Sergeant Joe Friday, threatening to take her in and then recapping all the pitfalls associated with marijuana use. He was straight then, always playing it by the book, but those jock days of high school were an eternity away from him now.

The dumbfounded look of his father's face jarred him like the hot kiss at the end of a wet fist. His mind raced from the ugly past to the present, which was not much consolation. He had a term paper overdue. He had lied to his ethics professor that his grandmother had died. It bought him time during the semester break, but he still had considerable work to finish. The home front was definitely not conducive to writing about ethics.

What in the hell am I doing here?

College was nothing but a self-inflicted ruse. Higher learning had been supplanted by higher living. Sex, drugs, and rock and roll had become a surrogate for a life best forgotten. Years of trying to right a foundering ship, its crew and captain lost in a fog of dark secrets and perverse rationale, had finally caught up with him. So preoccupied with navigating his family through a never-ending minefield, not once had he presence of mind to take stock of his own reason for being. He cast no blame, only doubts as to what he wanted to do with his life.

All the wrong reasons to be here.

Peer-pressure amongst his high school cronies festered in a kind of one-ups-man-ship, many electing to further their education. Will drained his beer and scored a two point hook shot into the wastebasket. Truth was, almost every swinging dick opted for college rather than roll the dice in the lottery draft. As long as one maintained passing grades, Vietnam's meat grinder had to carry on without them.

Last but not least was his high school sweetheart who was finishing her senior year. He was not about to disappoint her or her well-to-do family who had treated him like a son. That was a whole other issue that was going to have to be dealt with. She expected marriage. The prophetic words of her mother resonated:

"Oh, you kids. Just wait until he goes off to college."

The guy Charlene wanted to marry no longer existed. He had drifted far from what she thought still was. It was not that he no longer loved her. She was gorgeous, gave herself totally to him, and she and her family had been salvation from a maddening home life. He simply could not relate to her anymore; they had nothing but love in common. There were places to go, things to see and experience. Wanderlust and adventure beckoned him and he knew there would come a day when he was going to have to be one cold-hearted son of a bitch. *What a fucking mess!*

    Will jumped up, stripped, and made his way down the hall to the communal showers. Wrapped only in a towel, he was oblivious to the ogling of a few parents there to help move in their mid-year transfers. A couple of chicks took inventory, much to the vexation of their boyfriends. If not for the parents, the towel might have just come undone to liven up the place.

    His wardrobe was not exactly Saks Fifth Avenue: a dark blue turtle neck, beset by tight, threadbare blue jeans sewn together in a collage of patchwork designs. Donning his buckskin jacket with 'Jefferson Airplane' emblazoned across the back, he pocketed a joint and a four-way hit of Orange Sunshine. *That ought to do it.*

    The elevator door opened and the lobby greeted Will to a scene that looked more like that of an airport check-in counter than college dorm. A dozen or so second semester foreign exchange transfers had arrived en masse. *Rookies*, Will thought to himself, as he circumvented the pandemonium and entered the game room. The sound of a heated volley at the ping pong table drew his attention. Years of getting schooled by the old man had created a table tennis wizard. He was about to call dibs on the next game when the rack cracked behind him.

Slipfinger Nine

Angulated over the pool table and meticulously eyeing his next shot, was a most unusual looking fellow. Dudley Do-Right immediately came to mind: angular chin, course orangey hair and bushy sideburns. The raw-boned chap banked the five in the corner pocket as if routine, his deft execution making it plainly obvious he had game.

His hand spread like a tripod, the cue glided through gnarly knuckles that surely would do damage in a fistfight.

Will grabbed a stick off the wall and chalked the tip. "Feel like a game?"

"Sure, why not. Play to fifty? You can break."

As usual it sounded good, but no results. "Name's Will Bradford. Haven't seen you round before."

"Karl Smith. Six ball in the corner. Yeah, I missed the first semester, got caught up working on my stepdad's farm in Dover. Friend o' mine just got drafted, so I figured I better beat Uncle Sam to the punch."

Will watched Karl methodically sink three in a row. A nice combination, a cross-side bank shot, followed by a long one down the rail, and Will knew he was the sacrificial lamb.

Five racks later and the mercy killing ended at 50-21.

"So, where's the action around here?"

Will considered getting even with the hustler at the tennis table, but opted to play entertainment director.

"How 'bout I show you round the campus, student union café is always a good place to start."

"That's right neighborly of you. Mind if we stop by my room first?

"Nope, lead the way."

"Excuse the mess, haven't had the chance to unpack. I think I lucked out."

"Yeah, how's that?" Will fired up a joint and handed it off.

"I got the place all to myself. Seems like my roommate dropped out." Karl was tearing through his gear, the extra bed serving as a catch-all. While he rifled through his footlocker and duffle bag, Will was giving him the lowdown on the college scene:

"Slick and the 'Plane 'graced' us last year..."

Karl snorted in acknowledgment of the reference.

"Miles Davis played here last month. Totally wasted, the cat could still play a mean horn. We really caused a stir when Ravi Shankar and his sitar-playing entourage came out. We were laid out, front row in the auditorium and half way into the first song they all get up off their magic carpets and walk off. One of their security people tells us we insulted them by exposing the bottoms of our feet. Hell, we didn't know Indian culture. Anyway, the show went on after we put on our shoes. Got a good house band...Gunnison Brook. 'Bout twice a month they'll play here or ten miles up the road at Tenney Mountain ski lodge. And if you're really desperate for something to pass the time, our first-year football team can show you a hundred different ways how to lose sixty to--"

"I found it!" Officially unpacked, stuff strewn everywhere, Karl produced a small sheet of blotter acid with a dozen gun-blazing Yosemite Sams spaced inside the perforated squares. He tore off two. "Open your mouth and say 'ah'..."

Will felt a kindred spirit, inasmuch as Karl's stint here seemed to be for reasons other than the institution's intended purpose, but there was more. "Well, Smitty, you ready now for the tour?"

"You bet." Karl donned a baseball cap and flashed a Snidely Whiplash grin. "Let me know when you start to get off."

En route to the coffee house they came across a debonair-looking fellow sitting on a bench in the commons. Knee-high jackboots, dark blue full-length drover with sewn-in cape, a red sash cinched around the waist, the longhaired Union Field General was immersed in Nietzsche. Roger Kaswell meticulously fingered his goatee and mustache when two pair of feet came into view. He looked up. Mischievous blue eyes engaged the intruders. "Well, look what the cat dragged in. Where'd you find this rodent?" Roger stood and embraced Will. "Welcome back, stranger."

"Good to be back, Kaz." Will introduced the two, who sized each other up as equally strange in appearance. "We're headed up the hill. Join us for some coffee?"

"Sure, why not." Kaz collected his reading materials. "Let's go."

Will caught Karl's eye and without saying a word it was agreed they were both on the launching pad, ready to blast off.

Kaz's companions were having a bit of a time keeping their footing. It had snowed the previous night and today's flurries did pose traction difficulties, but not THAT bad. Will laughed at Karl when he almost fell on his ass. Karl shoved Will into the snow bank.

"Hey, are you guys on something?" Kaz had not slipped once and his footwear was not exactly made for the conditions.

Will dusted himself off and approached, unable to shed his grin.

"I shall not tell a lie, we dropped half an hour ago." He reached into his coat pocket. "Here, I got a little something, if you care to join us."

Kaz waved him off. "Thanks man, but no thanks. I tied one on last night and only came down an hour or so ago. But if you got a little smoke, it would really even me out."

A stone's throw from their destination, the three stood huddled, smoking the joint to a nub.

CHAPTER THREE

The basement of Blair Hall was once again the center of entertainment for the weekend holdovers. Neither Beatnik poetry, nor a Peter, Paul and Mary rendition, could upstage the show now in progress. Standing on a table was an unassuming, scrawny man with a bible clutched in hand. Will and his cohorts pulled up chairs outside the perimeter of believers and scoffers who were putting the self-proclaimed Christ to the test. Some were laughing, others angry, but most were simply enjoying the bizarre dialogue, considering it cheap entertainment. A bystander asked what kind of drug he was on and would he sell some. Another asked for a miracle on his midterms.

"What gives you the right to proclaim you're Jesus Christ?" a petite blonde was overheard.

"Man, what a trip! This is too much", exclaimed Karl.

"Pretty weird, huh?" Will responded with a cringe as he thought of Marx proclaiming religion to be the opiate of the masses. "Man, fucking zealots give me the creeps."

"No, I mean this acid is gooood! I'm off like a rocket".

Kaz was intensely engaged with the ongoing challenges. "Wow, this is just like it was two thousand years ago."

"What, you were there then?" Karl flashed back the most stupefied inquisitive expression.

Will endured a tremulous chill rushing up his spine and wondered if the guy had freaked out, gone crazy or, for a fleeting moment, the insane thought came over him: *Shit! The dude might just BE Jesus.* "Guys, I'm outta here. Scene's too heavy." Will's self-induced flight from reality was experiencing severe turbulence. Evasive action was required.

Kaz replied nonchalantly. "Happy trails, man. I'm gonna stick around and see where this is going. Besides, I won't be able to relate to you guys much longer. Send me a postcard when you reach Pluto."

"I'm coming with you," Karl said quickly, "this cat's a real bummer. Hey Kaz, lemme know if your time machine circles back."

A curt bird-over-the-shoulder flicked the two sojourners way, as Roger kept his eyes locked on the 'Son of God'.

Outside, the two chaps were greeted with a winter wonderland: huge snowflakes floated deftly down. The wind had ceased and, being mid-December in New England at five o'clock, dusk had set in. A slate-gray sky, the campus blanketed in white, the only sound was that of their crunch-packing footsteps in the freshly fallen snow. The ladies' dormitory was about two hundred yards up a moderately steep hill, but it seemed further due to their improper footwear. Two steps forward, half a step slipping back. Returning the earlier favor, Will shoved Karl into a snow bank, precipitating a snowball fight at point-blank range. In their altered state, the two-hour battle royale lasted all of one minute, when a truce was called. Two foxy ladies strode past, dispensing hostilities in response to errant throws.

"Well that made a hell of an impression." Will raked remnants of a snowball out of his hair. "Hey, there's somebody I want you to meet. Plays a mean game of pool, you up for it?"

"Play better when I'm high, so let's do it."

"Geez, if that's the case...."

The lobby was a veritable smorgasbord of women coming and going. Will acknowledged a number of acquaintances, two in particular who had snuck him in after hours for in depth physiology studies. In light of his altered state, now was not the time for stimulating conversation. Furtive glances sought an out from a potential awkward situation. *Thank God.*

Frenchy was in the side room lining up his next shot, the parlor being his favorite haunt. *Was it the close proximity to the babes, or the seldom-used table's consistency that was so appealing? Probably both*, thought Will, as he exited his self-awareness, leaving Karl to absorb the scorch of deprecating eyes scrutinizing the intruder.

Will reveled in playing the instigator. Introductions made, he stirred the pot promoting the other's skills and goading them into a cash-backed game of cutthroat. Clearly the underdog, Will's intent was to stoke the competitive fires of two very good players. While they beat each other silly he would operate incognito and hopefully be left with a lot of easy shots. It was the only option.

An hour later, down ten bucks to each, Will sought to recoup his losses. "I'm done. There's no way I can compete with you guys." Standing at the end of the table, he fished out a couple balls and placed them precariously on the lip of each corner pocket. "All right you guys. How's about double or nothing if I can pull off a trick shot?"

His adversaries demanded details.

Will centered the cue ball about a foot of the end rail and lined up his stick. "I will bank the cue ball off the far rail, bring it back sinking both while putting the cue ball in a side pocket."

"Yeah, right. You have a hard enough time making a simple combination." Frenchy deferred to Karl. "What do you think?"

"Easy money. I'm in."

"Great." Will relieved Karl of his stick, "need to borrow it, man." Laying the cue across the table so it was kissing each ball, he prepared to shoot.

"Whoa, wait a damn minute!" Frenchy's stick interfered. "This is bullshit. The ball goes up, comes back, hits the wood and taps them in."

"Correct. But how the hell's the cue ball gonna end up in a side pocket? It'll just die there."

Karl was high enough to fall for it. "Or fly off the table. Okay...you're on, let's see it."

Will parted the two, who had encroached on his space. "Spread out, boys. I need room to operate." He leaned over the table, stick gliding back and forth, occasional adjustments made to the cue ball using the stick's tip. The only purpose was to piss off his roommate, which it did.

"For Christ's sake, hit the damn thing!"

The ball ricocheted off the far bank and was on the horizontal cue in a wink. **Clunk**. Airborne a couple inches,

Will snatched it and jammed it in his pant's side pocket. "We're even, and I'm outta here!"

"That's bullshit, man!" Frenchy's advance was halted, having to catch the white ball lobbed at him.

Will grabbed his coat and headed for the exit. "You guys coming?"

"Yeah, wait up." Karl was eager for a change of scenery.

Frenchy, still miffed, declined. "I'm not on the same page as you two. Guess I'll hang around here, maybe get lucky."

Karl shook Frenchy's hand. "You shoot a good game, let's do it again sometime."

The steep incline down into town provided a slick venue for skiing without skis on the street. No longer only flurries, the now considerable snowfall had already deposited three inches on top of parked cars. The few autos on the road scrunched their tracks, as the pavement was cold enough to prevent the accumulation from turning to slush. A velvety squabble between blue jays and what little activity there was on Main Street played out in mime. A mischievous trio initiated hostilities with a band of pedestrians on the other side of the street. Snowballs thudded cars and storefronts, jocose battle cries were muffled in the fluffy air. To the cosmic travelers, the setting was all too surreal. It was as if the small town was encapsulated in a child's snow globe, the existence of the outside world unknown to its Norman Rockwell inhabitants.

"Hold up," Will said, entering the gazebo. "Let's burn one".

"That's great. Smokes got wet." Karl scrunched the pack and tossed it in the receptacle. "Got one?"

Will's own box had kept the cigs dry, but condensation underneath the cellophane had turned its magical contents to a pasty orange.

Firing up, Karl considered the colorful waste. "Ah, looks like your stash is trashed, man."

Will took the Marlboros and gently tore the cellophane from the box. Licking the residue off the cardboard and splitting the wrapper in half, he offered it to Karl. Enough truth serum for six, the adventure seekers sat on the railing awaiting the Doorman to beckon with impunity. The smokes dragged on forever. Mired in introspection, Will glanced at his traveling companion whose face was etched in a faraway stare.

"Where you at, man? You okay?"

Smitty flicked his butt into the snow and shot Will a bothered glance.

Anyone who has ever tripped knows what it is like to reach a level where two people become almost telepathic. Will sensed his newfound friend was grappling with something beyond the present.

"Hey man, what's buggin' you?" Will fired up a joint, hoping to take the edge off the mounting intensity.

Karl took the handoff, toked deep, and felt small. "Did ya ever feel like you were outside the grand scheme of things? You know, kinda like you're the observer of some tragic comedy?"

Will offered no response. The question hit too close to home.

"I've always felt as though I was looking at the big picture from outside the box."

Slipfinger Nine

    Will leaned back, hands clasped behind his head, his thoughts drifting with the snowflakes. His screwed up home life had many times made him question his purpose for existing. Was his life an exception to the norm, denying him the simple pleasures of youthful innocence? To what purpose did he endure the years of such disturbing realities? Was he a survivor, or damaged goods? He felt damned to these questions that had no logical answers.

    Karl had begun sharing his life in a monologue meant for no one. "I 'been ping-ponged all my life. My father and mother divorced when I was four, an only child raised in the Wyoming outback. Old man was twenty years senior to ma and to this day I can't figure out how or why they hooked up. For all I know a one night stand, me being the bi-product. Pappy, that was what everyone in Dubois called him, was a holdover from the cowboy days. Was a stunt man in a lot of westerns and actually hobnobbed with the Duke. In his prime, Pappy made numerous trips east to the big city performing at the Polo Grounds and Madison Square Garden's annual rodeo show. Anyways, ma left him and his bottle to start over back east. Two half-brothers, two half-sisters and I, the oldest, lived our school years out on a small farm in Derry. Every summer, I'd get shipped back west for the duration. Didn't matter much to me where I lived. Here I was the black sheep, in Wyoming...well, I was pretty much on my own. Putting up with the cantankerous old fart was a trade-off for the summer reprieve in the great wide open." Flicking the finger-burning roach into the snow, he considered his newfound friend who was immersed in contemplation. "A Man Without a Country."

Karl's novel quote retrieved Will from far away. "What'd you say?"

"Hell, I don't know what I'm saying, man. My dreams and aspirations just don't match up with my options, you know? It's a shitty catch-22. I'm a top-water plug getting jerked across a mirrored surface in an endless routine: cast out, reeled in, no takers. I know there's something big down there but dang it, all I seem to attract is a bunch of puny baitfish. Must be the action, maybe size and color, or perhaps I'm out of season...all I want is to score that one big fish then call it a day."

Will looked at his quizzical, comedic-looking friend. "Strange analogy, man. Personally, I think you'd look exquisite in chartreuse." Will did not want to waste a good buzz on such a downer conversation. The whole reason he dropped was to check out for a while, cleanse the mind of haunting memories, and hopefully get a fresh perspective on things. "Hey man, lighten up."

Karl floated out from his fogbank. "Wuzzat?"

His quick exit from the gazebo signaled Will was ready to relocate to a safer haven, FAST. A twinge of fear told him they had done way too much and it would not be long before reality became incomprehensible.

"Come on, Smitty. There's someone I'd like to turn you on to."

Jumping off the railing into the rising blanket of snow, Karl fell in behind Will. They walked the length of Main Street, no words spoken, as the new guy made note of what little the town had to offer.

It was a quarter mile to the edge of town. The storefronts abruptly ceased and Main Street melded into a country road. Two and three story clapboard houses stood weathered on each side of the road. The onward trek took them into an ever-growing encroachment of tall, heavy timber as the houses became more dispersed. The great north woods closed in on the road as they trudged on toward the last visible outpost of humanity. The century-old, three-story house looked like a quarantined garrison. A good two hundred yards separated this lone structure from the dwindling others. Beyond, Mother Nature ruled supreme.

Kappa Zen Phi was one of six Greek houses, evenly split for gender equality. This particular frat house was the pariah of the lot. Shunned by the locals, feared by the establishment, treated with distain by the governing student body, Will likened it to Alice's Restaurant where you could get anything you want. Searchers, misfits, and adventurers sought refuge in the house of dreams. It was funny, the core group of charter members was made up of heads, hippies, and political malcontents whose ideals were the antithesis of anything the "establishment" adhered to. Yet, at any one time, it was not uncommon to see rogue jocks, curiosity seekers of the straight set, and even a few professors make clandestine cameo appearances. Their reasons varied: enlightenment, escape, rebellion, quenching of the curious mind. Whatever one's agenda was, one thing remained a constant at the "head-spa": upon admittance, you would tune in, turn on, and check out.

Will led Karl up the porch stairs as a distant Grace Slick envisaged their evening to come: a white knight walking backwards, red queen on her head. Will rapped the brass knocker shaped like an Indian peace pipe. The door opened a few inches to a female wearing a beaded headband keeping in place what looked to be a Guinness record for hair length. Smiling diamond eyes at Will, she then shot a furtive glance at the stranger.

"He's cool," motioned Will to his companion. "Social call, to see the good doctor. Is he in?"

"I haven't made it up that high today." Almost undetectably, her head moved in the direction she threw her voice, her eyes caught in a fanciful stare somewhere in-between, "Anyone here know if the doc's in?" The inquiry went unanswered amongst the twenty or so people gaming at foosball, pool, and ping pong. The spaced out chick shrugged her shoulders and stepped aside with the opening door. "Couldn't tell ya. You'll have to go see for yourself."

Will led his friend into the twilight zone and left the maiden at the gate to contemplate the doc's whereabouts, or whatever else her drifting mind had moved on to.

The house was a three-tiered social event. The higher you went, the higher you got. The first floor seemed more like a jock's haven of beer, whiskey, and occasional joints. They made their way to the stairs and as they climbed Will turned to Karl, "You all right?"

"Man, I'm ripped. Cold Italian pizza...could use a lemon squeeza."

"We'll get something to wet our whistle, cool out." Waving a pointy finger in time with the Stones, Will signaled upward: "must go higher."

The second floor was incense-laced, with beads on every doorway. Grateful Dead atmospheric. A place for lovers to play out their fantasies, a refuge for crashing trippers, and a quiet sojourn for board game enthusiasts to find seclusion in their surroundings as well as in their own minds. Will acknowledged a nod from an acquaintance looking up from a chessboard's embattled engagement.

"Still not there yet," he lead his bedazzled follower to the narrow stairwell. Will was enjoying playing the part of pied piper. He remembered his first tour. The physical world, or more accurately his previous misconceptions about it, his outlook, and overall persona were never quite the same after his first night in the attic cabin.

The third floor had a mystical Indian flair: sitar music, black lights highlighting neon depictions of the metaphysical, and pillows-upon-pillows. They entered a side room.

"Holy shit, man" muttered Karl. There were three or four girls, two of them already topless and two half naked guys sitting in a circle partaking a hookah pipe that had to be five feet tall. The bowl itself was a glowing campfire that sent billows of smoke funneling up to the ceiling, permeating the room in red wine and red Lebanese. Will recognized one of the topless gals and nodded subtly to her, knowing all too well that to disturb the moment, to utter even a 'hello', would destroy their karma and probably their evening. She looked up at Will with a dreamy smile and deftly waved her hand, beckoning them with their indulgence. Obligingly they stepped forward, squatted, and sampled complimentary tokes. The sweet taste of wine mixed with potent hashish was numbingly exquisite. The stationary travelers floated with the music; there was no need to speak. Time elapsed unrecorded. A sitar somehow condensed eternity into an instant...or was it the other way around? Will drifted to his feet and felt a white out coming on. A minute passed as if an hour as he struggled to regain motor skills, his body numb with pins and needles. He tried to focus on the others' faces to see if they had noticed his incapacitation: *hell, they're just as stoned as I am.*

Will placed prayer hands together and offered a bow to his hosts, and then slow-motioned to Karl it was time to move on.

Through darkened rooms with incense and smoke-filled air, simple forward motion was made precarious. Of course their induced state had nothing to do with the difficult navigation; rather it was the gooey airborne molasses-molecules that restricted forward progress. They shuffled their way towards the black hole at the end of the hallway.

The ascent into pitch was tedious. Half way up the steep, rickety ladder, Will felt his heel clip Karl's jaw. The clop sound was followed by Karl lunging for a handhold. Instead of ladder, he grasped an ankle and the leader went face first into a rung. There were no expletives exchanged, all was quiet except for the far away sound of sitar. Will's head bumped into the trap door. Fumbling the wall, he found the switch only a few knew about. Turning it on flashed a warning light inside the doctor's abode announcing there were visitors. The miniscule bulb of black light exposed white teeth suspended in space where parted lips of pain had betrayed their location. The vain attempt to stifle a snicker did them both in. The hilarity, combined with the forced suppression, brought forth stomach wrenching, snot drooling jags followed by shoving admonitions to shut the fuck up. Finally, Will reached into the dark and grabbed a handful of hair.

"Man! Cut the shit. We got to keep...." Will busted out laughing again.

Slipfinger Nine

"Where the hell we goin'?"

"We've reached the summit, come on." Will pushed open the trap door and hauled himself up onto the attic's planked floor. Karl followed, feeling his way in the dark. He let the trap door slam behind him, scaring the crap out of Will.

"Son of a bitch! Be careful." A pause in Will's words gave separation between them and whatever it was that had gripped them both so vehemently only moments before. "There it is, see it?"

Will directed Karl's head toward the thin slice of light that outlined a closed door. Dimension and relativity being skewed, twenty paces to the light could well have been a half-mile as they shuffled toward their objective. A thousand thoughts ran through their minds, all of them unspoken yet many of them shared, before they reached the door.

Karl ran his hand over the side of the structure and flipped when he realized a miniature log cabin had been constructed in the center of the attic. Built acoustically soundproof, Alvin Lee's guitar riff was only as audible as Karl's whisper…"Nothing's real." A half-day till sunrise would pass before another word was spoken by either of them.

Logic and proportion was no longer in Will's grasp as he fumbled the intractable doorknob, simple motor functions being nonsensical. When the handle finally twisted the right way, a telepathic sigh clicked acknowledgement that they had reached a point of no return. Both were in dire need of solitude.

The door opened to a wall of sound that nearly knocked them over. Karl recoiled, closing the door with his back. Sanctuary had been mercifully reached. This guarded secret, familiar only to a select fraternity of campus heads and a couple professors, was typically accessed by appointment only. Will, being a close friend, was one of a very few considered a charter member. Barry Dillinger, aptly referred to as "Doc", sat cross-legged on the floor shaving shards of hashish into an exquisite hookah pipe. His patients, two girls and a guy, were laid back amongst throw pillows strewn about a plush Afghan rug. A stratum of bluish-white haze hung low, but Doc saw through it into the eyes of two sojourners who were way beyond resolve. He knew immediately what was required. Changing out the magnetic tape while the newcomers receded into pillow-piles, not a word was spoken.

Days of Future Passed to The Lost Chord from A Question of Balance; hours of Moody Blues would be required to shepherd the intense part of their journey out and hopefully back in. Two candles and an urn with burning incense complimented the room, serving to commingle the senses: smells were seen, sounds were tasted, thoughts heard. A few tokes, a shared bottle of red wine, and time passed immeasurable until the circle was broken.

One of the girls lay down with the nameless fellow who was by this time mumbling incoherently. Doc was in some sort of unspoken communal with his female counterpart. They had merged into one. A mile away, Karl was curled up in a ball against the log wall mesmerized with a hand-held fiber optics wand and getting blown away. He lightly blew the feathery fibers, tips aglow in multicolor light. He was gone, WAY gone.

Will collapsed backwards into pillows and viewed himself under an electron microscope. It was as if his eyelids had turned inside out...maybe they had. As he stared at the wood grain in the ceiling, its texture formed into graceful ocean waves. Knotholes were something to ponder, faces appearing and then melting away. He held his breath as fruit salad began pouring out, slowly burying him. Unable to move, suspended in animation, his inner-self was becoming light as a feather.

The Moody Blues' "Candle Of Life" flickered in rhythm to the numerous fire sticks already melting down around him. His gaze focused on one particular flame and pulled him straight into the fiery glow, as a tear formed in the corner of Will's eye. He was seven again laying in a field of hay behind his home, the late-afternoon sun warming him. It was his first conscious moment in life when he was acutely aware of his uniqueness, of life itself. He acknowledged the immensity of it all and the faint feeling that something unseen oversaw all that was being played out. He wondered what his purpose of being was. Was he any different? What was the basis of a young man's existence? Why was he here? "Time for supper" called his mother, off in the distance.

Fading into complete aloneness, Will shuddered and held a tight grip onto his sanity for fear it would fall away from him. *What am I doing? How'd I get here? Where am I going? Is there a destination?* Cognitive thought faded as the trip took him hostage, blasting forth into another dimension while reaching critical mass.

CHAPTER FOUR

    Summoned from college at their dying father's request, the brothers were on the road. The late night call informed them father had come home from a yearlong stint at Johns Hopkins that only served to prolong the inevitable. Radiotherapy with cobalt treatments could no longer keep in check the onslaught of throat cancer, doctors hedging he would not see the end of summer. Arthur Cromwell Blaine's amassed fortune as a shipping magnate could not buy his way out of an appointment with the grim reaper. Resigned to his fate, the wealthy widower insisted he would play out his hand in the comfort of his seaside home. A live-in RN was assigned to monitor his decline, attend to his needs, and dose him through the pain.
    "Thirty Days in the Hole" blasted on the radio as the joint passed between them. The '66 Corvette Stingray, ragtop down, made quick work of Route 132 leading into Hyannis Port. The old man bought Stuart the muscle car as a high school graduation present: 327, four-speed with Thrush side-pipes, Hurst shifter, and a modified engine with Mickey Thompson valve covers. James Dean lived again.
    A year younger at twenty-one, Rick rode shotgun. His graduation request was a customized Woody ideal for his surfing forays and ski trips to the Berkshires. Unlike his brother, whose pastime was making the scene and scoring with the babes, Rick preferred a more incognito lifestyle of

leisure pursuits. Oh sure, he got his too, he just did not flaunt it.

Silver-spooned, the brothers had bought their way into Harvard courtesy of their father's alumni status and powerful influence in the business community, not to mention a generous amount of elbow-rubbing amongst Beantown's bigwigs. Their patriarch's prominence also put his sons on the exclusive guest lists of the Cape's societal elite, garden parties and sailing regattas begrudgingly attended at their father's behest.

Stuart, presumptive of his fortuitous birth as first heir to be nothing less than the purposeful work of Providence, and all good favor rightfully his own, imbued a pretentious hauteur found grating to casual acquaintances.

Rick was the antithesis of his brother's vanity and egoisms. While being as much his own man, if not more so, he managed to exude confidence and sophistication that was not constantly choking on entitlement. Humble and low-keyed about his luck of the draw, he preferred to keep a discreet profile, feeling it was but by the grace of God that his lot in life was so magnanimous. Whether mingling with the proletariat at an Irish pub on Boston's south-side, chumming with weekend surfers invading the Cape, conversing with the retail girls down at Filene's basement, or just rubbing elbows with commoners at any chance was what made him feel real. Hell, not commoners....*REAL* people. Nevertheless, playing the consummate chameleon he could hold his own at high-society social events.

His brother on the other hand, could be abrasive, aloof, and obnoxiously overbearing at times. Calculating and self-serving, especially in the company of other snobs, he always sought the best angle to leverage his own ego.

If ever there were two identical peas in a pod, the Blaine brothers' husk did not contain them.

The estate came into view as the Stingray rounded the bend on Shoreline road. Stu downshifted into third and motored the remaining one mile at a rumbling thirty-five miles per hour. Rick stared out at the goldenrod and sea oats that covered the rolling landscape down to the sea. He thought of mom. A decade had passed since a brain aneurysm had come like a thief in the night, but it always seemed like yesterday when returning home after a stint away at Harvard.

Pulling off the pavement onto the quarter-mile driveway, Stu downshifted into first, grimacing as the tires crunched the hard-packed seashells. Five miles per hour or the black pearl paint job suffered a beating behind the rear wheels from kicked up shards. *Brilliant idea dad*, he thought as he coasted the remaining distance.

The three-story white mansion with evergreen shutters overlooked Nantucket Sound. Built atop a sloping plateau nearly a century ago, the ole homestead's constant maintenance defied time and elements. A testament to a bygone era was the widow's walk cantilevered off the roof's backside. Accessible from the attic, it was the boys' favorite retreat where they would concoct dreams of high seas adventures and faraway lands. On clear days, the expansive vista stretched from Nantucket Island to Martha's Vineyard's Kennedy compound, perceived. Springtime found mother and sons, field glasses donned, panning the horizon to witness one of nature's prized spectacles: the migration of the humpback whale. White plumes jettisoned, the voyeurs would focus in anticipation of a mighty breach. First to witness would invariably holler bragging rights.

Stuart circled the spewing fountain centered in the heated concrete reservoir and parked in front of the tiered terrace built from monolithic slabs of polished white granite. Rick stared in retrospection at the mini-rainbow as Stuart sat for a moment gathering patience to endure his father's incessant diatribes. Both wondered if this summons was to be the precatory announcement they had been planning for.

Butler and maid met them halfway down the steps.

"Master Stuart. Master Richard. It is with much sorrow we welcome you home. Your father insisted that he see the both of you as soon as possible."

"How is he, Albert," Rick asked as Stuart greeted Gretchen with a peck on the cheek.

"Considering, he is doing surprisingly well. I believe his coming home is somewhat therapeutic. He has been enjoying the bedroom view."

"What's his prognosis?"

"Let me introduce you to our lovely nurse Glenda who will be staying with us. She will answer all of your questions."

Once inside, Albert led them through the atrium and into the parlor. He seated Glenda and motioned for the boys to do likewise.

"If you will excuse me, I must finish preparing lunch." Gretchen ruffled Rick's hair. "You boys look like you have not eaten in a week."

The RN fielded an hour of bottom-line questioning with clinical response: Yes, it was terminal...six months, tops. No, he would not feel pain; an IV drip of graduated morphine would ensure his comfort. Yes, he is completely lucid and should remain so through the ordeal, almost to the end. Spirits were good; he is being pragmatic about the situation. Not to worry, he vows the final days would not be devoid of dignity.

Rick shook his head. "That's dad, stiff upper lip no matter what."

Lunch was devoured. After reminiscing a bit with Albert, it was time to see the king. Up the winding staircase to the second floor and down the hall, the door opened to a bedroom accommodating a dying man's every wish. The heavy mahogany bed was centered in the room, affording a panoramic ocean view through the floor-to-ceiling glass. Father appeared to be dozing as the IV slowly leaked its mercy, yet he was not. Sensing their presence, he raised his arm to signal and got it caught on the oxygen tube, pulling the line taunt..."God-damned contraptions."

"Damn, he looks small," whispered Rick.

"Yeah, he sure looks wasted. Still ornery though." Stuart moved out of the way so the nurse could untangle the testy patient.

"Beg your pardon boys, not decommissioned quite yet." The raspy voice and intermittent gurgling made it hard for the boys not to wince. "You know, lying here, seeing water and sky...feels like I'm flying this bed right through those clouds. Sure beats the view I had at Hopkins."

Stuart closed in on the morphine drip. He jiggled the connection and saw it was indeed fulfilling its purpose. "Where's your flight heading, father?"

Slipfinger Nine

"They haven't told me yet, son, but accommodations are first class cozy." An ugly cough put to rest any further attempt at levity.

"How are you doing, dad?" Rick kissed a clammy forehead and brushed aside wispy strands of stark white hair.

Albert pulled up a couple of chairs and motioned the boys to sit.

"Oh, you know. Pretty nurse, good drugs, and a great view...got it made in the shade." The chuckle brought forth another coughing jag. After waving off their relief attempt, it was a good minute before he regained his composure. "That was unpleasant, excuse me." Timeworn eyes looked through them into infinity. "Besides visiting with my two boys, there is another reason I summoned you here—"

"Dad, perhaps you shouldn't try to—"

"Now listen, I'm short on breath and my throat's sore, so try not to interrupt while I speak. I know my time is borrowed, but I'm at peace with that. Only two things I'll miss in this world. There were three, but I know soon I'll see your mother. You boys, and my mistress..."

Rick caught his brother's raised eyebrow and shook off the sign...

"...*Slipfinger*. I'm commissioning you both to roust up your buddies who've sailed with us before and soon as school's out, high tail it down to the islands, bring her back home, and sail her right past my window. I'd like that to be the last thing my eyes see before they close for good." The wilted hand slowly waved across the vista then plumped to the bed.

Rick's eyes glistened, the watery veil not shielding him from the harsh reality that lay before him. Stuart listened, all the while staring out into the dark blue Atlantic. There was a brief respite to siphon some water before their father continued.

"I'll have money wired to our bank in St Thomas and enough up front to cover all expenses. I'd suggest a crew of ten would be sufficient, provided you enlist wisely. Five thousand apiece, airfare, and a lifetime adventure should be enough to persuade your blokes to forego summer frivolities. You boys know the routine. We've made this trip a dozen times before."

The coughing and labored breathing increased. Albert and Rick propped him up with an extra pillow as the unsettled Stuart retreated to the window for a better outlook.

"Best damn summer vacation any young man could dream of. As co-captains and inheritors, I know she'll be in good hands and treated with respect. With your training, knowledge, and worthy skills, I have no reservations whatsoever about your competence in fulfilling my request."

Another sip of water and the boys could tell the dissertation was wearing him out.

"Dad, you should know that Rick and I have anticipated this and have been making preparations for some time now. Except for rounding out a crew, we're good to go."

"See, I knew I could count on you two. Good planning makes for smooth sailing, son. Who's your complement?

"All the usual suspects: Artimus, Barry, Jason, and David. You remember them, don't you?"

"Sure do. Good boys. Are Jason and David still playing ball for B. C.?"

"You bet. Playing good enough to keep a scholarship, but I doubt they're major league material."

"Hmm. How 'bout Artimus? Is he still at MIT or did he find a way to expel himself yet?" The self-amusement achieved by his own dig was just about enough to do him in, that and the blood and phlegm battling to drown him.

"Chemical engineering. R&D in molecular reconfiguration. He hasn't blown up the laboratory yet. Oh, and Barry's way the heck up in the north woods, haven't spoken with him in awhile."

Rick saw his father's eyes fighting closure. "Dad, don't worry about a thing. We're on it, and we'll keep you posted. Now get some rest. You've got a great nurse here...do what she says, and don't push it. You need pain relief...ask for it. Love you."

The face was etched in the peace of his sons' reassurance.

"Love you too, Pops, everything's under control. We'll keep in touch." Stu doubted his words were heard as they took their cue to exit.

"Look, let's get something straight. We may be co-captains, but I reserve the right to make final calls.

"Whatever swizzles your rudder, brudder. Go ahead and call Arti, see if he can hook up with the BC boys. I'll get us a couple ales and meet you up on the roof for old times' sake."

"Now that's a command decision I won't challenge! Be up momentarily."

It was mid-afternoon and a six-pack later when they pulled out of the drive. Priorities had been set, options discussed, and matters of immediate importance agreed upon. Stuart would journey up north and pay a visit to his wayward friend whose power of persuasion last Christmas had introduced the brothers to a weekend-long acid trip. It was then that they revealed to Barry future plans to which he had committed immediately.

Stuart let his brother drive until they got pulled over for excessive speed. The cop recognized the name on the license and let them off without even a warning. Life of privilege sure had its rewards.

CHAPTER FIVE

The last few months of half-hearted studies found Will feeling vacuous. Having to take pre-requisite courses felt like advanced high school and he was bored to death. Statutory and corporate law, with a minor in political science, was his intent, but impatience undermined perseverance. Classes were skipped, books were not purchased, yet somehow he still managed passing grades.

"Strawb—Strawb—Strawb—"...

"Strawberry Fields" was stuck just like his studies, which were going down the drain. Will lifted the needle out of the rut in the vinyl. *Yup, pretty much sums it up.*

The funny farm had stagnated into a redundant cycle of sex, drugs, and rock and roll. Three months had passed since the otherworldly episode inside Doc's padded cell. Will had concluded that such a trip could never be duplicated again. He had seen it all, been to the other side, and considered himself damn lucky he made it back with his sanity relatively intact.

Diversion, more like salvation, had been found nearby on the many slopes. Posting an ad at the student union, he offered free ski lessons, and stayed busy. Clients would provide passage, pay for his lift ticket, and buy lunch. Tips were unexpected but appreciated: cash, a little smoke, an occasional sorority babe showing him her room...all 'perks' of a day's work. "Business" lasted until mid-April.

Nearly six months of winter and the last vestige of snow banks left the streets wet. A toasty spring day thronged the campus with a flush of hibernators: girls catching rays, their pasty white skin reddening beneath a cloudless sky. People studied for finals amidst floating Frisbees and errant footballs. An impromptu concert, courtesy of a local band, serenaded the festive crowd.

Will was still fuming over the altercation with his ethics professor. He had nailed a thesis paper, or so he had thought, on standards of conduct in a capitalistic society. When his exposé came back carved up, not for grammar or structure, but purely on opinion and ideology, Will made sure the professor got an earful after class was dismissed.

"D-fucking-plus?! What the hell is that supposed to mean? I sift through your pompous, skewed, sanctimonious lectures on how *you* perceive things while being challenged to think for myself. I addressed all your talking points, but apparently you're too damn opinionated to find validation in any opposing views. Tell you what. Either reconsider and merit my work a C, or please do me the favor and flunk me right now."

"Fine Will, I'll see your request for a failing grade. Have a nice day."

Huffed, Will plunked down on a bench outside the professor's hilltop redoubt. Observing the carefree crowd below, he replayed what had just gone down and realized that his college days were numbered. Lack of interest, misplaced priorities, a growing wanderlust for adventure, and he blamed only himself for his conundrum. Lighting up, Will recalled last week's hair-brained attempt to sabotage the Biology finals.

Recruiting Smitty and three other equally concerned classmates who were ill prepared, Will had devised a secret mission to postpone the exam. Under the cover of darkness, they "borrowed" a local farmer's swine and hauled it back to campus in the pickup truck of one of the perpetrators. After a clandestine raid on the cafeteria's discards, an inordinate amount of Ex-Lax was blended in with the swill and the bloated hog was good to go. It would be an explosive night in the plush lecture hall.

The brilliant strategy backfired. Next morning, the biology instructor, accompanied by a furious Dean of Students and an incredulous custodial crew, surveyed the amphitheater.

"Jeezus Christ, look at this goddam place!" If the dean had had any hair, he would have yanked it out. Greasy excrement was everywhere. The foul stink was overwhelming as they attempted to corral the pig and lead it outside. Finally, after many spills, they managed to divert the spent sow out the emergency exit. It was decided then that the show would go on. Those held accountable would be charged, fined for damages, and expelled. But in the meantime, everyone would suffer through the testing, courtesy of those responsible.

Struggling through the stomach-wrenching finals, hasty retreats and hurried answers hurled the entire class into a dismal sub-par performance.

With the coup's delay tactics a bust, priority shifted to anonymity. Tight-lipped, Will and his cohorts kept their distance from each other all week. So far, the college dicks were chasing ghosts.

The grin that delineated his face while recalling the feces-fest evaporated when he saw her coming up the path. His high school princess was turning heads as she walked his way. The gorgeous busty blonde had a knack for causing neck strains amongst the male populace. Hippie chicks looked on with disdain: mini-skirt, heels, and a tight cashmere top made her presence a well-observed affair.

He had anticipated this eventual moment, but the uninvited surprise still caught him off guard. Visits back home had all but ceased and he had made it clear that his college life was not conducive to furthering their relationship. The rift was not her fault; it was he who had changed into someone foreign, and in some ways even to himself. They had become oil and water, constituting divergent worlds of opposing tastes best summed up in music preference: acid rock so diametric to the Bee Gees, Neil Diamond, and the up-chucking Archies. "Just wait until he goes off to college." Oh, how they both had scoffed at her mother's absurd statement, now prophetic.

Bewildered innocence came to him with open arms. What he did next was so out of character, a knee-jerk reaction unforeseen, and a final act that would haunt him for being such a heartless bastard. All the love she and her family gave him. The countless trysts in her daddy's Lincoln making them the last to leave the drive-in. The routine rocking in her ski boat, situated behind the island out back and shielding them from views from her parent's house. The adopted good fortune was a godsend from his familial hell. All of this was to be unceremoniously trashed in an instant by way of a tirade of undeserved condemnation. Cold and callous, with no definitive explanation, Will backed away from his love of four years and walked out on the only life worth remembering.

Charlene walked the commons to her car, holding back tears for the sake of mascara. There was not a guy in the immediate area who did not twist his neck in sympathetic concern, only to feel the dig of his girl's elbow-jab moments later.

Word got around campus. Some found his performance ignoble and crass; others begrudgingly acknowledged him as a tool. Notoriety as a heartbreaker brought unsolicited advances from ladies seeking a challenge, the unwanted scrutiny leaving him feeling like a caged animal in a petting zoo. A month to go and if not for two finals, he would have packed what he could carry and split to destinations unknown. A future uncertain, a past best forgotten, Will found himself frozen in the moment, dreading another weekend of the same old shit. He stared at the cluttered student union's message board: a half-covered index card caught his eye. Folding back an ad for used books revealed a hand drawn American flag with a peace sign instead of stars:

Riders wanted.
Share expenses for trip to
May Day Demonstrations,
Washington, D.C.

Will had lucked out, or so he thought. This would be a much needed diversion.

Friday morning. Backpack shouldered, Will waited for his ride. Doc came rolling up the steep hill and pulled curbside, cranking down his window.

"Hey man, where you headed?

"Catching a ride down to DC for the weekend."

"Oh right, the demonstrations. Far out man, should be a blast. Wish I could join you."

"Yeah. Might not be Woodstock, but there's gonna be a shit load of people."

"I bet, sounds like a trip." Doc snuffed the spliff in the ashtray. "I'm glad I caught you. You'll be back by Wednesday, right?"

"I better be back by Monday night. Got an English Lit final Tuesday that I should nail. What's up?"

"Close friend's coming up from the Cape with an intriguing proposition I think you'd like to hear. Smitty, Kaz, Frenchy...all said they'd be there."

"What the hell is it?"

"Can't say, but it's something to do about a summer job. I guarantee it'll blow your mind. Wednesday at seven?"

"Count on it. I got nothing to get home about."

"Strawberry fields forever, man. See ya when you get back."

Doc pulled out, making room for Will's ride. The van's side door slid open and released Jim Morrison, crooning about strange people. Slinging his gear in the rear, Will climbed in and settled into a legless, beat up recliner. Chauffeur Ralph and shotgun Eddie nodded a dazed welcome from a cockpit already up in smoke. A peace flag with the words "D.C. OR BUST" flew from the antenna, garnering mixed reviews as they drove through campus. It was clear reciprocating V-signs and propitious well-wishing outnumbered the curses anchored on middle fingers.

Will hoped the pennant would get blown away once they got on the interstate. He could not allay the bad vibes emanating from the insignia which was sure to attract unwanted attention. Although he was captive in the mobile gas chamber, offers to partake of the pipe were declined. *Damn numbskulls'll get us busted, or KILLED.* Pulling out Vonnegut's *Slaughterhouse Five*, he kicked back and braced himself for a visit from a state trooper looking to make his mark.

The journey south would have been uneventful except for one hair-raising incident. Leaving interstate 93 to pick up I-95, a pit stop was made to satisfy the munchies. Will slept soundly as Ralph and Eddie procured a bag full of junk food. After gorging themselves on Twinkies, another pipe-load was fired up and a clambake ensued in the parking lot until all the windows were an opaque white.

In a coughing fit, Will awoke to a fog that made no sense at all. Ralph was bent over the wheel, lights on and wipers dragging glass that glared with the bright sunshine. Driving past the entry ramp, the wrecked navigator and co-pilot inadvertently took the exit ramp, which was devoid of traffic. Eddie reached back for a beer as Ralph shifted into high gear and whipped into the freeway's fast lane. Locked in a tunnel-vision stupor, he was oblivious to four lanes of traffic coming the wrong way.

"Holy shit, lookout!" Eddie's beer was up for grabs as both hands went for the wheel. Will catapulted out of the easy chair and lunged forward, his arms enveloping Ralph's head. The battle for control careened the van off the concrete barrier; sparks flew, along with cursed accusations. Conflicting evasive action from all three sent the van swerving at sixty as Eddie and Will fought towards the left and Ralph held a death grip back towards the wall. It was an out-of-control maneuver Steve McQueen would have been hard pressed to emulate. The only thing saving the trio from becoming statistics was a slight break in the wall of oncoming traffic. Slicing diagonally across four lanes: a left, a right, another left, they slalomed in between five cars and spun out, off the shoulder into a swale. Airborne dirt clods plastered the wave of unswerving motorists.

"That's it! I'm driving the rest of the way! You guys wanna stay wasted, get in the back!" Will yanked the catatonic driver out of his captain's chair as wide-eyed Eddie peeled his hands from the wheel.

"Stupid shit could've killed us," mumbled Will. He eased out of the ditch and onto the breakdown lane while making adjustments and praying for no cops. Back up the ramp and across the bridge, Will turned onto the ramp normal people took when headed south. He shifted into fourth gear at the bottom of the gradient and as he reached merging speed, acknowledged an annoying conclusion: *Going to be a long-ass drive in the slow lane. That's if we even make it.* The beat up van was in dire need of a front end alignment.

CHAPTER SIX

Artimus Stiles pulled his Jaguar into the ball field's parking lot, still fuming over the dirt-churning idiot who had served up the rock he received while doing seventy. Point of impact almost dead center, he eyed the spidery cracks that fanned out across the windshield. He wished he had gotten the tag number, but the logjam of morning commuters had him boxed in. Still, it brought him a minor amount of pleasure imagining all the ways we would have gotten revenge.

The call from Rick the night before necessitated he split MIT in haste and, under the guise of being homesick, visit his retired folks in the upscale suburb of Wellesley. Mission accomplished, at the expense of a busted windshield, the Jag's trunk was stuffed with all his seafaring gear.

"Sorry Mack, rules are rules."

Artimus was being forced to fork over full price for a game paused for the seventh-inning stretch. It was not so much the petty five dollar admission as it was the unbending pinhead behind the ticket window that had him conjuring up injurious ideas...hangover effects from the highway hell. Except for pocket change, he only had hundred dollar bills and the gatekeeper had already cashed out. Instead of simply waving the fee, the control freak called his superior for sufficient funds to break a hundred. Artimus had half a mind to cram a Franklin in the fool's fork-hole, but he decided the fiend was hardly worth it.

Twenty-minutes of contentious detention later, he ploughed through the turnstile. Storming down the stadium steps past an usher who thought it best not to challenge, the pissed-off patron claimed an empty seat right behind the dugout.

Eight innings and the Golden Eagles led 3-2 over cross-town rival B.U. Jason Crandall was in a two-out jam with a man on first and third when he caught the batter looking at a called third strike. The players hustled off the field to grab lumber and get the job done.

Artimus refrained from any attempts at contact; now was not the time.

Thanks to the obliging old man who apparently missed his calling as a play-by-play announcer, by the time the Eagles went three and out to end the inning, Artimus felt like he had been there since the first pitch. Their catcher, David Shoemaker, had smacked a bases loaded double in the fourth, accounting for all their runs. They managed only one hit since. The pitcher, still gunning for a complete game, had been in and out of trouble the whole way. Allowing only five hits, it was the six walks that had his infield bailing him out with three double plays.

Top of the ninth and the kindly gent was incredulous the bullpen remained inactive. "Dagnabit! Hey coach, you got a closer down there pulling his pud!"

The inning began with a leadoff walk that really ratcheted up the old man's blood pressure. Artimus nudged his shoulder and pointed down the right field line. Finally, there was action in the bullpen. The next batter went down swinging, the runner stealing second. A routine pop-up to second brought the crowd to their feet.

A pinch-hitter was announced sending David and the head coach to the mound. The conference brought to Artimus a flashback of bygone youth: the three of them always on the same pickup team reenacting the Red Sox in the neighborhood field, with Monbouquette pitching, Pagliaroni behind the plate, and Yastrzemski shagging fly balls.

"Never mind the runner, he's not gonna steal third. Gimme a fastball high and tight, then we'll work the outside of the plate. Nothing but trash, okay?" David glove-whacked his pitcher's butt just as the umpire reached the mound.

"That's it fellas, break it up."

Jason had retreated to fondle the rosin bag and the catcher was halfway to the plate, stranding the ump in comic ambivalence.

Jason delivered a brush-back fastball followed by a whiffed slider, low and outside. A foul tip into the stands and the count was a ball and two strikes. From the stretch, he looked back at the runner leading off second and then seemed to hurry his delivery. David was set up for a fastball outside but the pitch came right down the middle. The batter timed it perfectly, a mighty blast over the left field fence. Jason knew at the sound of contact it was gone, and dropped immediately into a crouched position, his hand cradling his head. The coach leaned out from the top step of the dugout, as if believing he could 'will' the ball back into play. It was not to be.

One pitch and a ground ball to short ended the inning. Too little, too late.

Jason stormed off the mound, pegging his glove into the dugout and disappearing below. Sounds of batting practice on the water cooler resounded as players filed in cautiously. David nodded acknowledgement to Artimus before going below to expiate his anguished pitcher.

The closer for B.U. did his job, striking out the side ending the Eagle's dismal season at 5 and 15.

Artimus stood, replaying in his mind Jason's misstep. Yogi Berra's adage, *it ain't over till it's over*, came to mind. "Helluva game, eh?"

David was taking off his gear as he walked to the corner of the dugout. "Damn Art, what a way to wrap up a season, huh?"

"I bet Jason's really bummed." He leaned over the fence and shook David's sweaty, clay-covered hand.

"Yeah, I'd say he's just shy of mass murder at the moment. I figure I'd let him blow off steam before trying to cool him down, really takes things personally. Too damn hard on himself…he's already hinted at hanging up the cleats." David pitched his gear into the dugout. "Man, it's good to see you. I thought you'd lost interest in sports. Surely you didn't come all the way down here to see us blow it again? What's up?"

"Got a call from Stuart last night. It's time."

"Are you serious? You talking 'bout what I think you are?"

"Yup. Looks like their ol' man's on the way out, might not see the end of summer."

"Jesus. We really gonna do this?"

"You betcha. The plan's already being implemented. Get Jason and I'll wait for you at the gate. We'll go have a couple beers, on me, and I'll fill you in."

"Good idea. Gonna have to rinse his mind of this shit before we get anywhere with him on new plans." David looked over his shoulder for his teammate, then came back around. "Hey, I got this new Camaro, I'll drive." David rubbed his stubbly chin in retrospect. "You know, this is perfect. I was wondering what to write about come fall semester."

"What are you talking about?"

"How I spent my summer vacation report should earn me an A plus."

"I forgot. You jocks have such high academic standards to fulfill."

David flipped him the bird then disappeared below.

Hours and pitchers of beer later, the collaborators emerged from Frankie's feeling no pain.

Jason's surly mood over "the pitch" had been tempered due to the information overload Art had presented, not to mention the boilermakers.

It was dusk when David pulled into the vacant stadium parking lot.

"Oh shit! Somebody busted your windshield."

"Freak accident on the way down here."

"That really sucks, man". The sincerity was shot down by the swallowed chuckle. "Tell you what….you headin' back to Tech?"

"That was my plan."

There's a glass man a couple blocks from here that can get you fixed up in a day. I'll take her in first thing in the morning."

"A righteous gesture, sir. Here, this oughtta cover it." Arti forked over ten one-hundreds. "Call me tomorrow when it's done."

"Gotcha. Hey, keep the tach below four thousand. I'm still breaking her in."

They piled out of the Camaro, items of importance transferred and keys swapped.

David sat in the Jag making adjustments. Arti caught Jason at the passenger door.

"Hey, even Koufax got rocked, so don't go doing something stupid. See it through next year, and baseball will have paid your college."

"Yeah, I know. Just getting tired of it all. Remember how much fun it was when we were kids? I sure miss those afternoon pickup games."

Arti clasped his friend's hand, "A simpler time for sure. Hey, but dig it man, we're gonna have one hell of a summer, aren't we?"

"Bet your ass we are. Can't wait to get away from it all."

CHAPTER SEVEN

Having washed off "The Weight" of D.C. grunge, The Band pled for relief from some room down the hall, as Will emerged from the dormitory's community shower feeling five pounds lighter. Five days of dirt, sticky sweat, and crusty blood in matted hair, had been rinsed down the drain. The ratty clothes were all he had returned with and these he stuffed in the trash bin. Dripping wet, he walked with impudicity down the hallway clogged with footlockers, stereos, and duffel bags. Those who had concluded their finals were getting a jump on summer break, which officially began in three days.

The door was locked. Taps turned into knocks, and then beatings. He contemplated going out the window next door and shuffling across the narrow ledge seven stories up. He always left the room unlocked, contrary to his paranoid roommate who envisioned dubious characters attempting a harrowing rip-off of his stash. "Dammit, French, wake up!"

The door opened and Will crashed through with a clenched fist that narrowly missed his roommate's groggy face.

"Holy shit, man, where the hell have you been? Rumors flying all over the place! Saw your ride roll in Sunday night...they were real evasive, acting strange. Asked 'em what happened to you, said they lost you and thought you split. Dudes wouldn't even look me in the eye, ally keyed up. No one's seen 'em since. Think they checked out or something."

Wrapped in his bed quilt, Will waded through Frenchy's chaos of half-packed belongings and returned to the cubbyhole study. Mini-fridge raided, he emptied into the hardback chair while sliding open the window with his foot. Will tilted back, feigning attentiveness to the incessant grilling while biting his tongue. *Chicken shit. French had been all gung-ho about going, but at the last minute bailed with a lame excuse about meeting with counselors to sign up for fall classes.* Will knew damn well the admin offices were never open on the weekends.

"If you don't mind, I need to crash for a while. Wanna know what went on down there, why don't you go get a paper and read all about it."

Will's tone, followed by an awkward silence, told Frenchy that it was best he vacate the premises. "Hey man, you going to make it down to Doc's?"

"Wha- ...what'd you say?" Will was somewhere yonder in the mountains.

"Doc wants us at his pad by six. You forget about it?"

"Forget about what? Ah shit! Yeah, I guess I'll be there. If I'm late, just start without me."

"I'll set the alarm..."

"Man. I said I'd be there."

Frenchy caught the drift. He collected what he needed and then bowed out, closing the door on a dorm room suddenly growing cramped.

"Oh...FUCK!" His left foot drove the realization into the window sill. He had missed the one final he knew he could ace. *Great.* A fitting end to a freshman year he knew would mark the last of his ill-fated college career. *Well, wonder how long before Uncle Sam comes calling.* Disillusioned over the whole Washington incident, Will floated in ambiguity as he recalled the play by play:

Upon arrival Friday, considerable time was spent on a stroll of the Capitol grounds. The cherry blossoms were in full bloom as Will stood at the feet of Lincoln, feeling small and watching the influx of protestors swell the ranks by the hour. Staking out a piece of turf by the Washington monument, he pitched his tent amongst a sea of humanity.

Saturday's concert. Best seat in the house. Perched high in a massive oak overhanging the stage, sharing the huge limb with two lovebirds peaking on acid, kindness was reciprocated with an offering for him to indulge. The festive atmosphere lasted well into Sunday until darkness came with night.

Growing ire filled the smoky air, caused by hundreds of small campfires reminiscent of a civil war encampment. Ralph and Eddie were acting squirmy. Mayday Tribe zealots congregated, coordinating plans to shut down the city; volunteers would drive into Virginia and Maryland, then return during morning rush hour, backing up traffic. All seven bridges were to be shut down, keys thrown into the river. A few planned to set their decrepit vehicles ablaze, taking one for the team. Mob mentality simmered beneath it all with a brash indiscretion. The party was definitely over.

Monday dawned, his head thumping with the sound of choppers beating the air into submission. Crawling out from under the plastic tarp, revealed Ralph and Eddie had cut and run along with half the weekend revelers.

ASSHOLES! Nothing left, not even his wallet. He was at ground zero, and an unwilling conscript in a depleted army of thirty thousand Yippies and other hardcore elements hell bent on anarchy.

"YOU HAVE ONE HOUR TO DISPERSE AND VACATE THE PREMISES!" The loudspeaker ripped asunder any remaining hopes festivities would continue. These guys meant business, and that was heard loud and clear.

National Guard and riot police advanced in rank, initiating a mass retreat to points unknown. What ensued was two days of bedlam.

Trashcans hurled off bridge overpasses onto oncoming traffic, not good. City streets choked with tear gas. Innocent bystanders and rock-throwing malcontents alike suffered burning consequences. All day and into the night, running. Anyone with long hair, motley dressed, or just looking suspicious, rounded up. Georgetown's soccer field became a gulag, jails overflowed. Late night: exhausted, lost, and hungry, walking a side street, the smell of gas, sirens close and faraway.

Eerie beginnings of "Gimme Shelter" echoed softly from a brownstone building's open window...he indeed felt like a stone rolling with no bearing, a rolling stone in need of a place to rest.

Angel of mercy, cute blond, approached and offered asylum for the night. A safe house. Must have been a hundred people crammed inside. Half dozen televisions, different stations broadcasting live, Nixon evincing his resolve and declaring zero tolerance. Cronkite. Another room, a makeshift triage: ankle sprains, cracked skulls, broken bones, puking and labored breathing from burning, gassed lungs. A cache of small arms lined a bedroom wall.

Ham radios monitored, Black Panthers dressed in military fatigues. *DAMN!* Now holed-up with some serious radicals.

Tuesday, daybreak. Bologna on bread never tasted so good and all he wanted to do was get the hell out of town. Filing out of the brownstone building along with fifty others, no sooner had they hit the street and squad cars and paddy wagons converged. Pigs swarmed while dispersing pepper spray, flailing nightsticks, itching to unleash snarling attack dogs. It was every man for his self. There was a mad dash, cutting left and right. Down an alleyway, colliding at the corner with a cop. Face bloodied. Massachusetts Avenue was in full riot mode. Guardsmen squared off with an unruly mob refusing to yield. More tear gas, another hasty retreat. Hours of zigzagging through war zones trying to make a way out of the city.

High noon at DuPont Circle. Trying to get bearings, cops pull up to the curb. One 'brilliant' miscalculation of asking which way to the interstate. While talking to the officer riding shotgun, he was oblivious to the driver who had gotten out and came up from behind. Head split, Billy club cinched across the throat, thrown in the back of the cruiser with another brutalized catch.

Jail was a madhouse: two-man cells packed with twenty, pigs spraying irritants through ground level windows, neck and back on fire. Next cell over, epileptic girl passes out standing up. Packed like cordwood. Five hours of screaming profanities reciprocated by police brutality, finally processed and charged with disorderly conduct.

The hitchhiking was a blur. Hell, anything coulda happened to me. Was it four or five rides? His chair pitched back precariously, feet on the sill, Will conked out.

CHAPTER EIGHT

Following two comatose hours in the wooden chair, *so this is what rigor mortis feels like,* the long hike to Doc's was therapeutic.

Will leaned against the steep stairs, the trap door denying entry. He pulled the cord that tinkled Japanese chimes inside the cabin.

"Are we fashionably late now," asked Stuart, swirling a martini.

"Hey man, at least he made it." Smitty snuffed his butt, already perturbed with Stuart's stuffy arrogance. "I'll get him. I think last week fucked him over pretty good, so cut him a little slack, man."

Having not seen his wayward friend for a week, he could not resist the inane routine. "Don't crush that dwarf..."

"Cut the crap, Smithers, and open the frigging hatch."

"Not without the password."

"Hand me the pliers," Will's voice sighed in resignation as the trap door opened to an outstretched hand. "Man, this better be worth it. You mind filling me in?"

"Haven't a clue dude, been waiting on you."

"Sorry 'bout the delay, didn't know if I'd even make it," Will's laissez-faire entrance affronted the pertinacious ringleader. Stepping over and around the lazing group, catching a beer hand-off from Kaz, he squatted against the log wall. Smitty echoed everyone's sentiment.

"Poster boy for Gimme Shelter, man you look like shit."

"Thanks brillo-head. Should've been there, could've used you to run interference."

"Alright gentlemen, can it." Doc pitched out to Stuart. "It's all yours."

Stuart nodded, killed his drink, and opened with a jabbing lampoon to the latecomer.

"Anyone incapable of adhering to schedule and protocol best bow out now before I begin."

"Whoa, dude. You're lucky I made it at all. So just cut the pompous crap and deal, man."

"From what Doc's told me, you blew your hand first year in college, and you're lucky I brought a new deck. So if we could dispense with the bullshit, perhaps you'll allow me to proceed."

Pegged, Will conceded. "Well, you got me there. By all means, carry on."

"Excellent. Before we go any further, do I have everyone's solemn word that what's spoken in this room remains confidential? Our mutual acquaintances have vouched for you, and if you care to respect that trust, you will maintain tight lips."

A unanimous assent gave Stuart pause to freshen his drink. Kaz and French exchanged quizzical glances. Smitty blew smoke rings, the Camel floaters zeroing in on Stuart. Will tapped Doc, whispering, "I get it, premiering your nightclub with stand-up comedy and we're your first patrons."

"Yeah, right. You're gonna love the punch line." Privy to the bizarre scheme two years in the planning, Doc repositioned to observe the audience's reaction.

The proposal was crafted such that the gist was presented, yet particulars were reserved for those who signed on. Stuart began with a question:

"Has anyone here sailed before?"

Will broke through the silence with a meager response. "Gramps had a sloop. Showed me the ropes at his summer cottage on Squam Lake."

"Is everyone willing to learn and get paid handsomely?"

All hands signaled on deck.

If he never stepped foot in a phone booth again, it would be too soon. While his brother sought recruits, Rick had spent the better part of two days feeding coins into pay phones; no two calls made from the same locale. First and foremost was hooking up with their island confidant, Zal, whom they had befriended many years ago. It was he who had turned them on to an enterprising, albeit bizarre, proposition. A Jamaican transplant attending Saint Thomas College, the Rastafarian was closing in on a four-year liberal arts degree. Paying his way through college as first mate aboard a small-time commercial fishing boat, four years of weekends trolling the archipelago made him an invaluable informant. His knowledge of charts, accessibility to the eighty-odd islands, and even Coast Guard activity, was critical to formulating their strategy. Zal also kept abreast of the local agriculture, and one crop in particular was key to his spiritual roots.

"So sorry 'bout your fatha, Masta Rick. But if it had to haa'pen, coulda' not chose a bedda time cuz it been a banna' year for ganja. Looking forward to your return, mon. Have beaucoup information you and your brutha need. May Jah be with you, then you and I celebrate maybe, yah?"

The call gave Rick the green light to proceed. The past few years he, his brother, and Artimus had made "connections" while canvassing the college scene. It was a hit list of prime customers, and the boys were quite particular and discriminating in their selection, having landed on a half-dozen candidates who fit their criteria: out of state transfer students of an enterprising nature with little family connections, or very close friends trusted, residing along the eastern seaboard and owning vessels suited for off-shore ventures. Intentions premised and sworn to secrecy, the like-minded adventurers committed to a pact that would be privy only to the Blaine brothers and Artimus, as clandestine preparations were formulated.

It had been eighteen months since the senior Blaine was first diagnosed; his stubborn, year-long denial of a pesky cough sealing his fate. They had expected old age, not cancer, to be the signal it was time to act. The circumstances as they were had differing impacts on the sons: Stuart's matter-of-fact summation that everyone goes in the end and pop's misfortune only served to move up the timetable. Such cavalier coldness deeply disturbed Rick who, from that moment on, reserved judgment on his sibling's morality.

Contacts cued, Rick returned to the cape. Holed-up in his father's study, he gathered nautical maps, schematics and maintenance records for the schooner. Pouring over the latest on maritime law and boundaries, he sat at the desk comprising a check list and itinerary. It was late afternoon when the maid came calling to see if dinner was in order. Gently lifting his head, she placed a pillow underneath and freed the pen from mid-sentence.

Doc and Stuart had stepped out for a bite, leaving the dumbstruck time to digest the outlandish proposal. They would each have to ante up before the stakes were raised and the particulars divulged.

Once back in Doc's cabin of countless dreams induced, it was the moment of truth. "Alright you guys, who's in?" Glances were exchanged, the wheels still turning as they mulled over the prospect.

Will raided Doc's fridge and cracked open a Schlitz. "Okay, I'll kick it off. I'm in regardless what the rest of you decide. For me, this is like drawing an inside straight. School's down the drain, dumped my girl, and returning home is not an option. I've been stewing over what to do and where to go this summer." His beer raised acknowledging Stuart, "you solved the mystery. Adventure, new horizons, if what little you've disclosed is no bullshit; extensive planning and a ready crew who, from what you describe, have a hell of a lot more to lose than I...yeah, count me in if you're that confident in its success." The desperado stood alone in thought, a moment of silence ensued as the others weighed their own decision. *Got nothing to lose, no bridges left to burn. Best get onboard or suffer a self-imposed exile on my own island, void of any promise.*

"Damn the torpedoes, full speed ahead!" Smitty stood with Will and clinked bottles. "Count me in. Sure beats a summer in Wyoming shoveling stalls of horseshit and castrating baby bulls. Not to mention enduring the old man's drunken laments. Get to learn how to sail *and* make a boatload of money to boot? Hell yeah, or I'd be looking a gift horse in the mouth!"

Kaz was caught up in the enthusiasm, but clearly anxious. "Sounds too good to be true, but I just can't bring myself to pass it up. As long as we're back in time for fall semester, guess I'm along for the ride."

"French, how 'bout it?" Will could tell by the expression that asking was a mere formality.

"Excuse me for saying this, but you guys are fucking nuts. Too many variables, too much to risk. I honestly can't believe you all are sold on such a hair-brained scheme. If something **was** to go wrong, and there's plenty of opportunity for that, you guys could be spending the rest of your life behind bars!"

Will volleyed back a response in an attempt to stymie the negativity. "It sounds like more than just a calculated risk, man. Look, mister aristocrat here probably has more to lose than all of us put together. Why would he gamble his privileged lot if he wasn't so cocksure of its success? There are four other high-rollers that apparently are sold on its feasibility. Come on French, it'll be a gas."

"Nope. Can't do it. Maybe I don't have brass balls, but I just got a bad feeling about it. Besides, my old man depends on me to help run his hardware store. He and ma leave me in charge for two weeks so they can take a much needed vacation." French got up and bid the sailors of fortune good luck. "I'm outta' here guys, gotta pack up and head on home. If I don't read about you in the funny papers, you can tell me all about it when you get back." French passed Doc and Stuart, wished them well with a 'thanks-but-no-thanks', promised to be tight-lipped, and left the cabin to descend back into the real world.

"If anyone were to bail, I'd have picked Kaz. So much for character analysis, eh?" Doc scratched his head while muttering to Stuart.

"Hey, three out of four isn't bad. Sure, it will be a stretch, but we can wing it with a crew of nine. Look at it as one less slice of the pie. Let's toast to the new crew, and then I'll brief you all on next week's itinerary before I split. Got to get back home, still have a ton of details to iron out."

Will was in no hurry to join the exodus from campus. Frenchy had cleared out the night of the meeting, Smitty and Kaz were off the next day to make ready for the big summer event.

Friday morning on his way out, Doc stopped by Will's pad to give him directions to the Cape for next Thursday's inaugural crew meeting. "Man! Looks like a rummage sale. What gives?"

"Records, stereo, ski equipment, books...even party favors, all being sold at discount prices. I figure to pocket three hundred and I've got an idea how I can extort a grand from dear ole mom when I get back home, going price for abortions in New York."

"Man, you shitting me? Who'd you knock up?"

"No one I know of."

"That's pretty cold; you know it'll break her heart. You can live with that?"

"She'll probably be plastered when I tell her. It'll just give her a reason to really tie one on. Besides, I've caught my folks in lies so many times, I figure turnabout is fair play."

"Sounds pretty fucked up back home."

"Yeah, but it has its advantages."

"How's that?"

"Madness, insanity all these years…hell, what we're attempting to pull off seems tame in comparison." The straightforward retort left Doc with no doubts about Will's hell's-bells commitment to the cause. The two shook on it.

Will stood in the near empty room, the hallway echoing with fading footsteps. The thought of returning home was unthinkable, so he lay down on his bare bed. He would sleep until the custodian or some administrative hack evicted him for vagrancy.

He dreamed of tall ships, blue waters, and booty.

CHAPTER NINE

"Jeez, Will! You look like Ryan friggin' O'Neal. You had to get a haircut to go fishing?"

If he only knew. "Nope. Didn't want to hassle with it any more, that's all." The guise was a prerequisite to deliver the deception: collegiate yachtsmen in training, honing their skills.

The day before was quite a scene at Goffstown's local barbershop. Ancient Henry had not seen Will in years, his freak-flag living proof. When told he could take all but two inches, the barber nearly fudged his pants. Three old coots, familiar to Will since he was a little tyke, simultaneously lowered their newspapers to witness a hippie being defrocked. *Reforming? Military?* Will sat unflinching as ten inches were pruned to the floor. The usually verbose shearer-of-locks was engrossed in the moment, jubilant at the prospect there was still hope for the generation he could not understand. Yes, the rare event would be celebrated at the ole red and white for quite some time. The codgers bearing witness would recant the shearing snip by snip, year after year.

John backed out of the driveway, stopping at the end to engage Hendrix into the eight-track and fire one up in a purple haze.

"Man, you *ever* gonna get your own wheels?"

The question went unanswered. Sister and brother stood on the front porch looking forlorn.

For years Will had been their buffer zone, doing what he could to shield them from the ugly, sometimes violent, domestic conflicts. He would station them in their bedrooms and position himself on standby, his bedroom door ajar, listening to the escalating war of words beyond. An obnoxious drunk, mother would beat a dead horse, driving father to the brink of madness. The son-of-a-bitch deserved it though…he taught her how to drink. Will pressed his temples as the flashback threatened to bore its way out of his head:

"*I can't take it anymore you fucking bitch!*" A loud slam reverberated down the hallway, followed by a grotesque moan from mom.

Twelve year-old Will raced down the hallway to intercede. What he found were two flounders loaded to the gills…*how the hell can two people polish off a half gallon of Scotch in a weekend?* The red-glared eyes of a man possessed flashed in the corner; father had her in a stranglehold. Her head was pressed against the dining room wall, and a free hand was poised to knock her block into the next room. "*Dad, stop it! Leave her alone!*" The intrusion redirected the rage.

There was total disconnect in that moment as father knew not son. The death-grip was quick as he rose and chased him to his bedroom. A bed was all that separated a little man with pissed pants from the approaching devil. Through squinted eyes he heard the bedsprings creak and awaited the impending onslaught of drunken rage…it never came. Eyelids gave way to light and the reveal that the monster was felled incoherent across the bed.

He moved down the hall and retrieved his slumped mother, carrying her to bed. It was a hard night curled up on his little brother's floor, but he was protector, and they needed him.

Fond memories such as these Will could discount as just a bad dream, but what his sister confided to him during the tearful goodbye left him feeling sick to his stomach and contemplating revenge. For all his trials and tribulations, the totality paled in comparison to what had been kept secret all these years. Molested repeatedly by the sick bastard, many times while everyone else was asleep, Will was livid that he had not been told, but the explanation given he could not refute. Having witnessed her older brother sneaking out of the house many times with pop's twelve-gauge, successfully bagging partridge and pheasant, sister was afraid of what might happen. *She was right. Would've blown the son-of-a-bitch into the nether world! So help me, when I get back I'll find him and there'll be hell to pay!"*

Rubbing the back of his neck, Will sighed away a life bereft of rationality. "Thanks for the lift, Johnny." Will palmed a C-note, along with a joint. "Here, this should cover it. Now let's get the fuck outta here."

"Righteous, my man, I take back slamming you about wheels. Hey, how's your ma?" The Volkswagon van whined in reverse out of the driveway.

Will could not bear to look back at his siblings. "Nine a.m., third Bloody Mary. She'll be toast by noon." He donned his shades and muttered, almost imperceptibly, "Prick's gonna wish he never lived."

"What'd you say?" John lowered the music. "Two riders were approaching and the wind began to howl, hey...HEY..."

"Ah, forget it. Hey, you mind making a pit stop at Charlene's? There's something I need to do."

"Uh, sure. Just make it a quickie, eh?" John had no idea the couple were no longer an issue.

"Don't be a smart ass, I just want to say goodbye."

It was a short drive to what used to be his sanctuary. Throughout high school her parents' home had become his; a safe haven where he had been accepted almost as a son. Will knew any attempt at damage control was futile; it was abject guilt he hoped to assuage. His first love deserved a heartfelt apology for having been treated so inexplicably rude. Now that he was divested of college's chemical engineering department, the fogbank he had lost himself in had lifted ever so slightly, enough for him to admit transgression worthy of the most sincere apology. The van drove up the long driveway, which Will now felt in his gut was no longer inviting.

"Stay here. I'll be right back."

Will got out, walked around a strange car plastered with Marine logos, and entered the garage. He was greeted at the door by his almost mother-in-law that was to be no more. Bitter hurt for her daughter radiated as she told Will to leave. What he had done and the manner in which he did it was unforgiveable. Will insisted he owed Charlene an explanation; all that did was draw out the ire of a protective mother. The standoff called to duty a burly stranger, accompanied by his jarhead buddy. They both sported white tee-shirts stretched to seam-busting limits by abounding muscle mass. They piled out the door, backing Will into the driveway. Words were exchanged. Will hoped Charlene would appear and call off her dogs, but no such rescue was in the offing on that day. Instead, there was a curt warning to leave immediately or he would find himself being hosed off the driveway and rinsed down the gutter. *Pretty clear on message*, Will thought.

"What the fuck you lookin' at, faggot?"

Sitting on the front fender, poor John never saw it coming. The chiseled marine walked right up to the neutral observer and unloaded a haymaker to the face. John went flying across the windshield and landed face down on the pavement.

"All right, that's enough, you made your point!" Will hustled to his downed friend, picked him up, and quickly deposited him in the passenger seat. "Fuckin' assholes! Didn't waste any time movin' in, did ya?" Readying for the assault, he walked past the pugilist and his mute sidekick. Sliding into the van, he was at the same time surprised and relieved to be departing unscathed, but it was a real kick in the crotch there was no sight of the girl who once loved him to death.

The jarhead's shit-eating grin accompanied a farewell: "Payback's a mother, ain't it? Now get the hell off the property."

"Fuck you!" Will revved up and backed out of the driveway, leaving the goon squad in blue exhaust. He was pissed off. Not so much at the ignominious scene as he was at his own lack of foresight. *Reap what you sow, asshole. Should've seen this coming.* "Jesus, Johnny. I'm sorry." His friend's cheek was swollen, lip split open, a mouthful of blood expelled out the window.

"Ya, what the hell did *I* do?"

"Beats me. Maybe he just didn't like your face." Will grabbed the retired, oil-stained Red Sox jersey off the floorboard. "Here man, use this. Just sit back and cool it, I'll get us down the road a bit."

Will could not argue with "Me and Bobby McGee", Janis was right about when you had nothing left to lose.

The aborted attempt to apologize his way out of town was the proverbial nail in the coffin, strangely freeing him of anything else to come home about, the town having grown minuscule, complete with a covered bridge that could safely be considered burned. But what REALLY spurred him on to get the hell out of Dodge was the offer from the gracious sheriff who had known him since he was knee high to a grasshopper. A week earlier, having been busted for ten pounds of Columbian Gold, he was presented a get out of jail free card with a non-negotiable option: leave the state within the week. It was that decree that had made the conscript Will an unflinching participant in the face of the hazardous venture awaiting him. Besides, he had no place else to go. The unknown of what lie ahead was even more so now anticipated with enthusiasm and wonder.

Will relinquished the wheel at a gas station just outside of Derry and placed the call.

"Hey Smitty, ready to get it on?"

"I've been ready, and it's about time! The old man's really pissed about me going, says you're a bad influence and the summer job's nothing but a ruse. Just a bunch of incorrigible hippies on a lark. I think the only thing that kept him from taking a swing at me was my damn haircut. He's out plowing the back forty, so I suggest you get your ass over here quick. Kaz is with me, our gear's staged at the end of the driveway."

"Right, be there in a flash. Hey remember, our driver thinks we're working the cod boats. See you in ten."

"Just hurry up."

So I'm a bad influence, huh? I didn't twist anyone's arm to enlist.

Two hours later, thanks to the usual screwed-up Boston traffic, Will co-piloted John through Hyannis down to the waterfront where directions said to pass the two parallel piers. Not a hundred yards further, he saw the timber-framed establishment named Sea Basstion's Tavern. Once inside, they would be directed to the private luncheon reserved in the back room.

For someone to have kindly offered his services, regardless of the hundred-dollar compensation, the trip to the Cape ended with a brusque farewell. John expected a farewell drink for services rendered, but the troupe remained stationary by their gear, a ruse intended to give the impression they were awaiting a supposed transfer to their trawler. Something other than the raw egg smell of the Atlantic reeked of subterfuge. *Why the hell were they so adamantly opposed to a farewell drink in the tavern?* John could not help but feel slighted as he drove off fingering a salute. "Sayonara, cod heads!" Rubbing his swollen cheek, he vowed retirement as designated driver.

Jason Douglass

Awkward vibes called for a precautionary smoke and small talk before entering the tavern, just in case their ride decided to double-back. Once assured, they hoisted their belongings and entered Herman Melville's world.

Established in the 1830s, Sea Basstions' original single-room bar was an historic landmark. The bartender acknowledged the patrons from behind his dory-shaped enclave. The rough-hewn timber and dark mahogany absorbed the lanterns' candlelight, immobilizing new customers until their eyes calibrated. Gaffs, cobwebbed nets, marlinspikes, and even a hurled harpoon stuck in the rafter, lent credence to a seafarer's retreat. Hanging from the walls were old photographs of whaling ships and blubber yards, complimented by news clippings dating as far back as 1852.

"What'll it be, boys, dining room or are you old enough for the bar?"

"Blaine party, miss," responded Will, turning away from obituaries of sailors long ago lost at sea.

"Ah yes, indeed. Please follow me."

The creaky floor had a discernable slant downward leading them past the main dining room to smaller quarters that extended out over the waterfront. Constructed almost a century after the original pub to accommodate private parties, the addition was a gift from a regular patron: Arthur Cromwell Blaine. The huge, pile-driven timbers that supported the overhanging dining area were losing their integrity due to forty years of incessant tidal flow and storm-pounding surf. The slope and noticeable, yet gentle, sway affected a knee-jerking sobriety check on all landlubbers, and was soothing assurance to sea dogs groggy from splicing the main brace. These soused sailors would find comfort in the cadence.

Rick met them at the room's floor-to-rafters swinging saloon doors.

"Thanks, Millie. Please tell the waiters they can serve lunch now. Four more pitchers should take care of us for the time being."

"Sure, sweetie. Give your father my regards. Tell him we sure do miss him around here."

"Will do, ma'am." Rick turned to greet the latecomers with a handshake. "Welcome aboard, mates, take a seat and I'll introduce you to the crew."

Seating around the massive driftwood banquet table had been integrated in order to facilitate acquaintances. Stuart stood at the table's helm, framed by a circular window, its glass overlain with radiating wooden spokes. Rick co-captained the other end, the newcomers filled in slots on each side of the table. Conversation flowed with the beer as two waiters humped trays of crab cakes, fish sandwiches, and plates pyramided with steamers.

Smitty and Artimus immediately hit it off, debating cosmic consciousness crap. An avid baseball aficionado, Kaz could not get enough of Jason and David's exploits. Their talk evolved to the major leagues and both ball players were amazed as they tried in vain to stump the veritable stat machine with trivia. Rick and Will were engaged in casual conversation, debating the merits of snow skiing and surfing. Doc and Stuart tossed around hypothetical scenarios pertaining to the coming venture.

Will tipped his mug towards Rick. "My compliments on your choice of venue, sir, I take it you frequent this place?"

"You could say my brother and I are charter members. Back in the forties, father rescued this place from the wrecking ball. A benevolent contribution restored the landmark, revered for generations by local fishermen. I remember coming here as a little tot on Friday nights. Pops initiated weekend poker fests and rousing cribbage tournaments that have been a mainstay ever since. You play cribbage?"

"Only cutthroat. Ten cents a hole, dollar a game, double for skunk."

"Great! I'll bring a board along with us so I can relieve you of your cash."

"Perhaps, but I doubt it. I'm quite proficient in the art of pegging my opposition into whimpering surrender."

Rick laughed, then switched the subject to sailing. He wanted an idea of how much training would be required to convert the three recruits into functional shipmates.

"Oh, enough to know bow from stern, I guess. Had a summer cabin on a lake and gramps used to take me sailing on his small sloop. He taught me how to tack, jibe downwind, positional difference between close reach and close-hauled, how to pinch the wind. Showed me some sailor's knots, but I don't know if I remember. Hell Rick, it's been ten years. Smitty and Kaz...professional landlubbers."

"Needn't worry, swab, it'll be my responsibility for getting you guys up to snuff along with the others who'll receive a refresher course."

Stuart chimed the meeting to order. As Doc circled the room handing out envelopes containing details of the schooner's specs, layout, glossary of nautical terminology, and one-way airfare on Eastern Airlines, the crew was briefed on all aspects of the itinerary that were not incriminating. The dicey details would be discussed later, not in a public setting.

Stuart looked at his watch. An hour from now, transportation would be arriving for portage to Logan airport. "Gentlemen. We haven't much time so allow me to speak uninterrupted. Any questions will be addressed in due time. The information packets are for your benefit, I suggest you familiarize yourself on the flight down. This operation will require all hands to be proficient in their primary tasks but also dependably versatile. Rick will coordinate training and serve as instructor." Pausing for effect and a swig, he continued. "Years of planning and preparation, risks calculated, everything from charts updated to contacts confirmed…if everyone does their job and stays on task, success shall be assured. Once we…" the constant hand gesture was becoming a real pain in the ass.

"What is it Mister Bradford? Apparently you do not listen very well, as I said no questions at this time."

"Understood, but there's something that's bugging me. From what Doc's told me, you and your brother are sitting pretty…so why in hell are you guys doing this? It doesn't make any sense.

"Because we can." Stuart knew he should have anticipated such a query, but it was the source posing the question that was flustering. *What is it about this guy?* It was all he could do to remain calm as he purposefully talked down to the one whom he perceived to be an insolent wise guy. "I know you can't relate, but what you envision as a life of privilege is not all that it's trumped up to be. You're expected to tow a certain line, walk in the footsteps of someone else's success, think and act according to what others regard appropriate and befitting a 'gentleman'. Imagine watching yourself in a movie and you already know how it's going to end, pretty fucking boring, huh? Is monetary gain our reason for such a bold undertaking? Hardly, just icing on the cake as far as I'm concerned. It's the challenge and the opportunity of autonomy that in itself is the reward. It's the absolute genius of the plan we've so meticulously pulled together. After college, when we're all some sorts of corporate cogs subjected to rules and regulations, the fact that we bucked the system on our own terms will be the hook I proudly hang my hat on. Besides, when we pull this off, which I assure you we will, it'll make for one hell of a story to tell someday. Does that satisfy you, *Mister* Bradford?"

"Works for me, if it does for you Mister Blaine. Personally though, it's the money that makes it worth the risk."

Courtesies feigned, Rick sensed the negative charge and intervened. "Just remember gentlemen, we operate as a *team*. To promote collective soul, proceeds from this enterprise will be equitably split. It is imperative everyone realize we--"

"Excuse me, boys. Your transportation just arrived."

"Thanks Mil," replied Stuart, regaining the helm. "Tell the drivers they can load our gear. Do you mind putting all this on father's tab?"

"Taken care of. Just be sure to stop by when you return and fill me in. You lads are in for a trip of a lifetime. May fair winds blow you safely home with god-speed so your dear father's request will be satisfied."

"All right then, it's a wrap. I had intended on giving a brief outline for the benefit of the new guys," Stuart shot a glance at Will. "You can thank me later for the furnished material. Familiarize yourselves with it on the way down and for Christ's sake be cognizant of those around you. Refrain from discussing anything about this on the plane."

Few words were spoken during the one-hour caravan to Logan. Cabbies are excellent listeners.

CHAPTER TEN

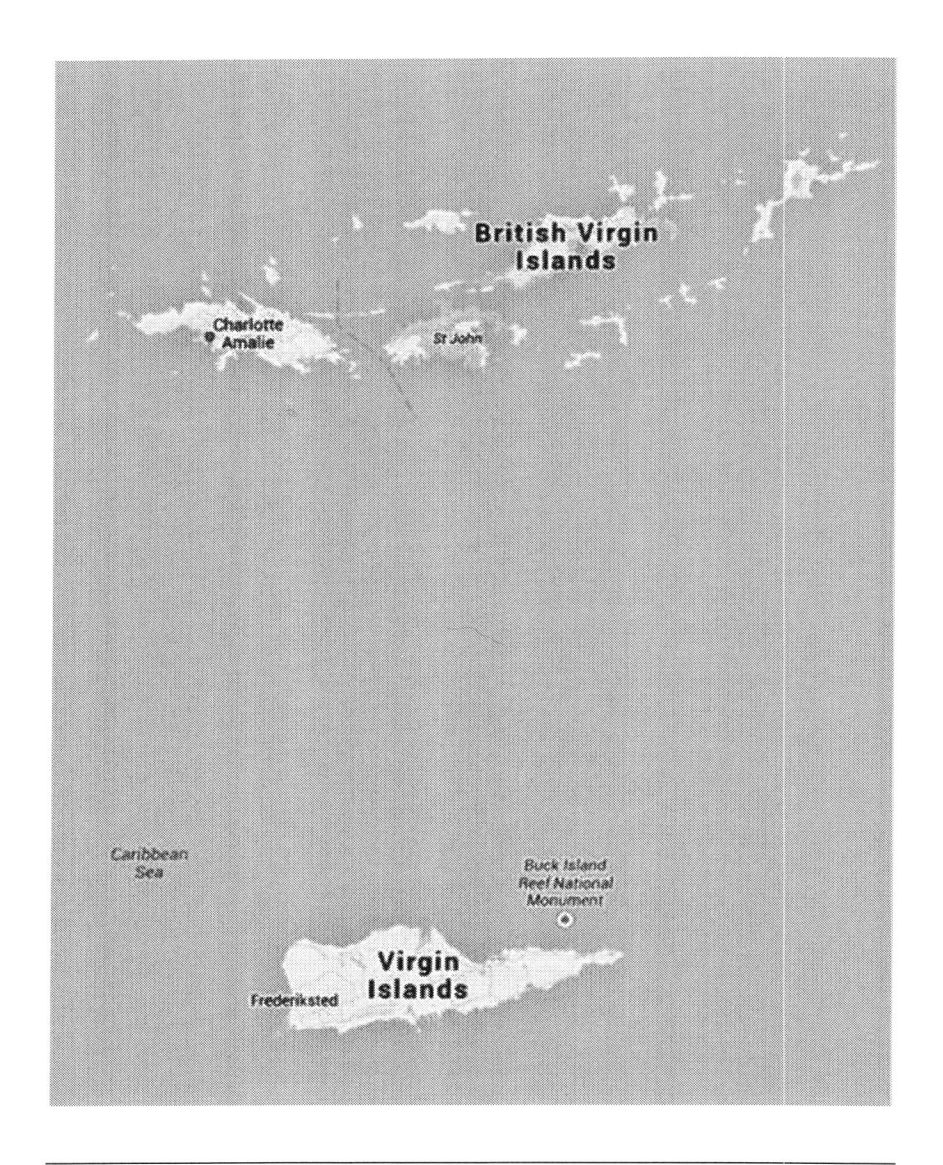

United States Virgin Islands.

Saint Thomas, St. John, and St. Croix, along with eighty non-descript islands and cays, comprise an archipelago which is part of the Leeward and Lesser Antilles. St. Croix: arid. St. John: two-thirds tropical jungle nature preserve. St. Thomas: commercialized, touristy. Two islands, Big and Little Hans Lollick, a couple cays large enough to warrant names. The remaining miniscule outcroppings, mostly undeserving of map recognition.

Most were comprised of volcanic soil-rock, the lowest lying lands mostly sand too briny to sustain anything more than mangrove and the hardiest indigenous flora. However, a select few with elevation had workable soil enhanced by fertilizer. These were unincorporated and tax exempt farms exclusively utilized by the pharmaceutical industry as well as military R&D. What was grown? Hybrid plants, referred to in popular culture as weed, various strains crossbred and cultivated for their chemical compound THC. It was all for research, exploring the wide-ranging beneficial medicinal uses: pain management, glaucoma, diabetes, perhaps even treatment of psychological disorders. One would think since hemp had been utilized since early Egyptian times, the potential would already be widely known.

So remote and inaccessible, these "funny" farms were kept secret, or at least denied. Many islanders considered any postulating as simply rumor or folk-lore. Still, many others wondered about the wonder-drug plantations' existence. One particular dreadlocked captain's mate, with a nose for ganja and eyes and ears receptive to the faintest scuttlebutt, new better. After years of enlisting on various fishing vessels combing the territorial waters, he knew Coast Guard routes and routines. He was familiar with backwaters to the point he no longer consulted depth charts. Yes, Zal was a logistical goldmine who had an incurable itch to rip off The MAN.

These well-concealed farms were located on remote, uninhabited islands. Access was tricky, but attainable. Scheduled patrols in the areas of interest had been documented. Charts were updated. A half dozen prospective islands were identified. They would hit those most feasible then make a beeline to Florida where they would cruise the eastern seaboard well outside the twelve-mile jurisdiction. Committed clientele would rendezvous at predetermined coordinates with insistence that they be in International waters. Arrive at the Cape, clean as a whistle and all the richer for it.

The dog and pony show while in the islands would be intentional: they were a collegiate yacht team in training. Their itinerary involved cruising the archipelago to work on tacking maneuvers while making periodic stops to dive, fish, and perform routine maintenance. At dusk they would conduct their forays, and harvest however much they could before dawn.

The brief prospectus, one page glued to the inside of three scoffed-up travel brochures, had been put together by Rick once current intelligence was received from some mystery dude, name not divulged.

Will, Smitty, and Kaz sat in silence. They had just entered the loop where the other six did not require any explaining.

Will spoke softly. "Well, Smithers. Perfect timing, huh? We agreed there was no backing out once made privy. No wonder Rick waited 'til now."

"No shit. 30,000 feet up, haven't seen anything but ocean for how long? So much for parachutes."

Kaz sat across the aisle, pale-faced. He looked like he needed a drink and that is just what he called for from the passing stewardess. "Rum and coke...uh, double."

A couple rows back, Doc was somewhere out the window, immersed in thought. His focus had nothing to do with the familiar scheme, but rather the seating arraignments. *Some things never change,* he thought. The partition that separated them from their blue-blood colleagues, toughing it out in first class, was grating in symbolism. He was not pissed, how could he be while flying free. *It is what it is.* Doc floated above the clouds, recalling his sixteenth birthday:

Pa surprised him not with keys to a new car, but an invitation to sign on with other fathers and sons for the annual summer trek up the coast. Far removed from the social elite, the only commonality they shared with this part of the upper crust was the boys' friendship that had been kindled throughout grade school. Doc was always considered one of the guys, but when it came to family functions and social events, economics and privilege reared their ugly heads.

So memorable, that summer cruise of '64 haunted him. Although they were welcomed as part of the crew, father and son could not help but feel somewhat slighted by the rest of the sailing party's hauteur. Reality of caste forced a bond between father and son outsiders who had for some time drifted apart like so many Generation Gap casualties. He and dad actually related, realizing they had more in common than not. *I finally had the ole man figured out,* or so he thought.

    No sooner had *Slipfinger* docked and their separate cars been loaded, than did dad unload a bombshell. Goodbyes were exchanged and son, feeling like a gun, leaned against his set of wheels and watched the bastard drive away memories of a trip now forgettable. His mind had been blown numb, the drive home...surreal. Dad was leaving mom. Said he got things sorted out before their trip. *Son-of-a-bitch was so nonchalant about it! Well, hell of a farewell tour. So happy for you and your mid-life crisis!*

    It was soon after that when his tango with mind-bending drugs began. *Correlation? Perhaps.*

    Doc returned from the clouds. Six years since that last voyage and it was not rusty sailing skills or rubbery sea legs that concerned him. It was that damn barrier separating the four of them from their first class counterparts. He hoped the symbolism was just a misread on his part. *'Be a wicked long time at sea cooped up on a jammer.*

    Will reached into the seat pouch; the in-flight magazine would do as a diversion for a mind spinning imagined scenarios. He wanted to shut down and snooze, and whatever advertisement fodder was contained within should suffice just fine. Leafing through the first few pages, retaining nothing of the prop for idle hands, his mind drifted to the seat assignments as well: *It's a bit of 'us-versus-them', isn't it? Hell, first class was probably full anyway, and besides us peons can't bitch. Got a ride to paradise and one hell of an adventure...free of charge.* Still, he could not shake the thought that if the shit hit the fan, the expendable stooges were riding coach. *Fall guys, fucking cannon-fodder.* He thought about broaching the subject with Karl, but checked himself, downing his second high altitude rum with a splash. Besides, his friend had Kaz and a stewardess engrossed with another of his bizarrely hilarious, believe-it-or-not tales of childhood gone stupid. Will was fairly certain he had heard them all and had to admit they were a riot, though questionable as to authenticity.

On cue, the cabin signs illuminated the call for seat belts and no smoking, just as he turned another page. The "ping" for descent was really the sound of his jarred brain tilting when the centerfold advertisement for Virgin Islands Getaways nailed him with hard sell sensory overload. "Beauty and the Beach" captioned the alluring picture, her intent look captivating and holding no prisoners. He could not tell whether she was coming from, or going into, the frothy turquoise surf. Knee-deep, oncoming breaker, she stood sideways with arched back; her jet-black long hair proving a steady breeze. Bronze olive skin glittered with flecks of beach sand all the way up shapely thighs to a white bikini bottom which tortuously left to the imagination one hell of a nice derriere. The profile of her bikini top proved to be more cruelty to animals. Her posture seemed to exude confidence, and danger worth any risk.

Jaguar eyes...no, the welcoming gaze on the whole of her face, solicited him out of playboy mentality. Her parted lips facilitated imagination of kissing, there was a nuance in her look that said both "come" and "leave me be." *Damn she's gorgeous **and** haunting. Sure would be a handful.*

The enigma held him a willing hostage until a hard landing and reverse thrusters yanked him out of his nosedive into the magazine.

CHAPTER ELEVEN

The bright sun softening the tarmac was quite pleasant as it patted down the shoulders of the arrivals. Towering coconut palms rustled credence to the incessant trade winds providing relief: eighty-eight degrees and not a wisp of cloud in the sky. For the first-timers, 'paradise found' somewhat mollified trepidations of there being no turning back. They were now committed.

Baggage claim projected a compliment of dialects: a soothing English lilt seasoned with Creole, mixed in with the melodious pitches of Dutch, Spanish, and French.

At the curb, two vans would be required for the six-mile transport to *Slip's* berth in Charlotte Amalie. Even then, it was a tight squeeze with duffel bags, suitcases, and carry-ons. Once again, as on the plane, they crew rode separate.

Named after the seventeenth century Danish queen, Charlotte Amalie was a popular cruise destination and home to a multitude of high rollers hiding their tax-sheltered yachts from the inclement northern winters. A labyrinth of tight alleyways funneled down to the docks, where cruise ships rotated in and out, releasing passengers to lose themselves in search of duty-free bargains: cigars and liquor a favored quest. Rustic, actually rusting, warehouses lined the waterfront, backed up by a cornucopia of quaint mercantile exchanges, boutiques, open-air eateries, and hole-in-the-wall bars.

After negotiating the hustle and bustle leading to the marina overlooking Hatch Cay, the cab-vans pulled alongside one of two long piers jutting out into the bay.

Fares paid and taxis unloaded, Stuart told his brother he would meet up with them dockside. Crossing the street, he entered the turn of the century two-story blockhouse. Having accompanied his father many times, he knew the routine. He presented personal credentials proving ownership, and the port master reciprocated with critical information: maintenance logs, condition of the ship, repairs performed, and pending work necessary in order to confirm her seaworthy. Stuart filled out the required customs paperwork and entered into the Coast Guard logbook a tentative departure-arrival schedule along with projected course headings; a precautionary formality to facilitate search and rescue.

Rick led the crew down the wharf which thrust itself a full football field's length into the bay. The new guys straggled, gawking at the floating fortunes lining the boardwalk.

Rejoined three quarters of the way out, Rick relished the introduction. "Gentlemen. I present to you our lady of the winds, her majesty of the seas, *Slipfinger*."

Kaz's jaw dropped. "The nine of us are going to sail **this** monster?"

"Nah, we'll lasso a whale for a tow home." Arti turned at the gangplank. Come on guys, let's check her out."

Jason, David, and Doc slung their gear and filed onboard. The new guys just stood in awe: Will and Karl captivated, Kaz clearly intimidated.

"Damn! No wonder your dad calls her his mistress, she's magnificent."

Rick acknowledged the compliment. "That she is. Let's go onboard and get acquainted."

Commanding the gathering at the bow, Rick commenced his impromptu spiel.

"She's a forgiving vessel with a first rate disposition. Take care of her, respect her, and she'll respond obligingly. Quid pro quo. A true gaff-topsail, twin-mast schooner, *Slip's* overall length is one hundred thirty-five feet, deck length a hundred ten, and twenty-six feet across the beam. Half full or half empty: a draft of twelve feet. Look above you and you'll see the rigging tops out at a hundred ten."

Trout-mouthed, the newcomers gazed skyward. Karl pointed out the crow's nest. "Must be one hell of a view up there."

Rick noticed Kaz's pallid face. "Hey man, you okay?"

"Heights don't agree with me, there's no way I can handle that."

"I appreciate your candor. We'll work something out."

"Thanks. I'll do anything to get out of that detail."

"Can you cook?"

"Standard fare, sure. But if you're thinking gourmet, you'll be sorely disappointed."

"A work in progress. You just found your niche." The unexpected handshake preempted any response to contest the assignment. Rick continued where he had left off. "You'll be instructed on climbing technique and I advise you to hone those skills while in port. When at sea, pitching and rolling, you guys best know your hand and footholds blindfolded.

"Full sail deployment area coverage, five thousand four hundred fifty feet. Proper unfurling and retrieval is essential in preventing unwarranted repairs. She displaces one hundred ten tons and has newly rebuilt two hundred fifty horsepower diesel engines. The hull, as most every other surface, is all wood and it will be everyone's daily task keeping her finish swabbed.

"Now, a little background you may find interesting. Built at Plymouth, Mass in 1913, she was commissioned as a dory fishing vessel and served twenty-seven grueling years on the high seas from the Cape to the Great Banks before being mothballed in 1940. A year later, a group of investors converted her into a Windjammer, pleasure-cruising passengers off the coast of Maine up to Nova Scotia. Seventeen sea-worthy years and once again she was retired; dry-docked in Hyannis Port. That's when, in 1959, my father bought the aged vessel for a paltry hundred thousand and began restoring her nobility. A million bucks would be a conservative estimate eradicating years of neglect.

In the first year, the bow and stern were rebuilt, replacing all wood which was weathered beyond repair. The following year, both the port and starboard sides were rebuilt to eight strakes below the waterline and all stanchions, bulwarks, and rails from the break in the deck to the stern replaced. The year after that, almost six figures spent on Danish white oak lumber to refurbish the deck. 1962 was completion year. Foredeck rebuilt, and all the planking below deck replaced. The cabin configuration was drastically changed, sleeping quarters downsized to accommodate only those not on watch duty. Eliminating one of the heads, and a redesign of the galley; all this was done to increase the cargo hold area and to compensate for increased ballast due to added upgrades such as a motorized winch for cargo loading, heavier sails, and a shitload of teakwood to trim her out regal righteous."

"Why the need for all the cargo capacity?" Smitty's inquiry was expected.

"Father's plan all along was to offset the cost of his hobby by providing long-haul shipping services from the islands to the states. And that he did. Over the years, he more than recouped the initial remodeling investment. One client in particular, an Antinguan expat with a specialty shop in Manhattan accounted for forty percent of all *Slip's* shipping revenues in the last ten years."

Will could not resist stating the obvious. "Shit, guess it wasn't a long leap to get to this current scheme—"

Stuart appeared out of nowhere. "Got that squared away, we're good to go. You guys conducting a séance?"

"Captain's giving us a little background and details, quite informative, impressive, and greatly appreciated," replied Karl.

Acknowledging the compliment, along with the disparaging glance his brother shot at Will, Rick realized there were two problems to contend with: the dicey concept of co-captains, and a clash of two particular personalities. "I'll meet you below after the two-dollar tour."

"Get on with it then. I'll be in our quarters making sure charts and maintenance logs are up to snuff." Stuart walked off in a huff.

Karl backslapped Will. "Like oil and water. I don't think he likes you very much."

Will shook his head. "Can't win for losing, Smitty. I don't even have to open my mouth and I seem to piss him off."

Bar Knuckle's proprietor, a dead ringer for Burl Ives, was stocking the bar in preparation of the marina's dinner patrons when the haggard bunch filed in. Norm Bartlett made a cursory note and went about his business. The hostess acted as if they were invisible, flitting about empty tables nudging chairs.

Rick and Stuart lagged behind, engaged in a heated discussion about the obvious: what was it about Will that stewed Stu so? There was no definitive explanation, and Rick told him that whatever it was, he should get over it and knock it off.

The brothers' entrance flushed the old codger out from behind the bar, in an instant becoming 'Uncle Bart' and receiving both boys in open arms. Numerous apologies were delivered to the motley crew, his jarred memory now recognizing Artimus and the baseball duo. When told of senior Blaine's plight and last request, the owner insisted food and drink were on the house.

It was a gratis feast as marina customers started filing in, many recognizing Rick and Stuart, some even the other young men they had seen over many summers. The party held the waitress willing hostage and Uncle Bart's big mouth made sure the boys were celebrities...upcoming voyage all theirs----*if he only knew.*

Indulgence had stuck a fork in a long day begun predawn, latitudes away. Calling it a wrap, Uncle Bart refused gratuity, but when he turned his back to wish Stuart fair winds, Rick slipped the waitress a day's worth of tips.

"You really took excellent care of us, thanks."

As was tradition, the bartender tolled the brass bell. Whenever someone was to embark upon a long-distance voyage, glasses were raised toasting good fortune and godspeed. The last to exit was Rick, who made known to the remaining patrons their appreciation and that while they were still in port, all were welcome to drop on by.

One person in particular would do so, their waitress.

It was lights out early, except for Will. As tired as he was, his blurred vision saw him through a third and final read of *Slipfinger's* diagrams, schematics, situation sail deployments, and nautical nomenclature. Hell bent on becoming an immediate asset, he would be damned if ineptitude on his behalf would allow an opening for Stuart's haughty-ass demeanor. *The guy's got 'insufferable asshole' potential and it's not going to be at my expense, no sir.*

Chalking it up to disparate personalities that would somehow need resolving, Will fell asleep with the study papers sopping up sweat from his chest.

CHAPTER TWELVE

Thursday, June 3rd. 04:00 hours.
Five hours of fitful sleep and Will lie sweltering, contemplating putting his foot into the sagging bunk above him. Smitty's snoring was off the Richter scale. The warm, stagnant air and close confines induced a claustrophobic chokehold on breathing. There was something else irritating the crap out of him. Sporadic thuds invaded from the other side of the bulkhead. *What the hell is that? How can these guys sleep?*

Sitting on the side of his berth dressing, he wondered how well the brothers slept in the spatial, well-appointed confines of the captain's quarters. He also realized why Jason, who last night lost the roll of the dice and was banished topside with bedroll, accepted the assignment heartily. While in port, not being on shifts meant the six-bunk accommodations left one man out. He claimed first dibs and moved out before anyone could challenge. Will got it; until they got out into the air-conditioned open water...the hard deck under stars was where it was at.

Rick slept hard, but the anticipation of the day's packed agenda had him up and dressed an hour before the alarm. With diligent furtiveness, he closed the cabin door on his comatose brother, heard the ladder creak and saw the heel of someone stepping topside. *Excellent, someone else is ready to get it on.* He would join him once the coffee was brewed.

On their way back last night, he had had the foresight to branch off and pick up pastries and fresh-ground Columbian. While the coffee dripped into the stainless receiver, he took stock of the galley: *pots, pans, utensils...all there, cups, bowls and plates...sufficient.* Barren of foodstuffs, one of the day's priorities would be collaborating with their newfound cook on an extensive supply list. Mugs in hand, Rick headed up to join the early riser.

"Couldn't sleep, huh? Trust me, once we're out to sea there's good flow-through ventilation down there."

"Yeah, pretty stuffy right now. Thanks for the coffee." Will was leaning over the side, engrossed in the action. "I heard the thumping from below, get a load of this!"

Twenty feet separated them from the slightly smaller schooner in the next berth. A dock floodlight situated between the two mighty ships illuminated the waterway, attracting a zillion baitfish and a couple dolphins on a feeding frenzy. Will pointed straight down into the emerald, phosphorous-rich water.

"Damn, these guys are fast! Watch 'em turn on a dime."

Below the surface the dolphin duo were wreaking havoc. Out of nowhere they would appear, slashing through the school, then whipping one-eighty turns, their tailfins occasionally slapping *Slipfinger's* side.

"Hmm," Rick murmured, "this is good and bad."

"How's that?"

"Well, I've always felt that dolphin sightings, especially in uncommon places, are good omens. But these creatures are far from stupid. Watch the ship's side next time they whack it, you'll see the bait fish congregate around the immediate area. The hull has algae buildup and I hope to hell we don't have barnacles on her belly. We're going to have to break out the diving gear and do some scraping before we take her out."

"Count me in. Scuba diving's something I've always wanted to learn."

"Excellent. Consider yourself enrolled." One of the predators did a slow surface roll. Rick pointed to its unique markings, "they're striped dolphin. See the black line going down the side? Looks like she's got mascara 'round her eyes. Dig this: did you know dolphins constantly exfoliate, shedding skin every two hours? That's why they're smoother than a baby's butt. Also, dolphins sleep with only half their brain. If they should go unconscious sleeping as we do, they'd die. So they float at the surface, keeping one eye open, and rest the other side of their brain. Then they alternate."

"That's bizarre. I read somewhere they don't take too kindly to sharks. Is that true?'

"I've seen them go at it a couple of times when they're competing for the same food. Sharks don't hang around for long. You can hear thuds. Once I saw a shark slammed completely out of the water. When it comes to speed, agility, and hard-hitting action...there's no contest."

"Whoever got the coffee going...brilliant." Artimus, mug in hand, came up behind them. Pulling out his pocket watch, he scratched his go-tee. "Should see first light any minute now." A slight pause gave way to reveal the gears that were turning. "I don't know about you, but a morning dip sure would be a great way to start the day." A devilish grin conveyed intentions. "Come on, let's get Jason off and running." The "lump" lay atop his bedroll. Rick and Arti lifted from both ends, struggling to keep from busting out laughing.

Will unlatched the gated railing. "Man, he's gonna be pissed! Hope he doesn't drown."

"We'll join him." Arti nodded to Rick, "ready...on three."

Discharged off the stern, the vivid sensation of flying ended abruptly in a wet dream. The back flop was a rude awakening. Jason, breathless after the wind was whacked out of him, inadvertently inhaled and sank like a rock.

"Man overboard!" Will dove in for retrieval.

Arti cannon-balled.

Rick opted out of the free-for-all; *marina bilge water, no thanks*.

They surfaced.

Jason puked, his flailing arms grasping at air. Garbled profanity ensued as the useless life-guards treaded water just out of range from balled fists. "Assholes! Dickheads!" Jason choked threats of payback in-between a barrage of traded splashes. Will's attempt at playing Samaritan earned him a choke hold, then a shove down deep when a foot found the top of his head.

Artimus wisely kept his distance." Take it easy man! Damn if it ain't a great day to be alive, huh?" The two exchanged dueling splashes as Will surfaced, gasping.

Rick called for a ceasefire, extending a hand to Jason who still had not run out of profanities. "Come on guys, let's go wake..."

"Rise and shine lug heads! Time and tide wait for no man!" The raucous affair topside apparently raised Stuart from the wrong side of the bed, as he sought to end the rest of the crew's slumber by banging pots...right out of the old man's playbook.

Stuart chaired the briefing. Bent over the galley table, Rick charted the sequence of events, detailing assignments and responsibilities in preparation for Saturday's shakedown voyage to Saint Croix. The new guys, including Doc who requested a refresher course, would remain on board learning the ropes under Rick's tutelage. Jason and David's duty was procuring supplies, the extensive inventory would keep them humping all week. Stuart and Art would assist in the foraging and loading, branching off mid-week to rendezvous with Zaldavar. There would be various clandestine meetings: first for intelligence such as updated charts showing the archipelago's channel depths, locations of enterprising interests, and the all-important law-enforcement patrol schedules which during his commercial fishing forays, Zal had duly logged. The following day, the three of them were on a small charter plane to St. Johns.

When asked the nature of that venture, the brothers and Artimus traded glances. Stuart off-handedly replied Zal had turned them onto a fresh produce market and cannery that specializes in outfitting long voyages. "Also, mates, photo reconnaissance from above the maze of channels, documenting the lighter and darker hues for ease of navigation when we get in close...an invaluable tool."

"Yes, you certainly don't want to run aground out there." Rick flinched at the ruse, but had caved in to his brother's and Art's insistence some things were best kept under wraps until due time. The REAL reason for Zal's needed presence was to mediate the art-of-the-deal and make sure the two Yanks came back in one piece. *Secrecy, lies...not exactly the way to garner trust and solidarity.* Rick bit his tongue and swallowed his principles along with the last stale donut. Segueing from his uneasiness, he drew an arrow to the top of the chart. "Priority number one: stocking the ship with food and supplies." He then announced their volunteer cook, which earned a complimentary golf clap and more than a few snide remarks. Kaz acknowledged, with a warning not to piss off the chef or they would suffer serious consequences.

Stuart rose. "Well boys, that wraps it up. Any questions?"

Will chanced starting the day off on the wrong foot. "Yeah, I got one. Cooped up on this boat all week, you think we might be able to squeeze in a little shore leave?"

The query was seconded by others, prompting a response from Stuart. "Well, Mister Bradford, that all depends on you guys learning the ropes and the ship getting outfitted on time. Right now, R and R is reserved for Friday, provided we remain on schedule. Incentive enough?"

CHAPTER THIRTEEN

Slipfinger's deck resembled that of a disturbed fire ant mound. Townsfolk and those seasonal inhabitants of the marina speculated as the flurry of activity signaled an impending departure. Consensus was large in scope and it had to be soon. What foreign port or great purpose awaited her? The non-stop action caused more than a few to wonder if they were witnessing preparations for circumnavigation. Whatever their endeavor, these boys were not messing around, methodically readying the schooner to be a tight ship.

Jason and David had left immediately after breakfast to rent a flatbed truck, their entire day devoted to supply runs. Food staples were bought in bulk: flour, powdered milk, juices, dried fruits, beef jerky, dried beans, peanut butter, bread, cheese, canned goods, a hundred pounds of beef steaks, blocks of ice, a case of rum, wine, and a boatload of beer were requisitioned during the initial foray. Petrol was next: ten fifty-five gallon drums of diesel and several cases of thirty-weight oil.

Subsequent excursions would become more and more specialized: new generator, a few hundred feet of cordage, material for sail repair, miles of the strongest test nylon line they could find, rolls of heavy-gauge plastic tote liners, swivel clips, plastic cinch-ties. Fishing tackle was replenished, machetes and leather gloves procured, along with binoculars, flashlights, and extra batteries. Finally, a complete scuba outfit to go with the two already onboard, three extra air tanks, and a weigh scale capable of registering up to a hundred pounds.

    Each delivery offered the trainees respite from their instruction. Supplies had to be unloaded and palletized. Jacks were used to roll equipment out the long boardwalk and onto *Slipfinger's* parallel pier. The davit's winch, now motorized, hoisted cargo onto the aft staging area where items were broken down and stored accordingly. Fuel drums swung over the cargo hold were carefully lowered and secured. The schooner's draft increased.

    Further on into the week, procurement focused on smaller and smaller details along with a few added requests: medical supplies, two-way radios, deck-varnish, and a case of candy bars for quick pick-me-ups. Speculation ensued among the crew as to just how much the old man had forked out to his sons. Surmising they had been granted carte blanche, Doc was willing to bet the house that the captains had an open checkbook.

    Will, Smitty, and Doc spent hours aloft acclimating themselves to the harrowing heights. Rotating out, they would join Kaz on deck as they deployed and furled sails to Rick's satisfaction. Various knots were practiced, ropes spliced using a marlinspike, and routine maintenance was performed, including swabbing the deck.

    The most important phase of their training took up the better part of a day. On the foredeck, Rick conducted a seminar familiarizing the plebes on terminology. Throughout the course of instruction, he would single out someone for a definition while illustrating its function and application on a makeshift easel. Working the riggings for maximum efficiency under every possible wind and weather condition detailed, scenarios were presented compelling the crew to work out the solutions. With such a steep learning curve, college now seemed like a walk in the park.

After placing a call to the originator of dreams one smokes in a pipe, Stuart and Artimus caught a cab for the meeting downtown. Giving only an address, Marin Zaldavar had instructed them to remain at the drop-off and wait.

"Here be your stop, Yanks."

Stuart handed the driver the fare plus an additional twenty, obliging him to return in an hour.

"Mighty right. You're on my ticket, I look for you, one hour."

The searchers got out and stood on the sidewalk, surveying the scene: Stuart donned his shades. Artimus mouthed his drooping pipe.

The bustle of sidewalk pedestrians and a street clogged in traffic created the perfect screen for Zal, who was lolling at the outdoor café across the street. Minutes passed while sipping coffee and observing his connection until he felt all was cool.

A break in the traffic congestion allowed for visual intersect, and Zal beckoned with a raised mug.

"Che Guevara with dreadlocks, give me a break," uttered Stuart.

Artimus was locked onto a babe window shopping a boutique. "Huh? What?" He turned to Stu who was already in the middle of the street.

The Jamaican, donning a beret and wearing olive drab fatigues, greeted them with his memorable smile and motioned for them to sit.

"Ah, I see you even in disguise. Excellent idea, mon. Hard to believe it's been a year. I like the look, Van Gogh."

Artimus patted the host's shoulder, "Good to see you too, wild man. How's the revolution going?"

"How's it hangin', Zal?" Stuart flagged the waitress for service. "You should come out and see the ship and the crew. You know, take a break from your idle leisure and pitch in. Get a nice work-out while darkening your tan?"

Zal laughed. "Mon, the last thing you need is the likes of me hangin' around ole' *Slipfinger*. All those high-rolling country club elite down at the marina, shit mon, stick out like a dangling turd. No, I think it best we keep our distance. It be bad karma and besides already boo-coo shit could go wrong. Less we seen together, betta for everyone. We play this close to da vest, unless you looking to make headlines in da funny papers, yah?"

"More coffee?"

Once the server departed, Zal produced a manila packet from inside his jacket and slid it across the table.

"Everything you need is here. Maps of the islands with updated charts: channel drafts, accessibility, marine patrols, you name it. Tomorrow we get good aerial view where you be sailing, oh, three hundred bucks get us over and back." Zal shifted in his chair, eyeing his surroundings. "Dis was not easy, my friends, getting the deal set up. I introduce you, but you best be careful bargaining with these people, they are resolute and don't fuck around none, ya. You pay attention, I signal you if you're out of bounds. You be wise to make only a one-time counter-offer, take what they insist, and we get out of there with our eyes peeled in back of our intact skulls...if we still got 'em."

With the caveat duly noted, Zal proceeded.

"We meet in Red Hook, dawn. Blue and white floatplane, don't keep the man waiting. Fly over to Cruz Bay, I got address where we get picked up. Deez people trusting me are not too keen on new faces, so be cool, know what you want, and just go with the flow."

Stuart folded the envelope and thanked the friend they had met on a beach what seemed like so long ago now: they were seventeen when innocence got chucked out the window. It had been a work in progress ever since. The handshake greased Zal a thousand. "Consider it gratuity, my old friend."

"Jus send me a kilo and Rasta will look favorably on you and your journey..." Zal's classic smile: wide grin, head tossed back flailing dreads, minus the boisterous Hua-Ha. "We meet here first light, okay? I got a friend who's gonna take us to da plane, so, until then, yah?"

There was no debate Zal was an original. Stu and Art watched their friend, lanky and a head taller than most, meander off into the sidewalk crowd. Not until he disappeared around a corner two blocks away did the boys flag their waiter, twenty bucks for three coffees negated any need for a bill.

Two-days-plus of non-stop activity, and for the first time the entire crew was awake and reunited. One by one they filed into the galley from the marina's hot showers...much needed, even if the water smelled of sulfur and rotten eggs. Hard water made lathering soap an exercise almost futile.

Dinner was Cuban sandwiches and a case of beer, which spared Kaz any smart-ass culinary critique.

It was a temperate roundtable meeting; status reports garnered congratulatory kudos...they were ahead of schedule.

Rick acknowledged his apt pupils' near seaworthiness, a work in progress still requiring some fine tuning. Only once they were underway could skills be refined as they would acclimate to actual conditions under sail. Tomorrow the newbies would receive a crash course in scuba diving. Will and Smitty caught the exchanged grins of the seasoned crewmates but played dumb, sensing they were being set up. Something smelled afoul, and it was the pervasive scent of rotten eggs.

Jason and Dave gave a detailed summary of the ship's inventory. Most requisitions having been obtained, they enlisted their services to get *Slipfinger* spit and polished.

Stu and Art divulged intelligence, courtesy of Zal: detailed maps of the eighty-plus island archipelago and depth charts spread atop the table. Three WPB Point Class patrol boats, one always in port on standby for distress calls. Spread thin, such a vast area encompassing the territorial jurisdiction gave hope they may avoid the heat all together. Maybe.

"According to Zal, the maze of tiny islands we hope to operate in initially can get tight, but is navigable by dingy. He did say it would be wise to bring a compass, easy to get turned around and you end up coming out into open water opposite where you went in." Arti grabbed his beer as if in a toast, "down the hatch…. He's even provided us with the Coast Guard call signs and frequency so we can monitor their whereabouts." Nodding to Stu, "It's all yours, El Capitán."

"As you can see, gentlemen, we have not been fiddle-fucking around." He tossed another map on the table, showing a half dozen landforms highlighted. "Accessibility, cover, and the level of security will determine which ones we hit." He paused to assess the crew's disposition: *receptive, but guarded.* "Tomorrow, Arti and I wrap it up with a trip to St. Johns for specialty items not available here on St. Thomas."

"Female companionship for the long trip? Excellent idea, sir." Doc's guess was cheered on.

"In your dreams, quince head. Everybody chop-chop tomorrow, and Friday's all yours. Maybe you'll get lucky."

Frustrated, Will butted in. "Well, what specialty items? Why the cloak and dagger bullshit?"

"It must have been a real pain in the ass for you on Christmas Eve."

"You have no idea, captain."

"You awake?" Smitty joined Will on deck, where he had opted out of the stagnant quarters below.

"Barely. It'll be good to get underway…fresh air, dammit."

Smitty lay back to join in the star-gazing. So far removed from northern latitudes they were accustomed to, led them to ponder the heavens as if it were the first time. *Where the hell was the Big Dipper?* There was a long interlude as both tried to connect the dots and imagine constellations unfamiliar.

"You still awake?"

"Nope." Will was contemplating what he thought might be Orion.

"Do me a favor, man. If this goes south on us, can we agree we got each other's back...you know, if there's one of those every-man-for-himself scenarios."

Will reached out his hand and clasped Smitty's." We're tight."

"You think we can really pull this off? Kinda surreal, like we're pirates incarnate on a ghost ship, or a bunch of dicks chasing a white aberration with a fucked-up name. Moby, know what I mean?"

There was no answer. Smitty released the limp hand, fixated on a star-cluster that had to be part of some constellation. A meteor streaked bluish-white. On high, one of the masts creaked to the warm breeze. He drifted away with the receding tide.

CHAPTER FOURTEEN

The day kicked off with a killer breakfast: coffee, French toast with powdered sugar and cinnamon, bacon, cheese omelets, and fresh cantaloupe. Any reservations the crew might have had about the cook's culinary capacity were dispelled, and Kaz accepted the accolades, with conditions.

"All right, all right, thank you very much. Here's the deal: I don't do lunch, everyone fends for themselves. Also, when the bell clangs, best get it while it's hot. I cook once, and none of this cooked-to-order crap. Finally, don't piss off the cook. I'm not your galley bitch, so clean up your own mess." Being the cook did carry some weight.

Jason spent the morning fine-tuning the ham radio. The installation of a booster antenna high atop the rear mast enhanced range. He actually made contact, though garbled with static, with their Floridian counterpart. Frequencies were established and vague schedules agreed upon. ETA and coordinates for rendezvous would be updated once the islands were vacated.

As planned, Will and Smitty received a scuba tutorial from David. The conscripts' dive lesson came at a steep price: a very labor intensive shit-job. The three divers spent two tanks apiece while hovering in *Slip's* shadow. Armed with a long scraper and wire brush, they worked in unison from bow to stern, chiseling off pesky barnacle clusters. Smoothing the surface of algae growth attracted blennies to feed, the shimmering baitfish streaking in and out of the divers' head-mounted lights.

By noon they were finished, the near four-hour rubdown assuring the schooner optimum speed and agility. Lounging on deck, Rick, Doc, and Jason had just completed swabbing and were kicked back enjoying a cold one when the divers climbed aboard.

"If that don't beat all! Enjoying your mint juleps, Mastas? David dropped his gear, visibly irritated. Smitty, then Will, added to the pile.

"Better back off Cousteau, or should I say 'JACK'? You're not the only ones been busting ass." Jason pitched beers out of the cooler, while speaking to himself, "geez, damn deck's so clean you could eat off it, WOW!"

"All right guys, nobody slacked. Take an hour, grab a bite AND Kaz. Meet me topside and we'll run through one more time everything I hope you've learned." Rick's diktat was ill received. Body language spoke dog-tired.

"You think you're beat now, just wait until we're underway."

Time-wise, the excursion to Red Hook dispelled the theorem that the shortest distance between two points was a straight line. The overland route weaving through the interior of the island was a royal pain in the ass. The washboard road riddled with potholes and deep ruts punished both car and passengers.

Though dependent on tourists, the indigenous driver masked his disdain for Yanks with feigned courtesy. It was the disparity between the haves and the have-nots: the haughty attitude of vacationers who rarely venture from their seaside resort and their naïveté to the fact that what they perceived as paradise exists only in their privileged high-life surroundings. It annoyed him to no end. Duping customers into taking the "scenic route" was his way of exposing them to the other side of island life. Riding shotgun, Zal's presence did smooth conversation as they neared the low highlight. Deep in the heavily forested hills was Tutu, a ramshackle village he proudly proclaimed as home. The effect was always sobering. So dirt poor was this harsh reality, the intention never failed to garner sympathetic tips from the very generous, and Stuart was no exception. The brandished arrogance, and gaping breath-hole, nine times out of ten meant deep pockets of money to burn. Zal kept his smile looking forward; he admired the driver's technique.

    Early explorers discovered it. Pirates treasured it. Sportsmen and pleasure-seekers inherited it. Red Hook's harbor, Vessup Bay, was a veritable parking lot of yachts and fishing boats. On the other side of a jutting peninsular more vessels anchored in half-moon Muller Bay. Further out, Red Hook Bay opened up to Pillsbury Sound. Barring hurricanes, a flotilla of two-lane traffic came and went round-the-clock.
    As instructed, the driver dropped them off at the floatplane, twin props began spinning as soon as Zal was seen exiting the taxi.

    The flight over would have been up and down if not for the sightseeing request. The pilot asked his passengers if they worked for National Geographic, there were so many pictures taken at three thousand feet. When they landed just outside Cruz Bay and taxied in between two jetties, the pilot indicated the quoted fare needed to be renegotiated, adjusting for fuel. Stuart was one step ahead of the pilot's concern.

"Great flight, man. This should cover the extra fuel, and here's another hundred for giving us the grand tour." Before being last man out, Stuart thought to suggest something as insurance. "Hey look, if you don't get a call that squeezes in another flight, why don't you go into town. Eat, drink, but don't get too merry…you just make sure you're ready when we get back. Three, maybe four hours, right?" Before the pilot could nod, two more hundreds greased his palm.

"I buy you guys some really fine rum so flight back be more first class, yes? Moreau Distilleries, best in the islands for sure!"

"Right. Just be here and able to fly."

"Doan you worry, Mister Blaine. I fly dis route so many times, probly do it blindfolded…AND drunk."

Stuart laughed along, disingenuous. "Great, that's reassuring."

Zal knew the way. He also knew that this side of town was not exactly tourist friendly. Down the trashy street, cross, a right then first left brought them to their destination.

"No smart-ass shit. Gotta be cool…and LOW profile, got it?"

Blackbeard's was not the kind of establishment one would find in a travel brochure. Wedged in between dilapidated shanties, a flickering 'COLD BEER' sign was the only inkling of commerce in the narrow back alley. Stu and Arti entered the dank, musty watering hole. It took a moment to adjust to the darkness before seating themselves at the table nearest the door.

Zal grinned pearly whites, sensing their apprehension.

"Okay, Zal, what now? Where are they?"

"Doan you worry, mon. They be here, an' I promise you they have no trouble knowing you are who they seek."

Doctor Livingston and associate waited to be presumed and just like traipsing around dark Africa, there was no doubting recognition. It was not long before they realized there was no table service, only a shadow figure unmoved behind the bar. Zal motioned for them to sit tight and moseyed on up.

"Three rum-runners."

Two patrons observed from a corner table, only the whites of their eyes betrayed their existence as they glared at the seated intruders.

"Six dolla."

Zal thought it best just to drop a ten and walk away.

Any reference to feeling so out of place was a foregone conclusion, so they killed time talking softly the trip to Saint Croix. Both agreed that once they reached the island they would anchor and wait till sundown to return.

Arti downed his drink. "Yeah, it makes sense. It's a whole different animal navigating at night. The new guys need exposure to…"

Floorboards creaked. A hulking silhouette filled the doorway, all but blotting out the sunlight. "You boys come with me." The husky tone commanded compliance.

Readjusting to the blinding light, they hustled to follow the leader who had just turned the corner. Into the alley strode the anxious duo, both wicked glad for Zal's foresight to accompany them.

"Been nice knowing you," muttered Arti.

"Cut the shit, man, we got Zal. We'll be fine." *I hope.*

The faceless giant stood at the alley's other outlet, looked to his left, and signaled. "Stop right there! Turn around and face the wall." The trio's approaching footsteps halted in their tracks.

The scene mirrored unspoken sentiment as they were blindfolded. *What the fuck did we get ourselves into?* Reggae hummed, Zal was being Zal.

Herded into a back seat, the sound and smell of their ride indicated a vehicle long overdue for maintenance. A few French words were spoken to the driver, as heavy footsteps faded away.

A labyrinth of turns, and five minutes later they stopped to the sound of a heavy roll-up door granting entrance. Not until they came to a halt and the door winched to a close did the driver confirm he was not mute.

"You can remove blindfolds now."

Stuart Bla..." The introduction was cut short.

"We know who you are. You Americans would not be here if not for Rasta Zal's endorsement." The boss man showed civility only when doing some greeting ritual with Zal. "You crazy, mon, just like always. You look well."

That was it, as to the formalities. The buyers were instructed to keep it strictly business, no small talk, no bullshit. "No one knows shit...better for everybody, got it?"

Artimus made a note of the two sentries posted each side of the garage door, and then fell in behind Stuart. They were led to the other end of the gutted auto shop where a dim light from a hole in the concrete floor showed the way down creaky wooden steps into a defunct oil and lube pit.

"Watch your head."

Stu's forehead caught the tail end of a rusty exhaust pipe, dangling off the partially dismantled pickup straddling the hole. "Son-of-a BITCH!"

They followed their guide to the far end, the false wall cordoned off by tool carts, hoses, and a stockpile of lubrication. Padlocks were keyed and a door opened to blackness until the cord yanked light on an earthen cache, twenty by twenty. Stacked crates lined the walls. Ordnance depicted, most of the contents were labeled 'United States Army'. The rest of the hardware: party favorites of the Communist Bloc.

"Impressive. How's 'bout a look-see?" Penchant for weaponry, due to his dad being an avid collector, the array of armament mesmerized Arti into total focus.

Stuart was handed an oil rag, a finger pointing to his forehead where blood leaked from a gash over his eyebrow. As he patted the wound with the least grimy part of the rag, he made out a corpulent figure sitting in the corner. A wide-brimmed straw hat concealed the eyes.

"My prices are non-negotiable. You may find market prices more reasonable, but considering these are hot, and many illegal, serial numbers burnished off, and the risk involved in my private enterprise...consider the cost compensatory surcharges." Man With No Eyes belly-laughed behind a plume of cigar smoke. Shifting in his creaky chair, spittoon in range, a grotesque sound of phlegm coughed up spittle. The loud planting into the brass urn gave proof through the dark that the discharge was one hell of a wad. Stuart felt queasy.

"We deliver dockside before sunrise Saturday. That service rendered is going to cost you extra. Ferry over, got to rent a flatbed, third party mules paid to deliver...if anything goes wrong, that's your problem to contend with, not mine."

"We assume all risk."

"You're damned right."

"Understood." Stuart was joined by Arti, who had befriended an XM-177E2, 5.56mm Colt Commando.

"We buy two, right away. Look at this baby." Arti checked the action, held it to his shoulder then side-winded at the hip. "It's like a shortened M-16. Telescopic stock, gas operated, magazine-fed, capable of semi or automatic. Effective range...what, three hundred meters? Practical rate of fire...five, maybe six hundred per minute. How much?"

"Four-fifty."

"For two?"

"Still four fifty apiece."

"Throw in the rounds?"

Wanting to ward off any growing irritation from their dealers, Stuart interceded. "The man said no bargaining.

Why don't you pick out what we can use and we'll decide what's in our budget."

The word "budget" budged the boss to stoke further purchases. "Fine. I throw in a thousand rounds."

Arti moved on to other items: two Browning forty-five pistols with rounds, a nifty large-bore M79 launcher with a dozen 40mm grenades, and two M3A1 Grease Guns tapped out the finances. A dispute ensued between the buyers.

"Dammit, man! What good are the M3s when we don't have enough money for ammo? We're going to have to cut something from the list."

Arti bemoaned the fact: "seven pieces, nine guys, you do the math."

"So what! We're not going to fucking war for Christ's sake! We could probably get by with one or two."

The sole purpose of their black-market purchase was precautionary. Too many stories of lawless transactions, especially those of such magnitude and rare quality, not-so-funny things are known to go down when a boatload of money and contraband are being exchanged. If their clients send out desperados to do the dirty work, risking all for a comparative small pay-off, the possibility of foul play could not be discounted.

The wrangling ceased with another repulsive expulsion, from Coughing Man. Sensing buyer's remorse, the boss blew a cloud of cigar smoke that drifted along with an offer to seal the deal. "Tell you what. You give me what you got, and I'll throw in the ammo for ALL the weapons."

"Deal." Art beat Stuart to the proposition.

What once was a billfold fat with tens of hundreds, was now reduced to a teenager's first wallet and first payday at minimum wage. "Last time I take you shopping with me. Jeezus, Art."

A different ride back dropped them off at an alternate location, yet not far from where they were picked up. Blindfolds were removed, no sweet goodbyes. The sound of rubber crunching seashell surface, it figured the vehicle had no license plate.

"Man, What a rush!" Arti was jacked as they walked down another tin-pan alley. "This'll really blow their minds."

"No doubt, but we keep it a secret 'til we're well on our way." Stu was relieved when they turned a corner and saw, off in the distance, the floatplane still there and the pilot conducting a preliminary check. The ordeal they had just gone through left him thinking one thing: getting smashed.

The flight back DID have rum onboard and the pilot was right on two counts: the booze was REALLY good, and it was just an up-and-down puddle jumper. Straight up, bottle passed three times, each gulp smoother and more substantial than the previous...when they floated up dockside, the parting of ways with Zal was but a slurring of appreciations for his mere presence.

Late afternoon, and the crew raised their beers in a toast: they were ready, the ship was ready, and all that remained was waiting on Stu and Art's return so they could hit the town and celebrate.

Will's challenge brought the crew to attention.

"Come on, Smithers, I'll take the foremast, you the aft. We race to the top and back down to first foot on deck. Loser buys the first round."

"You're on! Hey Doc, you start us off." Smitty grinned, "I can already taste victory."

Jabs were exchanged and side-bets wagered, the contestants were off positioning at the base of each mast. At the count of three, Doc dropped the bandana. Will timed his release perfectly. Smitty's foot missed the first rung, spotting his opponent a head start. The commotion drew the attention of nearby yacht owners as the two raced to the top. From the onset, Will maintained a rhythmic pace contrary to Smitty whose reckless attempt to make up ground only widened the lead. Ten feet from the top he caught sight of Will, who at the same height was going down.

No way can I catch him. Unless….

Touching the top, he took a deep breath and reached out for the backstay secured to the stern far below. With legs wrapped around the rope, it was immediately evident he had screwed up big time. He thought his sneakers could control his descent, but the angle was too steep. Will was half way down when Karl attempted an `inverted` Karl Wallenda tightrope act…the contest, all but conceded, would hail as one of the greatest come from behind victories of all time.

Out of control, Smitty zipped down the line. Two handholds away, Will heard the dull thump of feet slamming the back deck.

Victory may be sweet, but in this case it was bitterly painful. The backstay had sagged enough for touchdown a few yards before the stern, but forward momentum

Slipfinger Nine

launched him on the run into and over the waist-high parapet. Comically contorted, Smitty's triple forward flip propelled him out of sight. There was no cheer from the winner, only a splash.

Will cited a foul, raising his hands as the self-proclaimed winner. Half the crew saw it differently, but it was the agonizing scream that left the tale-o-the-tape disputed. Everyone rushed aft.

Dave and Kaz bent over the stern with a gaff.

"Son of a bitch! My hands, they're burned up!" Salt water magnified the pain, bloody hands unable to firmly grab hold of the rod.

Will jumped in. Wincing with pain, Smitty wrapped his forearms around his friend's neck.

"Like I said, I got your back. Jus' take it easy, I'll get you out, man." Will grabbed Doc's outstretched hand, "Someone get the first aid kit!" The rope had gnawed through the flesh, leaving it raw: *seared tuna garnished with steamed cabbage* came to mind.

"Damn it, Smitty! No gloves? What the fuck were you thinking?!" Rick was livid. "Now you can't even pull your pud."

Laid out on the deck, not uttering a peep, the contorted face spoke incredible pain. Jason side-stepped the gathering, making it to the side of the ship just in time to puke.

"Take it easy, cap'n, we'll get him fixed up." Will had both wrists pinned down. "No man, you don't want to see."

Kaz returned, bitching about the need to station the medical kit somewhere other than the cupboard containing

139

cookware. By this time the pasty swivel-kneed injured was steadied on his feet and flanked for support.

His composure regained, Rick assumed command. "Alright, let's get him below and out of the sun. Hey Doc, gonna need you to break into your stash. He'll need some of the good stuff."

Smitty was eased into a bunk. The tight quarters were jammed with the concerned.

"Holy crap, look at this!" Jason had removed the sneakers and held one up for inspection. Smitty's vain attempt to slow his decent had grinded grooves in the shoe's insteps. "Now THAT'S rope burn!"

"Burn rubber, man!"

"Spread out!" Doc wedged through, hydrogen peroxide in one hand, Tequila and a Quaalude in the other. "Here, man, down the hatch." Doc was ready to douse the raw flesh. "You ready to do this?"

"Fuck, it hurts! I need another swig." He gulped as if it was water.

"Whoa, buddy, take it easy." Will cut him off.

Watery eyes scrunched shut. "Lez do it."

Peroxide effervesced over the raw meat, the cleansing action fizzed audibly. Smitty writhed in silent anguish, body English akin to Joe Cocker's Woodstock plea for a little help from his friends.

"Hang on, man, we gotta do it again."

The second dousing sat him straight up, a guttural moan escaped through gritting teeth. Will brought a towel to the contorted face, which was now bathed in sweat. "All done. Breathe."

Once the searing pain subsided to tolerance, Will laid him back onto the bunk. Kaz began slathering on the antibiotic ointment and Will followed by gently rolling on the gauze. Doc conceded the patient another belt.

"Alright, man, you're cut off. You're gonna be comatose and end up pissin' the bunk."

Jason considered the mummified hands, "Jeez. Better gets his pants off. When he does need to go, no way he'll get his wang out in time."

"Doan borry, I figger it out. Woan ask you to hold it." Smitty was fading fast. He looked at Will, who was tearing the gauze to tourniquet around the wrists. "Tarzan good, but Cheetah faster."

"Cheetah cheat, but I'll still buy you monkey juice, provided you stay put and rest." Will gently positioned the bandaged hands across his friend's chest as if readied for a sarcophagus. "You are one crazy fucker."

"Yeah, the son-of-a-bitch could've killed himself." Pants off, Jason noted the black and blue score just below the waist. "Railing's busted, I heard the crack. Could've broken a leg or a rib."

Stuart's going to have a shit fit. Rick could see it now. "Alright, break it up! I suggest we get that parapet repaired before Stuart gets back."

Everyone dispersed except for Will, who took an adjacent bunk. "I'll stay with him, it was my stupid idea."

"Yeah, well, if you admit that to Captain Bligh, be prepared for an earful." Kaz led the procession out of sick bay.

"He's already got it in for me, so what else is new."

Rick looked at their comatose mate and shook his head. "I'll be in my quarters if you need me."

Rick was right, and the crew steered clear of a Stuart gone ballistic...except for doped-up Smitty and Will who were captive in sick-bay. TWICE the belligerent captain entered, increasingly inebriated.

Will remained impassive, enduring the haranguing that was excruciatingly reminiscent of his mother's obnoxious refusal to just **let it go!** Refusal to engage only heightened Stuart's combative demeanor. *Jeezus! No wonder the old man acted like Ralph Kramden. Bang! Zoom! To the moon Alice!*

"Give it a rest, mother!"

"You calling me a mother? Fu--"

Rick intervened just in time to usher his brother out of the area. "He'll sleep it off, Will. Don't sweat it." Token resistance, the nuisance was escorted to quarters.

Smitty was out like a light. Will leaned back in the adjacent bunk, wound-up and certain of one thing...exclusive rights to the booby prize: member of the most fucked up home life on the planet.

He was wrong. Someone else, not far from their berth, had him beat.

CHAPTER FIFTEEN

"You ungrateful, insolent bitch!"

The vicious backhand landed her splayed on the dread bed, blood trickling from the corner of her mouth. He thought about it, her listless body his for the taking. The fiery glare of steely dark eyes told him it would be one helluva of struggle if he chose to get some. He resumed packing the overnight bag.

"I give you everything a woman could dream of and I expect obedience and respect in return." Forty-three year old Alaine Moreau sensed his wife had plenty to say, but she elected to remain silent.

Nicole demonstrated wise restraint that betrayed her twenty years. Knowing that to bite her tongue would hasten his departure, she lay there tolerating the tirade. A year of marriage, an arrangement she had little say in, had evolved into a continual day and nightmare.

"I absolutely forbid anymore shoots. Travel brochures, swimwear...huh! Nothing more than pictorial wet dreams for jack-offs and I will NOT be the subject of public ridicule as the husband of other men's fantasies."

"Excuse me, sir," the butler eased in to zip the bag and carry it down to the idling Mercedes. "It's time."

Alaine pivoted at the door for a final admonishment. "So help me, woman. Disobey me, and there will be hell to pay. And not just your Catholic hell. Horror-flick, fucked up shit hell!"

Why don't YOU go to hell, you bastard.

Noontime Friday, and Will, with the help of Jason, had finished repairing the railing busted by Wildman's plough-through. Everyone found something to occupy their time: refilling the scuba tanks, picking up extra fishing gear, more supplies for the galley which Kaz declared a necessity. Stuart was still in a foul mood, mostly due to a raging hangover, but thanks to Smitty raising himself from the dead and toughing it out, the captain came to accept the incident as a lesson well-learned.

Smitty stood on deck admiring Doc's handiwork. Re-wrapped hands allowed fingers to bend at the joints. They were still burning and he hope what little skin was left would graft quickly. He forced himself into good spirits and lied about the pain. Fidgety with cabin fever, he feigned a patient with unbelievable recovery powers.

"Alright, that's it! I got a hankering for good medicine: ice-cold beer and oysters on the half shell. See you clowns at the bar."

"Hey wait up!"

"The crip's ready to party!"

"Fuckin eh, abandon ship!"

"Outta be a real hoot watching him shuck an oyster."

The crew filed out. Smitty, still dopey, was half way off the wharf, not exactly walking a straight line.

Dinner was a low-key affair. Will and Stu kept their distance. The brothers sat at the end of the bar mulling over a map, quietly discussing their course of action. Will, Doc, and Kaz got a kick out of Smitty's dining frustrations. They did take turns pouring the pitcher of beer for him, but until asked, they were content to watch the man-versus-oyster battle. Jason and David sat in a corner, engaged in a lightning-round game of cribbage. Arti was outside on the deck, a fruity beverage quenched his way through the last chapters of George Orwell's Animal Farm. Diversion was attained each to their own.

In a strange way, the leisure time was more strenuous than the days of frenzied preparation. Soon to set sail for a shakedown sprint to St Croix, the mounting tension was admitted by no one as they contemplated their trepidations of coming exploits; nobody flinched behind a veil of bravado. What few unattached female clientele were present offered a playful distraction.

The debate over who had won had been beaten to a dead horse. Will rose from his chair conceding under protest though he knew the desperate maneuver warranted honors, and drink. "Here, that outta cover it. You got balls, Smitty, I'll give you that."

The scene had grown stale, Will's overwhelming urge to be alone could not be denied. Something, nothing, beckoned.

"Man, where you going?" Doc was returning with pitcher in hand. "A couple ladies at the bar want to join us."

"I'm sure you guys can handle it."

Will checked in with the brothers on his way out. "Going for a long walk, I'll be back ... whenever."

Rick nodded.

Stu looked up from the map. "Try and stay out of trouble and don't get fucking lost, will ya?"

"That will be one of my objectives, sir."

Jason Douglass

Will had a way of being misunderstood. Always sincere, his delivery seemed tinged with a mark of sarcasm, if not arrogance, yet he intended nothing of the sort. Most found it quite entertaining, but those who really struggled to understand him found it most irritating. It was clear Stu fell into the latter category, as he burned holes with his eyes, straight through the back of Will's shirt.

If it were a nude beach, he would have complied. Longing to free his spirit, he would even shed his skin if he could. Destination unknown, Will stashed his sneakers under the boardwalk, tucked his shirt into his trunks, and headed east. Eyeing the coastline, he estimated two miles before development ceded to pristine seclusion...*solitude*. He skirted the waterline where the waves reached maximum extension before receding into the next surge. The breezy waft of salt air and crashing procession of waves seemed to clear his mind and soul of what lie ahead and all he had left behind. He had no home, nothing to go back to, and that suited him just fine. It made the adventure more inviting, the risks less daunting, and he could honestly say that not since he was a very young lad had he felt so unattached and free. The future was limitless and he considered anything was possible.

The beach load of late afternoon sunbathers thinned out the further he walked, giving way to the occasional shell seeker. Sandpipers scurried the edge of receding waves skewering the wet sand; their needle-beaks mini jackhammers. A squadron of pelicans swooped down into a trough, wingtips almost skimming the waves. Just beyond the sandbar, Will saw his first dolphin. *Awesome!* Diving headlong into a curl, he swam over the drop-off to the sandbar. He waded out neck-deep, and slapped his hands on the water. A porpoise closed in to investigate, then sounded. Will's heart pounded with anticipation. Seconds later, the majestic creature rocketed out of the water, its reentry splashing him a face-full. The exhibitionist surfaced and circled, emitting peeps of admonishment: *you are out of your element.*

"Show off!"

Rolled onto its side, the dolphin glided past then bid farewell with a tail slap. For a fleeting moment, Will thought there had been some sort of communication.

It was a good mile trek to where the coastline curved out of sight. He jogged. Arriving at the jutting point of land, he looked further and saw more of the same: *not a soul in sight.* In his mind's eye he was Robinson Crusoe, marooned. The shoreline was laced with drooping palms, and had a noticeable drop off, the breakwater more abrupt. Waves swelled quickly, and then became thick and tall just before caving into thunderous crashes. An outcropping of rock in the distance required investigating.

Maybe there I will find sustenance. Press on.

Since he was a tyke, captive in his house of daily horrors, Will's mode of escape and retention of sanity was to create his own world of made-up scenarios. If he could not roust up a baseball, football, or hockey game with the neighborhood gang, he would go it alone, sneaking out with his father's shotgun and playing Davy Crockett or Daniel Boone to bag a partridge or pheasant for dinner. OR, he would go fishing for that illusive lake monster only he had seen, and knew by name. Glen Lake's own Lockness Monster: Glen Nelly. If it were a school night and the home atmosphere toxic, his last refuge, due to time constraints, would be a retreat out back into their field where the hay grew shoulder high. He would lie on his back contemplating the cloud drift...the shape shifters were his friends...until dusk drew the curtains. Yes, to this day, he retained his resourcefulness. His imagination created dreams and adventures, to occupy and assuage a mind seeking nothing more or less than peace and harmony.

Volcanic slag jutted out into the surf, its farthest reach piled high. *Neptune's regal throne.*

He waded into a swirling tidal pool; the sight of small crabs scurrying along the jetty assured him he would not starve. The warm water engendered an irrepressible urge. Trunks yanked down, the soothing relief was almost orgasmic. Backing away from the tepid release, he stood content to let it all hang out...until a needlefish appeared inches from his pecker as if ready to joust. The thought of getting catheterized by this inquisitive creature backed him away in a hasty retreat to the jagged confines of higher ground.

Bare-footing gingerly, mindful of spiny urchins and snappish crabs, the castaway negotiated his way out to the rocky point. Waves slammed, soothing reddened skin with ocean spray. Waters shimmered with marine life. Baitfish massed close to the rocks in search of food, intermittent violent shifts lent credence to lurking predators, unseen. Speared assaults, the quarry would flash silver rocketing those in harm's way no other option but to go airborne. This drew the attention of circling pelicans that would hover briefly before dive bombing with precision. Success was validated by wagging tail feathers, head tilted with gullet outlining lunch. Seagulls joined in the food-fight, swooping to clean up the table scraps.

Will was lost to the raw spectacle until a rolling wave smashed the jetty, the soaking retrieving him from the National Geographic feature show. To his feet, salty eyes squinting sunlight, he thought he made out what looked to be a small sail beached further down the coast: *abandoned sailboat? Man, the boys would flip seeing me sail that back into port.* Tender footing the jagged rocks until reaching the shallows, he jumped in synchrony to a receding wave, the soft sand a soothing relief. He set out for the orange-yellow sail flapping a summons; the closer he got, the tinier the strange craft. Obscured by the sloping shoreline, it looked like the mast was planted in the sand as some kind of homage to a little sunfish sailboat no longer intact.

Cool, I've heard of this sport! Will walked around the modified surfboard admiring the artwork and what looked like inlaid strips of teak, grooved for footing. Cryptic symbols...*MAYAN?* He knelt to run his hand over the board's graphic design. The oddest sensation he was in violation akin to feeling up a total stranger halted the rubdown. Panning three-sixty, the vista west was blinding from the sun and its watery reflection. Will rose to his feet for another look, this time cupping hands over his eyes to deflect the glare. Left to right then back again, slower...

There! Dead center, fifty yards out. Must be a sandbar out there.

A well-proportioned figurine stood waist deep, facing out to sea: jet-black mane cascading down shoulders and forming a V, the spaghetti-strap turquoise bikini accentuating olive-bronze skin, heavenly body unyielding to the rolling waves. Gregarious when it came to breaking the ice with total strangers, something told him to approach with extreme caution. *If I'm intruding, the worst that can happen is a curt "fuck-off", right?*

Wading in and wondering if he was getting in over his head, Errol Flynn coming to the rescue of a damsel in distress raced through his mind. *Yeah right, get a grip!* Not wanting to startle her with a brusque introduction, he sidled up tenuously from behind and to her right, maintaining a respectful distance. The steady breeze and incessant din of small breakers over the sandbar negated the potential for awkward silence. There was no necessity to initiate conversation, at least not until she acknowledged his presence, if she would at all. They both just stood there in parallel silence, gazing out at the panoramic view.

Massive cumulous clouds and ominous thunderheads gave depth and dimension to where sea and sky met. The cotton ball behemoths slowly morphed into and out of abstract features: Snoopy, the Sphinx, a woman's knockers. Feigning detachment, Will mused his gambit while stealing furtive glances at her beguiling profile.

Damn, she's knock-dead gorgeous! Knowing the sticky web may quiver when he spoke, he readied himself for the worst. *Black widow, make it quick and painless.* He cast his fate upon the frothy waters that separated them.

"Never knew heaven was on Earth."

No response. *Well, that went over well.*

"Name's Will Bradford, Miss. Don't mean to intrude on your beach, just thought you might be in some kind of..."

She turned her head ever so slowly, and his bewildered expression forced the slightest of grins, attempting to be disarming.

Blown away and at the same time captivated, Will struggled to comprehend unimaginable beauty and déjà vu. *I've seen her somewhere before...Jesus, get it together quick!* "I got the strangest feeling I was led to this beautiful place, why, I haven't a clue. Are you alright?"

Will fell captive to the fluid grace that turned her to face him. Standing in the cross hairs of a full-frontal assault, sensory overload rendered him speechless. *Sweet mother of pearl, say something so I can awaken from this dream.*

Wading closer to his rescue, she mercifully spoke. "Alright? I don't know of anything in this world that is ALL right except for what we see before us. Take the human element out of the equation and yes...everything is all right."

She communicated as much through her emotion as she did with words. Will felt the hair on the back of his neck prickle. First words mouthed from lips so kissable...hauntingly understood. It was one thing engaging a total stranger impromptu, whose appearance alone was deliciously distracting; add perspicacity corresponding to exquisiteness and Will knew he best tread lightly and with tact. The biggest challenge was going to be stifling that irrepressible pain in his groin: lust.

"Yes, I know what you mean. The natural world seems to carry on in perfect harmony regardless of the meddlesome interference of man, which has sadly proven itself so damn defective. Maladies up the kazoo, from the perverse to outright madness."

Her expression was impossible to read yet something telekinetic seemed to convey understanding on a level both were painfully familiar with. He tried to stay locked on to the dark, provocative eyes, unintended seduction siphoning him off, but he could not resist taking inventory as the gap narrowed between them: *maybe five-eight, hundred twenty pounds, a touch of French mingled with Spanish and Creole, progeny of Sophia Loren? God, what a body! Risqué lips luscious and moist, a tiny diamond shaped gap keeping her lips, unsealed...oh so kissable.*

Sand shifted under his feet, *must be a cross-current riptide.* Refusing to admit to being a willing captive, and unconscious of his snail's pace encroachment, the space between them narrowed to arm's length. A space that was non-threatening, but VERY bold in that retreat was no longer an option. *Well, here goes*.

"Where did you sail from?"

Her warm lilt poured over him like honey. "Do you see that house on the point way down there?"

Will focused. Off in the distance, perched high on a cliff, sunlight glinted off glass exuding opulence. "Wow. Your parents look like they've done quite well."

"I'm married... well, sort of."

The response threw Will off balance. Having the presence of mind not to ask her age, *she can't be any older than me, for Pete's sake,* it was her indifference to the fact, the resigned tone, which stalled him as to how to proceed.

"Well, it seems you are truly blessed living high in paradise."

"Hah, paradise? All that glitters is not gold." She snapped her head back, not so much to clear her face of blown strands of hair, but to accentuate her contempt for what caused her to come to this place seeking solace. Then, antithesis to her demeanor, she wrapped herself in her arms...a noticeable shiver in spite of warm waters.

Slipfinger Nine

Will knew best to change gears. "Care to join me on the beach?"

"That would be nice, Will Bradford."

"How do you know my name?"

"You already told me."

Dumb-ass. He tried to play it cool, "that's right. Then I guess you owe me the same courtesy..."

"Nicole."

"Nicole what?"

"Just Nicole. Come on, I'll race you to my board."

"Wait a min..."

The false start gave her a body-length lead she never relinquished. Reaching the shore, his heart was in his throat. Not from the sprint, but the curvaceous derriere sashaying up the beach. Most delectable was the scant protrusion of flesh wedged out from her bikini bottom. *Suck-you-lent...* Will checked himself on the shaky tightrope.

She was an enigma; composed and pensive yet convivial and brazen in autonomy. Drawn to this place of solitude, neither felt compelled to force conversation. Unlike the norm of first encounters where silence begets awkwardness, the moments of silence were a mutual comfort, a respite for reflection.

Respectful of her privacy, Will made no attempt to pry into personal affairs. Instead, the tête-à-tête revolved around who he was and how he came to be here. He responded in kind, minus the real reason his being here. *We'll never see each other again, so what the hell.*

His unabashed candor and matter-of-fact delivery of a screwed-up life had an inadvertent effect. Nicole had never met anyone so sincere, baring ugly truths while somehow keeping it all in perspective. Instead of getting fed a line of the usual bullshit guys excelled in, claiming to be the charming prince whose world spun around himself, Will's candid admittance he was a rolling stone in search of something, somewhere, struck a raw nerve. When pressed why he was so far from home, his blunt reply was: "I have no home." He then laughed it off. So matter-of-fact was the response, its effect could not have been predicted.

She was intrigued by the originality, the sensation of something she longer for...*I wish I could be such a free spirit.*

He told her about their venture, well sort of. "I'll only be here one more day. Sunday we take her out for a shakedown to St. Croix and back. Monday, we depart for a very long sail home."

Dirty laundry, no future plans etched in stone, and now the convenient 'here today, gone tomorrow' number...Nicole did exactly what he anticipated: rose to her feet and offered a cordial farewell.

She stood defiant, a perfect complement to a gorgeous sunset. Will remained seated on her board, considered the view, and waited for the 'take a hike' that was yet to come. And then it hit him. *Holy shit!* Will recoiled backwards off her board; his butt planted in the sand, and leaned back on his hands. His expression and body language was as if he had just solved an insolvable problem. "The in-flight magazine! You're that model!"

Even her laugh was intoxicating, though fleeting.

"Until yesterday, yes."

"What do you mean? Why? Did you quit?"

"I didn't. He's forbidden me my one escape from that prison on the cliff."

"I...don't understand. Why don't you just..."

"I'd rather not talk about it, at least not now."

Dour in her request, Will knew best to drop it and back off the intrusive Q&A.

Both withdrew to consider the wondrous splendor going down. The fiery sphere that had chaperoned their meeting was nearing splashdown. Never tiring of a day's final act, it was for his benefit she deferred to the moment.

Will had never seen the sun kiss the ocean goodnight, his enrapture told her so. The merge looked to Will like a light bulb, *no...a nuclear test*. His heart raced with the realization: *she's going to have to go soon.*

Nicole eyed her prey. There was something about this welcome intruder that was refreshingly innocent. Comforting personality and physical attraction aside, it was boyish wonder she found so irresistible. She made her move. Palming his face, her soft lips conformed to his.

Will never knew a kiss so erotic. He pulled her in. The exerted pressure caused their lips to part in a crush. She bit his lower lip as he sought leverage. One hand to the middle of her back, the other cupping heaven below...the setting sun bore witness to the timeless union.

"I've got to go while there's still daylight. Can you meet me here tomorrow, early afternoon?"

"What about your husband?"

"He's in Jamaica on business. He won't be back 'til Sunday."

"Why don't we go out on the town?"

"No, you don't understand. He has people that shadow me when he's away. It's difficult to go anywhere in public without him finding out everything I do. That's why I windsurf." She pointed further down the beach. "See that leaning palm? There's an overgrown trail close by where I can hide my car. Just be patient and wait for me there."

"I'll bring a picnic."

"Don't worry about that, just be here." Nicole wet her finger and raised it to the wind. "The wind is with me. I'll be home before you reach the bend."

He steadied the board as Nicole positioned one foot and grabbed the mast's cross-brace. "I'm glad we met, Will Bradford. Funny...I don't believe in fate, do you?" She pushed off, catching wind and denying him the last word.

Will watched her angle her attack diagonal to the waves, speeding out past the breakers. He wondered what else she excelled at. The last vestige of light cast an orange hue from the beach out to where it met colossal thunder clouds, their size distorting distance as they flashed jagged lightning. Hearing no rumble assured him she was not in harm's way. He kept vigil until she disappeared into the eventide, her exit vaporous as was the entire encounter which now seemed unreal.

He jogged or floated all the way back, never breaking stride. His mind raced, consumed with what had taken place and oblivious his calves which were burning from loose footing in the sand. It seemed no time passed before he returned to reality.

Doc, Jason, and two lady friends were leaning over the pier railing when Will appeared out of the dark, limping from a bad leg cramp. He could still taste her as he shuffled up the ramp.

"Well blow me tight, it's the lone ranger. Where the hell you been?" Doc passed a joint.

"Swimming with dolphins, talking to a mermaid...usual beachcomber stuff." Will acknowledged the ladies and then fell silent, clearly detached. The uncharacteristic demeanor and faraway expression roused Jason's curiosity.

"Earth to Will. Man, are you on something?"

"Yeah, I'm on to something." Will looked right through Jason and bid an affable 'adieu'. "Ladies."

Jason looked to Doc who shrugged. "Maybe he drank too much salt water."

Hovered over the charts, Rick thought he caught a glimpse of Will drifting by their quarters. "Is that you, Will?"

The tired crewmember backed up to the doorway. "Turning in. I'll be up early to keep an eye out for that surprise delivery."

"Everything okay?"

"Couldn't be better. Really psyched about our maiden voyage Sunday. If there's any last minute details, just let me know."

Stu looked up from the table to verify it was Will who was so accommodating. *Something about his demeanor...*

"Ah, captains...if it's alright with you, mind if I cut out tomorrow afternoon?" Met someone I'd like to say goodbye to."

"Thought we'd all rally in town for a bon voyage dinner. Why don't you bring her along?"

"Wish I could, but it's a bit complicated."

Rick sensed his brother's concern. "Fine by me. Remember, not a word about what we're doing. Got it?"

"Yeah, I know, loose lips sink ships." *Oh, those lips.*

She would not leave him alone. It was a frustrating night counting stars.

CHAPTER SIXTEEN

The purveyors of armed persuasion arrived quayside, break of dawn. With the exception of Kaz, who was in the galley laboring away under growing angst, and Smitty, hell-bent on restoring his hands to usefulness, the crew filed out to secure the special delivery.

A few words of broken English were spoken as the large wooden crate was muscled off the flatbed and laid upon two pallet jacks. Arti nodded to the captains, "nice touch."

PEPPERTREE   CANNERY

FRUITS   VEGETABLES   MEATS

The stenciled artwork was a perfect ruse to deflect the attention of nosy mariners taking their morning coffee on deck. To the rest of the crew not privy the contents, it was a big letdown.

Doc spoke for all. "You got to be kidding me! All this secrecy...for this? I thought we were good to go on food."

Stu acted hurt. "What the heck were you expecting, torpedoes?"

Soon after the davit hoisted the crate on deck, a small tanker truck arrived, carrying potable water. The driver stretched a hose down the wharf and fed it inside one of the schooner's portholes, then into a five hundred gallon holding tank. The activity drew attention from more than a few early morning risers, some leaving their yachts to pay a social call. The captains took turns on the dock fielding questions about the upcoming adventure, the itinerary modified with discretion.

    Will and Smitty returned at noon, their requisition of last-minute supplies fulfilled: more batteries for the Ham radio, extra fishing tackle, and some over-looked items to placate an uptight cook. With the last minor details onboard complete, liberty was granted along with a decree that all must be accounted for by midnight. Come first light, they would be underway.

    "Hands healing nicely. Day or two, name's no longer 'Useless'." Sitting on the bunk applying ointment, he watched Will scurry about.

    "Where the hell's my wallet?"

    "Man, she's really got you worked up." Attempts to pry info on the mystery woman were ignored as Will rifled through his belongings.

    "Here it is!" He emptied his wallet, hoping he had enough cash. "Can you loan me a little? And spare some smokes?"

    "How's 'bout a description of her?"

    "Dammit, man! She's a thoroughbred. Twenty, going on thirty, tight and outta sight. That good enough?"

    Smitty fumbled through his gear and came across a pack. Tucked inside the cellophane were two orange tablets that were not baby aspirin. *Sweet 'sunshine', I forgot all about these.* He could not resist. *This should liven up his private party.* Smitty could see it now: she inquires, he balks, but her insistence to "check it out"...perfectly **'laid'** plans blown to what else...SMITHEREENS! *Hilarious.* Slipping a twenty inside to cover the parting gift, he tossed it with a straight face. "It's gonna be a long voyage so you better make the most of it, you dog."

"Thanks, I owe you."

"Ah, forget it. Just have a high...I mean...good time."

Across the street from the pier, Will's personal stash bought a change of clothes and a simple necklace, on which hung a Mother of Pearl. Rendered broke, only shrewd bargaining kept him from touching the loaned twenty.

Emerging from the bathhouse showered and shaved, he looked to see if the coast was clear. If any of the crew saw him he would surely be razzed: billowy silk shirt, drawstring khakis rolled up above his calves...the incognito swashbuckler. He made a quick exit down the boardwalk and onto the beach where the receding waves cooled the sand.

Coaxed by what he hoped was fate, he moved out, haunted: *What the hell do I have to offer her?* Never one to doubt himself when it came to fraternizing with the ladies, this time was different. He questioned himself, what he was doing, and whether he was going headlong into the incantations of a siren taking sport in luring her latest victim to their assured demise. It was because she was so alluring that he was `Will'-ing game.

Mid-afternoon brought about a discernible migratory shift amongst the locals and tourists alike. As cattle plodding in from pasture to a feed pen, two o'clock happy hour beckoned at The Shipwreck.

Trucked-in boulders had extended a rock pile into the surf, concrete and telephone pole piles lined each side of the jetty to brace the unique architecture. Built of salvaged lumber from demolished buildings, and boats no longer sea worthy, this replica of a windjammer rested on the edge of the sea, it's back broken. Her bow overhung the water and the aft portion was purposely severed low enough for easy access from the beach. Patrons filed in through an arched cutout in the stern. Melding the separated halves were matching sets of stairs accessing the second-story foredeck. A small pool and outdoor bar occupied the thirty feet of open space. Tattered sails flapped, moving shadows across the sun-drenched decks. As the pool gradually filled with half-naked bodies, mostly female, it was no coincidence the stairs and upper deck's parapet were congested with dudes appreciating the commanding view below: cleavage galore.

Smitty and Doc marveled at the engineering feat as they entered the cavernous, dark hold.
"Puts my attic cabin to shame, huh? What an ingenious concept!"
"A tale of two Alices." Smitty fumbled with his wallet. "Yours is a wonderland, this...a restaurant with a fucking five-dollar cover and no Arlo Guthrie." Smitty dropped a ten for their passage.
The stern section inside was darkly cool: cigar bar, bistro, and game room. Just outside: a small stage where a calypso band was tuning up under the cover of a patchwork mainsail. Umbrella tables and bikinis converged at the poolside bar. Forward, ingeniously concealed underneath the bow section, were the kitchen and lavatories. Above,

on the foredeck, sun and fun: shuffleboard for geriatrics and a regulation-size volleyball court complete with sand, its perimeter lined with half-round rubber tubing.

The unique venue was the perfect diversion for the crew to while-away anxious hours, tie one on, and maybe get lucky.

Smitty held court in the poolroom, one by one relieving his mates of most of their remaining cash. Even with mending hands, cue stick sliding smoothly between thumb and forefingers, his game found no equal. The clock-cleaning allowed him to play the benevolent philanthropist. He had no intention of going to sea with anyone's stake. Throughout the evening, the boys would return to the scene where the shark continued the bloodletting with anyone gullible enough to accept a challenge. Humble requests for fronts were denied, the cash-cow's insistence drinks be put on his tab made him MVP of festivities. His screw-up that had rendered him a liability was waived, in favor of his becoming a key asset. He was a true humanitarian.

The band played island music very well indeed, and would have done well to stick to their forte. The backbeat rhythm was simply not conducive to the mellowest of Stones' tunes.

"They're desecrating Ruby Tuesday!" Stu was aggravated, refusing to admit Smitty's game was far superior, but Rick knew that was not what had crawled up his brother's ass. They both had plenty of cash, so there was no groveling for a drink.

Rick leaned on the railing, looking down at all the cleavage aft. "Check it out. Looks like the jocks are working a perfect game. I think a squeeze play's on."

Jason and Dave flanked two ladies poolside.

Stuart huffed at their fortune and turned his back flagging down a waitress. "Another colada, double rum."

Rick knew all too well his brother's disposition; he was surly and intent on getting drunk.

"Man, what the fuck's eating you?"

Stuart had already consumed enough truth serum, any attempt at ambiguity was futile. "You wanna know what? What the fuck is Will up to? I mean, do you not find it rudely inappropriate that he's gallivanted off somewhere with no regard for camaraderie? This is NOT the way to kick off our venture."

"Not really. Besides, the way you've behaved towards him, he probably thought you'd appreciate his absence."

Stu paid the waitress and handed off a beer to his brother. "Tomorrow, these New Hampshire blokes will find out what high-seas sailing is all about. We'll push the crew to the limit and Casanova better have his mind right."

"You really got it in for him, don't you?"

"Nope. It's just that the smartass thinks he's so damn smooth up there in the riggings. It'll be a riot watching him aloft under full sail, pitching and yawing. Probably cry like a baby."

"Hey, just don't kill him, man. We're already stretched thin. Rick did not relish the thought of playing mediator and busting his ass trying to maintain a cohesive crew. On a journey of such extent, with so many variables and risks involved, two guys at odds could have a devastating effect their success, not to mention morale. The last thing they needed was a fractured crew. *Not good.*

CHAPTER SEVENTEEN

Rather than kick himself in the rear, Will reclined skyward on the trunk of the horizontal palm that was supposed to have been the rendezvous point. Salvaging his disappointment, he wrote it off as payback for the ignoble way he had dismissed his high school sweetheart. *Payback's a mother. Isn't it, shithead?*

An hour passed while he killed time collecting driftwood for a small fire pit and sweeping the sugar sand with a fallen frond. *Either she simply can't make it, or I've been stood up.* He tried to be pragmatic. *Hell, probably for the best. She's married, I'm leaving tomorrow, what good could possibly come out of this?* Envisioning the seductive beauty for the umpteenth time, with every passing minute her essence seemed to fade. What WAS clear though was his inability to refute his superficial reason for having come: there was no denying his fantasy. *What a selfish cad! Abandoned the crew in pursuit of a tryst that shouldn't be.* He awarded himself jackass of the day award; it was time to go. He knelt before the palm, placing the necklace on the trunk. Clutching sand, one word began funneling through his hand: **goodbye.**

The thick vegetation folded, giving way to a black Jaguar's stealth approach low to the ground. The growling purr ceased as visual contact was made through the dense cover. Shedding the vehicle, she made her move to the edge of the thicket to observe her unsuspecting quarry.

He had just resigned himself to the no-show, when talons came from behind, skewering his rib cage. A knee-jerk reaction from the surprise attack sent him broad-jumping forward; he did not clear the hurdle, and fell face-first on the other side of the tree. He struggled to gain his composure while on all fours, his heart pounding. He gladly endured the sweet laughter until its abrupt halt.

"What do you mean, 'goodbye'?"

Will rose to his feet. Fortified with a witty response, he turned, but his mouth would not function. He was rendered speechless by the beauty that stood before him...stunning elegance. Yesterday's dream paled in comparison to the here and now. He did not remember her being his height as he took inventory head to toe. Her silky black hair was pulled back and put up, with strands framing a face capable of launching a thousand ships. Just the right amount of mascara and eyeliner highlighted dark and dangerous eyes, luscious lips glistened with a moist, light red. Her olive-bronze skin was accentuated by an azure low-cut sundress, cruelly emphasizing her assets. Straps laced her ankles with pump sandals dug into the sand; her defiant wide stance *dangerously provocative.* Such was her presence as Will was sucked in, closing the gap by stepping over the palm, his eyes locked with hers in an unflinching face-off. Will stood before her, unsure of his next move. Mercifully, Nicole broke the silence.

"I'm sorry. I was followed and had to lose them in town. Didn't think I'd--"

Will sealed silent her irresistible mouth. One hand slid up her neck to where his fingers could manipulate her head to his; their mouths conformed, her fingernails raked his back. His other hand slid down the small of her back, which curved out marvelously. She pressed into him.

Fingers traced her dark eyes, while thumbs cornered the delicate mouth, slightly parting lips. An ever-so-gentle kiss static-snapped them into a fusion of swelling desire. She grabbed his hair. His hands slinked, tracing her shapely contour and coming to rest below a raised dress. He dared venture further. The salacious feel of soft flesh protruding from silk panties, color imagined, was tantalizing as he lifted her. She wrapped her legs around him as they fell against the tree, his intentions well noticed.

Expressing amusement at Will's predicament, Nicole wedged inside to halt the growing intent. "Whoa, not so fast, my stallion. Come with me." She noticed the necklace. "You're so sweet." Donning it, she gave him a gentle kiss, and then led him into the jungle.

The XKE convertible personified Nicole to a tee: sleek, sexy, and built for speed. Relinquishing their handhold, Will paused to admire the Jag.

"She's you on wheels…VERY nice."

"Gets me around. Here, come grab this."

The sight of her bent over to get a blanket and wicker basket from behind the passenger seat was mind numbing. *What did she want me to grab? Oh, right…the basket.*

With blanket spread, she arranged the cooler, picnic basket, and a lobster crate for a table. Sporadic gusts of sandy wind caused Will to spring into action. "I'll be right back."

Will foraged the tree line, returning with an armload of sturdy branches. Two more trips unloaded a pile of snapped-off fronds from scrub palms.

"What are you doing, nature boy?"

"Making the campsite worthy my princess. Just relax, you'll see."

Angled against the wind, long sticks were pushed into the sand and leaned against the tree trunk. More branches crisscrossed forming a grid. "Be right back."

Returning with an armload of fronds, he proceeded to weave them into the frame. Amused and impressed by his resourcefulness, Nicole joined in to fabricate the canopy.

The structure offered shade from the afternoon sun, an efficient windbreak, and privacy in the event a wayward beachcomber decided voyeurism was a bit more enticing than shelling. Finished, they stood back to admire their hideaway.

Will slipped his arm around her waist. "Not exactly the Ritz...does such a humble abode pass approval? I mean, I know it's a far cry from the opulent comfort you must be used to." Will turned to a warm smile.

"It's absolutely adorable, and cozy. Come on, let's sit out the hot afternoon."

Nicole dispensed a gourmet spread. Grapes, cut melon, finger sandwiches of fresh crab, French bread and an assortment of cheeses. Two bottles of red, crystal glasses worthy of the high dollar wine.

"I'm impressed. You put all this together?"

"Well, not exactly. My staff follows instructions accordingly."

Staff? Will uncorked and poured, contemplative, his countenance an easy read.

"I know what you're thinking, Will Bradford. Rich girl has it all. So, why am I here?" Nicole fingered a grape, put it to his mouth. "Do you know what I am?"

Risking offense, he offered, "a trophy wife?"

"More like a concubine to an insecure, controlling son-of-a-bitch. It's no wonder he was a mid-life bachelor when I met him." She looked away and drained her glass.

"You don't have to say anymore, Nikki." Dark scenarios could not hold a candle to what followed.

"Manipulating, possessive...**pervert!**"

Will winced. He lit a cigarette that was adroitly intercepted with a 'thank you'.

"What's funny is he's so jealous that he can't stand other men looking at me, yet he actually forced me once into entertaining a prospective client to seal a deal. I will never forgive him, and since then I've considered the marriage a farce. I don't acknowledge his last name, nor my maiden name anymore. My father married me off to save his failing farm. An arrangement, I call it; he and senior Moreau made this deal...think of old fashion dowry. I'm not a wife, I'm collateral. I had no say in the matter."

"Jesus, Nikki, you call that funny? Why don't you just leave him?" Her laugh and matter-of-fact deportment over her predicament spoke to Will of courage and resilience.

"Don't you think I want to? This isn't America. Customs and women's rights are quite different down here. Why do you think I was late getting here? I am constantly watched and followed. I'm now told I cannot have any life of my own to pursue my interests. He'll use me to his advantage, yet is so jealous and insecure if I'm not under lock and key, and my whereabouts always known..." she shook her head, "yet, the bastard had no problem pawning me off to promote his precious rummy business. It's as sick as his idea of love-making. I told him modeling was merely a stepping-stone. My real goal was to be a spokeswoman, head the tourism department that's been mismanaged, or should I say neglected. But HE denies me any pursuit of such things."

Will was struck by the realization she had yet to even mention his name; *Not only no love lost, she hates his guts!*

"So, see, we both seem to have a closet full of ugly, ragged clothes, huh?" From sitting to straddling him, her move was as smooth as her lethal thighs, which Will's hands now glided over.

Her English, the way she carried herself, Will had to ask, "How did you become so refined, so urbane?"

"Father sent me off to a private, I call it a finishing, school in Miami when I was thirteen. I've often wondered if it was done not for me, but for his future plan to raise me up for auction to the highest bidder." She grabbed his chest, fingernails threatening to pinch off nipples, "enough lamenting. Let's have some more wine!"

"One more question. What did your mother have to say about this?"

"Nothing. She died giving birth to me."

Good grief! Will thought he had an exclusive on a life worth forgetting. Suddenly the contrast of two people's veneer dissipated; *dealt shitty cards, two peas in the same rotten pod, kindred spirits seeking logic and meaning in an existence so convoluted, SO fucked up.*

He poured. She went for a smoke. Their thoughts mirrored each other's. Oddly, they both felt and knew it. The telepathy shared was but a harbinger of what was to come; something out of this world and unforgettable.

"Oh look! Is this what I think it is?"

Smitty's mischievous grin and well-wished "high time" replayed in his mind's eye. *Real funny. I'll get even with you, Smithers.* "Ah, a buddy gave me the smokes, probably aspirin."

Nicole thumb-nailed the orange tablets out from under the cellophane. "I don't think so, too small. Its LSD isn't it?"

Her quizzical look told Will she had never indulged.

"People tell me it's the new enlightenment, a fun way to escape for a while. They're so tiny."

"Look, I don't think it's a good idea..."

Before he could intercept, she popped one in her mouth and fell back on the blanket.

"Nikki!" He caught himself from scaring her. *Ah, hell.* "Don't swallow, let it dissolve." A year of pushing the envelope which culminated in the attic cabin, he considered himself damn lucky to have returned with his sanity intact. Having reached the pinnacle that was never to be surpassed, he had vowed it was his last trip. *Can't let her go it alone, damn you Smitty!* Via the outstretched hand, he received communion with trepidation. *Maybe the food will soften the intensity...ya right. Well, you're the idiot pilot now, so fly right.*

"I've tried cocaine, smoked a little grass, but this seems so exciting. At least you can say you spent an evening with a virgin." She giggled.

The first sign she was in countdown to launch: her dark eyes were beginning to dilate. Confirmation to blast-off was her wish they had some gum.

Will knifed the cheese. "Here baby, this'll help." His own clenching of teeth told him he was not far behind, they were on the precipice of no return. Scared for her, but no way would he show it; still cognizant, he reminded himself that the magical mystery tour embarked on was one he had traveled so many times, and often at warp speed. *I'm in control, she's in good hands. Just go with it, you know the flight pattern.*

And the crew partied on.

Smitty continued to bankroll the crew at the expense of local fish. Stuart was drunk, as was Arti, who was doing his best to temper the surly captain.

"Be cool, man. Last chance to get loose. Which is exactly what we're doing."

"Mother pucker's little foray better be worth it, I'll bust his ass tomorrow." Stu flicked his butt over the side. "I'm turning in."

"Christ, it's only eight!"

"You and Rick round 'em up before midnight, 'kay?

Arti steadied him down to street level and watched his captain slalom down the boardwalk to the pier.

He stopped by the billiard room where Smitty was setting up balls for some ridiculous trick shot.

"Looks like you've worn out your welcome. No takers?"

Slipfinger Nine

"Yeah, I think the well's tapped dry." Six-ball made the side. Three-ball ran the rail, but stalled on the corner-pocket's lip. "Must be the beer, that's it for me."

"Come on, let's gather up who we can for one more round. Meet you on the top deck. That waitress who's been my 'go-to' is looking better and better."

Gathered, one more for the road, they looked down on the battery still trying to pitch a complete game with the babes.

Kaz saw the action differently. "Funny as shit. Looks like their perfect game's gonna end up a no-hitter."

"Hey, that was pretty good, Kaz." Smitty looked to Artimus who was undressing the waitress while forking out a nice tip."

"Stu bailed early. He'll be all over us tomorrow." Frustration puffed a glowing pipe.

"Yup. I'm afraid we're all going to regret this in the morning." Rick raised his glass. "Bottom's up!"

Doc chimed in. "Yeah, what's up with AWOL Casanova? Where the hell is he?"

Smitty grinned, imagining just how far away they may be at the moment. "I got a feeling he's so far out there, prolly take him all night to find his way back."

Wonders so defined, they sat just out of water's reach, counting pinprick holes in a colorless sky. Racing hearts, perspiration moistening goose bumps, god-awful strychnine constricting them in a tight embrace...*could really dig some gum!*

"Stay right here."

"Oh god, I feel weird."

"I'll be right back, sit tight."

Will sprinted to the campsite and started a fire. There would be coals for when they returned...*IF we return!*

He felt he had it together, breathed deep, and stretched, wanting to pop every bone in his body.

"Will! Come quickly!"

The urgent call tripped a lysergic rush; *Houston, we have lift-off.* The fifty-yard dash in sugar sand was frustrating...akin to a slow motion dream never reaching the end. Another piercing plea. Will reached the crest at full speed, the downhill slope and hard-pack combined to blast him forth like Barry Allen, aka *The Flash*.

Nicole traipsed calf-deep in water, engrossed by the psychedelic light show her swirling feet created. She never looked up, and nevertheless somehow she saw him blur by and slam smack-dab into a breaker. The hilarious entrance, so cartoonish, brought forth uncontrollable laughter.

"MAN! I couldn't find the brakes! Are you all right? What is it?"

"No... I mean, yes," she managed between jagged fits. "Look!"

"Jellyfish? Get out of there!"

"No, silly. Look at the water!" The light show stirring by her feet was electrified. "It's phosphorous, maybe plankton." Entranced, she spoke into the sparkly watercolors. "I've never seen it so beautiful." She bent over and swirled her hands.

"Wow, it's like liquid fiber optics." Will stood watching her finger paint, regrouping.

"It's like it KNOWS us..."

"You scared the hell out of me." He took her hand. "Come on, I need to chill out."

They sat on the rise, gazing past planets into a fathomless infinity of a billion stars. Though a moonless night, the luminosity of so many suns reflected off the procession of breakers, the white foam giving dimension to an otherwise black void. The waves became a stairway as, hand-in-hand, they began to ascend. What ensued was an ethereal journey, conceiving the heavens clear of misty shrouds. Conversation was conducted entirely telekinetically, as they completed each other's observations. Sharing the view of a world growing smaller beneath their feet, they blasted forth through a chuckhole sky.

"Oh...my God...hold on to me." Her arm clutched around Will's waist, her fingernails making him well aware of reality.

"I've got you, baby." He pulled her tight, kissing her open mouth which seemed to scream silence. The ocean breeze added to the sensation that they were flying; her hair gently lashed his face. *Look down, Nikki! See the city lights?*

"Charlotte Amalie! It's so beautiful."

It would be so easy to love you.

Nicole shuddered a sensual moan. "I just had a mental orgasm."

Will's skin quivered as he sensed her ecstasy. He looked backwards to check the fire, hoping the diversion would make his thoughts unreadable. *How the hell am I going to get her back down?*

The answer came mercifully from the sea. A crashing breaker brought forth the rhythmic cadence that was frothing the shallows. It was as if a book was slammed shut, stunning the readers out of fantasy. He knew she was with him; relief sighed, they had both made the journey out and back in. Though they were still high as a kite, at least they were back on terra firma.

"Come on baby, time for a change of venue."

He drew her to her feet and held her close. The beacon of red coals gave focus as he guided her in. Neither spoke. Fathoming what had happened, any attempt to rationalize would be futile in their altered state. Will eased her down on the blanket. She seemed practically catatonic.

A comfort fire was in order, of which he took command. Another bottle of wine unsealed, he poured and sat down beside her.

"Here, drink." Unflinching dark eyes concerned him that she might still be out there somewhere. "Don't worry love. I'm right here with you, you're safe. Relax and we'll ride this out together."

"I feel so small." She sipped with two hands as Will spent the next hour talking her down with soft stories that drifted into the fire. Tactful perseverance gradually brought her back and when she finally spoke, it was not just what she said, but the provocative tone in her demand that compelled him to rise to the occasion.

"Make love to me, Will Bradford."

He obliged, taking her down slowly.

Sex on acid: Inhibitions melt. Corporeal overload. So acute the senses. Incredibly intense, heated passion plays out in slow motion that seems to last to...never-ending.

Multiple climaxes were reached, the finale ones timed in perfect unison, consummating a bond neither could refute.

"Nikki? You are too beautiful to forget."

"I think I love you, Will. Take me with you."

Will closed his eyes and for an instant wished he was somewhere else. "I can't do that. Not now anyway. But I promise I'll come back for you."

"Then take me again, now."

They grappled the night away, never reaching the end .

CHAPTER EIGHTEEN

"Baby, if I don't go now, I'll miss the boat." Will broke away from the warm embrace, donning his shirt over a crusty back. The high had waned, but so had the night. Neither had slept. The slightest vestige of dawn could be 'felt', not yet seen, through the trees to the east. "Come on. I'll help you pack, but then I gotta run."

Dazed, Nicole stretched and rose to her feet. "You're not running, I will take you. I'd like to see what you're sailing."

"Shit, Waddy, look at your gauge! Pull in that station and I'll make a call while you gas up."

Manny stepped into the booth, cussing their situation while slotting a coin. "Come on, idiot. This was all your fault, answer the fucking phone!"

The dolt who should have been the one searching his ass off answered: "Yeah, you found her?"

"No, Rico, I called to see if she's home yet. Damn it, man, how could you let her slip out? Where the hell were you?"

"Hey, wait a minute, bub. If you guys hadn't left the cottage fucking empty; no food, nothing to drink, out of smokes, I wouldn't have stepped out. SHIT, I wasn't gone thirty minutes!"

"Hey asshole, we've been all over this island casing clubs, her photo shootin' buddies' homes, hotels. It's like she just vanished into thin air. Pretty much like you're gonna do when the boss finds out."

"How hard is it to find that car of hers? There ain't another like it nowhere."

"Listen to me, Rico. If we blow this, the two of us over here are out of a job, but it'll pale to what the boss has in store for you. So, I suggest you get off your goddamn ass, head east, and look for the broad! Might want to call in Stubby and Bobo and tell them to get on the road...NOW!!"

Wad was paying the attendant for gas when the Jaguar cruised by, wedged in traffic. "Keep the change!" A mad-dash to the booth resulted in folding doors crashing inward. He slammed Manny into the pay phone. "Come on, she just drove by!"

"Rico! Stay put, we're on her." Jammed, Manny kicked the doors back outward, one side coming off its hinges. "Son-of-a-bitch! Let's move!"

Rubber peeled, the sedan swerved onto the main drag. Weaving in and out of Ocean Boulevard's two-lane traffic and barely avoiding a couple of head-on collisions, awarded them verbal rebukes and fingered salutes, which Manny viscerally reciprocated, as they managed to close within eyesight.

"There she is! Get closer, a couple cars' separation."

Idling for an opening to turn onto the marina's access road, Nicole and Will were silent, neither wanting to acknowledge the inevitable farewell. They were oblivious to the surreptitious duo lagging two cars behind.

"Oh shit," exclaimed Wad as the Jaguar made the turn. "Looks like little-miss has a playmate. Get the camera ready for a drive-by."

Nicole pulled alongside the wharf. Smitty and Doc were on the bow coiling rope when they heard the engine's growl. "Hey Doc, check out the ride."

"Don't cut the engine, Nikki. It'll be hard enough saying goodbye."

"I can't get last night out of my mind. I feel like your leaving is taking a part of me I've never known. I feel a tiny hole growing inside of me I don't think I can stop." She pulled him close, "I can be ready tomorrow. I know how to sail and I won't get in the way."

"If wish it were possible, but no way. Baby, I can't tell you why, except that this venture is no place for a lady like you. It's not gonna exactly be a pleasure cruise."

"But..."

Will kissed her just as the sedan motored by, the Polaroid clicking off shots. "Christ! Shit's gonna fly when he sees these. Keep movin'. Drop me off up ahead and follow her. If she's going home, check in with Rico then come back for me. I'm going to snoop around for a while, try and find out who this guy is."

"It happened so fast, it was crazy. I swear what we shared won't be a one-night stand. As soon as we get the ship back home I'll come back for you. Just promise me you don't do something foolish. Don't provoke anything. Here, write down a phone number where I can contact you and I'll call the minute we get into port."

Will got out of the car and walked around to her side. Doc focused in on the Jag. "Well I'll be. Check this out." Smitty received the field glasses and zeroed in just in time to see her kneeling on the seat. Will embraced her, hiking the dress. "Wow, nice...no wonder he's late."

Doc wolf-whistled, drawing the others' attentions. The long goodbye earned a rousing round of tawdry accolades.

"See what I mean? No place for a lady." He backed away stealing a famed line: "I shall return." He could not resist one more kiss. "You make it so hard."

Manny sat inconspicuous on a bench, flicking off pictures of the embraced couple and boisterous revelers on the big schooner. *Damn! Hope it was worth it.* Out of film, Manny decided to stroll down to the marina's harbormaster to see what information he could glean on the ship, its crew, and their intentions.

Will walked the plank, enduring gibes and boorish innuendos from the peanut gallery; he could still hear the Jag speed shifting into a dream. The celebration of hair tousling and backslapping was muted when Stuart appeared topside. His expression of disdain spoke general quarters to the crew, leaving Will in a face-off.

"You're late!"

"I doubt any apology would be accepted. Give me ten minutes to clean up and I'm at your service."

Will peeled his shirt off on his way to the hatch, unaware of the dried blood from raked claw marks. Doc commented, "God dam! Must've been one hell of a..."

"Break it up!" Steamed, Stuart shot a glance to his brother, "Take her out."

Eased out of the berth, *Slipfinger* motored past early risers bidding farewell and good luck.

"We'll be back tonight," hollered Rick.

Stuart strode the deck, barking orders. Like a bride swarmed by attendants in preparation for her big moment, *Slipfinger* began a sequential deployment of sail while the diesel motored them into the bay's expanse.

Passing through the buoys demarcating open water, Stuart shouted all remaining sails be unfurled and the diesel shut down. Arti came topside, wiping his greasy hands. "Purrs like a kitten, gauges all centerline."

"That's good." Stu gave a pat on the shoulder. "You mind working the ropes with Smitty, looks like he could use good hands."

"Right." He looked skyward. "I see you got your boy right where you want him."

He grinned, "Yeah. Think I'll keep him up there for a while. A LONG while."

Zephyr winds had given way to more robust easterlies of fifteen knots. Rick had the mahogany-spoke wheel locked on course, due south. Forty miles to St. Croix, he estimated ETA sometime around noon.

Slip glided smoothly through the swells, at least it felt so for all on deck. Assigned look-out duty, Will stood queasy in the crow's nest. He knew exactly what Stuart's intentions were. *Be damned if I puke, but if I do he'll be the first to know.* Looking down for the captain's whereabouts only exacerbated his condition. Crashing hard from the all-nighter, he closed his eyes and realized immediately it was not a viable option. The methodic pitch and roll: ten feet port, ten feet starboard, was anything but lulling. Focusing on the horizon was all he could do to keep from spilling his guts. *Fuck you too, cap'n.*

Under full sail with no land in sight, it was easy to summon up great explorers of a bygone past: Magellan, Cook, Columbus, and a host of others were brought to light. However, considering their own mission, while being furtively disguised as nobles; other, more colorful Caribbean characters were raised from darkness: Blackbeard and Calico Jack.

"Yeah, what about Sir Walter Raleigh, Drake, Hawkins and Kidd?"

"Pirates indeed," chimed Arti, "but not of these seas."

The history lesson was cut short. "Hey cookie, I could use a hand!" Kaz rushed to assist Doc, who was engaged in a losing battle of tug-o-war with the mainsail which was trying to take slack.

An abrupt change in wind direction had whiplashed the mizzen topsail, fouling the halyard around a handhold on the mast. Stuart yelled skyward. "Hey, lover-boy! You're gonna have to climb up to release it!"

Will was not about to give him the satisfaction of his chickening-out, even though leaving the crow's nest to climb another ten feet flashed life before his eyes. *Well, here goes.*

"I need slack in the fucking line!" Will's legs vice-gripped the mast, one hand white-knuckling a grip. "WHOA SHIT!" He struggled to free the halyard while swaying far and wide. Nothing down below was helping, Jason's and David's retorts...barely audible.

"Hey! You alright up there?"

Hell no. But I will be if- when I get the hell down from here and strangle mister dickhead! Will had no energy to vocalize expletives. Drenched in sweat and shaking profusely, he took time out to regroup. While doing so, he noticed something: when the ship leaned to starboard with the wind there was a brief interlude of slack line before pitching back to port. Riding the pendulum back and forth, he timed the window of opportunity. *Maybe three seconds.* Climbing one more rung and leaning out from the mast, he waited for the next cycle. Back to starboard, a timely tug of slack line, "Ta Da!" cordage was extricated. It was a damn good thing he released immediately or he would have been ripped from the mast pole.

"Not bad" was all a begrudging Stuart could muster as the others acknowledged with resounding applause. "Alright, alright. Within the hour we should be half-way there. Hey, Dave. Your turn to relieve Jason on the aft riggings, if the need arises."

"What about Will", asked Smitty?

Stuart looked high, suppressing amusement. "Looks like he's nestled back in. I think he likes it up there, but if he cries uncle, Doc...you be his alternate."

Except for Kaz getting blindsided by a boom when the wind shifted direction, the voyage progressed with no further mishaps. Cookie's lesson earned him a bruised rib cage when he got knocked silly into the foremast's fife rail.

Will knew he was being made an example of for what Stuart deemed as conduct unbecoming. As tired and stiff as he was, caving in was out of the question. *I'll be damned if I give him the satisfaction. A*nother hour maybe? He looked forward to the first sight of land and the victory of yelling down to Bligh, LAND HO! "Wooden Ships" had been rehearsed to perfection, emulating Stephen Still's voice, mercifully inaudible to those below.

Anticipating first sight of St. Croix, Will's attention kept reverting back to a vessel keeping pace off starboard. What had been a dot on the horizon an hour ago had gradually taken shape. He took the collapsed spyglass out of the holster and zeroed in. Still too far off to identify key features. T*oo big to be a pleasure craft. No outriggers, so nix commercial fishing vessel. Not a freighter, too small.* Frustrated by the sun's glare reflecting off the water and the unidentified craft, Will kept disengaging to rub his eyes. The fact that he had gone thirty-six hours with no sleep, AND residual effects from a little orange tablet, did not help. What remained of the water bottle he poured over his face, eyes open. Again he focused, this time recognizing true colors: orange and white. *Be cool.* Taking a moment to compose himself he scanned forward. *There*!

"LAND HO!" He paused for the cheer. "We also got company closing, maybe three…four miles off starboard. Looks to be the Coast Guard!"

The celebration was short-lived.

Jason was monitoring the short wave radio, and conversing with some of the local traffic, when a call intruded:

"This is United States Coast Guard *Yellowfin* calling. We have visual on your vessel currently four miles east our position. Please identify yourself, over."

Jason pushed back in his chair and barked topside. "Uh, Captain, I've got contact with the Coast Guard. You better get down here…quick."

Stu was down the hatch and in the cubicle in time to hear the second transmit:

Jason Douglass

"*Yellowfin* calling...requesting confirmation of last transmission. Please identify yourself, over."

Stu grabbed the mike, adjusting the squelch, fine-tuning the frequency. "Copy that last transmission *Yellowfin*. This is *Slipfinger*, over."

"Roger that, *Slipfinger*. What is your objective and destination? Over."

"En-route to St. Croix, turnaround back to Charlotte Amalie. Trial run breaking in a new crew and readying our ship for long voyage to Cape Cod, over."

"Request that you trim your sails and decrease speed to five knots. Prepare for rendezvous thirty minutes, over."

"Ah, copy that *Yellowfin*. Is there a problem, over?"

"Negative, just routine inspection, over."

"Ten-four *Yellowfin*, will comply."

"Thank you for your cooperation, over and out."

Stu cradled the mike. "Come on, Jase, let's get this over with."

"Hey, Will, need you on deck pronto!" Rick yelled for all hands to trim the mainsails and prepare for boarding. Stuart joined his anxious brother at the helm.

"Well, better now than later. We're clean, they check us out, and hopefully for the duration we're down here we can operate with impunity. We'll be logged, legit."

"Damn! What about the crate?"

"It's sealed and is what it says. Even if we broke it down and they decide to board us, it wouldn't matter where we stashed the stuff, they'd find it. We're just going to have to chance it, and play it cool."

"Yeah but what if..."

"Well, brother, then it's fucking ballgame. OVER."

The eighty-two foot WPB Point Class Cutter came alongside. Except for Rick maintaining course, Stuart had the crew lined up smartly, identifications at the ready. The encounter required that protocol be exemplified. Slack sails flapped to the deep growl of the patrol boat. Arti whipped out a whistle he had fabricated out of a shell casing. With naval verve, he announced the Guard's arrival. It was a nice touch that the dressed men no doubt appreciated.

The crew's deportment did in fact impress the officers. Chief Petty Olsen acknowledged with approval the clean-cut crew's esprit de corps.

"Mighty fine presentation, young men. It appears this beautiful lady is in capable hands. Who's the captain of this majestic schooner?"

Stuart replied back while pointing to his brother, who waved at the helm. "I'm Stuart Blaine, my brother Rick is here with me. We share that duty sir. Our father is terminally ill and commissioned us to retrieve his ship so he could see it one more time."

"Is this your full complement of crew?"

"Yes sir."

"A bit understaffed for such an undertaking, don't you think?"

"Negative, sir. We've sailed this journey with our fathers many years over summer vacations. We are trained and know exactly the efforts demanded for a safe journey."

"When do you plan to set out for the Cape?"

"We're going to spend a few days in preparation, working out any kinks. Maybe get in a little diving and see what we can of these beautiful islands, for perhaps the last time."

"I commend your prudence; preparedness and discretion are vital when undertaking such an extended voyage."

"Thank you, sir. We've already filed our itinerary with the harbormaster back in Amalie. We'll be returning there tonight. I can provide you with a copy of the details if you like. As for now, we're going to drop anchor off St. Croix, perform some routine maintenance, spiffy her up for journey, and wait for dusk so we can get a little nighttime navigation in. You're welcome to drop on in if you're in the area, give you the two-dollar tour of dad's vintage ship."

JEEZUS CHRIST, Stuart. Shut the fuck up! Rick cringed at the gambit gone way over the top. The rest of the crew was rigid at attention as if corn cobs had been rammed up their backsides.

There was a pause, a pivotal moment, as the captain talked to his petty officer. . .

Bullhorn raised, the captain replied. "Stuart and Rick Blaine, sons of Arthur Cromwell Blaine?"

"Affirmative, sir," replied both.

"I thought I recognized *Slipfinger* from afar. Sorry to hear about your father's plight, it's been a few years since I've seen him sailing these waters. I remember you boys when you were mere sprats. Please give my regards to Mister Arthur Blaine upon your return. I apologize for the detention; you have our frequency if for any reason you need assistance while in the islands."

"Thank you, sir."

"Captain Melvin Hargrove. You may remember me."

"That's right! I was a lot younger, but I do remember you now. We'll be sure to convey to father your best wishes."

"You do that, son. Remember those pesky afternoon thunderstorms, just get to Florida and hug the coastline. You'll do fine."

"Thank you, cap'n. It's reassuring to know you guys are out there."

"'To protect and to serve', that's what we're here for. I bid you farewell, steady wind, and smooth sailing."

Twin diesels growled to life. *Slip's* crew did their best impression of the Beverly Hillbillies wave: 'ya`ll come back now, hear?' The orange and white faded, roaring off into the sun in search of law-breaking scoundrels making their presence essential.

"You almost out-did yourself." Rick wiped sweat from his brow.

Main sails reefed, jib and topsails doused, when the schooner came within a hundred yards of the rocky coast, Rick brought *Slip* around into the wind, employing a "back and fill" tacking maneuver and using the outgoing tide to keep them from stalling out. It was high noon.

Once the ship slowed and settled, order was given to drop anchor into the deep water. They would moor away the afternoon, taking in some much needed R&R.

Discussions of what went right and wrong were engaged over lagers. The dingy got its checkout, ferrying excursions for buccaneers wanting to lay claim to the rocky, narrow beachhead. There was a diving exhibition off the foremast's crossbeam, while a couple rods cast silver spoons aft, and yes, a siesta or two ensued.

    The previous night, still unforgettable, returned again to haunt him. Will lay on the bow, gazing over the side. Blue waters, almost transparent in clarity; what may have been a depth of a hundred feet looked like twenty. Immersed in the water world, he fathomed what she was doing and was she consumed as he was with that magical night. *Will I ever see her again? Will she want me to?*

    Smitty was at it again, never missing an opportunity to segue into another insanely ridiculous childhood tale. Arti, Jason, and David asked for it and left an opening; now they were going to get it.

    Will lay flat on his stomach grinning, his arms were dangling overboard. The arrested listeners were hunkered down, their backs against the riser that separated the bow and midsection. The story teller was barely audible, but it did not matter, Will knew the story forwards and backwards. He actually welcomed it, hoping the diversion might free his mind of her, at least long enough to fall asleep. *Damn, my head aches.*

    "How Dick Longwell became famous, aside from his name..." comments and chuckles from the peanut gallery expected, Smitty drained his beer before continuing. "Gentlemen, please. This is serious stuff. Dick had just turned fifteen and, as a show of confidence, his folks left him alone at home while they traveled to Boston for an overnighter. They were to return by noon the next day. Well, needless to say, it was a bad judgment call. Against orders, he invited some friends over. Man, we had a blast!

Poker game, food everywhere, then we raided the old man's booze. Couldn't understand what the folks found so appealing, tasted like shit. Vodka mixed with rum, bourbon with gin, all sorts of ghastly concoctions. Late night horror flicks, rumbles on the living room floor, we were wasted and the place was trashed. Then everyone got wicked sick. I don't know who the last person standing was, but I woke up the next morning in the upstairs bathtub. I stumbled downstairs and saw we had two hours, tops, before the folks would return. Two choices: run like hell, or suffer the brutal hangover and get rid of the evidence. Well, I woke everybody up and it was decided we save Dickie's butt. We fanned out, starting upstairs and also downstairs back of house working our way out of the god awful mess. When I got to the living room, there was Dick. I'd woken him up, but apparently he collapsed right back onto the couch. Clad only in underwear, one of his nuts was dangling in plain sight. He was comatose. I even checked his pulse to see if he was dead, because if he wasn't, he surely would be when his parents got home. I was steamed. Here we were in high-gear damage control and sorry-ass was too wasted to care less HIS dire consequences! I moved in with the vacuum I'd been running. It was one of those caster floor models where the bag expands when full or clogged..."

"Get the fuck outta here, you didn't!"

"Oh come on, man, the noise didn't wake him up?"

David spewed beer all over Smitty's leg, laughing so hard through what he predicted was coming next.

"Hey, what the hell else was I gonna do? Wasn't about to throw a bucket of water on the couch, that would just add to the mess! Look, I gave him one last chance:

shook him, yelled at him, maybe I should have slapped the shit out of him. Screw this, I thought. Took the head attachment off and sucked his 'nad right up the pipe."

The audience went wild. Will snored.

"It was great! He rose from the dead, wide-eyed into instant action. Airborne off the couch, screaming like a girl, he hit the floor running with the darn roller vacuum dragging behind, between his legs. I chased him down when he ran out of the room into the back of the house. Finally cognizant, realizing the sucky situation, he took matters into his own hand and grabbed the pipe." Smitty stuck a finger in his cheek and pulled to deliver a loud POP for effect. "Hole-lee shit! The blue gonad looked like a deformed, long, but not-so-well second dick! I just stood there dumbstruck at what I saw until the weirdest, or should I say murderous, look, transformed his face. I was out the door and down the street into the woods before daring to look back. If he'd had shoes on, I think he would have killed me."

They were rolling on the deck. Jason posed the question if Dick recuperated back to normalcy.

"Dunno. We fell out after that, but in high school, he was a legend with the girls." The jester left all to ponder its implications.

The anchor weighed at twenty hundred hours. Smitty insisted on the crow's nest, wanting to show his hands were capable of the climb, but also to spare Will the possibility of being Stuart's amusement again. The ascent was not pleasant.

The only hassle the crew experienced was the unseen swells posing a question of balance keeping everyone on their toes.

A moonless night revealed stars too many to comprehend. Constellations were easily discerned, coordinates plotted to coincide with compass headings. So clear the firmament, mere particles of grit could be seen, streaking to burnout. Yes, it was true: Mother Earth sure does catch a lot of crap from on high. Halfway back, celestial navigation became superfluous. Stuart kept the bow pointed towards the soft glow of Charlotte Amalie's lights miles beyond the horizon.

When they reached dockside, celebratory beers broke out. "Not bad. Got back almost a half hour sooner than expected."

"Yeah, brother, not bad at all, considering you could have gotten us busted if they'd taken you up on your offer."

"It worked out, didn't it? Sometimes you've got to go with your gut and play it cool."

"You went overboard, we were lucky."

Stuart sauntered off, calling for lights out as soon as the ship was secured. "Five hours and a wake-up!"

Everyone crashed hard from the day's trials. Will, in particular, was grateful for the dogged workout. Her apparition faded to black, his sleep too deep for dreams.

CHAPTER NINETEEN

Sixth ring, lucky seven would be her last.
Please, PLEASE answer the phone, damn it!
A fumbling sound, muffled French cussword, and the jarring noise of the receiver saying hello to a hardwood floor, broke the suspense. Nicole breathed.

Groping, Jacque felt the cord and hauled in the handset. "NOT a good morning."

"Jacque, wake up! I need you to meet me at the studio...now."

"Nikki? Do you know what time it is?"

"Five-thirty, and I'm headed out the door. Park in the back alley, I'll be at the front door in thirty minutes."

"What's wrong?"

"Just be there, please!"

"Don't tell me, your old man again? Are you..."

Click.

No headlights, foot off the gas, the engine purred. Down the long driveway, past the cottage she referred to as the guard shack; when rubber met the main road, only then was Nicole conscious of her own breathing. Another five minutes into town, no one in the review mirror, *relief*; escape undetected...so she thought.

It was Manny's rotation. A light sleeper, early riser, and a proclivity for beating dawn to the punch over coffee with a side order of coke, he was in the process of chopping two lines when red tail lights flashed at the end of the

Slipfinger Nine

driveway. Still in his shorts and in the midst of his ritual, there was no way he was going to be denied his routine. Even if he did break with custom, she had way too much a head start. Manny cradled the phone in his neck and continued dicing the white stuff into a fine powder.

Jacque opened the studio door, his greeting could not match her hurried entry.
"Nik, you mind telling me what's going on?"
She paced back and forth. "Alaine was supposed to be back last night, but something came up. He'll be returning home this morning 'round nine. Is your jeep out back?"

As she explained her strategy, a black sedan took up surveillance at the end of the street.
"Yup, that's the bitch's car all right. Call Manny."

Easing out of dockage, Rick maneuvered the marina's largest vessel with meticulous skill into the narrow waterway: forward, reverse port, forward starboard, reverse, then more of the same until centered between the two rows of yachts.

Word had spread throughout the resident grapevine of the youthful crew's formidable commission. Though barely dawn, well-wishers rose to acknowledge the departure with Bloody Marys and Irish coffees toasting good fortune. The ranks of salty-dog veterans were never derelict in commemorating the departure of one of their own, the empty slip leaving a hole in their community. It was tradition that on such occasion fanfare and well-wishes be in order. To some, it was superstition; to not pay tribute cast a pall on the voyage. It was a long-standing ritual and the crew of *Slip* acknowledged with reciprocating farewells and appreciative gestures.

Whenever the Port Authority was notified that one of their maritime mainstays would be departing never to return, fliers circulated informing who, when and where.

Numerous boats fired up and backed out of their slips. Encircling as escorts, they guided through the seafarers between jetties and into the bay. Chugging along at three knots, an hour would pass before they reached the choke point to open sea: Hassel Island. Local fishing boats joined in the festive flotilla, forming a growing armada of revelers.

Rick got on the horn and called up his brother who was in his quarters going over charts. "You and Arti get your asses up here, you gotta see this!"

The wind gauge high atop the mainmast registered ten billion butterfly sneezes on the anemometer. That did not deter Rick from wowing the revelers. He ordered full deployment of sail as a gesture of gratitude for the escorting fanfare.

"All right tars, let's dress her out!"

Sails were unfurled in methodical precision. Rousing cheers and horn-blasts saluted the command performance as *Slipfinger* pulled away from the armada, entering open water.

Slipfinger Nine

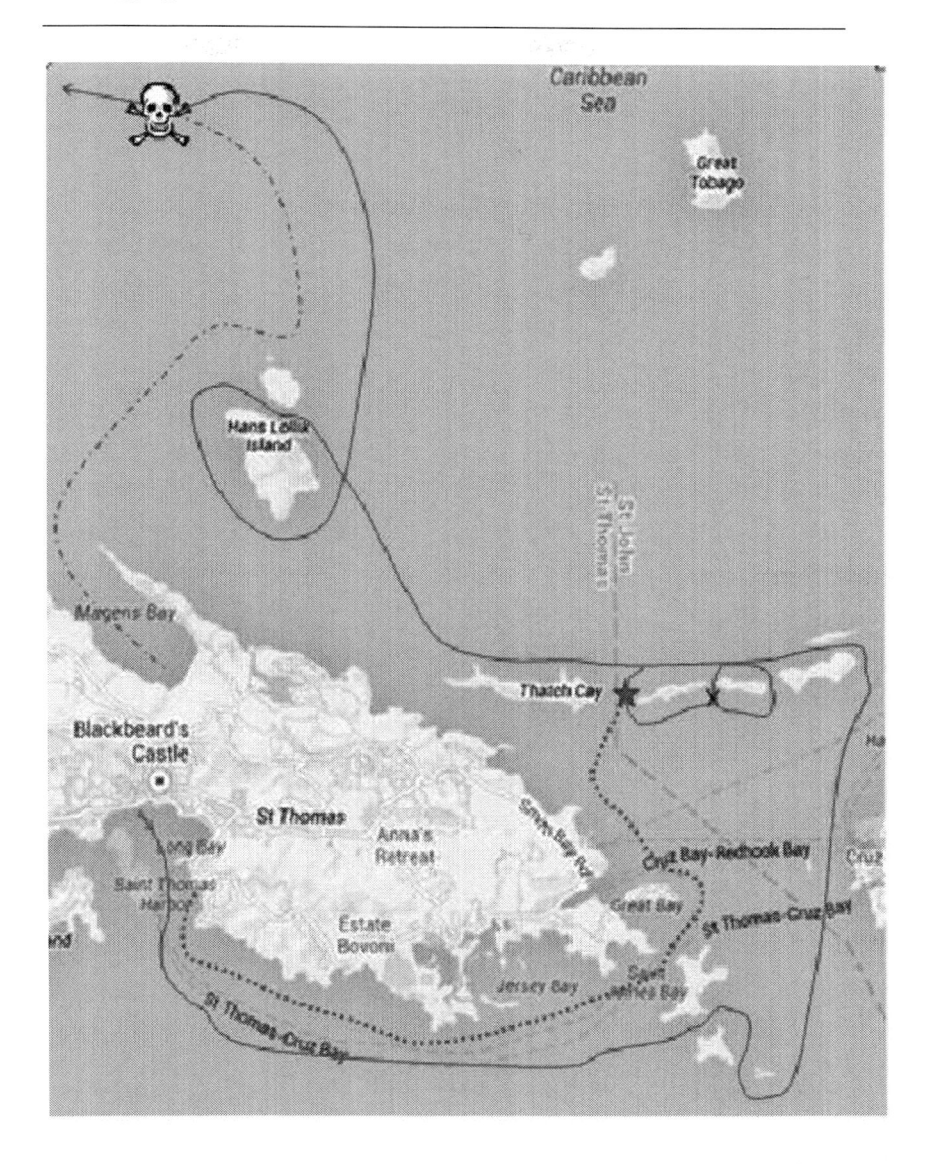

The jeep idled away a 'bon voyage' to the fading clipper. Nicole acquiesced to the probability that their wild night in the sand amounted to nothing more than a one-nighter. There were no regrets; the diversion had been a welcome respite from her dreaded captivity, doubtful a way out. *Maybe in another life, Will Bradford. Goodbye."*

The dutiful lackeys fidgeted in the car, patience growing thinner with the last shade of darkness ceding to morning light. An hour's vigilance and binoculars detected no movement whatsoever through the studio-front windows. *Naughty girl...your husband's going to come undone when he finds out your screwing around on him.* Harlan was about to give in to temptation, the passenger door handle drawn.

"Hey, where you going?" Waddy grabbed his partner's arm.

"I'm gonna play voyeur, see for myself." Harlan was half out in a tug of war when the jeep pulled up behind the Jaguar.

"Hold it!"

Nicole got out and was met at the front door.

"We've been had. How the hell..."

"Shut up, Wad, get down." Both snoops sank eye-level with the dash.

"...I won't be doing any more work for you, Jacque. The bastard's forbidden me."

"Jesus, Nik. How long are you going to put up with that son-of-a-bitch?" Why don't you just leave him?"

"And go where? I don't know what I'm going to do."

"You have many friends here. We could put you up, move you around until we figure something out."

"I know you would do that for me and I appreciate it, but you don't know Him. There's no telling what he's capable of, I wouldn't want to see my friends get hurt." She leaned over and kissed his cheek. "I've got to go, I'm sure his dogs are looking for me and you can bet they'll slobber their master with all sorts of trumped-up details."

Harlan had captured the kiss on camera, as Waddy put the car in reverse and slowly backed around the corner. "Hope it was worth it, Missy. There'll be hell to pay when your old man sees this." A U-turn made at the main street intersect, they awaited the tug on their line.

Buck Island off their starboard marked the halfway mark en-route to the narrow strait between Great and Little Saint James Islands, and the gateway into Pillsbury Sound. Sailing headlong into easterly winds required a constant tacking to maintain modest forward progress. The crew roamed the deck per shouted orders; trim and tuning of sails, standing riggings secured, heave-ho on the mains; it was a work in progress, or more accurately...on the job training.

They plowed through a massive feeding frenzy of mackerel slicing and dicing through a corralled school of baitfish. A plethora of seabirds joined the carnage, dive-bombing for freshly shredded sushi.

Artimus came up from the engine room wiping his hands with a grease rag. In typical his off-handed manner he reported; "fabricated a gasket, found where the oil leak was. Other than that, the engine's overhaul was a righteous one. She's a clean machine."

"What's Stuart up to?"

"Fiddling with the charts. Heard him bitching about his old man's antiquated caliper, so I just fingered the hinge with my oily fingers. He's happy now."

Stuart splayed the suite of reconnaissance photos as if a deck of cards to be flipped. Settled back in his chair, he picked from the line up corresponding snapshots and positioned them on the chart's cluster of cays ten miles east-northeast of St. Thomas. *We hit these first. Remote, and appear to be unguarded.* He made note the light blue hues depicting shallow waters. *Have to anchor off here, ferry in with the dingy.* The logistics sucked: coral reefs, oyster bars...a veritable maze of seclusion. *Perfect. Won't be easy, but feasible. Go in at dusk, out before dawn.*

Stu used the slide rule, drawing a straight line northwest to the Lollicks: Big and Little Hans. 'Big' was the mother lode, its co-ordinates duly marked. *Dicey-difficult. Get out of there undetected, home free.*

Jason hollered out from the radio cubicle. "Hey, Cap'n. We're nearing the strait. Meet you topside." He signed off with the fishing charter that was in direct line with their approach, informing Rick of the draft required to navigate the passage.

"Ten-four. See you up top."

All hands were needed on deck in order perform a ninety-degree turn to port to line up entry. The crew readied for radical transfer; headwind to starboard blow.

The exercise was a flawless execution. Revelry was short lived.

Arriving in the narrow strait, a tidal flow was at its apex to meet them, flushing Pillsbury's contents out with the old and in with the new. Entry could not have been more ill-timed. Infusion equaled displacement, so there was no issue of depth, but lunar effect manifested itself unanticipated. The massive volume of water disgorging from The Sound created a turbulent maelstrom: swirling whirlpools in the deep center, rolling river-like whitewater along the shallower outer edges. It was a slog fighting midway through the channel.

Slipfinger leaned with the wind, her deck slanting steep to port. "Ease the sheets out, head's up for the boom," yelled Rick.

Too late.

The ship stalled in the tidewater's onslaught, its canvas luffing in the wind. Try as he may, Rick could not keep her steady. Gyrating to port, the undulating currents pounded the broad side of the hull, and not only were they being pushed backwards, but the schooner was being subjected to precarious listing.

"Ah, Captains, I do believe there's a distinct possibility we may capsize." Arti's of-the-cuff manner in which he stated their dire predicament was almost comical, if not for the accuracy of his observation. Both captains yelled out for all hands to get on fore and aft masts and release them perpendicular to the wind.

Canvas billowed with the directive; it was all everyone could do to hold the booms to a draw. Squeaky sneakers burned on the tilted deck. Stuart rushed aft to a losing battle...the extra muscle managed no more than a stalemate.

Rick started the engine. "Fuck!" He spun the wheel hard right in a last ditch effort to turn headlong into the torrent. *If this doesn't work, we're going back out.*

Jason Douglass

"She's coming around!" David was at forty-five degrees, rope lashed around his waist as he gripping, white-knuckled, the boom's line.

Rick had all his weight on the wheel, driving it hard to starboard, the distance to shore closing. *Turn baby, turn*.

"Look out!" The foremast's boom swung around from over the water almost taking Will's head off and belly-flopping him to the deck.

Just when Rick resigned they were going to beach and probably rip open *Slip's* underbelly, the whirl of mast pirouetted the schooner's bow dead ahead into Caribbean's mini-version of the Colorado River. The diesel went full-throttle.

Minutes of organized chaos brought *Slipfinger* into resolute conformance back inside the channel markers. Sails left slack, it was left up to the diesel to see them through. There was nothing to do but lean on the wheel's spokes at ten and two, and power forward at a whopping two knots.

Arti went to the aft hatch to listen to the engine's response to the test.

"How's she sound," inquired Stu.

"Growling on all cylinders, so far. Engine's not built for this wide open shit, hope she doesn't throw a rod."

"Man! We almost bought it back there." Doc was sweating profusely. "Talk about right place, wrong time. Should've gone further out in the channel before making the turn."

"No, what we SHOULD have done was avoid this all together." Rick was visibly shaken. "God damn this dual-captain shit. I told Stuart we should have gone farther south, but he wanted to test *Slip's* capability to navigate a tight squeeze." Rick jabbed the handwritten small map tacked to the railing. "We're headed south anyways to scope out Dog Island and a bunch of little cays. We should have just gone south of Little James and we'd be there already. But NOooo...had to..."

"Whoa, be cool. We made it didn't we?" I'll take over for a while." Stu edged his brother away from the wheel. "Couldn't have asked for a more perfect day. Hell, any day on the water is a good day, right?" Rick was in no mood to joust, instead he was already gone in response to Arti's beckon.

"If you say so, cap'n." Doc scratched his head. Nonchalant after near disaster, erratic disposition made note of from the start: *great! Schizo at the helm.*

"Yeah, what's up?"

Celebratory pipe fired up, The Sound finally achieved, Arti advocated disclosing the crate's secret. "Now that we're in the clear, it'd be a good time for show and tell."

Rick was hesitant.

"Man, sooner or later. Now's as good a time."

"Hell, guess so. Worse that can happen is a mutiny, huh? I'll round up the troops."

Holding a slow and steady course, only the mainsails set, Stuart listened to the Articulate presentation. It was the crew's deportment the captain paid close attention to.

Each weapon was exhibited; features and capabilities thoroughly explained, then passed around.

Itching to fire off some rounds with one of the M-16's, Doc asked for a clip.

Rick interjected. "And wake up the neighborhood? Brilliant, Doc. Not until we're long gone out of these waters will there be any such thing." Rick returned a side arm to Artimus. "Jeez, damn arsenal's a trifle overkill, don't you think?"

"Nope, not at all, cap'n. After comparing insurance plans, we decided to go with full coverage. Besides, we can make a hell of a profit selling this shit back home."

"O, God."

Smitty and Jason rifled through the cache of weapons. The over-under grenade launcher fancied Smitty. "You've got to be kidding me!"

"Sure beats fruits and vegetables." Jason hefted the Thompson. "Awesome!"

Will and David stood outside the gathering. Both grasped the implications of disclosure. "Holy crap, Will. Talk about a game-changer."

"Yeah, as if the stakes weren't already high enough. Nice timing, huh? Now that we're on our way, there's no turn..."

"Oh, this is just great!" Kaz's sunburned face had flushed pallid. "I'm not buying into this. No one said anything about going to war!"

Kaz's vehement objection sparked a vociferous free-for-all.

The situation deteriorated rapidly. Will and David engaged Rick, wanting reason for the cache. Art was trying to cool down Kaz.

"You're damn right I'm uptight. I'm not buying into this shit!"

Doc, Jason, and Smitty wrangled over weapons of choice.

From his vantage point above, Stuart tabulated the mixed reviews: Kaz was adamantly opposed. His brother appeared apprehensive making him a difficult read. David and Will were detached, absent enthusiasm. Doc, Jason, and Smitty were immersed with the crate's contents. *They're in.* The way Stu saw it, five to four at worst.

Two fingers to his mouth whistled a halt to the commotion. "Alright. Knock it off!"

Will responded. "Explains the cloak and dagger, nice ploy, skipper. Get us out to sea where there's no turning back."

Art intervened, thwarting another certain clash between the two. "Everybody cool out! This is strictly precautionary, boy scouts. Always be prepared." He relieved Doc of his weapon as Rick proceeded to do the same with the others.

"They get stashed below. Weapons are off-limits to everybody until we reach international waters." Rick pried the grenade launcher from Smitty's firm grip.

Will sought more clarification. "So, why the hell are we packing heat? You just raised the ante big time. Smuggling weed, especially STOLEN weed, buys us more than enough potential for serious repercussion. Running guns too? This is uncalled for...and fucking crazy!"

"Got that right, if we get..."

Stu cut off Kaz. "For those of you that just don't get it, I'll spell it out for you. Yes, I'll admit we went a little overboard; quantity got us the best deal. But if you think for one minute the people we're going to deal with won't be carrying weapons..."

"Hey, wait a minute! I thought these connections were all good buddies of yours."

"Close friends", Stu tempered his response. "The buyers are, Dave, but not the third parties risking the rendezvous. No telling these characters' disposition and if something were to go down, don't you think it prudent we protect our assets AND asses?"

Kaz was incredulous. "Wait a minute. You spent almost three years planning this and you don't have a clue who we're dealing with?"

"By design, no one knows anyone. If the shit were to hit the fan, the heat won't be able to connect the dots. The only way we could negotiate a firm commitment was on their terms, which I can understand. It's the middlemen that are of concern."

Made sense to Will. He was about to make reference to bringing a knife to a gunfight when he spotted the channel marker dead ahead. Both he and Rick yelled the same three words.

"Quick, right turn!"

It was too late. The ship's hull obliterated marker number seven.

CHAPTER TWENTY

Mid-afternoon and they were right where they needed to be: northern sector of Pillsbury Sound. Plenty of daylight hours allowed them to thrice circumnavigate Lovango Cay and the cluster-maze of lesser landforms: miles of narrow channels, treacherous oyster beds and from what they could see, gnarly mangrove shorelines. The shallows surrounding the archipelago of interest limited their approach to a quarter-mile at best. Had they arrived eventide, their keel would have been plowing furrows in the sandy bottom, mollusks scaring *Slip's* underbelly. There was little room for error in these waters.

With their briefing adjourned, standard operating procedures and contingencies checked off once more, it was time. Will prepared to board the overloaded dory in what felt like a scene out of *Sands of Iwo Jima* with John Wayne: troops crammed into landing crafts, everyone silently numb. The shore party's reflective demeanor: contemplative stoicism masking prevalent angst. Everyone kept to themselves their trepidations, knowing full well they were about to cross a line of which there would be no return.

"Shove off." Will crammed in next to Smitty at the bow. Doc throttled the thirty-horse Johnson, backing off when water began to spill over the stern. *Slip*, skeleton-crewed by the captains and Artimus, headed two miles east under one mainsail where they would anchor in the calm waters off the western tip of Thatch Cay.

Will keyed the mike. "Radio check."

"Check." Rick scanned the horizon. Sailboats, yachts, fishing boats flitted about; most fading away back to port. "Looks all clear out this way. We'll let you know how the fishing is. Good luck."

"Roger that. "

"Ten-four, out."

The labyrinth's narrow channels required Smitty to straddle the bow as lookout for shallows. Doc steered accordingly. Crystal clear, azure waters made it difficult to ascertain depth; ten feet looked like two. Will and Jason kept referring to the sketched map comparing it to the aerial photos, both in agreement they were somewhere in the vicinity; one large cay in a maze of many. What they were looking for showed up in the photo as a sliver of a channel, slicing into the cay that meandered inland to slightly higher ground. Elevation was key in order to rise above the salt-saturated soil conducive only to indigenous vegetation like...

"Fucking mangroves! How the hell we supposed to find something we can't see?" Doc was clearly frustrated, unable to see a yard into the interior. No wonder they picked this place. Only *reasonable* way in and out is by chopper!"

"Natural deterrent, impossible to get to, and camouflaged up the ass." Jason stood up, whipped it out, and arched a stream over Kaz, pissing him off. "Ask me, the foray's a bust!"

"Right! So let's get the hell out of here before..."

The distinctive aroma silenced Kaz. A sudden shift in the wind wafted the herbal bouquet. Their objective was close.

"Hello....Mary Jane." Will leaned back, fingering the map in Doc's view. "Round the bend and keep starboard."

He's right, Doc." Jason noticed the darker blue in the photo. Channel deepens, shoreline concaves to where the inlet is."

Smitty guided Doc underneath the overhanging canopy to within arm's length of the bank's thicket."

Doc eased the throttle to near neutral, his hands grabbing the overhang and pulling them along.

"There it be, boys." Smitty seized a branch nosing the dinghy into the tiny estuary. "Cut the engine!"

"You call this a channel? It's a friggin' ditch!"

"Shut up and pull. Maybe it opens up."

So narrow, branches could be reached from both sides. In less than a minute the boat dragged bottom.

"Great, now what?" Kas was becoming more of a nuisance than the black flies and muggy air.

Rather than tell him, Smitty jumped off the bow into knee deep water. "Guess we're here."

The cue prompted everyone to do the same. Will stood to bail out and caught a glimpse of daylight through the wall of mangrove.

"Hold it!"

David had just jumped in. The rest did what they were told. Minus the weight of two, the dinghy wobbled now free from the bottom.

Will wanted to make sure, not wanting to be the latest object of everyone's snide aspersions. Side to side, up and down, he found an opening big enough to confirm what he hoped he saw.

"HOLE-LEE-SHIT! It's right there, not thirty yards!"

Those remaining in the boat crowded in for a look, the combined weight leaning to one side pitched Doc and Jason overboard. The mishap was not even acknowledged.

The operation presented plenty of difficulties.

They backed the boat out to where it could be turned around and looked for where the mangrove was less dense. There was not much difference, but all agreed on one path of least resistance. They had three, maybe four hours to prep the staging area and cut through to the field before nightfall.

Doc and Kaz assigned themselves to clearing the landing area and organizing the material to pack and transport. Jason and Dave set in to hacking a pathway to the clearing. Will grabbed two machetes, "come on, Smitty."

"Where you goin'?" Doc was rummaging through his satchel and pulled out a small Mason jar."

"Well, there's no room here, so we'll fight through this tangled mess, recon the area, then clear our way back to Jason and Dave."

"Strategic." Doc extracted a glass vial buried in salt. "Hey guys, time out. Before we get the show on the road, I brought something to keep us jacked through the night." After spooning each nostril, Doc passed the white powder.

Faced with the arduous task at hand, everyone indulged Doc's foresight.

Will was the last to partake of the still plentiful vial. "You sure live up to your handle, Doc. Well, let's get it on."

Darkness had come long before sundown at the estate.

Primed with pictures, Alaine fumed in the back seat as he listened to the driver's embellished discourse of his wife's escapades. His tan complexion reddened to near scarlet as Manny displayed his colorful exposé, adding in a few made-up facts for effect.

She stood with resigned indifference in the cavernous foyer, regarding the Mercedes' deliberate approach as it chauffeured down the long drive. She 'felt' trouble coming to a halt in front of the mansion's multi-terraced entrance; engine idled, tinted glass veiled her nemesis. Only when he appeared, (she knew the '**look**' all too well), did Nicole withdraw to higher ground half way up the curved staircase to make her stand. From the landing, through the floor-to-ceiling window, his expression told her there would be no negotiating, only war.

Even the house staff knew best to take cover. Alaine let himself in, their absence further exacerbated his demeanor; the indignity of not being properly received only fanned his fire to a raging inferno. Nobody dared referee or interfere. In times like these, they had a propensity for busying themselves with some menial task far and away from ground zero. Even then, no refuge could be found to escape the audible tirades.

His wrath battled her counterblasts as vilifications were exchanged in a cursed war of damnation. Nicole fended off allegations with stinging jabs of ugly truths that were indisputable, the acrid denouncements negating his gambit. Innuendos of impropriety were retaliated with scathing recriminations and pent-up grievances that poured gas onto the pyre. Incredulous over the mounting challenge and caught in the crosshairs of hell's furious scorn, Alaine burned in the lava flow cascading down the risers. The rancorous *bitchkrieg* of irrefutable grievances stymied any attempt at rebuttal.

She could have been dressed barefoot in a gunnysack, it would not have mattered. Her endowed sensual beauty, corporeal assets frustrating even the most chauvinistic of pigs, Nicole's defiant stance aroused more than rage and provoked him to charge the high ground. Brute force, bolstered by carnal lust, overwhelmed her attempt to thwart the advance. Each step surrendered tenaciously, her dogged retreat was halted atop the balcony. Bruised and bloodied from the pummeling, she cursed her assailant, blood spewing from the corner of her mouth. Alaine intercepted a face slap. Twisting the intent wrist, he wrenched her arm behind her back. Nicole's free hand reciprocated with slashing fingernails that raked his face. That did it. He yanked her arm causing her to spin around into a vicious roundhouse that greeted her face. She careened off the balustrade and collapsed facedown, unconscious. *War's over. Let the games begin.*

He scooped up the limp body and carried it into the dread-room. Tossed on the bed, she regained consciousness only to suffer perverted abuse. Nicole endured by checking out, devising escape in her mind's swollen eye. She might as well have been a mannequin, and being so, probably shortened the torment.

His pathetic self-gratification attained, she was left an unresponsive doll, as he headed down to his study where the next thing he would ravage was an un-opened bottle of very expensive Scotch.

The first shuttle had been a logistical cluster-fuck, putting the raiders behind schedule. The chokepoint: an underpowered, thirty-horse Johnson making a four-mile round trip was not going to cut it. Towing six bulbous tote bags, each the size of a VW Beetle, by the time delivery came alongside the schooner it was clear that the ship would have to reposition a lot closer. Doc had seen a cove not a quarter-mile from the covert action and it was agreed *Slip* navigate to this point.

"Jeezus, Doc! Did you have to haul the whole farm in one trip?" Each heavy gauge plastic sack, cinched watertight, was winched aboard. Rick read the hoist's scale: each weighed in at just over three hundred pounds.

"Nope, there's plenty more where this came from. Never seen plants so big and bushy. What we got here is almost a hundred percent smoke. Got a smooth operation going; cut and bundle, drag to the staging area for processing...nothing but the choicest part of the plant packaged." The play-by-play spoken in rapid succession was impossible for anyone to get a word in, except Arti's one question.

"Hey man, are you speeding?"

Doc rambled on. "...damn stalks the size of my wrist. Massive buds. We're buried in the shit...just the smell's got everyone stoned. But focused. No worries there."

Stuart returned with gas tank refilled. "Alright man, we'll move in closer, call us when you head back out."

Doc finished coiling the rope used to tether in line the payload. Zoned, an acknowledged nod, and the little outboard that could revved a fishtail disappearance into the night.

"I do believe the whole bunch is jacked on rocket fuel, courtesy our resident medicine man." Pensive, Arti stoked his pipe then added, "A damn good plan, I must admit. Higher production through chemistry."

"Come on you guys. Let's find that cove." Stuart challenged his brother rock-paper-scissors to avoid anchor duty with Arti. He lost.

Doc returned to the staging area that gave proof through the night the boys were still there doing nothing. They had run out of room.

"This isn't gonna work, Doc, we're way ahead of you."

No shit, William Sherlock! I've got this all figured out so be cool, man. You guys got two loads already staged. One of you come with me, I could use an extra set of eyes. He gets dropped off. Same thing on the next trip while the rest of you bag a fourth load. That way there's less ballast and hopefully the last load we can pack without swamping and still tow the load. Makes up for the lost time."

Smitty could not resist. "Hey, Doc. All this time I took you for just the 'head' of operations. You got this figured out, Admiral."

"Yeah, well I had plenty of time to think, going all that way and back. Come on, we gotta MOVE."

The last tote was winched up and over the hatch, the contents spilling into the aft cargo hold.

"A little over three and a half tons!" Artimus penciled down the math: 7,560lbs, $100per... "$756,000."

"Man, this stuff's so potent, $300 an elbow...EASY!"

"No doubt, Doc, but that's on the street for just one. You're forgetting the bulk rate, plus the cut our clients are paying third party go-fers."

The shore party was dog-tired, but still wired. It had been a discriminating harvest: instead of clear-cutting, they cultivated every third or fourth plant making the theft not so obvious from the air. They even camouflaged the narrow path they had cut into the crop. As they went, they had strewn mangrove branches above their head and tossed leftover debris on top, forming a canopy. It had been an afterthought well worth the added effort, even if it gained them just a few extra hours to detach from culpability.

Once the dory was hoisted and secured, course was set west-northwest. Still dark, the narrow passageways and unmarked shallows dictated caution. The slow retreat was frustrating under the one mainsail; putting distance between them and the depredation before daylight being on everyone's minds.

Having been spared the night of grunt work, Arti still accepted a couple spoons of wake-up from Doc. They went below to calibrate the precision weigh scales and experiment with compressing and packaging manageable fifty-pound bricks, a process critical to expediting transactions. The task would rotate shifts non-stop throughout the duration of the voyage until completed.

The rest of the crew remained on deck, briefing the captains as to what went down: problems encountered, lessons learned, and injury reports.

Kaz hacked his leg, just above the knee. Bandaged and sore, he would be okay. Jason got spiked by a small stingray while wading, tying off totes to the dory. The swollen ankle had been lanced and was draining yellow pus, but was now cleaned and taped. Twice he had wretched his guts of toxin, undoubtedly exacerbated by what went up his nose. Everyone suffered a zillion bites from pesky little gnats. One conclusion had been drawn from the experience: hauling expectations would have to be downsized given the single dinghy was their only mode of conveyance.

The sun's crest broke water and it dawned on Will this was his second all-nighter in three days. *Not like back in college, sleep walking through classes or missing them altogether.* Twelve hours of hard labor and he, along with his partners in crime, was spent and spread out on deck like a landed fish after a grueling fight lost. Woozy from exhaustion and feeling sick to his empty stomach, he staggered to the stern where marginal shade cast from the bulwark would do just fine. A gentle roll did not have to rock him to sleep.

CHAPTER TWENTY-ONE

The sound of anchor chain paying out roused him from a three-hour coma. Nestled in a secluded cove, somewhere north of Red Hook Bay on Saint Thomas' eastern shore, Rick and Arti were positioning the ship. "Sorry 'bout that skip, I just fell out."

"It was a tough night. Everybody's in pretty rough shape, that's why we're holing up here to recuperate." Rick cut the engine and waited for the anchor line to draw tight.

"Anchor's set," affirmed Arti. "See you below."

He and the captains, though a tad groggy, were in pretty good shape. Their grueling night that finally reached the end was in no way comparable to that of the others. Exempted from manual labor, the time between deliveries was wisely spent; one man stood watch, the other two copped a few zees.

The walking wounded and the rest of the dog-tired sore stumbled around the galley downing coffee and bread, whatever could be scrounged. Kaz had informed the group where they could shove special requests; the cook was toast. In various stages of consciousness, there was one commonalty that kept them roused...constant itching of the little bastards' assaults.

"Now I know why a flea bitten dog chews itself bloody!" David went from scalp down to privates. "Shit! I down this coffee and I'm going overboard. Maybe the salt water will help."

The mention of 'dog in agony' was Smitty's opening to start the new day off on the left foot while everyone finished chewing coffee grounds floating in their cups.

"Only creature I've ever known to hang tough, through to the bitter end. Note I didn't say 'dog'. This is the true story of an animal named Von, who morphed himself and became worthy of a new name: Aardvark."

Will grinned. *Here we go again*.

"What kind of fucked-up name is that for a dog?", asked David.

"Which one, Aardvark or Von?" mused Doc.

Though he knew the shag-dog story, Will could not resist watching Smitty's animations. Comical as the stupid stories themselves, not to mention the skeptics' comebacks, made it well worth the admission price of hearing it for the umpteenth time.

"Quiet please. There was this neighborhood dog, see. Owners didn't seem to give a rat's ass about him, just let him run wild. No doghouse, no leash, I doubt they fed him either. Poor bastard was left to forage. Cats, squirrels, rabbits, turtles...his favorite was skunk."

"He ate skunks?" Rick spat a coffee ground in doubt.

"Von didn't always *eat* his prey; his owners were too cheap to buy him play toys. Whenever a neighbor's dog went missing, Von was always the prime suspect. He was half shepherd, half Dane, a veritable rogue monster easily a hundred-fifty pounds. You could always tell he was coming: ground vibration and smell of skunk his calling card. Upon approach, first-timers would freeze in disbelief or get the hell out of his way." Smitty lit up, relishing the pregnant pause. The fish were hooked and willing to be reeled in.

"I don't know who adopted who, but Von became a mainstay with the neighborhood gang, accompanying us as scout, intimidator, or mascot. Football and hockey pick-up games against rivals, the opposition always wary we might call a "sic-em" audible after flagrant fouls. Army games in the woods, the enemy dug in thickets...Von would smell 'em out and plow ahead; the growl and snapping of branches always rendered a whimpering surrender.

"No retreat?"

"And risk becoming his latest play thing?"

"Okay, but what's up with the name Aardvark?"

"Transformation began in sixty-three. Bunch of us were playing basketball, the driveway's backcourt delimited by the main road. Von would play guard, blocking any errant throws from going into the street. I guess he got bored and wandered off up the middle of the street and out of sight. There was this sound of screeching rubber and a wicked loud crash then the weirdest sight of a hubcap silently rolling past the driveway, comically, as if trying to distance itself from the scene of a crime. We ran up the street and there's Von standing stolid, faced off with a pickup. The old man was frozen, white-knuckled at the wheel, his eyes big as golf balls. The truck's front end was caved in, radiator belching steam. Von just stood there shaking his head, one shepherd ear broken straight down. Snorting at the inconvenience, he left the scene, probably with one hell of a headache.

"He took on a truck and all he got was a broken ear?"

Smitty left Jason to ponder the plausibility. "That summer he went nuts with high temperatures and fleas, but figured out a solution to both. Anticipating the coming day's heat, under the cover of nightfall, Von would select a neighbor's lawn to excavate a crater and cool out in. Needless to say he became public enemy number one with the dads. One neighbor got so pissed he declared open season for dog."

"Did he get shot?"

"Once. But the bird shot was just an annoyance, thanks to his thick coat. It was the fleas that really got to him. Kinda weird how the smallest can drive the mightiest to the brink of madness. He gnawed his long, bushy tail off, leaving a six-inch stub, which the owners did nothing for and we weren't about to. Von eventually chewed the hair clear off the stump, leaving nothing but a white boner to bleach in the sun."

Silence. Faces contorted, visualizing the disturbing amputation.

"Winter came, and with it a *new* diversion. Von loved to play catch with snowballs, thrown at point-blank range. I don't know who started putting rocks inside, but...."

"Man, you gotta be shittin' me!"

"Hey, the dog loved it. I think it was the sound, proving a good catch. Anyways, we thought the good times would come to an end with the snow melt, but dang if Von didn't insist the game of catch carry on with just rocks. We tried tennis balls, but he liked the hard stuff and it didn't seem to bother him. Sure did a number on his teeth though. Canines were worn down to nubs, the front teeth were all squared off like a human's...the metamorphosis was complete. Town folk seeing this freak of nature would pause, perplexed, and ponder the origin of this ghastly being. Children cried. Aghast, mothers tried to shield their young until the disturbing mutant lumbered out of sight. Yup, the name Von just didn't suit him anymore. Could've called him 'It', 'Thing', or 'Gorgon', but none of those seemed to suit. So we decided on Aardvark. Poor Aardvark: one ear up, the other down. A white bone sticking out of his ass and now, a mouth full of teeth flattened out; no fangs, incisors blunted. When he bared his teeth, the grin looked almost human. Strangers gave him a wide berth when he snarled his hilariously hideous grin. It was rather cartoonish. Heck, cars would stop in the middle of the road just to make sure what was witnessed wasn't a species never recorded. You know, like a Sasquatch. Deemed a public nuisance, the city council considered euthanizing the creature."

The visual had David in hysterics. Kaz choked on snot.

"Dammit, Smitty, you're so full of shit!" Jason's face hurt.

"So, did they put him down?" Even curmudgeon Stuart was sucked in.

"No, Aardvark would go on his own terms. It was an unfortunate accident that did him in." Smitty tamped out his smoke, his demeanor went dark for effect. "Me, Liquid, and Dowrinkle..."

"Who?"

"Stupid nicknames. We were down at the lake, spring thaw. The middle of the lake was free of ice. The dam's floodgates were wide open, the current strong. At least a hundred feet of ice from the shoreline out remained, maybe a half-foot thick. We were talking about fishing and how long it would be before we could get a line in the water. It was then that an idea came to us: we'd use

Aardvark as an icebreaker. Skimming rocks out on the ice, Aardvark couldn't resist retrieval. We could hear the ice cracking under his weight. It became a contest as to who could stop their stone closest to the edge of the ice pack. Every time Aardvark got to one another would zing by, further out, which he just couldn't refuse. The plan worked. Sections of ice broke into bergs." Smitty paused to reflect. "Should've stopped and called him in, but it was too late.

"Aardvark went adrift on a calved slab of ice and got caught up in the current. We called for him to make a swim for it, but he was frozen, trying to keep his balance. Statuesque in all his glory, he stood defiant as we ran down the shoreline. His one good ear looked like a signal flag of distress, white bone sticking straight up in a final salute, and rock in mouth bearing a grin of victory. He held up his end of the bargain, always faithful, to the end. He was a good dog. The best of dogs. He bid us a fading farewell. We kept running the shoreline, pleading he swim for it, but the iceberg took him to the far side where the dam's intakes that powered the turbines were. Last we saw of him before he disappeared...bravely facing headlong his destiny; solid as the rock he clenched."

"That's it? Man, what a bummer ending."

"Didn't you guys go look for him?"

"Couldn't, it was getting dark. But a few weeks later in that cold spring, we were down at the dam fooling around. From up high, we noticed something strange wedged in the boulders way down below on the far side of the dam. It was the sun glinting off it that caught our eye, so we went to investigate. Son-of-a-bitch if it wasn't Aardvark, partially encased in a block of ice! Guess he avoided getting chewed up in the turbines, but where he went over was the dam's highest point. Must've been one helluva a ride down."

"Man, you're cold."

"No, but Aardvark was. Frozen in time, only his white tailbone sticking out of the ice like a middle-finger goodbye, he STILL had that stupid grin, minus the rock."

"Jeez, he might have swallowed it. Did you at least bury him?"

"Of course! We weren't about to leave him like that, but the ground was still too hard, AND he was too far away. Plus, we didn't have shovels. So being near the river's headwaters coming out of the dam, we decided on a sailor's funeral. Took us an hour to haul him out and slide him down to the river where he floated away. For weeks we expected to read about someone finding a strange anomaly, but that never happened. I like to think he made it all the way to the Atlantic. A damn good dog, faithful to the end."

The crew filed out mumbling uncertainties as to the narrative's validity.

"I could walk backwards on crutches faster than this. Think we ought to power-up?"

"No, let's hold off on the fuel."

The chain of islands, barely discernible on the horizon, marked the northern boundary that separated the Sound from the Atlantic. Stuart kept the bow aimed for the gap between the last two landforms: Thatch and Grass Cays.

"They don't seem to be getting any bigger."

"Come on Art, you remember how it goes; it's the calm before the afternoon storms, typical noonday conditions."

Rick came up from below with an idea. "Hey, remember those jib sheets the ole man had stashed in the forward bulkhead? We've got plenty of guide wire and extra cordage. Might buy us an extra knot for later, once we make it to the big pond."

"Excellent idea. Calm winds, be a perfect time to get it done."

Smitty sat on the aft-mast's crosstree, screwing in an eyebolt. Will ascended with boltrope tied around his waist along with a guide wire. Dave and Jason had fixed the foremast's jib, now feeding the guideline through the eyelets and securing the end to the bowsprit.

Sail hoisted, the duo remained aloft, gazing back at the Sound's expanse. Boats flitted about the seascape: yachtsmen working their sails to capture what they could of the gentle wind, fishermen in search of their trophy, and pleasure cruisers in party mode.

Smitty lit up a joint. "Figured we'd give it a try. Doc and Art tried a little when they were calibrating the scales, said they got wasted."

Will could tell it was lethal by the potent smell and Karl's bloodshot eyes after just two hits, even high off the deck. He took the hand-off and braced against the mast.

"You know, we get back to Beantown, it'd be smart if we go our separate ways for a while till things cool off. You know damn well sooner or later the heat's going to put two and two together." Will took a hit and for the hundredth time imagined her, each visual a little blurrier than before. "I could live down here." Second toke, a twinge of vertigo,

Slipfinger Nine

and he became one with the timber. "I'm good. Here, take it. That's some potent shit, man; they ought to renegotiate at two hundred a pound."

One more hit and the joint went airborne with the breeze. "Dig this. Old man's up there in age, lives alone in Wyoming and not doing so well...willed his hundred-acre homestead to the only mistake he ever made, me. Hour south of Yellowstone, thirty miles as the crow flies east of the Tetons in the middle of nowhere. Fucking awesome. Step out the back and fly-fish the Wind River. Got a few horses...there's an extra saddle if you're interested. If you're looking for a place to get lost, perfect place to go incognito."

"It's an idea, thanks man. Tell you what. I made a promise I intend to keep. Pending the outcome, might just look you up." Will surveyed the Sound's expanse while Smitty resumed his monologue, painting God's country in wild-west images.

Wooden ships glided free and easy, a contrast of white sail across pastel blue skies. Anglers dotted the Sound, trolling or fixed, over tried and true holes. Speed junkies spoiling for a challenge, raced. Runabouts moved from one spot to another: *lovers desperately seeking seclusion.* Will could still taste her cocoa butter skin. He grimaced, wondering if he would be able to make good his promise; *Bastard of the Year Award if I don't.*

Realizing he had been following a particular boat way off in the distance, he grabbed the binoculars from the hook on the mast and zeroed in. Running pell-mell, apparently harboring an interest in sailboats of considerable size, the harasser twice circled his second victim before breaking off. Heading north up the far side of the sound to another schooner anchored off a small cay, Will mumbled; "what an asshole."

"Hey! You listening?"

"Yeah, I'm with you." He watched the interceptor close in, circle, then veer off. *Damn!* Will tried to focus in to see if the driver was in uniform. *Please don't be the law!* The boat was still too far away, but it was heading in their direction.

"We had this jet black collie named Whitey, wouldn't stop running other ranchers cattle so we had to put him..."

"Check out the madman across the water." Will passed the binoculars.

"Jesus, look at that rooster tail! Sucker's flying, and heading right for us! Oh shit."

Hands cupped over his eyes, Will felt like a helpless sailor watching a torpedo dead set on its mark. The inboard's growl grabbed the attention of those below. Activity ceased.

Smitty sounded like a broadcaster calling a horse race down the stretch. "Coming on strong, looks like a ski boat. Cat's really hauling ass, heading straight for us."

Maintaining distance in order to circle wide-open, the dude was wearing a baseball cap with a pony tail flailing like a horse's mane as he came down the stretch. He throttled back on the second pass and closed. Around the bow, down the port side, once rounding the stern the craft slowed starboard, matching speed.

"Is there a Will Bradford on board?"

There was no immediate response; everyone was preoccupied, taking inventory.

Slipfinger Nine

Smitty turned to Will, but he was gone, literally. Oblivious to the danger, Will found himself standing at the end of the yardarm grasping a guide wire.

"Man, are you crazy?!"

Thirty feet up, he aimed for the space between the two vessels. When the ship leaned to starboard he let go, diving headfirst as far out as he could.

Nicole was engaged in a stare down with the crew when the body flashed by, followed by a "man overboard" from on high.

"What the fuck is this all about? Who the hell is she?" Stuart stomped aft to give Will an earful, or better yet, to not see him come up at all.

The Chris Craft roared, veering off for recovery. Lifeline and float in hand, Doc rushed aft, followed by others. Will surfaced as the boat pirouetted and came alongside for rescue. The crew marveled at the sight receding aft; tight white slacks framing a lusciousness that was bent over to retrieve her catch.

Slip continued on its slow course. Hauled in and coughing up salt water from the high dive that sent him deeper than he had imagined, Will got to his feet and yelled; "Keep going, we'll catch up!"

The attentive crew stood erect in more ways than one. Stuart stormed off, seething over Will's kismet. *Not part of the plan, there'll be hell to pay!* Loathe to playing second-fiddle, voyeur to someone else's fortune; scenarios of unfortunate accidents flashed through his mind. *Son-of-a-bitch won't see port.*

One of the housemaids entered the gloomy first-floor study to shed some noonday light on what had otherwise been a very dark last twelve hours. Drawing of the wall-to-wall curtains evoked a curt rebuke. The cradled scotch bottle rolled off his chest and spilled onto the floor what would have been last-call.

"Heaven mercy! Mizza Moreau, I didn't know you..."

"Jumped up Jesus Christ! Dam Ellie, close the drapes and fetch me some coffee!" Alaine lurched up on the couch, pausing for his head to join him. "Has princess had breakfast?"

"Tis pass noon, sir." She paused at the doorway, "Missus locked herself in, left a note under the door saying she not feeling well and wishes not to be disturbed. I think she very upset, but note says she expects you join her for a civil dinner at six. Please, señor Moreau, for everyone's sake, I think it best you leave her alone until then."

"Relax, Ellie. Bring me toast with the coffee. I've got business to attend to, so plan dinner for seven."

"Yessum. I bring fresh clothes and dinner jacket when you freshen up later."

Business was an out to sober up, and conjure up an apology for what he was trying to remember: inexcusable and unwarranted behavior.

CHAPTER TWENTY-TWO

From initial embrace, their impassioned reunion was frustrated. Everywhere he grasped caused a noticeable reflex; more than once a diminutive moan was misinterpreted for sensual compliance. Vanity was short-lived. Desiring to gaze into her unforgettable dark eyes, he deftly removed the chic sunglasses, and then recoiled. Nicole's left eye was swollen nearly shut. His gaze drifted downward, where it discovered a delicate neck gripped with black and blue imprints. Only then did he realize why her kisses had responded to his so delicately. Will now felt a tinge of shame as he realized his passion had been so desirous and of such single focus, that it had re-opened her split lip.

"Jesus! What the hell happened to you?" His hand grabbed her shoulder to pull her in and she winced. "Sorry." He raised her sleeve and saw the baseball-sized bruise. "Good God, Nikki," his other hand went to her thigh and again she flinched.

She took his hands to halt the painful exploratory proceedings and elected to enlighten. Nicole spared him the sordid details, but filling in the blanks was excruciatingly easy. The hurt in his expression quickened her to give account of the escape which had been so resourceful.

A determined Will questioned his worthiness of such fortitude.

After the onslaught and subsequent rape, she had collected herself under a near-scalding shower. A note was written and passed outward under the locked bedroom door. Two changes of clothes and bare essentials were packed; the shoulder bag went out the second story window into shrubbery that lined the back of the manor. She dropped a back flop into the shrubs, cushioning the blow. She passed down the long pathway, praying that if her staff did see her, they would be sympathetic to her plight. Disappearing over the rise, she made quick work of the down-slope to the boathouse where, luckily, the boat was waiting. She eased out and set a course east. All she could remember from Will's sketchy itinerary was that they would probably spend a couple days in Pillsbury Sound, working out the kinks before setting out on the long journey home.

A full throttle away from hell, either she would find the schooner or run out of fuel. No matter the outcome, no way would she ever return unless drowned and delivered in a body bag.

Will gently held her while wrestling with a thought: *one incredible night together. Can it be love this soon? Am I just a ticket out of a living nightmare? Or, is it a combination of both? I guess only time and trial will tell.* There was one thing about which he had no doubt: *how could I not love her.*

Jason and Art were bent over the bow signaling evasive maneuvers through the shallow shoals. The sight of an old fishing vessel, back broken, her skeletal remains laid to rest atop one of many crusty oyster beds, was warning enough that they should negotiate the pass under auxiliary power only.

Fucked-up again. Should've gone west around Thatch Cay. Rick slalomed *Slip* between the last two cays stretching east-to-west and demarcating the northern boundary of Pillsbury Sound. Once cleared, he wheeled hard to port seeking refuge in what the aerial photo depicted as a deep cove recessed inland to Thatch Cay.

Engine cut, anchor dropped where the schooner drifted close in to the shore's curtain of tall, dense mangrove, it was there they would hope to hide and decide their next move. Stu appeared topside with an attitude that Rick was in no mood to entertain.

"I swear, if we weren't so shorthanded..."

"Knock it off. Let them say their good-byes. Meanwhile, we got a decision to make. And it's got nothing to do with them."

Much as they desired each other, the mere act of embracing proved painful. Moreover, everything she had endured: her fleeing quest from insanity, and the anti-climactic relief of asylum realized, Nicole was spent as she nestled in his arms. Will had thought it over: *got to come clean what we're up to. Doing so ought to give me some indication of her resolve, her true feelings. Well, here goes.*

"Baby, listen to me carefully. You don't deserve this, coming all this way under false pretense of what I told you. I didn't lie to you; I just didn't tell you the whole story of what we're up to."

Will laid it all out, periodically checking to see if she had not passed out in his arms. The details, so convoluted and bizarre, held her attentively silent, making her an impossible read. Even the worst-case scenarios presented did not move her. Again, he looked down at her beautiful face lying quiescent upon his chest.

"I'm sorry, Nikki. I don't blame you if you just dump me off and hightail it out of..."

"And go where? No, you listen to me Mister Will Bradford! What's that saying about burning bridges? Well, I don't have any left and even if I did, where is it I can go? There isn't a safe place for me here. You think for one moment what you've gotten yourself into is any worse than what I just got out of? Besides, it was **MY** decision to come. I hold no one but myself accountable if something terrible goes wrong."

Will gently kissed her bruised cheek, and then sighed. "Oh, brother. It'll be a hard sell getting you on board."

"No, it won't. I know more about sailing than most of you."

"No. I'm talking about one of the captains of this ship of fools. He and I are like oil and water."

Her hand slid somewhere to get his full attention, the seductive smile that had haunted his dreams whitewashed apprehensions of the upcoming face-off. "You're funny. After dealing with a tyrant old enough to be my father, you don't think I can handle a twenty-something jerk who thinks more with his other head," another gentle squeeze, "than where he logically should?"

Clearly she had a grasp the situation. He made a last-ditch effort to regain the initiative. "We're outlaws! We got contraband on board and plan to get some more. If things go south, I'd never forgive myself with you being involved."

Nicole fingered his lips, "So, I'm trading real trouble for possible trouble. That night on the beach you told me you were playing the cards you were dealt. Well, so am I. Besides, it sounds like you could use another boat."

Will looked off in the distance to where *Slipfinger* was last seen. Unwittingly, a slight shake of his head resigned himself that any further attempt to dissuade her would be futile. "All right. I guess I'm just blown out of the water that you're actually here." Will leaned forward pursing his sun-cracked lips to hers, so supple, conscious not to scruff her with bristly whiskers. Moisturized numb, lips managed to mouth: "this isn't the way I wanted to..."

"Shush. It's too late, cowboy. C'mon, introduce me to the crew."

Will skimmed the water at full speed while immersed in thought: *In possession of another man's wife, one whose standing in the community is well known and most assuredly has the wherewithal to do something about his loss. Just another reason it's 'the quicker the better' we vacate the islands.* He knew that would be the ace Stuart played denying her passage.

"There she is". The declaration raised Nicole's sleepy head off his shoulder. The tops of the masts could be seen above the low-lying cay, sparing Will the dilemma of whether to go left or right of the pass they had just cleared. Nicole sat upright on the leather bench seat, and as women do, primped for a first impression. Entering the cove, Will wisely chose to ease the Chris Craft alongside in between *Slip* and the dense overhang of mangrove...out of sight.

Hands reached out to assist Nicole on board, but it was egoist Stuart who interposed, negating her choices. Aggravated as he was with the intrusion, he could not resist dominating her presence; putting on airs reeking of self-indulgence.

Standing before the crew, sunglasses adding to the mystique, she withstood the unstated consensus that Will had landed a trophy catch…suitable for mounting. Savoir-faire guided her through the obvious ogling as introductions were made. She only offered a slight smile in return, due to her split lower lip.

Pleasantries exchanged, Stuart immediately started in on Will. He had every right to answers explaining what this was all about. So out-of-the-blue was this mystery woman, it was a legitimate concern that her presence stood to jeopardize the entire campaign. It was not the grilling so much, but rather the manner and tone in which it was conducted that made so obvious the opportunity taken by Stu to humiliate and belittle Will in front of Nicole.

Will's composure only heightened the haranguing until Nicole had had enough. She knew exactly what was taking place and would put a halt to it immediately. For effect, she intervened between the two while removing her sunglasses, yanking a short sleeve above the concealed black and blue shoulder, and at the same time lifting her shirt to expose a taunt belly that was also bruised.

Doc whispered to Rick. "Holy shit. She's STILL a knock-out."

The confrontation lasted about as long as Clay versus Liston. Though looking like a prize-fighter on the losing end of a fifteen round bout, her exquisite beauty and alluring comportment was so disarming, and this put Stuart in his place: against the ropes.

The gripping soliloquy was spoken calm and collected. It beguiled not only Stuart, who was caught squarely in the crosshairs, but the entire crew. It was all Will could do to maintain a deadpan look while watching mister big-shot be for once at a loss for words.

Nicole took full responsibility for her being there, making it quite clear Will had nothing to do with it. She then switched the gears towards pointing out deficiencies in the way some of the riggings were improperly tied off. When someone muttered "how the hell did she know..." Nicole turned in the direction, replying: "my father taught me how to sail when I was seven and the bastard I left has a schooner not quite as large, but I can sail it solo."

Assuming she had not a clue as to what they were up to, Stuart interjected. "Lady. You have no idea what's going on here."

"Don't I? Will, just moments ago, told me what you're up to, in an effort to protect you and try to dissuade me from coming along. But from what I can see, after last night's episode, you guys could use another boat if you expect the payoff to be worth the risk." Her nonchalance about the potential danger and high stakes dumbfounded all, except Will, who had waited for such an opening to slam the door shut on any further debate.

"If she's not welcome, for her safety, I'll have to leave with her."

Nicole looked at Will. There was that same sensation experienced on the beach when telepathy was achieved, causing a momentary lapse in his train of thought.

Do you really mean that?
Yes, I love you.

Stuart was a millisecond away from taking Will at his word when Smitty joined ranks.

"If Will goes, so do I."

"Fuck that! If you guys are bailing, then so am I." Kaz fidgeted like he had ants in his pants. "You guys talked me into this daft undertaking, I'll be damned if..."

"Alright, cut the shit! She stays."

Will tried to stifle a grin. "Well, Cap, guess that settles that. I'll get her set up below. Smitty, you mind refueling her boat?"

"If you know what I mean", the remark from Doc was subtle, but still heard by most.

"You got it, mate."

It was the first time Rick saw his brother at a loss for words. Nicole approached, having disposed of her detractor and feeling drawn and quartered. Will held his ground in a stare down with Stuart as the rest of the crew scattered, smothered by a feminine finesse never encountered before.

"Thank you for being so understanding. If you'd be so kind as to allow me a little rest, I'll ready to be of service all the sooner."

Enamored, all Rick could muster was an obligatory "whatever you need, just ask," his dumbfounded look getting the best of him.

She swiveled and swayed away in her exit from the deck.

Approaching Stuart, who was preoccupied with her rear view departure, all Rick could say was "Guess you showed her, huh?"

Doc had no reservations about relinquishing his berth. It had been added as an after-thought years ago and was separated from the main sleeping quarters by a partition. Will hung a sheet from the rafter providing some sense of privacy.

"You get some rest, baby. I'll be topside if you need me." They kissed. He stroked her hair. In no time she was asleep.

Pow-wow at the bow...
"Okay, Romeo. You tell me if I'm missing something here. Your damsel in distress seeks protective custody. Let's just call it what it is: stowaway. Jilted husband, possessive and jealous as shit, and who's got plenty of resources, no doubt...and by the looks of her, a very short fuse. He's got boats, goons, and how she describes him, can be a real son-of-a-bitch when he wants to be. From what I can tell, if he hasn't already found out she's split, when he does, then he'll come unglued. In other words, thanks to you, we got a boatload of **MORE** trouble and the quicker we get out of here, the better."

"Erring on the side of caution, you pretty much summed it up. Look, I didn't plan for this to..."

Stuart waved him off. "It's done, so now we go to plan B."

There was an awkward pause akin to an actor forgetting his lines. Rick sensed his brother fighting the urge to unload on Will.

"I got it from here."

Stuart abdicated, but stepping aside he could not resist speaking his mind as if to himself: "Hope that snatch was worth it."

"What the hell's that supposed to mean?"

"Figure it out, Casanova."

Rick took command, thwarting any further salvos. "Alright, listen up!"

The change in itinerary was received with unanimous approval and yes, Will caught Stuart's drift. Nixed were two intended forays, both as hard to get to and diminutive as the first. They would proceed directly to the big mamou: Hans Lollick. No time to dilly-dally, for time was of the essence.

Rattle of anchor chain, commands shouted; it was the diesel roaring to life that mercifully woke sleeping beauty from the lurid nightmare. *Oh my god, he's coming*. Realism blotted out the pain of injuries, fright supplanted sleep deprivation; her ready-for-action appearance topside astounded all with her gritty tenacity.

"Damn, that's one tough broad," remarked Arti. "She might just show us all up."

Stu stewed dark thoughts of making a play for her when the opportunity presented itself: *gonna be a real kick in the crotch, Wiliey Boy.*

Chris Craft in tow, a course was set west-northwest that was expedient in that the mother-lode happened to be in direct line of their route into the Atlantic. Within the hour, Big Hans Lollick would be circumnavigated.

High noon, and plenty of daylight hours to reconnoiter and coordinate the bold undertaking, once again Nicole was beseeched reassurance. With conviction, she calmly elucidated to both skippers their concerns about what could possibly be expected due to her defection. She owed them the worst case scenario, but moderated the tone of her delivery. It was a multi-task not easy; the dream still fresh in her mind.

"Seven o'clock, he'll be awaiting my appearance, probably halfway drunk. Being the stickler he is for punctuality, I doubt a minute will pass before he sends one of the staff to get me. No answer, door locked, he'll charge upstairs and end up busting in the door. When he notices the open window, he'll probably tear the room apart. The extent of what he could see missing, which is next to nothing, I hope will clue him into thinking my leaving was temporary...my way of saying 'fuck you'. He'll call out the goon squad and search every square inch of the island. All my known acquaintances will be paid a visit. It'll be late in the evening when all possibilities are exhausted, and then it's just a matter of time until someone checks the boathouse. That's when he'll connect the dots and redirect the search. His yacht is berthed on the north side of the island which will take time to get everyone up there. His helicopter buddy who he calls on for island hopping will be called into service, but that'll be put on hold till daybreak."

"Sounds like you got him figured to a tee."

"He's so predictable...and crazy. Now if you'll excuse me, some of your boys are bungling the riggings."

Both left to ponder the situation, Rick broke the silence since his brother was entertaining something else: the way she moved. "Well, there it is. We make the most of it and make damn sure we're long gone come morning. I'll say this, her boat will speed things up and by the looks of it, we just gained one hell of a sailor."

"Huh, yeah right." Stu was obviously distracted.

"Did you even hear what I said?" Rick relinquished the wheel to break the spell. "Here, take over." Then he lied. "Must've been something I ate, gotta pay the head a visit. Tell cookie to get his butt down below, we might have some food gone bad." Feigning stomach cramps, he left his brother, who was now occupied with navigating.

Actually, Rick only half lied. He was in fact suffering discomfort. He knew his brother all too well, the fixation so evident...*oh man. This is going to be one big pain in the ass.*

Saint Thomas was visible south on the horizon as Little Hans was cleared off the starboard. *Slipfinger* made a ninety degree turn north for a run up the leeward side of Big Hans. Unremitting trade winds from time immemorial had dusted off the island tops, spreading terra particles across the waters creating shallow shoals extending hundreds of yards from shore.

Field glasses raised, Rick surveyed the coast. Doc joined with a spyglass. It had already been agreed upon the narrow channel between the two islands was not suited to a ship their size. Halfway up Big Han's west side, a wharf jutted into baby-blue waters, indicating only boats with a shallow draft could gain access. From there, a switchback road traversed the steep slope leading up to a lone concrete structure. Fine tuning their sight, what appeared to be a chain link fence of considerable height began at each end of the blockhouse and extended the perimeter of the high plateau before curving out of sight.

"Well, this side's a wash, be like breaking into Alcatraz."

Doc collapsed the spyglass. "More like Devil's Island or Gibraltar's little brother. No wonder they chose this place."

The objective had grown small on the horizon when orders were given to ready the riggings for a course change due east, headlong into the wind. It was purposeful they had sailed so far north...so as not to be so conspicuous in their stakeout.

Smitty was about to ascend and assist Will in the riggings when her delicate touch shivered a halt.

"I'll go up."

"Bit risky up there, wind's picked up."

Nicole's smile subdued any debate. "Nice of you to be concerned, but I can handle it. Besides, I want to show these guys I can earn my keep."

"I think you already have..." head jerked upward to a delectable view. *Lord have mercy.*

One by one, the crew paused in their duties to marvel at how cat-like she scaled the mast, but it was 'that' view that strained necks, not to mention the unmentionable.

David joined Smitty. "Damn. Wonder if she packed a bikini? Sure would like to see that!"

"Man, this is torture enough."

Petite, white short-shorts lent proof she packed light.

Seething with envy, Stuart envisioned Will's demise. *Better watch your step, buster. Be a real bummer having to swab your splattered guts.* "All right you guys, stop fiddle-fucking around! We'll be turning south in ten minutes!"

Doc and Jason were shamming difficulties with the boom vang that just happened to be attached to the mainmast directly under Nicole.

"This is exactly why she shouldn't be onboard."

"Take it easy. The novelty will wear off." Rick could not help admire the blue sky that just happened to be in the direction everyone else was looking. "Man, couldn't ask for prettier skies, huh?"

Another turn to starboard, adjustments made accordingly, *Slipfinger* headed back to the scene of their potential crime.

Will enveloped her from behind; the wind tickled his face with her silken hair. The view from on high: liberating and appreciated. "Nikki. When we get to the Cape and get our cut, how 'bout we split to the Big Apple incognito? You know I can't compete with the life you've been accustomed too but..."

Didn't the Beatles say love is all you need?" Nicole turned and kissed the troubled look from his face. "Money? Look what it's gotten me. We can make it work. Money comes to those who try. She squished against him as the schooner leaned hard to starboard. "I love you, William Bradford."

His year of running pell-mell to nowhere came to an abrupt end. In that instant, the past that had haunted him so...ceased to exist. Purpose overwhelmed him. Her 'being' was a godsend, though a trifle intimidating. *Time to get serious, do what I know I'm capable of.*

"I love you too, Nikki."

Slipfinger Nine

It was an intense kiss that did not go unnoticed. Stuart whirled the wheel hard to port, tilting the mast. The attempt to break it up only caused the two to become more one. Their fortuitous bond heightened Stuart's lust to possess what he deemed suitably his. Accustomed to getting what he wanted, spoiled by status and wealth, the concept that such a jewel was infatuated with someone of inferior caste caused his jealousy to fester like a cancerous tumor, untreatable. He found it insulting. *What a mismatch, he's so way out of her league!*

The windward side of the island was a different world: deeper water, a rocky coastline, in many places defined by a fascia of two-story cliff. Surveillance concluded, only one site on the entire coast appeared worthy of consideration.

Halfway back up the island's coast was a comma-shaped indentation into the shoreline. Protruding rock created a breakwater for a cove smaller than a tennis court. On deck vantage, twelve feet high, enabled them to see over the natural jetty: a narrow beachhead, but to any passerby not as close in and in a lower profile boat, activity would be concealed. Other than the tight staging area, the only other drawback was the twenty-some odd feet of rock they would have to scale. That was Will and Smitty's forte, having spent many weekends getting high naturally on the face of Mount Washington's Tuckerman's Ravine. Both assured the crew that makeshift grappling hooks and rope would render the obstacle a piece of cake.

The clincher that decided it was a go: inaccessibility combined with the utter audacity of their scheme. Who in their right mind would be that stupid to chance spending thirty years in the hole? Consensus: nobody.

Slipfinger veered off the southern tip of Big Hans, heading out into open water to disassociate from their intentions and gear up.

CHAPTER TWENTY-THREE

Anchored midway between their objective and a marker denoting British Territory, preparations for the incursion were underway. A hefty roll of plastic tote bags, machetes, bolt cutter, ropes tied to two gaff hooks removed from their poles, canteens of water, radios, and a box of sugar-rush candy bars were distributed into the fully-fueled boats. Everyone going ashore dressed to blend: gray, brown, tan. The wiriest of the bunch, Smitty, loaned Nicole a shirt, since her own, scant wardrobe was bright or white.

Kaz's latest concoction: a hodge-podge of perishables both he and Rick had agreed best be eaten 'now or never' were crammed into funky-tasting bread rolls that everyone inspected for mold in-between bites.

The dory was hauled over the stern and secured alongside the Chris Craft. Few words were spoken as the boats were boarded. They had gone over the game plan thrice; everyone knew their part. The prospect of failure was an option no one dared broach. Even doomsayer Kaz managed to keep a stiff upper; negative waves might affect their karma. Contingencies accounted for, watches synchronized 1800hrs to adhere to a rigid timetable, and the boats disengaged.

Six o'clock. Nicole shuddered to think; *a little over an hour from now...*

She rounded the breakwater out of sight of the dory which lagged a quarter mile behind.

Will and Smitty went overboard to walk the Chris Craft through the rocky shallow to the shore.

The last of the supplies were being unloaded when the dory entered the cove. Heavy laden, the crew should have paid more attention to the submerged boulders instead of Nicole's bent-over transference. The sound of wood meeting rock was followed by the splash of Jason flying headfirst off the bow.

Provisions having been staged, and the ascension detachment geared up, the drill was gone over one last time: base camp would be staffed by Nicole, Doc, and Kaz, who would be on the receiving end of Will, Smitty, Jason, and David's exploits up above. An area was selected for a drop zone. This time the whole plant would be reaped, the pruning conducted below. The inboard's superior power would expedite transfer to *Slip,* unobtrusively adrift from afar. Upon being radioed, the transfer would know it was time for a return to shore, thus adjusting haul sizes according to the pace of the harvest...a nonstop operation throughout the night, leaving enough time to close shop and be out of sight by dawn.

Slipfinger shined tiny on the eastern horizon, but not on the shore party existing in the shadows of the island's rock face. A time check told them they had two hours to get situated, and as soon as darkness provided cover, the undertaking would commence.

Will felt her goose bumps. Diffused light and ocean mist added to the unease as the four climbers prepped for the ascent.

"Don't worry, we can do this. I'll be on the radio if you need me."

"No, it's not that. I just realized that right about now he's probably discovered I'm gone."

"It'll be okay, love. We'll be long gone before he even knows where to look." Their bodies melded, fused lips saying a passionate goodbye. Will plucked the machete from its sheath in the sand and slid it behind his back into the rucksack. "Time to go."

The rest of the team was already negotiating the cliff when Will fell in behind Dave. The climb was deceiving, a mere thirty feet, but almost vertical. Smitty followed a fissure running diagonal; an added bonus was a sliver of ledge running parallel below for footing. Like a mountain goat, he clambered on and was about to yell down 'slow and easy, piece of cake', when the ledge fizzled out and the cleft shrank to finger-hold. His head a mere five feet from the top, Smitty stalled. *You've got to be kidding me!*

Everyone bunched up.

"Hold on! Got a problem here." *A problem for me.* Analyzing the situation, he realized there was only one way out of the predicament and it was not going to be easy. His right leg stretched out, he tested the only foothold available. He was unable to put much weight on it, so it would have to be a leap of faith. If it held, there was a protruding rock within reach above. If that held, he would be able to pull himself up to where he could wedge the other foot into a reliable-looking cavity. *If* he made it that far, he was home free. Everything but rope was passed down to Jason. "Well, here goes." Oh, to be nineteen and invincible.

Focusing on the do-or-die feat, he took a deep breath and committed to fate. The transference went so lightning fast there was no time for second guessing. The next thing he knew, he was sprawled out on top of the plateau, trying to recall the details of what got him to where he was.

"Hey, what's going on up there? You alright Smitty?!"

"Kissing the fucking ground! Just hang tight for a minute while I scope it out."

An access road separated him from a solid wall of green gold so tall he had to rise to his feet and jump in order catch a glimpse of the far side of the island. Only the rooftop of the concrete structure was visible, estimated distance: mile and a half. Tire tracks camouflaged by tall grass half at attention told him the perimeter was rarely patrolled. *Maybe twenty feet:* the distance to an eight-foot chain-link fence. *Damn, wonder if it's juiced.*

The shock through his leather climbing gloves would not be too bad, especially on the back of his hand. One touch and...nothing. It was on. Secured to the metal post's base, he crawled the rope back to the edge and began to lower it.

Packs were hauled up first, and then one by one they heaved themselves up and over the edge.

The party was now hunkered down at the base of the fence. A time check indicated there may be an hour of daylight left. It was agreed a probe be conducted while bolt cutters performed surgery on the galvanized lattice.

Slipfinger Nine

Hugging the fence line, Will went left while Jason took off to the right; no more than thirty minutes out for a look-see.

A disheveled and enraged Alaine imprecated a plethora of threats mixed in with directives.

Manny stood in the middle of the bedroom enduring the tirade, but it was the silence between outbursts that was nerve-wracking. The rhythmic drip of water into an overflowed bathtub reminded him of a ticking time bomb. He moved quickly to diffuse his boss's growing angst.

Both bedroom and bathroom doors were splintered at the casing from forced entry. Alaine had exploded into a fact-finding rampage. Dresser drawers, closet, toiletries were trashed. He could not tell what, if anything, was missing. Exasperated, he came to a standstill in front of the unlatched bay window. He fondled the tied-off bed sheet, collecting his thoughts while Manny stood at attention awaiting orders.

"Find the goddamn wench! Get the others. Check that fucking studio, clubs, hotels."

"But her car's still here. How could she..."

"Then **someone** picked her up down the road...or..." Alaine wedged in between the dresser and the splintered door still wondering how she managed to muscle the heavy furniture. *I must have REALLY pissed her off.* "Call when you find out anything."

"Right boss. Hey, where you going?"

"To the fucking boathouse!"

Downstairs, into his study, he sought company from his desk drawer: Smith and Wesson.

He sat on the fuel storage tank tapping the gun barrel in a rhythmic shit-fit. His thoughts ran to the small outboard runabout as a means to search the five-miles of coastline leading into town. *Waste of time, she's not that stupid.* Gut instinct told him she was long gone. What was required was a phone call to the harbormaster's office, and if he was not there, he would be after a not-so-social call to his house.

Will had run out of road and fence. A straight drop-off into a ravine prohibited any worthwhile surveillance of the guardhouse off in the distance. The side of the building facing him was void of windows; there was nothing to be gained by sticking around. *Well, if we have company, it sure as hell won't be coming from this direction.* He headed back.

Jason had his back against the other end of the fence as he peered around the northwest corner of the plantation's exotic crop. Field glasses dialed into the second floor window indicated two men. A television kept one glued to a stool; the other looked to be cleaning up the evening slop in a cubbyhole kitchen. As far as he could tell, the odd couple was the island's gatekeeper.

Fifteen minutes of observation and Jason came to a conclusion: *they must be bored out of their minds stuck on this rock.* The guy watching the tube looked like a mannequin...*he hasn't moved a muscle!* The one at the sink looked to be stuck in slow motion. *Son of a bitch! I bet they're stoned!* Panning the grounds for any other activity, he was positive they were all there was. The immovable object got off his ass and stepped out onto the balcony. Jason wanted a close up look at the sentry, but wisely refrained. The last vestige of sunlight from beyond the horizon might reflect off the glass. Stock-still, he waited for him to finish the smoke before retreating.

Alaine stormed out of the port authority, charts in hand, having had his way intimidating the poor office jockey. The harbormaster who also served as the marina's landlord had answered the call, but by the time Alaine got there he had conveniently been called out on a family emergency. The cantankerous Moreau knew exactly the ruse; a few years back they had had it out over complaints his parties were excessive and late into the night, too colorful for the neighbors. Hence evicted, to this day bad blood flowed and was the reason his yacht's berth was on the opposite side of the island. It really mattered not to Alaine, for the big game fishing was better up there. But what still stuck in his craw, *the audacity of such a prick;* such a humiliating scolding he had not experienced since he was a teenager being dressed down by his father.

His cigar lit and the rogue Yanks' recorded itinerary in his possession, tires smoldered a spin out of the parking lot and fish-tailed onto the coastal road. *I won't kill the bitch, just the thieving punk.*

Alaine whipped into the circular driveway, spraying the car and two stooges with seashell fragments. The other two gumshoe thugs were still out there somewhere.

"You found her?" Manny asked cautiously.

"Does it look like it?"

Manny knew he stepped right in it with that one.

"But I know HOW to find her. Where the hell's Rico and Wad?"

"That's why we came back after casing all the joints in town. We hoped they already back here."

"Well, as soon as they get here, get ready to move out."

"What's the plan boss?"

"We're going fishing!"

"What?" Harlan looked to Manny for verification he heard right.

"Harley, you're one dense mother-fucker."

"Listen up. When the others get back here I want you guys to haul ass to the yacht. We ain't moving out till dawn, but get *Happy Hour* ready, load up with enough grub and drink to last us all the way to the Bahamas. I'm going in to call Leonard and tell him to have his ass in the air first light."

"You coming with us, boss?"

"No, I'll meet you guys up there." Alaine did an about face for the house, leaving them with one final directive: "pack all the heat you got!"

Alaine bounded up the steps and was met in the foyer by the butler. "Inform the staff I will be gone for a while. Any business calls, I'm in Miami. There's an important conference about new tariffs on exports."

Jeeves was not about to challenge what he knew to be a ruse. "I will pass the word, sir. Have a safe trip." He feared for Nicole...*Godspeed, Missus.*

"Hey, where the hell are you guys?" Jason stumbled upon the opening in the fence.

"Psst...couple a rows straight in."

The dense mass of cannabis, easily two feet above Jason's head, was a blind man's maze in the evenfall. The pungent smell was a head rush as oozing resin slathered his groping arms. He would have tripped over the squatters if David had not flicked the flashlight on-off. Crouched, a purplish bud the size of a corndog thrust inches from Jason's face, Smitty's white teeth grinned endorsement. "Stout. Robust. Aromatic. What we have here is a Christmas tree farm of kick-ass, primo shit. Jackpot, boys."

Jason fondled, smelling the baton. "Damn. Don't even have to smoke it to get a buzz. And who ever said that government couldn't do anything right?"

Will called the play: "Two cut, two haul. We'll alternate on the hour. Work the entire width, but no deeper in than halfway. Start each row staggered first, second, third; take every third plant each row. Thinning it out like that, it'll take more than a glance to realize what's gone down. Work quietly, radio volumes low, and unless you cut your leg off, or you get punch drunk and walk off the cliff...no stopping."

Smitty snorted what was left in the vial. Everyone was fortified, their eyes acclimated to the faint light from a rising half-moon...perfect cover...and the harvest onslaught began.

The lessons learned from their first exercise were employed in the layout of the new base camp in order to facilitate an expeditious operation. Foremost among them was staging equipment ahead of time for easier access.

The beached dory's aft end was stuck out into the water, offering a buffer against the remnants of broken breakers. What rocks could be removed were forming a depression deep and wide enough to float the huge totes as they were stuffed. Nicole's boat was moored off the point of the jutting rocks, and a towline stretched to the beach, with half a dozen clasps tied in at intervals.

The good doctor offered a bump of the white stuff to Nicole; it was politely declined with her stating the insanity of what they were doing had her wide awake enough.

While waiting on the first payload to come raining down from above, Kaz leaned against the cliff in his natural state: fidgety. The staging area flickered faintly from a solitary lantern; Nicole's silhouette helped pass the time.

"Look out below." The initial delivery missed the drop zone, soaking in salt water.

"Not good. Go ten feet to your right next time," radioed Doc.

"Copy that. Be happy in your work."

"Come down and blow me. That'll make me happy."

The next load crash-landed on soft sand.

"Spot on, but how 'bout giving us a head's up. You almost flattened Kaz."

"Oops."

And so the process continued, leveling out into a rhythmic routine: every fifteen minutes or so another load of six, seven footers fell like manna from heaven. Only bud-laden, leafy stock was crammed and stomped into the tote bags...100% green gold.

When it was time to ferry out the first load of six, it became clear a change in staffing was in order. This crop was indeed heavier than the shakedown harvest. And now with Nicole indisposed for the rest of the night ferrying consignments out to the schooner, there was no way the two guys could keep pace. By the time they readied the first ferry, wading out to feed the tethered line of bulbous bags until taut, and then watching Nicole's slow-but-sure departure clear the jagged rock barrier, the pile had doubled in size.

Doc called out to her. "Tell Rick we could sure use an extra hand!" The crushing sound of another load did it. Doc got on the radio. "Hey up there, no fucking way we can keep up."

Will beat the others to the call. "Hold on, Doc. We'll regroup up here and send someone down."

The group convened and it was decided a rock climber make the decent in the dark. At Will's insistence, a certain someone made it a no-brainer to the others.

Going down was tricky. The rope only reached a few feet farther down than where Smitty had played orangutan. He would not chance a twenty foot drop in the dark, not with rocks strewn all over the place. Like a pendulum, pushing off with his feet and holding on with one hand, he groped for that cleft. Third try he found it, on the fourth he went for it. One hand, then immediately the other, held him long enough to find a footing on the narrow ledge below. A brief timeout was taken in order to breathe deep and have an epiphany: *no way in hell doing that in the dark, have to be first light so we can talk Jase and Dave through it.* Will made his way down, imagining Stuart going ape-shit about the delay. *Screw you, can't sail Slip without us.*

The communiqué having been received, *Slipfinger* met Nicole halfway for the transfer. Rick climbed down to assist her and was immediately asked if he could return with her to expedite the operation. Stuart offered his services, Rick stopped short of saying 'I bet you will.'
"She asked me, and I'm already on board. Just drop anchor right here and hold the fort."

Nicole appreciated Rick's coming to her rescue. "Thank you," she whispered, as she bent over next to him to secure the first sack.
Stuart winched. The davit's weigh scale marked each at close to four hundred pounds. Guiding the loads over the hatch, the underbellies slit to spill the bounty into the aft hold, Arti did the math.
"According to my calculations, six trips times six, times four hundred...righteous! How's seven point two TONS grab you?!" Mister MIT kept crunching the numbers; *14,440lbs at $100 per= $1,444,000. Add the other haul's estimate...*"we're two million, two hundred thou!"
Stuart was at the railing watching the white wake trail into darkness. Arti joined him. "Hey man, did you hear what I said? This stuff is SO killer, we ought to seriously reconsider dealing at two hundred a pound."
"Nice way to start a gunfight. The deals went down at a hundred because of the risk. But, that doesn't mean it's not worth suggesting we renegotiate. After they try it,

they might be so wrecked we could sell them catnip for two."

Four AM. Half the plateau had been selectively thinned. The guardhouse had remained 'lights out' throughout the night's undertaking.
Radio check above and below, and again yonder on the water: Nicole was on her way with the next to last haul. The harvest had ceased per order of base operations. They never could catch up with the deluge of crop raining down. The heap remaining having been sized up, they were doubtful all of it could be taken out on the final trip.

Up top, Smitty, Jason, and Dave were running on fumes. Taking great pains to make sure no tools, no clothing...nothing be left behind, they made their way out the fencehole. Dave tossed a bolt cutter, machete's, and a bag of candy bar wrappers over the edge after getting the all-clear go-ahead. It took all three to perform the meticulous task of pulling taunt the slashed heavy gauge fence while stitching it back together with snipped pieces of chain. Pliers twisting, Smitty couldn't hold back.
"Hey man, you losing it? What's so funny?"
"I couldn't help it back in there."
"What are you talking about?"
"Man, when we got the call it was a wrap, I fucking celebrated, leaving a part of me behind as a thank you."
"Oh crap."
"Precisely. A steaming heap."
"Jeezus, Smitty. What'd you use to-"
"The leafy greens, of course. "

The last bundle was hooked up and Nicole climbed aboard making a beeline below. There were personal matters she could no longer endure. Arti was swinging the load over the hatch when he saw Stuart in hot pursuit. *Oh shit.*

She opened the door to the head for relief then was immediately startled as she walked right into the ambush. Stuart grabbed her wrists and pinned her to the wall.

The coercing triggered a flashback: survival instinct was immediate. "Get your hands OFF of me!"

"You're with the wrong guy, Nicole. I can give you everything you need." Closing in on lips he had fantasized about tasting, the puckish grin instantly contorted when her knee met his crotch. On his way down, Nicole was still in reactive mode from the day before, and she raked his cheek with her talons.

Nicole was already at the hatch's stairs when his labored admonition gasped. "You mention a word of this and I promise the two of you will be cast adrift in the middle of the fucking Atlantic."

Her composure regained, she stopped on the first step. Not turning around, purposeful body language signified an unspoken 'bastard'. "So un-captain-like. Now, if you'll excuse me, there's still work to be done."

Not a word was spoken or eye contact made, yet her hasty departure left Arti to prognosticate about what had taken place. When Stuart clambered topside and walking a bit bow-legged like John Wayne and sporting a clawed cheek, Arti fired up his pipe and wisely digressed.

"Gonna be light soon. Think I'll unfurl the mains, leave 'em slack so we're ready to move out."

Stuart lit up. "I'll join you in a minute."

Clearly not an 'after-sex' smoke, Arti left him to recover. *How's he going to explain the face?*

The dory was loaded and the last of the yield bagged and tethered to the Chris Craft. The holdup was sitting on the edge waiting for the first vestige of light. It was decided that Rick and Kaz would head out with Nicole. Will had considered joining them, but with the treacherous descent, he thought it wise he stay behind to spot their holds. He detected an odd agreement from Nicole that it was a very wise decision. Somewhat placated by her kiss, he watched the departure until the call from above snapped him out of a trance he knew was really sleep deprivation. Knowing his spaced-out condition for what it was, it was still most disconcerting. He approached Doc.

"Bad vibes, man."

"About what?"

"Are you tired?'

"Beyond tired, feel like I'm sleepwalking."

"That's what I'm talking about." Straining to focus in the marginal light, Will could barely make out the fissure they would have to transfer to from rope. "Give me that radio."

"Yeah, I see it." Smitty was on his stomach nearly half over the edge.

"Don't you think you better go first?"

"We talked it over. From up here I got a good read, Jason wants to go first so I can talk him through it."

"Alright, it's your call. Just worried about everyone being dog-tired. Might want to slap each other silly. Be careful!"

"You ready, Jase?"

"Let's do it."

Dave lay over the side to watch and learn. When Jason reached the end of his rope, Smitty started swinging as Jason pedaled the cliff wall. Will kept calling up how much further to the handhold. Smitty did likewise. Back and forth; *damn it, one of you guys SHUT UP!* On the fourth swing Jason's outreached hand realized the mark...*shit, here goes*. Taking the fifth, he pleaded mercy.

"Son-of-a-bitch!"

"You alright?"

The question came in stereo form above and below.

"I'm talking, aren't I? Gimme a minute to reposition." Jason inched down to where more firm hand and footholds secured him, and yelled up to Dave. "Hey man, don't worry. I'm locked in with a free hand to grab you if you need it. Rock's a little slippery, just get mad at it and dig in." Jason felt his left hand ring finger's nail split in two. So concentrated on his buddy's welfare, he felt no pain. The strangest thought came over him: *since grade school he's been catching me, now I'm catching him.*

Dave dangled, visualizing the tricky maneuver that would have to be performed on impulse. There would be no time to second guess. "You got to be shitting me, Jase."

"Just like I did it. You let me know when you're ready to let go."

Smitty called down, "hey Dave, you ready?"

"Ready to get it over with."

Heaviest of the crew, it took seven pendulums to get Dave to commit on the eighth. The notion 'suicide' just crossed his mind.

Dave did access the crevice, but a split second question of balance and the mist covered fascia panicked him into letting go in favor of the outstretched hand. His foot slipped, lessening what should have been a firm clasp of sweaty hands.

"David!" Jason almost went with him. Swiveling a face plant against the cliff spared him the gruesome sight, but not the grotesque thud and what sounded like a dead branch being snapped in two. The immediate summoning, JESUS CHRIST, froze Jason one with the stone.

Doc and Will rushed to the scene. The horrific sight dropped both to their knees.

"Oh my God!" Will ripped off his shirt. Doc was trying to find a pulse.

Smitty rappelled, mindless, through the danger. "Damn it, you gotta move!"

Jason was still fused in place.

"Snap out of it! I'm coming over and if you don't get the fuck out of the way, both of us are going down!" Smitty started swinging.

"He's got a pulse, barely." Doc could not find one on the extremities, but did on the neck.

Will tied off the shirt. It was not a tourniquet, but a veil cloaking a sight so grotesque; the visual incomprehensible. David's skull was split wide open like a hickory log requiring one more whack of an axe to finish the job. As horrific the injury, it was the comprehension of peering into squiggly composition of gray matter...his **mind**...that seemed so intrusive, incorporeal.

Jason, Smitty right behind him, crowded in.

"Oh, God, how bad is it?" Jason was freaking out. "This is all my fault. I should've..."

"No man, it should have been me to go first."

"Fuck that. I was the one who insisted..."

"Shut up, it happened. We got to get him in the boat and get the hell out of here! Doc, raise the ship and tell them to come in as close as they can." Will saw Jason going for the shirt, "NO, don't look at it!"

"Is he still..."

"Yes, but if we don't get him out now and stabilized, he might not be. Everybody grab hold, easy on three."

Doc tried his best to soften the jarring blows. The sun's peek on the horizon added to the tension; *should be onboard and out of sight by now*. Crisscrossing at full speed, the diagonal approach to swells may have lessened the slamming rise and fall, but herky-jerky sideways motion was probably just as detrimental.

"What the hell's wrong with them? Are they drunk?" Stuart yelled for the engine cut and ladder deployed. "Sons-a-bitches are way overdue!"

There was a dead-pan expression on Jason's face as he cradled his friend's bloody head while trying to compensate the whiplash sway. Will sat next to him, ready to thwart a look-see. *If he saw what we saw, he surely would come unhinged.*

The scolding Stuart was about to unleash was immediately muzzled. The urgency in Smitty's demand that the boat be immediately lashed alongside and all hands be of assistance, silenced all queries as to what happened. Hoisting dead weight while trying to be as careful as possible, delayed any explosion of interrogations and accusations, until Dave was secured on deck.

"Now what do we do?"

"What you think Kaz, we high-tail it outta here!" Stu was about to order everyone to man the sails when Jason jumped up from the motionless body and got right in the captain's face.

"No fucking way. He's got to get to a hospital now!"

"Oh, and just sail back into port with a boatload of grass? Or, do we spend the whole day getting rid of it, meanwhile missy's madman comes to the party."

"Okay, I'm out. Get him back down into her boat and I'll take him."

Doc and Rick were oblivious to the free-for-all argument that was underway. What they both were aware of drew them into an unflinching stare off. Both their hands remained on the carotid arteries.

"We can't fix him. His frigging skull is busted wide open! I saw his brain for god sake!"

That did it. Hearing Will's description of the injury sent Jason over the edge. He was at the port side to reposition the ladder over Nicole's speed boat when the two words turned him into a pillar, and the commotion gave way to a pin drop.

"He's dead."

CHAPTER TWENTY-FOUR

Early morning blues: a cloudless sky and the pang of conscience with which everyone dealt in their own manner of coping. The island had just disappeared on the horizon, but remembrance of its cruel sendoff lingered like a pall. The morale...there was none.

The scuttling of the Chris Craft had offered a diversion, though temporary. Just before setting sail, Nicole had opened the drain plugs and Rick assented to Smitty's plea to try out the grenade launcher. Everyone, except for Jason, who asked to be left alone so he could write a eulogy, gathered at the stern. Towline cut, separation sufficient, the blooper demonstrated its capability. The boat shattered in two. Weighted down by the inboard, the aft end sank immediately but the bow bobbed. Arti had anticipated such and got a bang out of unloading the Thompson, riddling the hull with holes.

What weighed on everyone's mind now, besides reaching the safe confines of international waters, was the disposal of David's body. The mention of bringing him home was out of the question. The nature and extent of the injury would raise serious questions and undoubtedly call for an investigation. But also, there was the unpleasant reality of a corpse's quick decomposition in the summer heat, not to mention the smell that would announce their arrival back home long before they got there. Doc's offhand comment put a lid on any further discussion.

"I'm not making light of this in any way, but excuse me if I'm blunt. Unless we ditch all the perishables and put the body in the meat freezer, if he'll even fit, there's no way. It's not an option, and I've smelled decomposition. We store him below, no matter how we wrap him up, **in THIS heat…no sir!** He'll foul the entire ship. Forget sleeping down there. I guarantee even if you think you're immune to sea sickness…you won't be. And last, but not least: it won't matter how much seasoning Kaz puts on his concoctions, I don't want to be reminded of Dave with every bite."

Jason and Nicole had already removed themselves from the unpleasant discussion; the rest now adjourned having no stomach for continuance.

So it was decided: body wrapped in bed sheets, temporarily laid to rest under the dory's shade, there would be a sunset burial at sea before the body could begin leaving a lasting impression. Morbidity would rule the day.

The Bell helicopter dropped down from on high and was coming straight at them.

"Oh shit, we got trouble!" Kaz was their resident doomsayer, always expecting the worst; the proverbial glass-half-empty, sky-is-falling, worry wart. Nevertheless, all eyes looked in the direction of the rotor blades chopping away at the humid salt-air. The sound grew in a direct line with the sun.

"Be cool, Kaz." Stuart shielded his eyes, all he could make out was the glowing orb of reflected sunlight.

"*Happy Hour*, do you read me?" Alaine pressed the headset to his ear to muffle the aerial disturbance. The pilot pulled back, leveling the copter into a circular pattern above the schooner. "*Happy Hour*, come in, dammit!"

"Go ahead, boss."

"Found them! Twin-mast schooner no more than fifteen miles north the Lollicks. Stand by." They circled the stern. "Yup, confirmed. *Slipfinger.* That's a fucked-up name for a boat. I count six, no seven, on deck. She's probably below, keeping out of sight. Looks like they're making a run for it, north. Returning now, prepare for immediate departure. Out!"

The whirlybird finished what the crew on board hoped was a passing fancy admiring a vintage schooner's magnificence. The only markings on the bird were tail numbers. Nothing signified law enforcement, the guy in the right seat was seen smiling, waving, and signaling a 'thumbs-up' before veering off to the south.

Tension lessened, commensurate with the fading hum of the interloper: diminished, not dissolved.

Stuart hollered for the crew to get back on task. Everyone complied, except Will, who was stock-still pensive, locked onto the gnat-sized helicopter. An ominous sensation washed over him. He was glad Nicole was below, out of view. *We better get far away from here, **FAST**.*

Smitty approached with a nudge. "Hey man, you okay? What is it?"

"Just got a weird feeling."

"Oh, that. It's natural...just means you're finally becoming a man." The sideways glare told Smitty that Will was in no mood for childish jokes. "About what?"

"Everything...nothing. Hell, I don't know, I can't put my finger on it." Will forced a grin, feeling underhanded about not coming clean with his best friend.

"Yeah, everyone's pretty messed up about Dave. It's a bad trip, man."

"Sure is." Will did not want to dwell on the subject he was trying to scrub from his mind. *Dave's brain*. The last of the Marlboro was finger-flicked into the wind. "Well, we came, we saw, we pillaged. Now let's get the fuck out of here."

Rick joined his brother at the helm. "What do ya think, an hour before we clear the territory?"

"Plus a half." Stu eyed the gauges. "Mid-morning breeze steady-but-light, at seven-to-eight knots. Bow's riding a tad high due to all the stash in the aft hold. I think we move everything not nailed down: weapons, the spare anchor and chain, cordage, extra sail, any drums of water; all that shit as far up in the bow as possible. That'll help level her out some. Should've fucking done that earlier."

"You know, I was thinking. We may only be able to do ten, twelve knots, but when we get in the Gulf Stream and start dealing off this load, I'll bet we can do it fifteen." Rick paused, another subject needed addressing, and he chose his words carefully not wanting to even mention Dave's name. "I've already run this by everyone except Jason, and it's my call. After sunset when it's done, we go into shift mode. Me, Smitty, Will and his woman got night duty."

Stu knew the reasoning behind his brother's thinking and the scratches on his cheek were one of them. The tragedy, the busy work getting *Slip* underway, sinking the evidence linking Nicole to her whereabouts, the mystery helicopter that was in the back of everyone's mind as to who and what it could mean...not once did anyone ask about the lacerations. They were all too occupied with matters at hand. Only his brother broached the subject, and when he replied that one of the loads swung over the cargo hold had side-swiped him and the metal clasp raked his face, he could tell the story wasn't bought.

"Will and Smitty are tight, winds at night light, and she sure knows her way around the ropes; it's daytime you'll need a fifth hand."

Keep me and her detached as much as possible. Rather than challenge the obvious, guaranteeing an embarrassing confrontation about what REALLY happened to his face, Stuart let it ride. "Makes sense, brother."

"Good, that's settled. I'm gonna go check on Jason."

Nicole was doing just such when Rick joined the two of them below.

Jason struggled to verbalize what he was trying so hard to refute. Replaying over and over the missed exchange on the cliff fostered a guilty conviction. "There's no absolution...it's all my fault."

"It's nobody's fault, you've got to stop blaming yourself." Nicole's expression spoke apprehension over Jason's mental state.

"How are we going to explain what happened to him, why we didn't bring him home?"

"We'll come up with something plausible, Jase. Look I know you guys were like brothers, a diamond duo. But don't think for a moment the rest of us aren't pretty tore up also. Right now what's of everyone's concern is **you**."

"Should've been me."

"Yeah, well maybe we shouldn't have carried through with this crazy idea in the first place. Blame me and my brother."

A jaw-clenching head wag, a sigh of resignation, and Jason rose to his feet and exited the scene. Not until heavy feet ceased creaking on the steps to topside, did Rick speak.

"I'm sorry you're a part of this."

"I'm sorry if my being here has caused trouble."

Dazed from another all-nighter and the traumatic incident, he was at a loss for words and unwitting his stare as he regarded her flawless beauty.

Nicole was all too familiar with the scrutiny, but recognized it for what it was: a non-threatening, enraptured gaze.

"You are not at all like your brother," she said with a disarming smile.

"I guess I should take that as a compliment." Massaging a stiff neck and feeling the onset of something else stiffening, it was time to excuse himself. "I'll be in my quarters. Why don't you get some rest, we got night duty." He almost kissed her cheek, but resisted...*not at all like my brother*.

The sentinels had chosen the wrong night to tie one on.

Jason Douglass

Paul leaned against the deck railing, second cup of Joe doing little to alleviate the hangover. He felt sick to his stomach, not from the bourbon, but from the pinochle fiasco that went on hours after Johnny Carson signed off. *Two day's pay! Couldn't pull a decent hand all night!* Damned if he would admit the real reason: his partner just flat-out drank him under the table.

Tunney emerged, shielding his eyes from the nine o'clock fireball. "Darn good thing we don't punch a time clock around here, huh?"

"I should've clocked out with Johnny. You and your god-damned whiskey."

"Double-or-nothing before I check the perimeter?"

"Fuck you." Paul picked up the binoculars, more as a distraction than surveillance. His blurred vision was no hindrance. A Caribbean-blue was backdrop to wavy fields of dark green...*same ole shit, different day.*

Paul's third-year tour of duty watching marijuana grow to new heights had long since become mundane. So routine was the regimen, he could tell by where the sun hung in the sky it was ten o'clock. He surveyed the great beyond; a*ll those boats darting about, angling for position.* He considered the disparity of such a pastime...*sport or fishing as if life and livelihood depended on it*. One more week and the field hands would arrive: harvest, special fertilizer and chicken manure tilled into the soil, reseeding...all done in three days.

"Soon it'll be back to civilization," Tunney backed against the railing, "three months' freedom, then it's right back at it all over again."

Tape delay of the morning news televised reports that the *New York Times* had published excerpts from something called the *'Pentagon Papers.'* Next headline: U.S. believed to be conducting raids into Cambodia. The newscast wrapped up with live footage of demonstrators rioting; various cities and college campuses hosting the festivities.

"Geez, see what we've been missing back in the States."

"Long-haired, commie pinkos, Black Panthers, stinkin' hippies and yippies done opened up a second front. Fucking country's goin' to hell in a hand-basket." Tunney extinguished his butt and flicked it in disgust. "Give me those damn glasses." He focused his attention away from the tube. "Nixon inherited this cluster-fuck war, but mark my words, he'll be the one to get us out."

"Oh, you think so, huh?"

"Damn tootin! Troop reductions, dialogue opened up with the Chinese, Kissinger's doing his thing. If I were Dick I'd..." a ton of brick might as well have slammed Tunney.

"You'd what?"

"Fuck me!"

"You'd do yourself in the ass?"

In the background, Calypso music serenaded the tête-à-tête. Festively blithe, the chamber of commerce commercial about reinvigorating the tourist trade was a comical jingle to the otherwise stark realization; the both of them not only were caught with their pants down, but before long would be bent over and reamed out of a job.

Tunney was gone.

"Hey, where ya goin'....wait up!"

The jeep skidded to a halt, straddling a well-worn path from cliff to fence. Paul ran to the fence and climbed for a better look. Tunney grabbed the rope and leaned over the edge. The huge pile of denuded stalk lent credence to what he'd dreaded: *we are so screwed!*

"Hey, Tunney, get up here. You gotta see this! Looks like a beaver colony went on a rampage!"

Half the island had been thinned out in a semicircular arc.

Tunney joined in the stupefaction at the magnitude of this audacious incursion. "Only problem is, beavers don't exist down here."

"We're in deep shit. How the hell are we going to explain…"

"We're not. Come on, we got to get back and call this in."

"Son-of-a-bitch, such a gravy job. Guess this will be our last rotation."

"That's an understatement."

"Pharmacy's closed." Doc tossed the spent vial overboard. "Damn good thing I brought it. Two days of no sleep and we're still kickin."

Doc spoke only to himself. Kaz had not heard a word. Clinging to the davit's chain and fighting delirium from lack of sleep, he struggled to keep seasickness at bay. He found that setting his sight on the horizon, void of any landmass, helped somewhat. Having left the relative calm island waterways, the open-ocean's augmented pitch and roll was not well received. "I never liked roller-coasters. Man, I don't know if I can handle kitchen detail today."

"I'm sure everyone can fend for themselves, Cookie. You gotta roll with it, man, takes time to get acclimated."

"Don't mention 'roll'." Kaz's pallid face was tinged with lime green. He made it to the railing just in time. What little he had eaten since last night was hurled overboard, blending with the ocean spray as it blew by. "God, I hope I can sleep tonight."

The second shift crew had excused themselves to try and squeeze two hours rack time before the congregating for the dark ceremony ushered in the night.

Nicole's flight from hell that inadvertently enlisted her as co-conspirator of a heist unimaginable gave her ample worry for insomnia. However, utter exhaustion overpowered such disorder; she was down for the count.

Smitty's snoring denied Will any sleep. *Got a right mind to smother him with a pillow.* He could not take it any longer. Up and out of the bunk, Will retreated behind the partition and slid in to spoon her from behind. Denying carnal desire, the snoring not as audible, he dozed off into sleep, aggravated by a racing mind, courtesy the remnant effects of Doc's powder.

Alaine Moreau did not feel jilted, he felt robbed. If there was one thing he had no tolerance for, it was getting swindled, played for a fool.

Boarding his yacht, the crew was called front and center. The status report assured him the ship was ready to go: food and beverages stocked, weapons checked, loaded and locked. He rolled out a chart, pinpointing where contact was made and drew a line due north to where he estimated they would intercept.

"They've got a head start, but we've got the horsepower. They're east of our northern heading, but we'll cut ahead and already be in the area they'll have to pass through heading for Florida. I think a very warm reception is in order and if it's not well received, or these Yankee punks don't comply with unconditional surrender of stolen property, then we play rough."

Alaine plunked down in the sport-fishing chair, fired up a Cuban, and ordered departure. "Let's get these fuckers. Move out!"

Purveyor of rum, he had taste-tested enough to last lifetimes, yet his drink of choice to celebrate foregone successful conclusions: twenty year old, single-malt Scotch.

The glass swirled rocks, generating a mini-vortex and a smirk. *Smartass 'wife-nappers' are going down.*

CHAPTER TWENTY-FIVE

Diverted from its southern area of influence near Saint Croix, the patrol boat moored in Cruz Bay, Saint John. It had been on hold pending the hurried insertion of two federal agents. Rendezvous by helicopter, the WPB Point Class cutter's diesel roared to life for the half-hour dash northwest to Hans Lollick.

Facing the grim prospect that their cushy assignment was probably on the line, courtesy of the reapers, the guards conducted a preliminary investigation, hopeful their initiative might temper the inevitable interrogation. For a loss of anything better to do, they returned to the scene of the crime's great escape. Neither dared descend the frayed rope, and after a cursory review that yielded nothing useful, they once again returned to the west side, drove down the switchback, and walked the wharf's planks to face their fate.

"Pillaged and plundered. Now I know what it must've felt like back in the pirate days."

Tunney was not tuned in. The sight of the massive pile of denuded stalk brought to mind Joan of Arc's torturous demise; only they were the ones facing being burned at the stake. He envisioned a G-Man observing the roasting with stolid approval: a befitting atonement for derelict duty. Deflecting from the macabre image, he anxiously scanned the horizon for their executioners..."aw shit, here they come."

Paul rehearsed their story in his mind: *Perimeter patrolled mid-afternoon. Got back and found my partner balled-up with fever and a bad case of the shits, think it was the mayonnaise. I had to pull his shift. Conducted another security check just before the Tonight Show. Situation...normal. I don't remember Carson signing off.* The lie would have to suffice as a very pathetic defense.

It was a cut and dry meet-and-greet, immediately Paul and Tunney were separated. Done so to expedite processing the crime scene, both incriminates believed it was the old divide and conquer strategy: eliminate attempts to collaborate accounts of what happened.

Tunney drove two guardsmen and a DEA man up the switchback.

Paul was ordered on board. The patrol boat sped off for the opposite side of the island.

Atop the island, a walk-through of the guard station was accompanied by an unpleasant interrogation on the back deck, while surveying a boatload of private property that had been depleted. Then it was off to walk the acreage in search of any incriminating articles left behind.

Paul was in tow with investigators heading to shore via a rubber raft. He too had been grilled, the fabrication was what it was; they just flat-out blew it. Walking the site, the immensity of the operation made evident by the mountainous heap of hemp refuse, the combing uncovered nothing but footprints, some candy wrappers, and one incredulous question: *how the hell did whoever and how many pull this off!*

"Hey, you might want take a look at this!" Ensign Smoak bent over a bowl-shaped concavity in the rock slab.

The team of investigators grouped around the suspicious finding. "Jesus. That's a lot of blood."

Looking up to the dangling rope, another guardsman summed it up. "Some poor bastard took the quick way down."

"Yeah, question is: dead or alive?" Captain John Walker directed his summation to the two plainclothesmen. "The size and scope of this brazen action required many hands and means of transport...got to be one damn big boat."

It was agreed that an APB be put into local authorities to visit only the marinas substantial enough to accommodate large vessels.

"Destinations. Deportment and make-up of crews; we need to find out who we're dealing with ASAP!"

The agents concurred with Walker's approach. It would not take too long to narrow down the possible suspects: big ship, sizeable crew, probably charted for the most logical market...U.S. mainland.

Tunney and the DEA man were on the wharf, the patrol boat motoring in for retrieval. Two seamen remained up top until relief was flown in.

"Sorry, chumps, your personal effects will be collected and sent to you. We leave now." The Captain's curt response was best left unchallenged.

It was an ignoble departure back to headquarters for more debriefing. Standing on the aft deck, bamboozled over the outlandish raid that abruptly ended their laid-back occupation, Paul and Tunney bid a silent farewell to what now seemed like Shangri-La.

Walker was on the radio. He felt in his gut the scallywags responsible were well on their way north to the safe confines beyond Virgin Isle territory, but as a precaution he mobilized both patrol boats. One was in port, to which he directed a figure-eight recon of St Thomas-St John, and in the process potential hideaways in the cluster of non-descript cays. The other, already out to sea, was ordered south to traverse the periphery. Any boats of appreciable size were to be boarded and searched.

The command was more for show, a 'cover-my-rear' exercise in futility. Realistically, Walker knew they were too late, but at least he was working a couple angles. Once intelligence could ascertain ship, its destination, and the crew's M.O., he would have a better clue as to whom and where to place a heads-up call.

"Captain. SOL on the air recon you requested. One chopper is undergoing scheduled maintenance, the other just landed in Croix for refueling, but they said they could be in the air and at the northern perimeter in an hour."

"Tell them to do just that, go as far as fuel allows and report any curious sightings."

By the time they arrived at Charlotte Amalie, ninety minutes at full speed, information came to them from right under their nose. Across the bay was where just yesterday a large schooner with a strange name departed. It was crewed by nine college lads. Something about honoring a dying man's request. Charged with returning to Cape Cod a treasured schooner. The scuttlebutt floating around the marina and also the harbormaster was 'a mission of mercy.'

More like a mercenary mission of subterfuge. What a con. Walker forwarded the information: primary suspect, a twin-mast schooner.

"Get the harbor chief on the horn, find out if an itinerary was logged. Contact our eye-in-the-sky and tell him high altitude surveillance only. If he spooks them, they'll toss their cargo overboard and a hell of a lot of marine life will get very stoned. Report co-ordinates and heading ONLY! Little bastards probably already out of jurisdiction."

Stuart called out from behind the sextant. "Three, two, one, mark. Latitude 18.46, longitude 64.91." They had just crossed over into international waters. "Maintain course another thirty miles just to be on the safe side."

Artimus penciled in coordinates on the chart and drew a straight line due north into the Atlantic, Doc was at the wheel. It was decided they maintain longitude and go farther north to latitude 27.30 before changing course due west.

"That'll skirt us just north of the Grand Bahamas' outlying cays and put us in direct line with Fort Pierce." Stuart calculated the remaining distance to the east coast, considered the twelve-mile demarcation and doubled it. Coordinates marked, it was there they would execute a ninety degree turn north and make their run up the coast. "Two days max, let the vast Atlantic swallow us up into oblivion."

Their relief shift single-filed in from the hatch. It was time. Nicole insisted she take the helm, having not truly known the deceased.

The lifeless body lay on a section of gangplank, wrapped in a bed sheet and weighted down with spare anchor chain that was crisscrossed and secured with cable ties. Deference to the deceased, and surrealistic reality, imposed a stunned silence as the crew huddled starboard. The pallbearers stood on each side, balancing the board atop the gunwale.

Rick presided over the proceedings, offering a simple benediction. Jason stood, carved in stone, as the ceremony unfolded. "We commit our brother's body to the deep, but his soul-spirit sails with us to Cape's keep."

Trancelike, Jason stepped forward and gently put his hand on the shrouded head. "Goodbye, old friend. You caught a lot of my shit thrown at you, forgive me for not catching you." A single tear etched his vacant face.

The guilt-ridden farewell halted the final act. Hesitant glances were exchanged, as well as an understanding that something, ANYTHING, besides Jason's words be spoken before the send-off.

Artimus rescued everyone from the awkward moment that seemed to hold time hostage. He quoted a passage from a favored text read years ago:

> *All are born with halters round their necks;*
> *But it is only when caught in the swift,*
> *Sudden turn of death, that mortals realize the*
> *Silent, subtle, ever-present perils of life.*

This utterance, perhaps too cold, too real, was followed by an 'amen' here and there. Jason bent over whispering something, Rick gave the nod, and the housing of what everyone wanted to believe was that of an immortal soul, slid overboard.

Smitty's callous way of coping with such gloom was downright awkward. He could not shake a W.C Fields line: "It's a funny old world...a man's lucky if he gets out of it alive."

The weighted body speared the water mid-ship. All eyes considered the white bundle's immediate decent, but *Slipfinger's* forward progress left behind only imagination of the depths to which he would finally rest. Hiss of ocean spray displaced by the hull and sporadic flaps of sail filled the silence at last broken by Stuart's command.

"Second watch, remain on deck." The rest of you get some chow and shut-eye. Wake up's at o-four hundred."

"Come on, man. I got a little something that'll help you sleep." Like an orderly, Doc led Jason below.

Kaz willingly whipped up some grub...a welcome diversion as he came to grips with the reality of what just went down. Artimus and Stuart were at the helm updating the night captain on course headings and the latest weather forecast before they retired themselves.

Smitty joined Will and Nicole, walking the deck while inspecting sail and cordage in quiet reflection. The thought of lightening things up with another outlandish tale was nixed: *Comedy relief under such circumstances, a sure bomb.*

A midnight snack of leftovers was brought up from below as she did her best to mask exasperation.

Will detected a vibe that she was a trifle bothered, and inquired whether she was okay.

The fair maiden was not in the mood to repudiate the encounter, so, being accustomed to so much chauvinist 'pigism' of unwelcome advances she recounted, coolly detached: "I was in the galley, quiet, so as not to wake the crew. I thought it was you coming up behind me, but I could tell by the hands on my shoulders it wasn't." Omitted was the part about the unmistakable 'prod' at her backside. She knew better than to mention such lurid detail of a man clad only in his skivvies with a boner leading the attack. "I think Stuart must have been sleepwalking, but when I turned to face him with a knife in hand, it must have snapped him out of it." *Yes, and his heat seeking missile sure fizzled out.* "So that was it. He just startled me, that's all. He said something incoherent," this, another lie to prevent holy hell from breaking out, "and went back to his quarters like a 'good' little boy." Freudian slip? More like an intentional play on words, to placate her defender. The instant she said it, picturing Stuart's deflated ego, elicited an inadvertent smile that actually sold Will and Smitty the bill of bullshit. Nothing worth getting upset about, and anyway, Nicole found the incident rather comical...or so it was perceived.

Rick, however, did not buy it from the get-go. Poker-faced, he knew by her intermittent glances she was appreciative that he played along. *Incorrigible son-of-bitch! You're damn lucky she didn't cut you off, LITERALLY!* He admired Nicole's bravada, self-denial and sacrifice of integrity, all in the name of keeping a fragile peace. White lies, skirting truth, whatever it took to stave off a showdown between her lover and stalker...both realized the charade could only be played so long before Will woke up and smelled the skunk cabbage. Confined on such a lengthy voyage, it was only a matter of time before Stuart's obsession would manifest itself in some stupid, haphazard way and the duping of Will would no longer be viable. Little did they know Will was quite aware of Stuart's insatiable desires, he just was not privy to the extent of such flagrant advances.

Was he protective? Yes. Would he fight for her honor? Indeed. But what he would not do was show any semblance of the insecure, jealous, controlling asshole she risked all to get away from. No, Will was not about to exhibit such weakness. Considering what little he had to offer her, his only trump cards were a display of self-confidence, respect for her freedom, and above all...trust. The love she admitted was sufficient to overcome adversity and confide in him any concerns or reservations about her personal safety.

It was not as if lovers and brothers had an exclusive, privy to the soap opera that had no place in the grand scheme, chock-full of potential calamities. The entire crew was mindful of something brewing in the Stuart-Will pot that had been simmering since they first blended. The newly added catalyst that now made for a bad, caustic chemistry: Nicole. It was a personal affair that was no one's business to interfere with or even broach. All that could be done was to be held captive, a silent audience, and hope the sideshow gets resolved before things turned crazy in an ugly third act.

The general consensus was that it was all *unneeded* **NONSENSE**!

A blind man with autopilot could solo, so uneventful was the night. The consistent breeze was unwavering, and sails were set to compliance, as helm-duty was alternated among the four. Except for the occasional 'tweak', the crew meandered across the deck counting shooting stars and the interminable time between sightings.

Will could not resist what he knew would be a rare opportunity. He whispered an invitation to Nicole, who acknowledged with a mischievous smile. "Hey, Smitty. Can you run a little interference? You know, just shoot the shit with Rick while we sneak off for a little…?" The wink conveyed a single word: 'privacy'.

"Little?" Smitty could not help himself, measuring with a thumb and forefinger what was in store for Nicole. "Have fun with that."

"Thanks, dickhead." *Smartass.* "Just give a holler if you need me."

Smitty was happy for them, though unable to deny envy, so he offered one more jab in jest: "Yeah, sure thing. And you, little lady, just give *me* a yell if *you* need 'anything'.

"Always the comedian. Thanks, man, I owe you."

"I'm keeping a running tab."

Will led her by the hand to the only refuge offering a semblance of seclusion.

Rick made an entry in the logbook: *0300 hours. Steady going. North at ten knots; light easterlies. Two hours since running lights spotted southwest horizon, appears to be on similar course.*

When the day crew took over, he would suggest a slight turn west to better utilize the easterlies. According to his calculations, at current speed they still had eight hours of northerly run before making a ninety-degree turn west for the Florida coast. Arcing marginally into the westerly run would shave distance and time.

Smitty moseyed up to the helm. When asked about the others' whereabouts, he nodded his head towards the stern, "Will said there were a few issues they needed to address."

"Can't say I blame him. The likes of her, I'd be undressing hot issues also."

Neither mentioned David; for what does one profit from discussing a dead issue. Yet the tragedy did raise concern about the lasting effect it could have on Jason, whose demeanor was one of someone suspended between shock and denial, and the potential for becoming a 'loose cannon'. Resident curmudgeon Kaz was not fairing much better. To his credit, however, probably out of deference to Jason's personal loss, he kept gloom and doom to himself.

Rick was clearly vexed by the melancholy overtaking the crew. "Maybe we should take it as a sign. Forget the whole damn thing and bail out now while we still can."

The last thing Smitty needed to hear was doubt casted by one of the three brain trusts of a high-stakes enterprise that had been a guaranteed success. *Not reassuring. This calls for remedial action.* A mock laugh worked as his segue.

"What's so funny?"

"Man, your mention of bailing out reminded me of this picture I got framed. When we get back, I'll have to have a print made and send it to you."

"What are you talking about?" Too late. Rick should have recognized the set-up.

"Pa bought me a camera when I turned ten. For weeks, I walked around our Wyoming ranch taking pictures of everything, anything: blooming flora, wildlife, even cow patties. Man, some of those dumps have really weird designs to them."

"Oh, brother. I'm alone listening to this shit?"

"You bet, really great shit. Front and center, just for you."

Like everyone else, Rick refused to acknowledge that the stories had any redeeming entertainment qualities. But for Smitty, the laughter and groans confirmed for him they indeed did. Undeniable though was the fact that they were truly insane, and always left open the door for debate as to their authenticity.

Fortified with a lit Camel, Smitty continued. "I had just shot through three rolls of film. Luckily, what I hadn't realized was that one shot remained when I got back to the corral. Leaning against the barn, I noticed something strange. There was this long-necked gander perched on the corral's railing between the water trough and feed bin. Very abnormal for a goose, I almost took the last snapshot right then and there, but held up. The only horse penned up at the time was Butterball, a wide-assed mare whose voracious appetite for corn and grain made sharing with the other horses out of the question." Smitty paused for a drag, relishing the befuddled expression on Rick's face.

"So...you get a picture of the goose riding bareback?"

"Not quite." Smitty saw the dory's slight sway and could not resist sabotage. Moving in front of Rick to deflect the screwy yarn aft, he raised his voice a notch, and envisioned Will's frustration as Nicole laughed all the way to the climatic end. "Ole Butterball finished gorging on corn and alfalfa. I was waiting for what you assumed: a horsey ride to capture on film, but what happened next was far more intriguing. Unmindful of the gander on the fence railing, she pivoted from the trough. Her tail raised, snorting and stomping the ground...I think she was constipated. In her frustration, she'd backed up within range of the long-necked observer."

"You are so full of shit."

"No, but the horse was. With her anal cavity expanding, the stupid goose leaned in..." Smitty's silly grin and stuttered, laughter-filled, speech lent credence to the hilarity. "...with his long neck bobbing and weaving in anticipation, corn kernels embedded in the protruding turds proved irresistible. One thrusting jab shocked Butterball out of her dreamy relief. Must've been a reflex reaction, but her sphincter clammed shut, sucking the perpetrator into darkness. I don't know if it was the ramrod intrusion, flailing wings, or both...Butterball's eyes almost popped out of their sockets. I never saw a horse come out of the gate that fast! She whipped 'round that corral, powered by combative wings, and every time she bucked the long neck got shorter until there was no more. Numerous laps later, the gander went limp, ending Butterball's traumatic ordeal. Exhausted, her teeth bared in snarled disgust, she relieved herself. And the dangling duck plopped to the ground, buried unceremoniously in what Butterball was trying to get rid of in the first place."

"That's the biggest pile of crap I've ever heard!"

"That's what I thought...a 'goose enema'." Smitty could not help but grin, not at his true story that was too ridiculous to believe, but at the audible sound of a young woman's laughter. *Success*. "The picture I snapped is definitive: Butterball in full stride, wings attached and beating like a hummingbird, her ghastly expression, all caught for posterity as she rounded the bend faster than Seabiscuit coming into the homestretch...I just wish the camera had stop action 'cuz the wings were a bit blurry and her cue ball-sized eyeballs didn't reveal the proper graphic relief."

"You expect me to believe the horseshit?"

"Don't think I'm not appreciating all your well-laid puns. But you'll see, when I send you a copy. It makes for a great conversation piece. Hell, my old man actually had the picture blown up, framed, and on display in his study! Poor horse was the butt of many jokes."

"Touché. But how would I know it's not fake, some stupid, doctored-up picture?"

"It's authentic. I have the newspaper clipping recounting my story. You could say the event went down in the 'anals' of Dubois wild-west history."

"That's ANNALS, man." Rick's head was spinning, visualizing the corralled horse churning up dirt clods.

"No...'anals'."

"I get it. Man, you are one screwball defective."

"Nah, I'm good. Just had sort of an abnormal childhood, but I feel all the richer for it."

A torturous slow-ride left them bathed in sweat. It was not so much the act itself, but the extra effort it took to be discreet, that left them worn out. They had wrestled to keep the boat from rocking, while subduing their impassioned cries, more than once muffled by one's hand over the other's mouth. But it was Smitty's convoluted exposé that made concentration excruciatingly frustrating. Will imagined strangling the jester, but guilt overrode such a thought. *If I were any of the other guys knowing one lucky bastard was getting 'some'...yeah, I best just let it ride*. Though he knew damn well what his 'pal' was trying to do...impede on their night moves...he would NOT give him the satisfaction of knowing how well he had succeeded.

In the absence of pillow-talk, they lay face-to-face, gently swaying to *Slip's* rhythmic roll. Their lips converged, sealing an unspoken truth: the love was mutual.

She sensed something troubling him. "What is it?"

"I could make love to you three times a day, but I think it's best we cool it. You know, probably wouldn't be well received by the other guys."

Nicole understood what he was implying, "you're right. We're inviting trouble."

"Yeah. Not good for morale. Come on, let's rejoin the team."

Will searched for an intro into Rick and Smitty's conversation that would not be too awkward. He found it glowing on the horizon. "Isn't that the same light? I thought when we first saw it hours ago it was just a buoy. Looks like it's getting closer."

"We've been watching it, and it *is* getting closer. But I've slightly altered our heading in its direction. The blinking had to have been caused by the swells when it was barely on the horizon. Up-down, on-off." Rick raised the glasses more so to mask any tell-tale look of concern. "You know, it's rather reassuring that someone else is out here. If some unforeseen disaster struck, at least we know a distress call would be answered straightaway."

Stuart traipsed through the sleeping quarters rousing the dead on his way to the aft hatchway. His appearance topside coincided with a spectacle that was the last thing he needed to see. Arm-in-arm, the two of them stood at the stern watching the first hint of a new day dawning. He had had a fitful night, mortified and stubbornly obsessed, which ended with his getting up on the wrong side of the bed. Cantankerous from sleep deprivation, and unaccustomed to being snubbed, the blatant 'in-your-face' sight was the straw that broke his threatened machismo. Stuart just flat out snapped.

The confrontation that ensued fetched everyone else up to the deck.

Rick turned over the wheel to Doc as he rushed to head off a bad situation. He knew his brother all too well and could tell by his mannerisms he was itching for a fight.

Accusations were unloaded on Will, who stood his ground, enduring the tirade. The more he tried to mollify the Captain by accepting blame and apologizing calmly, the closer Stuart inched in. The crew closed ranks on the combatants. Words of caution were interjected in supplication that the altercation cease. Nicole stood by her man, seething. Stuart's dressing-down of Will was totally unwarranted, considering twice she had endured his unsolicited advances. She bit her tongue, but her unflinching eyes bored holes in their impetuous confronter.

To his credit, Will maintained composure until his adversary stepped over the line. In the heat of his diatribe, Stuart blurted the name "bitch." The next thing that came out of his mouth was a tooth, courtesy of a vicious right hook. Down went Stuart with Will going right after him. Everyone moved in to restrain the two.

"God damn you two, break it up!" Rick was livid.

Stuart sprang to his feet, spewing bloody insults and about to respond in-kind when Arti and Jason collared him from behind. Smitty put himself between the two.

"Tell you what. You two want to kill each other, wait until we reach the Bahamas and we'll drop you off on some deserted sandbar. This is total fucking bullshit and I'm making the call: from here on out BOTH of you stay clear of one another. Next one that starts anything...forfeits their share of the take."

Nicole had had enough. Reckoning the punch earned them castaway status in Stuart's eyes anyway, and Rick's decree being simply unjust in Will's case...the gloves came off. She unloaded the bombshells of unsolicited advances.

The public announcement infuriated Will, who now had to be kept at bay. The embarrassing accounts not only silenced Stuart, but shot to hell his credibility...except for with Artimus, who appeared to be unmoved.

Pulling no punches, the accusations shamelessly detailed, Nicole's testimony disbanded the jury to deliberate their private verdicts. One thing was universally in agreement: *better put a fork in it, or the whole crew might come undone.*

Nicole forced Will below; it was time for shift change anyway. Smitty stayed topside for a while knowing the two could use some privacy to sort things out. Rick also remained; he was not finished with his brother.

"Great way to start the day, huh?" Arti lit his pipe.

It occurred to Doc that in times of duress or touchy situations requiring contemplation, the pipe never failed to smoke. "That was some bad shit. You might need to talk to him. You're his best friend."

"I'll try, but he can be obstinate once he gets something in his head. I don't know if he's ever been told 'no'. Since we were kids, he always seemed to get what he wanted."

"Spoiled, huh?"

"Worse. Privileged, arrogant, and…"

"Narcissistic?"

"Very observant, Doc."

"What the hell's gotten into you?" Rick checked himself from an all-out chastising. Knowing how pig-headed his brother was, to do so would only escalate into a war of words… or worse.

Stuart wiped the rivulet of blood trickling from his mouth. He had no defense, except to say there would be no more display of lovey-dovey aboard his ship. "It's unfair to the rest of the crew and bad for morale."

"Morale? Coming from you Queeg, that's a doozy!"

"First hook-up we make, so help me, the two of them can hitch a ride out of here."

"Bullshit! We're shorthanded as it is and it's YOU who's obviously the problem. You've had it in for him since the beginning and it's got to stop...NOW!" Rick started to leave, "...and stay the fuck away from her! You're a goddamned captain, so act like one!"

Stuart knew he had no leg on which to stand as he stood alone watching his brother storm off below. He had made an ass of himself, yes, but an apology, especially to lover boy, just was not going to happen. *I don't eat humble pie, never have.* So full of himself, there was no room left to swallow wounded pride. He shrugged off the incident and strutted to join his confidant at the helm.

Looking forward to dawn when all remaining sails would be deployed and course heading adjusted to a more westerly run, Stuart hoped the activity might serve as a diversion to the unwanted consideration he felt from Doc and Kaz. Arti understood him. Jason was stuck in his own world with little to say and impossible to read.

The day that had started off on the wrong foot was a rude awakening, a harbinger of unbeknownst danger lurking ten miles behind and closing.

"Twin-mast, large schooner...it's got to be her." Shadowing all the while by starlight, the confirmation was gained when the eastern sky dawned a backdrop highlighting the vessel's configuration.

"Let's not spook them. Increase speed five knots. Slow and easy, we'll take them portside." Estimating two hours to bag his property, Alaine eased into the captain's chair grinning, and fired up a Cuban. He could not resist quoting a passage from Gaston Leroux's Phantom of the Opera:

> *"Here the sire may serve the dam,*
> *here the master takes his meat!*
> *Here the sacrificial lamb*
> *utters one despairing bleat!*
> *Poor young maiden!*
> *For the thrill on your tongue of stolen sweets*
> *you will have to pay the bill…*
> *tangled in the winding sheets!"*

The goons within earshot acknowledged the recital, impressed, and believed it to be an impromptu original.

"I didn't know you was a bard. Good one, boss." Manny bumped the throttle in anticipation of the impending doom that was in store for these punk-ass Yanks. *You boys might wish you were never born.*

CHAPTER TWENTY-SIX

Just in time for breakfast, Stuart got his wish. He had wanted attention diverted from his foolish folly, and he got it, **TWOFOLD**.

First there was the conspicuous high-flying chopper that could not be identified, but it sure as hell made it obvious they were of interest. Like a gnat too small to see, too pesky to snatch, it circled round and round driving the crew nuts to the point that Arti blurted out: "which of our ordinance has the farthest range?" What was freaky was as soon as he said it, the copter flew away south as if it had heard the question.

The immediate, more disconcerting issue was the cabin cruiser getting noticeably bigger in pursuit.

The bogie that they had been monitoring had not deviated from its course. It was S*lipfinger* that had done so. They were well out into international waters and through binoculars the encroaching craft was positively identified as NOT being law enforcement. *Who **ARE** these guys*?

Soon after the night crew retired, 0600 hours, Stuart had decided their flight north would be concluded. Sails were calibrated to accommodate the east-southeast zephyr; Stuart wheeled the schooner hard to port for the twelve hundred-mile western run to the Bahamas. Five degrees shy of ninety, Arti had calculated the slightest angle north of dead-reckoned west would sail them just outside British territorial waters. From there, almost a straight shot to their first rendezvous, offshore Daytona.

"If we average just ten-twelve knots around the clock and ruler of the four winds, Aeolus, is with us...five days."

It was a textbook straight shot, the shortest distance between two points. Problem was, the new heading looked to be setting them up for intersect with the cruiser which had not yet deviated from its northern track.

For the past hour, Jason had been trying to raise the mystery yacht. Stuart again called into the old-time voice funnel piped below into the radio cubicle. "Any answer?"

"Nope. I'm positive we're on the same frequency. Either their radio's busted, or they just aren't sociable."

Stu and Arti exchanged apprehensive looks. Art did not have to be told.

"I'll wake 'em up. Weapon preference?"

"Sidearm will do."

Doc collapsed the spyglass. "Hey, I count five onboard and there's a shitload of heavy tackle, rods and reels staged. You know, we're in primo marlin fishing grounds...probably after big game."

"Yeah, right. And we might be the ones on the hook cuz we got bait." Arti dropped down the hatch, but not before he heard Doc's reply.

"Hey, bring me up that Tommy."

Meanwhile, Coast Guard HU-16 Albatross reconnoitered...

"Send it."

The radioman called in the sighting: "twin-mast schooner and a large yacht in close proximity. Latitude: 21.78, longitude: 65.22. Both beyond jurisdiction. Suspect schooner on a westerly heading, yacht northerly. Possible rendezvous to transfer contraband. Returning to base."

At CG Headquarters in Saint Thomas, the Feds, DEA, and local authorities had compiled enough information to warrant the just-received communiqué as confirmation the perpetrators had been identified. The ship spotted fit the description and chronicled journey filed with the harbor chief. The rip-off of Big Hans was still being considered with incredulity when a fixed-wing spotter plane conducting a low level fly-by of the maze of smaller cays called in to report that what was just seen was hard to believe.

"Don't know how they got in there, but `C'-Farm's been gutted also. Half the crop's gone!"

HQ Commander Wallace was flabbergasted by the exploitation's magnitude, not to mention extremely vexed. The audacious sorties, estimated in tonnage...*Pirated right under my nose! Twenty unblemished years shot to shit!*

"Well, men, it's been a pleasure serving as your commander. Can't say the incident's out of our hands, because we never had a goddam grip on it in the first place. Sparks, telex Miami what we do know and what we suspect is their intent. Tell them to relay the dispatch up the entire east coast." Wallace knew the buck stopped with him. The only defense he could muster was shortage of resources and personnel. *Police action? Kiss my soon-to-be reamed ass, Vietnam!*

The misguided war, eight meat-grinding years and counting, severely thinned the reserves on the home front.

Men, material, and equipment had been funneled into the black hole of Vietnam. Stations were closed down. Those that remained were operated with skeleton crews due to reductions redeployed to the Far East. Key West and Miami bases remained relatively unscathed, but smaller stations all along the east coast were hit hard. Responding to SOS calls and conducting search and rescue was the extent of operations for depleted auxiliary units. Routine patrolling and drug interdiction were curtailed, if not discontinued altogether.

Wallace had to hand it to the buccaneering entrepreneurs...*such a sad state of affairs, opportunistic bastards timed it perfectly.*

Brunswick Georgia, Coast Guard Auxiliary.

Located on the Frederica River, which fed Saint Simons Sound before dumping into the Atlantic between Jekyll and Saint Simons Islands, the flotilla with its three cutters was one of a select few substations spared of the war machine's voracious requisitions. But with Jacksonville and Savannah gutted, the range of responsibility had spread coverage thinner than a wide-open sieve an aircraft carrier could sift through.

Admiral Frank Connor, fittingly dubbed 'The Walrus', due to his rotund build and white handlebar mustache, reflected before his office window. Loath to celebrations, he had conscientiously endured last night's surprise party commemorating thirty-five years of service and official senior citizen status. It seemed like just yesterday that he enlisted at the age of twenty. Time felt like an adversary no longer on his side. Puffing on a robust Honduran, he thumbed the tusk handle of the coffee mug presented to him by his staff. A closet Beatle's fan, the painted walrus with drooping tusks and the inscription "coo-coo-ca-choo," induced a slight smile.

He never married; his union was with the Guard. An unblemished record of staying the course and enumerable accolades for clutch search and rescues, his career felt wanting of a pinnacle on which to hang his soon-to-be retired hat. The myriad of routine calls blurred recollection: engine failure or out of fuel, inept sailors unable to tack their way back home, plain negligence, impending foul weather, booze-related mishaps. There was no defining mission that came close to measuring up to his dad's. As so often the case when sons aspire to follow in their fathers' footsteps, hero-worship damned him to fourth and long with the clock running down.

Frank stared out the window. He could not recall which jetty it was, left or right, where he sat perched on broad shoulders listening to the sagacious drone: "Red sky at night, sailor's delight. Red sky in morning, sailors take warning."

"Daddy, promise me you'll always come home." So long ago, and he could still recall the foreboding twinge staring past the dark waves and wondering what monsters lurked beyond the horizon.

The pact between father and son lasted seven years. 1928, thirty-four year-old Lieutenant Commander Tom Connor and crew vanished without a trace in the San Felipe Segundo Hurricane, also known as Hurricane Okeechobee. The torrential rains and storm surge breached earthen dikes and submerged south Florida under twenty feet of water where it claimed in excess of twenty-five hundred lives. It was the second deadliest storm in United States history. The behemoth tempest had sustained winds topping 160 miles per hour as it sliced through the middle of Florida before ripping up the eastern U.S. and Midwest and finally fizzling out in Toronto. In '28, forecasting was primitive at best, early-warning systems...non-existent. Any notice of approaching foul weather came in the form of a nasty skyline, and by then it was usually too late to do anything about it.

When coastal Georgians and mariners were caught completely off-guard, the base Frank now commanded sent its only life-saver to sea. His dad captained the rescue: a trawler thirty miles off Saint Simons was dead in the water, filling its bowels and sinking by the rear.

Twelve year-old Frank watched from his bedroom window, two blocks from the south jetty he now pondered, as his hero headed out to sea. Fifty mile per hour sustained winds. Ugly, ominous, dark skies churned frothy waters...he could still see the rescue craft pitching high on crests, then disappearing until out of sight into the maelstrom, never to be seen again. Ship and entire crew were literally gone with the wind.

Nothing, not even a piece of wreckage, was ever found. The memorial service displayed the crew of seven in photos framed by glorious wreaths and laid to rest upon easels. Departure was a somber procession of tacit condolences. Mother and son walked to the jetty's end, mindless of the dreary mist. They watched, along with the closest of other relatives, as the wreaths drifted out with the ebbing tide.

His mother had gone to the car to cry away her own grief, but Frank remained to the last, a little man firmly standing his ground and projecting a stiff upper lip. Not until the last sight of flowers disappeared behind the swells did the fatherless son consider turning away.

A gnarled hand placed itself on Frank's shoulder. It was Chuck, his dad's longtime partner and captain of the fleet's vessel, *Li'l Bit*.

"Your father fought to the end to save those men. He died nobly, young man, don't you ever forget it."

The scenario the young man now invented in his mind...a potential sequence to fill the void that was created when he was robbed of the opportunity to witness the passing of his protector, his teacher, his idol...his everything...was one he would recreate many times over in the coming years:

The bold darkness swept down on the rather small, yet sea worthy, coast guard craft. Neptune's left arm smashed down into the surf on their left side as Triton's reigned terror on the right. There was no escape.

"Commander, what's your command?!"

The Lieutenant stalled, only momentarily and unnoticed by the crew: "we can't run around it, we'll have to go straight through it."

The radar looked like cotton candy, the storm had engulfed them. Which way was straight ahead?

"Sir, we'll get rolled by these waves soon, if we don't back out of here..."

The Lieutenant knew they were in dire straits and at the mercy of the sea, yet equally important for the sake of the crew was for him to demonstrate some resolve. He knew if they sensed doubt in his mind; if they smelt so much as a tinge of fear emanating from his command….they were toast.

"Hard turn to the right, full bear on that crest!"

The stout craft handled well, in spite of the whirlpool of death it found itself funneling through. It was a cycle it could only maintain for a while before being swept asunder and engorged by the sea's angry belly.

No one, not one vessel in the Coast Guard's fleet had a chance on that day…. There are tales of such a rogue wave that burn on forever in the memories of families with lost loved ones. And this was a monster. A one hundred and twenty foot behemoth that raised itself out of the depths, unannounced, and with one focus, one solitary goal: to swallow up whatever vessel lie in its path at that time….or otherwise, to do nothing at all. It was the *Maiden's* unfortunate last hoorah.

The final view from the bridge: a disorienting bubbling up from whichever way was down…Tom Connor had made his last gasp of air a good one, knowing he would need whatever he could muster in order to rise back up to the surface and let his rescue beacon call on his would-be saviors. But it was not to be. He saw a crew member float past him, mouth wide open, eyes screaming a silent anguish that could only be conjured up in one's dreams. The wreckage of his mistress floating weightless and helpless all around him…the image of his boy, his darling boy, calling out for his promise to return home…and that was the sheer terror of it all…

Frank choked back some tears, feigning toughness in front of the salty old dog.

"...but he went nose-in to that black hole of the sea, and a rogue wave like that would chew up and spit out the greatest of sailors. And that's what your dad was. Truly the greatest." The family friend and confidant gave the young boy's shoulder a reassuring squeeze, and left him to ponder the thought.

Sixteen years old, and he had just become the man of the house.

Frank sank down behind his father's mahogany desk, the reverie dissipating along with the early morning fog. He repositioned his father's picture, a Coasties slogan tucked under the glass: "You have to go out, but you don't have to come back." It had taken thirty years for him to reach O-7. His young old man exited thirteen years duty an O-4 hero. *He'll always out-rank me, as it should be.*

Nearing a career's end, he was proud of his record: only four maritime fatalities on his watch. One never found. Two retrieved D.O.A., an apparent fuel spill caused an explosion, the bodies char-broiled. The fourth, solo, found face down floating in the backwaters. Empty bottle of Jack Daniels and numerous beer cans strewn about the small boat. An unlucky day of fishing had a funny way of driving a lonely angler to drink. All-in-all, Admiral Connor took pride in countless rescues and not one guardsman under his command suffered a fatality or major injury. What felt lacking was that one BIG call to action; something out of the ordinary on which he could hang his hat and feel worthy to mount his picture next to 'HIS'. *If it meant a full blown hurricane, so be it.*

Frank thumbed through the usual mundane morning report delivered along with coffee: *great...a personnel conflict...equipment malfunction issues...nothing out of the ordinary*. He looked over the updated forecast that would determine the day's modus operandi. A high-pressure system dominated the map showing clear skies and calm winds all along the southeast coast. Except for a tropical depression that had formed off western African, the chart showed nothing more than longitude and latitude lines sectioning the Atlantic into blank squares. It dawned on him he was long overdue for some R& R. *It's been two years since the ol' boat's been in the water!* Staring at the map, he focused on the inland waterways. A *week of fishing the backwater flats and bays would be a nice diversion*. An avid sportsman, the thrill was not quantity but quality of the catch he reveled in: twenty, thirty-pound Redfish deftly landed on ten-pound test line. A long, grueling battle wearing down a mighty tarpon: light tackle purposefully handicapping the titanic struggle...a true test of skillful play.

Imagining man versus beast, the questionable outcome was foiled when his adjutant encroached.

"Excuse me, Admiral, this just came in from Miami."

Handed the communiqué, the Admiral dismissed the aide and reeled himself back into the line of duty. Expecting another routine memo: *who's retiring this time?* Or the one he really dreaded being served...*another guardsman in that god-forsaken shithole, Vietnam, KIA. Not again.*

The dispatch had him hooked on the first line:

> [APB for the entire east coast. Be advised: large twin-mast schooner departed Virgin Islands protectorate heading west-northwest for U.S. mainland. Current weather conditions and forecast projects clipper nearing southeast coast within the week. Mid-Florida to Savannah considered high probability. Unconfirmed, but suspect vessel believed to be transporting large quantity of cannabis stolen from government-pharmaceutical research farms and is en-route to Cape Cod. Situation fluid. Intent to smuggle or distribute unknown at this time.]

Reading the rest of the report, he marked an "X" on the map in reference to co-ordinates of the air reconnaissance discovery. A second craft in very close proximity was cited, nature and relativity unknown. Lacking were the details of the heist and identities of the perpetrators. Connor thought to himself, *I wouldn't be broadcasting particulars of such a screw-up either, heads are probably already rolling. As far as the crew's M.O., hell, they're not even sure these guys are the culprits! Report says unconfirmed. Until it's verified, you can't just go pinning something this serious on John Q. Public.*

Studying the chart, Frank imagined himself a wind-jamming sailor. Since the days when tall ships ruled the seas, those voyaging from the Caribbean north to New England utilized the Gulf Stream for additional thrust and on days of little or no wind, the powerful current ensured at least three knots' forward progress. From the reported position, he scored a direct line west to the mainland, steering clear east of the Bahama jurisdiction. Using a bow compass, he scribed two one-hundred-mile arcs: one from Daytona, the other Jacksonville. He shaded in the area both arcs shared...*shortest distance between two points, that's where I'd be headed.* Anywhere in Florida, it did not matter, as if the ship(s) were running the coast all the way to Cape Cod, Brunswick Georgia CG Auxiliary would be standing by ready to host a warm reception, Southern style.

The prospect of playing spoiler to a smuggling operation of this magnitude was beyond enticing, a wonder drug that seemed to peel back the last five years that had relegated him to near desk-jockey status. Sure, Frank Connor had been promoted to the rank of Rear Admiral when he reached the half-century club, but such status at an auxiliary station meant rare moments at sea. It came to him as an epiphany and the reason for the funk. *Commanding from behind a desk sucks bilge water; got mold growing in my shorts, crab's legs, a walrus beached on the rocks, dehydrated and crusty.*

Thus was the drawback of being promoted to station commander. He had become sedentary, directing operations from headquarters. The last three years, the only time he had gone to sea was for the infrequent surprise inspection, appraising the seaworthiness of a ship and crew. Such was his commission, but it was about to change.

Ensign summoned, Frank requested an officers' meeting be scheduled: Captains and Lieutenants to be present. Only one of his four WPBs was out on patrol and due back later in the day for rotation.

"Arrange the briefing for seventeen hundred. Have status reports of each ship, charts, projected weather forecast for the next ten days readied in the situation room."

"Aye-aye Admiral. Will that be all, sir?"

"It'll be dinner time. Have something brought in. That'll do, Kendall."

Left alone, Frank Connor launched into formulating a plan of action. Not since having made honorary Seaman Apprentice for a day as a young lad while accompanying his father on a routine patrol had he anticipated going to sea with so much zeal. *Damn! I need to get out more.*

Before strategizing on how best to utilize his fleet, a couple of calls were in order: First, Group-Six Headquarters in Savannah, an auxiliary civil air patrol unit that had been deactivated in 1968 and recently reactivated under command of one LT David Pace. The call proved futile. For two months as of May 1st, the fledgling unit was comprised solely of a handful of cadets receiving training in a makeshift classroom at Hunter Airbase in Brunswick. Not until August could they hope to receive a pittance of decommissioned spotter-planes from Nam. Even then, overhauls would need to be performed, including patching up fuselages riddled with pesky gooks' small arms fire.

His request was simply denied: "Sorry Admiral, SOL."

The second call was dockside to the captain of *Sword*: Sloan.

"Captain, get Tarpon on the horn. Tell them to cease operations and return to port STAT. Expedite the routine maintenance on *Amberjack*, *Sword*, and *Tailfin* to level three. I want these boats first rate in forty-eight hours."

"Sir, they're not due overhaul for another month."

"I'm aware of that, Mister Sloan. I didn't say overhaul, but I do want them tip-top seaworthy. Something's come up and we're going to be conducting longer-than-normal patrols. Have the crews perform a weapon's check as well."

"Geez sir, what's this all about?"

Connor looked at his watch. 0930hrs, Tarpon's last - position was a good four hours out. "There'll be a briefing at seventeen hundred hours."

"Aye-aye, sir. Anything else?"

"Yes. You'll be filling in for me when I'm gone. You'll have Tarpon and the two Surfboats at your disposal for SAR."

"Admiral, sir. Did I here you right? You're taking command of *Sword*?" Sloan looked at the phone's receiver, tapped the cradle, "hello?"

CHAPTER TWENTY-SEVEN

Push was coming to shove. Flanked on their port side, *Slipfinger* was being herded farther north than their intended course. Follow-the-leader had evolved into an all-out race. The dogged pursuit had drawn the unidentified intruders too close for comfort.

"I don't like the looks of these guys. Got a wicked-bad feeling, man." Rick discarded the binoculars. Persona non grata now parallel, matching their speed with about a football field's separation, the glass vision only blurred details of the interlopers.

"All right, that's it. We can't keep going off course. Tell everybody to stand by and be ready for anything." Stuart's look caused his brother to caution.

"We're not starting anything. Let's just see what they want."

"I'll bet you my share it's her. And if it is, there's no fucking way these marauders are boarding our ship. She can swim over!"

"Alright, we play it your way, but I'm the one doing the talking, got it?" Unarmed, so as not to provoke, Rick left hothead at the helm and made his way mid-ship. Standing port, one hand clenching the gunwale, he breathed deep the encroaching unknown. He waved, feeling stupid. *Cordialities, my ass.*

Stuart yelled out to Doc and Kaz to release more main sail. Reacting to the unrelenting approach, Stuart kept veering starboard in a vain attempt to prolong the inevitable. With nearly all the cargo loaded aft, the uneven ballast pitched *Slip's* prow upward. Cresting undulations, crash-diving into troughs: fleeting moments of weightlessness were immediately followed by bone-jarring impacts. Kaz dropped to his knees, hurling, leaving Doc strained on the ropes. Kaz's stomach problems were as much due to mounting angst over the looming threat as they were to any seasickness suffered. Puked contents blended with ocean spray and emulsified into a greasy goulash that rendered traction negligible.

"Dam, Kaz, I could use some help here!" Doc had the line drawn taut when the foremast's main caught a gust of wind at the same time the ship's bow pitched downward. Resembling a water skier at the end of a towline, he skidded past weak-kneed Kaz, who was just struggling to his feet.

"Bring us alongside close as you can and hold course." Alaine Moreau kept his sight trained on the bumbling duo struggling on the foredeck. Rico held the wheel at one o'clock, slowly closing the gap. "Bunch of misfits. Got 'em scared shitless."

Manny, rifle shouldered, stuck his head in the cabin. "Boys are set up aft. I've got the bow."

"Good. No one makes a move unless I say so." Alaine traded field glasses for the bullhorn. "I doubt these punks are going to give us any trouble."

Helter-skelter.

"Hey, Stuart! We can't outrun them, so enough of the evasive action crap!"

Artimus came to Doc's aide. Mainsail slackened, *Slipfinger* turned more into the wind, billowed sails half collapsed as if acquiescing to a foregone conclusion.

"That's it, game over. Bring us alongside as close as you can." Alaine counted five. *They got her hidden below.*

Rick stood, unmoving, and not daring to look about to see who was where on deck.

Stuart held steady the wheel.

Both Doc and Arti had finished tying off cordage and smartly played footsies with their weapons, kicking them on deck to the port gunwale. There they stood: a knee-jerked reaction from being armed.

Kaz was out of it as he leaned propped up against the main mast awash in a shade of pale green, bathed in whatever was his last meal.

Jason peered out from the aft hatch; the Thompson locked and loaded by his side.

Wish I'd fired this more than once. Smitty chambered and collapsed the M-79 grenade launcher. Two more rounds into his pockets. *A cinch to reload.* The gang box in the captain's quarters served as a perfect firing platform, situated underneath the porthole. Latches unclipped, ever so slowly opening, he rested the tip of the barrel and knee-braced against the bulkhead so as to be unmoving. *Don't think they see me. Freeze.* A true stress test for leg muscles as he timed the pitch and roll.

Nicole, hands on hips, stood defiant. Will drew her into his arms and forced a smile. They both knew this was their doing and it was up to them to somehow, one way or the other, negotiate a way out of this mess before matters got out of hand.

"Damn, baby. We just had our first disagreement." He kissed her passionately. Face-to-face, Will remained unwavering in his demand. "As long as you don't show your pretty face, we don't know what the hell he's talking about."

"You don't understand. He's crazy! To come this far, he'll do..." she tried to push away, but he held on tight, enduring stabbing fingernails, "...he won't be denied."

"The bastard's NOT boarding this boat, Nik, plain and simple!"

"When he realizes it's you..."

"I'm pretty good at talking my way out of jams, he won't..."

"Oh, yes, he would...and I won't just stand by and let it happen!"

"Listen to me. I'm not going to play dumb if accused, it would only raise the suspicion of you being here. What I will say is we had a thing, which was my fault, but both of us realized it was wrong. We said our goodbyes and when I asked you what you planned to do, you mentioned friends in Miami you were going to stay with." The look on her face spelled doubt about the deception, and Will did his best to mask his own reservations. "Baby, just give me a chance and please stay out of sight."

Parallel at thirty yards, the cabin cruiser throttled back to match speed. "I count six: two on the bow, helmsman, smiley-face mid ship, one just sitting behind the mast, and I just saw a head peeping out of the aft hatch. I don't see anybody packing heat...no wait a minute, another one's coming out of the fore hatch.

Alaine acknowledged Manny's count and called out for everyone to keep weapons concealed.

Stuart watched with detached amusement as Will made his way to the port railing. *Should be interesting. Let's see lover boy talk his way out of this.*

Rick saw Will make his stand twenty feet to his right and had to admire the ballsy accountability while trying to blot out: *suicide by firing squad.* "Will. Let me do the talking."

"You're the captain. But if it comes down to it this is my burden, not yours."

Smitty had the launcher trained on the intruders. Wired tight over the prospect of conflict, his senses were further aroused by her proximity. A heady scent, breasts pressing his shoulder blade, it was her sultry low voice from behind that drew a bead of sweat on his brow.

"It's him. I'm going to have to go up."

"NOT a good idea. Just hold on and see what happens."

"I already know what's going to happen, Karl. If it means giving myself up to prevent people from getting hurt, so be it."

He grabbed her arm as she pivoted to jump off the box, "if it comes to that, I won't stop you. But in the meantime, I'd appreciate the company. Hopefully this'll all..."

The megaphone grated Nicole's attention. She bristled at the sound of his voice.

"Party's over boys! I believe you have something of mine and I'm here to retrieve it!"

Rick cupped his hands, "Sir, we'd be happy to oblige, but don't have a clue what it is you're after, or what you're even talking about!"

His laughter betrayed annoyance. "I don't have time for games, Yanks. You can produce her willfully for transfer and we'll be on our way, or I have other means to obtain the stolen property."

Will knew further denial was futile and felt horrible for putting Rick on the spot. "Mister Moreau. I'm the one responsible for causing you trouble. None of these guys know anything about what you are impugning. I met your wife on the beach, she was upset, and we just talked for a…"

"Nice try, mister. You think I can be played for a fool? What about the next night? I bet the two of you just wore each other out…talking!"

Will deflected the innuendo. "Sir, yes we met again. And from what she'd told me, I can't blame her for leaving you."

"What are you a marriage counselor, smart ass? You have no idea who you're dealing with, and if I were you I'd cut the bullshit and hand her over before someone gets hurt!"

"Even if I could, I wouldn't, but she's not here! She told me she was leaving for Miami to stay with friends."

"You're trying my patience, boy!" Alaine signaled his gunslingers to present arms. "I suggest you wife-nappers furl the mains and prepare to be boarded!"

"Go hide in the cargo hold! Nicole? Shit!" Smitty heard the footsteps racing up the hatchway.

The sight of guns drawn caused the on-deck crew to consider what could be the remainder of their lives cut down prematurely. Nobody moved, words were choked as they were apprehensive of the next move. Range closed to twenty yards. Up close and personal eyes were locked and time knew no boundary.

Nicole's emergence and mad dash to Will's side spared a triggered response.

"I came on my own volition! These boys had nothing to do with it. You might as well shoot me where I stand because I am done with you!" She hugged in closer to Will. "You're a sick bastard and your filthy hands will NEVER touch me again!"

A forced laugh bought him just enough time to precisely word his ultimatum. "You have no choice, princess. Either willingly or by force, you're returning with me!"

Will and Nicole locked eyes, and in that brief moment of exclusivity...a lifetime passed. Tunnel vision rendered all but themselves non-existent. In a whisper, he resigned himself to fate: "I love you, Nikki."

Turning to face the consequence, Will shouted back the unyielding reply. "You're an evil son-of-a-bitch and don't deserve her! She stays!"

Stuart stifled a grin, empathetic towards the jilted husband's dogged retrieval. If she were *his* trophy, he would do the same: no negotiation, game over. He was not about to meddle in this domestic dispute, especially after her repeated snubs. Ensuring the crew's welfare and safeguarding their assets superseded any attempt to mediate. *Well, lover boy, it's time to ante up.*

Rick sensed imminent danger. "We don't want any trouble, mister!"

"Too late for that, my friend. But you can cut your losses, if you simply hand her over!" Alaine directed his attention back to Nicole. "Thought you'd seen the last of me, my naïf coquette? Tell me love, did you fuck the whole crew for passage?"

Will lost it. "All right! That's enough, asshole! Just turn your fucking boat around and go back to whatever hole you crawled out of!"

"Hey, shit for brains, you best back away from her, or I'll have your gonads for a pair of cufflinks!"

"From what I heard, you could use some 'nads!" Defiant, Will stood his ground while wrapping an arm around Nicole's waist. She uttered something French and saluted a middle finger.

Alaine's patience had expired. He gave Manny the nod, growling the sanction. "Shoot the little prick."

At such close range, the scope was rendered useless. Manny eyed his mark, trying to line up his target with the sight tip. Nicole's proximity was not an issue as long as the two vessels maintained corresponding speed. What frustrated the shot was the out of sync pitch and roll. Up and down trying to follow Will's chest, he decided on a fixed aim dead center. Keeping the rifle stock-still, attentive to the rhythmic sequence, he timed the shot.

Will felt his hand squeezed, two words: "I love..." the impact blasting him off his feet. A one and a half spiral twisted him face down on deck.

The firearm's report was followed by a stunned moment of silence. What triggered the ensuing melee was Smitty's recoil at the sound of Nicole's hair-raising scream; a finger-twitch launched the grenade. Discharged unintentionally low, the fluke shot could not have been better placed. One skim off the water and it punched through the aft hull.

The initial explosion knocked the two gunslingers at the rear clear off their feet. Anguished howls from the shrapnel of splintered wood were mercifully silenced by the delayed secondary detonation: three hundred gallons of high octane petrol blasted the stern to smithereens. A titanic fireball mushroomed skyward. Burnt pieces of flesh and bone rained, unnoticed, in the ensuing gunfight, which lasted only seconds longer than the falling remnants of incinerated gunmen back onto the deck.

With both mains slackened, the winds having suddenly taken a hiatus, *Slip's* forward progress slowed to a negligible crawl. Separation between the combatants was minimal as bullets filled the air. It was not so much a gunfight as it was a turkey shoot slaughter. The cabin cruiser shook violently as the shockwave plastered Alaine and Rico into the cockpit's console and blown out glass sprayed Manny at the bow. The vessel immediately slanted steep from the inflow into a nonexistent stern. All but a few errant shots from the bloodied bowman laid flat on a near vertical incline, one hand grasping the railing. It was not murderous intent that emptied everyone's ammo, but rather sheer terror of such a horrific scene of carnage that stimulated adrenaline inexorable. To a mate, the only escape from the macabre nightmare was to shoot their way out.

Nicole knelt over Will, her hand pressed to his shoulder as it spewed blood. "Hang on...don't you die on me!"

Will grimaced. "Dam it, Nik! Get down before you get shot!"

She lay on top of him, her body a warm welcome.

"I'm cold." Will was going into shock.

The cruiser listed straight up. Manny's lifeless body slid, slamming into the pilot house. Another body slipped out from the cabin and into the water.

Spent, emotionally and munitions-wise, Jason, Arti, and Doc converged to console, but more so just to look away from the grizzly aftermath of blood now on their hands. Stuart had started the engine; they would circle the scene to see what evidence remained afloat. Attention was drawn to Will, as Rick and Kaz joined Nicole.

A hail of bullets strafed the schooner. Jason went down first, everyone else ducked for cover. Half crawled out of the windowless cabin which was now at water level, Alaine Moreau was not going down without a magazine full of parting shots and unintelligible expletives. He was more of a mess than he realized: one side of his body was flash-burned, searing pain emanating deep in his lower back. Blackish blood spewed the oddest reassurance: *I'll be dead before I drown*. The boat was now perpendicular, bobbing like a cork, trapped air in the bow. Vengeance was suspended as he was unable to see the schooner, but he could hear the inboard churning dead ahead. Alaine fumbled in his fishing vest and reloaded a new clip. *That's it, just come on around, fuck-heads*. "God damn, what the hell's stuck in me!" More blood passed through gritting teeth as he reached around and felt the splintered pole. *You got to be kidding!* "Fuck me with a gaff!"

Might as well. Smitty had just emerged topside brandishing newly nicknamed *'Liberator.'* Jacked from the decisive opening salvo, he swaggered port aft. *Slip* pivoted under diesel power. Still reeling from the incident that was a lifetime over and done with...dreamlike in seconds, the only ones not tending to Will and Jason were Stu and Art as they bore witness to the grenadier's closing argument. Taking aim at the craft's underbelly, the M-79 discharged its second barrel at close range.

'Bloop', 'wham-bam!' Smitty almost missed. Three feet below the tip of the bow disintegrated, the up-down bobbing not taken into account. It mattered not, the trapped air having been released; it only meant a prolonged *'ta-ta'*.

Arti was about to critique the lousy shot when rapid fire sent bullets whizzing high, perforating sail cloth and dropping everyone flat on deck.

Alaine felt the painful inhalation was to be his last. The absence of bow, a shard of which was embedded in his left eye which was quickly going blind, the only thing he could see on which to expend his ordinance was the upper half of the schooner's flapping sails. One more finger-squeeze as he faded, holding on to the 'click.' His last thought: *I won't drown.*

Nicole had removed her bloodied tank top, ripping it for a tourniquet. Rick was by her side sorting through the first aid kit for what was required. The bullet wound pulsed blood from dead center the left shoulder.

"Hold on, baby, just hold on." Gently rolling Will onto his side, she needed to see if and where there was an exit hole.

"Feels like a sledgehammer hit me," grimaced Will.

Kaz steadied Will on his good shoulder, as Nicole ripped open the back of his shirt. She fingered the hole, cloaked in blood, which elicited a yelp and spastic jerk.

"Sorry. Bullet went straight through. I got to do something, this might hurt." Fingers pressed both sides of his shoulder; Will writhed while grabbing Kaz's arm.

"OW, take it easy!"

"I think it missed bone. Blood is slowing, we got to hope that means the artery's okay."

"Might be one lucky dude, Will." Rick doused the shoulder with peroxide, waited for the effervescence to subside then doused again.

That broke Will's stare, which was locked onto a face he was trying so hard not to show his worry. *Florence Nightingale...* "Jeez, Rick. You gonna' drown me?"

"That ain't nothing. This might sting a bit." Rick poured povidone-iodine front and back. He was right.

Grabbing Kaz's neck, Will sat straight up. The sudden move was dizzying.

"Thanks, what a cooperative patient. Now we can get the dressing on. Wrap you up and get your ass below. I'm sure Doc has some good shit left for the pain."

"GOD, it fucking hurts!"

"Bet it does, but you're going to have to tough it out on your feet 'til we get you down the hatch. Try and focus on something."

"I'm doing just that, Rick." Zeroed in on Nicole's aqua bikini top as she leaned over, wiping beaded sweat from his forehead, the pleasant view suffered Will through the pain until gauze and bandages crisscrossed his chest, neck, and arm.

"Baby, I'm going to have to make you a sling. Can you stand and we'll get you below?"

"You taking me to bed?"

"I'm putting you to bed." Nicole was relieved by the grin and suggestive remark. *He's going to be alright...I hope.*

Jason was lucky, his wound bought him a superficial battle scar: outer right thigh grazed. Doc had him cleaned and wrapped, helping him to his feet.

"Hurt?"

"Just burns like hell."

"I'm going below to see what Will needs, I'll bring you up a nice downer."

Jason held on to the railing, seemingly unmindful of what had just been said.

"Hey, you okay? What is it?"

"I'll be damned, that's it."

"What?" Doc looked out over the side, a bevy of fins sliced the water. Meters below he saw a very large gray outline cruising slowly, he shivered in the high-noon warmth.

"I just figured out how to explain to Dave's family why there's no body for burial."

"Holy shit! Just spare them the details." Doc turned away right into Arti's plume of smoke.

"Where you going? This is National Geographic stuff."

Mute, sidestep, Doc left the scene but not the imaginings.

"That blast, hell of a dinner bell, huh?"

Jason acknowledged with a slow nod, absorbed in the confluence, at the same time a subconscious eulogy composed a funeral void in its entity.

Art puffed pensive, perceptive to Jason's thoughts. He talked only to fill an awkward void. "They seem to be scrounging table scraps. Those poor bastards blown to hell, scattered and seared medium well. Sharks mop up the appetizer, hopefully attention turns to the main course." A pause, tobacco smoldered. "Last asshole must have got hung up and gone down with the ship."

Stuart kept *Slip* over the wreckage, idling, every now and then a little power to compensate for drift. There were no longer any visible boat markings, only nondescript flotsam remained. Two bodies were afloat, and no one relished the idea they might have to riddle them with bullets. No one except Stuart, who was frustrated Will had not bought a date with his maker.

Two 'ludes and nearly a half-fifth of rum as chaser was not morphine, but it did the job well enough. Nicole sat on the bunk, her fingertips combing through Will's hair. Was that sweat or dried blood she kept getting her fingers caught in?

"Good work, Nikki. He'll be zonked for quite a while." Rick stood motioning to Kaz and Doc. "Come on, you guys. Got to assess damage and make necessary repairs so we can get the hell away from this spot."

"Thanks. I'll be up shortly, just need moment. I'm sorry for all of this."

"Take your time, rest if you need to. Might be a good idea anyway." His glance upward told her they were both thinking the same thing: *best lay low for a while*.

In a style developed as a coping mechanism that endured the travesty of a marriage in name only, she replied sardonically: "well, who said divorce proceedings were long drawn out affairs?" The impassive tone and unreadable face blanked everyone for a sensible comeback. Topside beckoned posthaste.

Left alone, Nicole needed the quiet solitude to regroup. She gazed at nothing, reflexively caressing a head out cold. It was not shock, surely not grief...*so long, you bastard*...more like a stimulus overload, then sudden release. Violently abrupt, everything happening so fast, and in the aftermath, bedside to a lover who willingly took a bullet and was now hopefully on the mend. Senses were dulled as the incident replayed in her mind's eye, but what consumed her thoughts most was the stark reality of her own autonomy that had been gained...*I am free. I am me*. All aspirations, desires that were until now only dreams denied, flooded her imagination.

How long had the bottle been there as a blurry focal point, a simple prop retaining unseeing sight? Reverie slowly faded, giving way to the here and now: **tat-tat-tat-tat**!

Oh god, still shooting?

The feeding frenzy swept clean unrecognizable chunks of human chum. One of the two floaters flailed like a rag doll. The food fight turned into a gruesome tug of war testing Art and Jason's intestinal fortitude and ability to endure. The struggle in the water matched the one of machismo on deck: who would be first to turn away. Engrossed in such grotesque ferocity that both secretly wished would hurry up and end, it was a monster shark that brought the contest to a final close and spared the onlookers' stomachs from roiling. A power ascent from the depths, the shredded body somewhat in one piece bobbed upward in a mighty breach. The carcass was enveloped in bone-crushing jaws, as the horror show's mash-ending back into the depths jolted Art to preempt another grueling performance.

"Fuck that." He picked up the half-spent weapon which still lie where Jason had gone down, took aim at the remaining cadaver, and expended the last of the rounds.

Nicole saw the smoking gun, caring nothing about the particulars of who or why. Resolute, her eyes fixed on both brothers at the helm; she approached with a simple request.

"Could we PLEASE get underway?"

Slip, now aptly coined *Swiss-Cheese* by Artimus, limped away. Her sails were shot full of holes, the portside hull riddled, several feet of cordage flailed in the breeze. There would be no rest for the weary minus one. Repairs would have to be made on the fly, as priority was given to distancing themselves from culpability. The last twenty-four hours of cat-and-mouse had set a significantly more northerly course and the pervasive beam reach wind from the south was not going to make it any easier to get back on track. Sails were configured to accommodate a gradual tack towards port, and a decision was made to maintain their heading until darkness. It was the first inadvertent

Slipfinger Nine

miscalculation that would sail them into a morass they would soon realize ships of the wind best avoid at all costs.

Some actions are hardly noteworthy; others live on to tell their tale in the indelible memory of recorded time and remind us for years to come of the importance of their impact.

CHAPTER TWENTY-EIGHT

Slip's bow was on a line with the setting sun.

Arti noted the console's compass. "Slight heading back to southwest, but damn if it doesn't feel we're being pushed farther west-northwest. Estimated speed, ten knots at best, wind's fading."

"What's our position?"

"I'm working on it."

The testy tone was dismissed. Frayed nerves lingered from the engagement annulling one woman's incubus; deportment of the crew was pensive. Tattered secondary sails above the mains would have to suffice as wind-sieves until the crew got back into sync. Shift-watch was in disarray; sleep would have to be a catch-as-catch-can affair at least for the time being. Rick's crew, down one, finally turned in mid-afternoon, a mere three hours before normal wake-up. Would just the three of them be able manage, or would it require staggered downtime to accommodate?

All because of a piece of ass. Stuart imagined his weight on a pillow balancing the crew four and four.

"A little out of practice, but I think I got it." Arti laid down the sextant and worked the protractor.

Jason's monotone weather update broke through, crackling over the comm. "Light easterlies downgrading to negligible. Clear skies. Low-pressure system moving southeast off Georgia coast. Marine advisory: dense fog ahead of the front."

"That's great, Jay. While you're at it, let me know what the weather's like in Trinidad."

"What? Why?"

"That's what I just asked. The forecast for the east coast makes as much sense as the Pacific Northwest! I don't give flying-flip about fog off the god damn coast, we'll be lucky to make it in three days. I suggest you stop moping around that cubbyhole of yours, go wake up what's left of the night crew and get your butt up here to relieve Cookie so he can fix us some chow."

"Intend to do just that, sir captain, sir." *Jeez*. Jason was not sulking, he was decompressing: feet up, eyes closed...*fucking monitoring the Ham*!

The only one needing rousing was Smitty, his snoring assured the others that sleep was no longer possible. Even Will, still dopey, was sitting up and being fitted with a sling, insistent he was able enough to offer one hand at the wheel.

Arti scribbled his calculations. "Got the coordinates, I think. Relative vicinity: 24.08 degrees latitude, minus 63.72 longitude, maybe a tad off." Using a straightedge, he drew a line east from the northern-most islands of the Bahamas, another slightly northeast from the Turks. Arti rubbed his eyes, "hope I'm wrong, but we might just be sailing smack dab into the dead zone."

Time check: sunset at twenty-thirty hours. A survey of the eastern sky behind them revealed the first of what would be countless stars twinkling through the black of night. Of the day's madness, the cordage had been mostly repaired or replaced, but a patchwork of sails still remained. Jason's sore leg was not an issue, but his growing cavalier attitude was most concerning. Stuart reckoned at least a day of intermittent siestas, when the work would allow, would be necessary to get shifts back on track. All complications he put squarely on *'his'* blown out shoulder; it was all he could do to veil his disappointment Mister Bradford was down, but not out, for the count.

Obstinate fixation welled in vengeance: *long night ahead, lonesome lady, opportune time for tact over a nightcap...* Although, much to Stuart's dismay and disbelief, the sling-armed Will had risen. Nicole's helping hand and Smitty's bringing up of the rear foiled his fantasy.

It was a brusque assembly. Rick insisted they had everything under control and the medicated Will, now a man of few words, affable and mellow, negated any potential for confrontation. Twice, snide remarks were blown away in the light breeze. Stuart realized that engaging in further attempts to bait Will would only shadow-box himself into a corner most unbecoming, not to mention self-defeating. Denied the satisfaction of exerting his prominence, he left in a huff.

Midnight on the Atlantic was eerily morphing into a resemblance: The Big Pond.

A glasslike surface and only the slightest zephyr made forward progress negligible at best. Will had been provided a stool on which to take off a load and steady him against the very gentle sway. Feeling puny, languid from Doc's 'under-the-counter' medications for pain and the mind-numbing boredom of holding course a ship moving as slow as a constipated turtle, it was the sporadic pang of muscle spasms gripping his shoulder that kept him alert enough to follow Rick's simple instruction: "just keep the bow in line with that bright star." In the hours that seemed to last forever, only once was it required that Rick choose a new pinprick of light as a heading. It was surely not due to their snail's pace progress, but rather *spin*ster Mother Earth turning on her axis.

Kaz came topside, too troubled to sleep. Vexed over all that so far had come to pass, distressed by an imagination running rampant of every worst-case scenario that could possibly lie ahead, his catatonic appearance was akin to Queequeg after interpreting the rolled bones and realizing they were doomed in their quest of the Great White Whale.

Smitty sensed the trepidation as Kaz joined the group lolling about on the foredeck. Nicole thought he was sleepwalking, but when prompted Kaz acknowledged with a blank nod that he was indeed coherent. Rick was in the middle of kudos on Smitty's fortuitous potshot...

"I don't care if it was luck, skill, or divine providence. It was a lights out, hot shot and quite possibly the reason we're still around and able to talk about it!"

Will chimed in from the helm. "Didn't see it Smithers, but sounds to me you were a one-man wrecking crew, a real show-stopper."

The accolades all started with Nicole's kiss on the cheek and a sincere 'thank-you.' By now, Smitty was looking for an out from the lavished praises and Will's only speaking engagement just opened the escape hatch.

"Nothing but a fluke, o' buddy o' mine. You say show stopper? I actually DID stop a show one time."

Opportunity was seized to delve into yet another ridiculous chronicle as Smitty rose to the occasion. The impromptu stand-up routine was not so much for the audience's benefit as it was yearning to change the subject. Rehashing the event was bothersome; he had disintegrated two lives and for all practical purposed doomed the others. Blood was on his hands and regardless the circumstances (*self-preservation*), he felt tainted and marked as an executioner. It turned his stomach and the karma was most disconcerting. Try as he may, he could not shake the notion that something dreadful lie in store as recompense. He was a modern-day Jonah and had subjected this crew to paying for it along with him. Not expecting any whale to come by, he threw himself at the next closest thing to it.

It was uncanny how his segues could catch an audience off guard. Even if they wanted to bow-out, the stories were so preposterous that everyone was hooked from the start and stood by to endure the absurdities so they could challenge the authenticity.

"Back when I was fifteen..."

"Oh no, here we go again. Nice going, Will." Rick plunked down beside Nicole. "This guy's incorrigible. I don't believe a word from his mouth."

"Me and Johnny Lamonte decided we'd head on into town for a little culture. Small town, and no wheels, meant no girlfriends, and in between football and basketball season, just another stir-crazy Friday night. Anyways, we hitched a ride to the high school and copped two tickets to the highly anticipated opening night of Oklahoma. I must admit, our school's thespians were deserving of mass appeal for the performing arts. Hell, the town would empty like Green Bay on Packer's game-day, the school gymnasium packed like sardines. Fold-out chairs covered every square inch of the court's floor, bleachers filled to capacity, standing room only on the back wall."

"Man, where you going with this?" Kaz's query was a relief to all, the story-telling monolog had cracked the shell, and the worry-wart was emerging.

"Patience, please." Smitty got a kick out of stringing them along, but it was Kaz's re-emergence that fetched a grin of success. "There we sat, dead center, on the gym floor. Regardless what play was being performed, knowing the actors and actresses made it all the more enchanting. To watch them in costume, taking on personas and acting so much as to convince they exist only in the characters portrayed, what a trip. It was the lead actress, Patricia, who captivated my attention. One time her brother had me over for the night. I walked in on her coming out of the shower and ever since then, even at fourteen, she left an indelible impression."

"Man, where are you going with this? Just a trip down memory lane for you?"

"Yeah, what do *we* get out of it?"

Smitty raised his hands in a 'whoa-take-it-easy' gesture, unable to suppress a grin that he had succeeded in frustrating the captain. "There she was on stage, a whirling-dervish spinning in dance. Now, I'm not a fan of musicals, but I must admit her do-si-do flashing lavender panties underneath a petticoat WAS a nice distraction. Man, did she have legs!"

Nicole's rolling of her eyes conveyed her bemusement at the simple pleasures of men.

Timing was everything. Before changing gears to the absurd, Smitty lit up a Camel. "So, there I was in my private fantasy, watching eighteen year old Patty do her thing, when mom's fire-brand chili started roiling down below. I was trapped. Thirty people on each side with hardly any legroom...doomed to sweat out the ultimate test of mind over matter. I started expanding, focused on only my stomach pain from the burning cauldron. Fidgeting in my seat, and jammed between my buddy and this old fart, desperation set in as I tried to delay the inevitable."

Nicole looked to Rick. "Is this like his other stories?"

"Unfortunately, yes, except this one might top all for a new low."

"There was Pat and her leading man, center stage. Music stopped, he had her in his arms leaning her back. You could hear a pin drop in the auditorium as he professed his love. I'd regrouped just a bit in my seat, settling in so I could bleed off some of the gas. At this point I didn't care who was offended, I was more concerned about shitting my pants."

"Oh, brother, you gotta be kidding me! Man, you're so full of it." Kaz stood to leave, but clearly it was a show of protest regarding the jester's legitimacy. He was not going anywhere until hearing the final act.

Unable to suppress a smile, Nicole sat captive while admiring crazy Karl's cleverness. Not so much the wacky, tall tale, or his delivery, but rather the inflection and animation that made him seem almost cartoonish. It was a realization that the funnyman's purpose had succeeded in having the desired effect. The shell of despair had cracked from the outside; Kaz unwittingly broke through from his cloistered confinement. Nicole returned to the farceur's foolish follies. *Way to go.*

"...I underestimated how explosive I was, big time. And it just so happened to be the moment in the play everyone had anticipated. You could hear a pin drop. Would they kiss? Leaned back into his arms, her lips so close to her lovers', tragically, they were never to meet. I detonated, fouling the impassioned scene. It was so loud that both actors stalled, looking out into the audience with pruned expressions. Like a rolling wave, starting with the row of old ladies in front of us, everyone directed their attention towards ground zero. Poor John was caught totally off guard, but I had my best poker face of innocence which deflected the scathing looks of disgust from me and onto my mortified fall guy. I got up, looked down disapprovingly at my shell-shocked friend, and swept my head back and forth in utter rebuke at his lack of self control. I was absolved of the flagrant interruption as the entire gymnasium zeroed in their disgusted discontent. I excused myself down the row, all the while shaking my head in disdain, making it to the aisle and never took my eyes off the exit sign."

Will thought he had heard all of Smitty's soiled soliloquies. He could not resist playing the straight man. "What happened to him? Did he get outta there and kick - your ass?"

"Don't know what happened to him, I didn't stick around. He did become somewhat of a small-town celebrity though."

"Yeah, I bet. What a pal."

"The weekly rag got a hold of someone's snapshot, gave him front page billing. Red-faced, veins popping out of his temples, and beads of sweat on his brow, the caption read: 'Explosive Outburst, An Untimely Show-Stopper!'"

"With friends like you, who needs enemas? Did you ever come clean?"

Smitty replied, throwing Kaz a knucklehead curve. "Yup, when I got home and changed my drawers."

"No, smart ass. Did you take credit for the deed?"

"Hell no, I made my buddy famous. Why would I deny him the notoriety?"

"Jeezus, Smitty. You ever think about taking your stupid show on the road?" Rick walked out on the end of the ludicrous yarn. Passing Will, he mumbled, "I'll take the wheel as soon as I relieve myself the bullshit. Going to the head."

The remainder of the night was mundane; the sedentary night crew's only duty was to spot each other sleep. Kaz finally found it, courtesy of the bedtime story. Nicole, Smitty, and Rick each took two hours at the wheel steering a ship that was barely making headway.

Will got a free pass due to his throbbing shoulder and requisite pain killers; he lay on deck. The wound never allowed sleep, only rest punctuated by bolts of stabbing pain. Careful not to disturb his sleeping beauty, he sat upright and considered her loveliness. It was indisputable. Was it worth it? *Without question.* Will winced at the thought it had nearly been his last day. Comprehending the close call, his existence seemed as ethereal as the surroundings. An unearthly contrast of color: pale blue-green morning sky, strange mercurial slate-colored sea of glass looking thick and heavy...*quicksilver* came to mind. Sails were rendered obsolete in the dead calm, intermittent swells creaked *Slip's* bones; a gentle rock-a-bye left him feeling like the sole survivor on a ghost ship.

To his feet, he surveyed the deck. Smitty was considerate; far removed and curled up at the bow, his snoring was a makeshift foghorn. Still woozy, *no more pills, please...just gotta buck up and deal with the pain*, Will floated his way to Rick who was slumped over the wheel, still standing.

"Captain, you alright?"

"Ah, yea...just dozing. How you feeling?"

"Shoulder hurts like hell, but I'm done trying to mask the pain...got to get my sea legs back. Need to eat something, but I don't know if it'll stay put." Will steadied himself, grasping one of the spokes. "What the hell did we get into? It's like a pond out there. Dead calm and hardly any noise at all..."

"Got chased too far north, we're obviously off-course. Sargasso Sea, Bermuda Triangle, Horse Latitudes, take your pick."

"What latitudes?"

Arti appeared out of nowhere. Smoldering pipe in hand, a prop replacement for cigarette, and an expressive look almost as lifelike as the inflection he articulated, the impressionist paraphrased a spot-on rendition Rod Serling's opening monologue; "We've traveled through another dimension, a dimension not only of eerie sight and absence of sound, but of mind. A journey into a wondrous water-world of boundaries, unfathomable to the imagination. There was a signpost somewhere in the dark of night that must have been missed; we've crossed over into an area of both shadow and substance, SCREWED...the Twilight Zone."

Indeed they had.

Rick explained, "In days of old, when voyagers were dependent solely on wind, this place was a kiss of death where intruders languished, facing dreadful alternatives of how to perish. Madness, dehydration, starvation; it was their horses, brought to the New World that were begrudgingly their last resort to salvation. Those they didn't eat were pitched overboard to salvage what remained of potable water. Hence, the 'Horse Latitudes'."

"Thanks for the history lesson. So now what do we do?" Will grimaced. He let go of his handhold to adjust the sling on his arm."

"How much diesel we got, Art?"

"Two fifty-five gallon drums and roughly another drum's worth in the tank. All that tooling around back in the islands, we've burned through one drum already. It's not exactly a gas miser. She's undersized, utilitarian for getting in and out of port, just not extended jaunts. Add all that extra ballast…three, maybe four miles per gallon. That means slow and steady, easy on the rpm's."

The sight of Nicole had them all contemplative. She sat up on deck, combing out her tousled hair with long fingernails.

A loud snort from the bow broke the spell. "Fucker needs a nose job. Will, go wake up Foghorn Leghorn."

Nicole waved Will off. It was her pleasure to interrupt Smitty's slumber for having endured shallow sleep thanks to the insufferable serenade. It was the trio's fancy watching her traipse with a purpose. Her sashay in skimpy shorts commanded their shared attention as Rick resumed his dictation.

"Get everybody up, Art, we got sails to furl. While that's being done, ready the diesel. Check oil, hoses, top her off. We'll power our way out of this morass or otherwise run as long the fuel lasts."

"On it."

"You feel up to taking the wheel once we get underway?"

"I feel useless as it is, Rick. All I need is something on an empty stomach, hopefully I can keep it down, and I'll be good to go as long as you need me."

"That's good, Will. Once we're underway, we'll set a compass heading straight ahead west and not deviate. I'll get cookie to whip us up some grub."

Kaz was in the galley, Arti conducting PM, Will getting together a mindset for a long day of weaning off the meds and booze. Both captains pitched in to expedite the furling of limp canvass that would only serve to be a drag on fuel consumption. The resistance of moving forward into stagnant air, *Slip* was stripped of her whites. Against a backdrop of placid, dark waters devoid of whitecaps, doing so also presented a much less conspicuous mark to any high-flying snoop. Such a prospect, unsettling, kept all eyes reverting to the spacious skies and festered contentious deliberation among the crew. Surely by now authorities were scrambling to ascertain probable suspects: *how many dots might have they connected? Process of elimination: how many vessels sighted in the area by local mariners were of sufficient size to make off with so voluminous a heist? Inquiries of who left when at which ports of departure. Then there was the issue of Nicole and the demise of her now insignificant other. Missing persons report filed on BOTH of them? No doubt.*

If they knew how spot-on their suppositions were, the Sargasso would be dumped on post-haste, aptly renaming the sea: Sar 'GRASS' o.

Interviews were just short of coercion: marinas, port authorities, local mariners on the waters in and around Pillsbury Sound. Additionally, associates of Nicole and a husband, both of whom now, after nearly seventy-two hours of having vanished, qualified for an APB missing persons report.

Too many clues paralleled in straight lines, the pathway was strewn with breadcrumbs. Even the Keystone Cops could flatfoot their way to conclusions that were NOT coincidental.

The information compiled was damning:

#1. A particular vessel with an odd name, uniquely crewed, cargo hold more than adequate to accommodate such an ill-gained windfall. #2. The Moreau estate's staff accounts of domestic violence in a relationship that never fully quantified a marriage. The fateful night that sent her packing and the subsequent pursuit of a very pissed-off, insignificant other. #3. Eyewitness accounts of clandestine meets: her beau just happened to be a crewmember of the suspect ship that was now long gone. #4. Where the hell did Alaine Moreau's stately yacht disappear to? SAR came up empty; port of departure known, heading unknown, it was as if the infamous Bermuda Triangle once again reared its ugly devil's head and consumed a boat and crew while leaving no trace. Until something evidential provided proof otherwise, the mystery would remain open to the probability that there was a direct link to the investigation that was now well outside their jurisdiction.

CO Wallace at Saint Thomas Headquarters ordered the detailed findings and suppositions be dispatched to

Miami, where upon the update was forwarded up the east coast.

The report captivated Frank Connor. Full of intrigue yet nothing concrete, no warrants for arrest: swashbuckling piracy on a grand scale, possible stowaway, husband of considerable prominence jilted then vanishes in pursuit...and yet, the entire message only surmised "possible" suspects. Nothing conclusive.

Again, these wild delusions of grandeur rivaled that of his father's heroic final call of duty and brought imagined feathers in his retirement cap. *What if the schooner and crew WERE the perpetrators, twentieth century pirates of the Caribbean? What if the lady in question wasn't a willing participant, but kidnapped? What if her prominent shithead of a husband and his cohorts were murdered? Talk about hitting the trifecta! What a bust it would be!*

One by one, sails needing repairs were dropped. Holes from the firefight were sewn with spare fabric in a patchwork fashion: efficient in utilitarian effect, deficient in aesthetics.

Slipfinger chugged along just shy of trolling speed, conserving fuel, easy on the diesel. Steady as she goes, the only time requiring deviation from an otherwise beeline course setting was to circumvent huge mats of sargassum, which guaranteed to entangle the propeller and shaft.

Besides the repair work and deck being swabbed of the bloodletting, one other priority was in due process of achievement: everyone managed to catch at least forty winks, and by doing so, officially ended the crying about sleep deprivation.

Meanwhile, Smitty had either run out of routines or the tension building about everything simply called for more sporting action. With nothing much left to do, Rick ordered a "fish-off." Three teams of three, one hour to test their angling skills; winners for largest fish win two pounds of profit from the losers' share. Stuart agreed, but only if there was no handicapping. Nicole and Smitty could NOT take the rod out of Will's cradled arm. If the fish was too much for him and he had to hand it off...forfeit.

Silver spoons of varying sizes up to six inches, single hook, thirty pound test line, and no weights due to the slowest of trolling speeds. Billfish, wahoo, tuna and dolphin, were potential catches.

Stuart made certain of his bragging rights with a good size wahoo that Roger promptly went to work on cutting into filets. Doc came up short with a dolphin; Rick got a hold of something that broke his line.

The final group closed out the tournament, which did serve its purpose. Late afternoon, the mind-numbing hours of tedium having been endured, and forty five minutes into their allotted time...not even a bite. Will had reeled it in, his bad arm sore from cradling the rod and wrestling with the lure's drag. Smitty commented on their shitty luck of the draw having coincided perfectly with the worst time of day for fishing: "must be a change in barometric pressure, shift in tide. Hell, if I was a fish, I wouldn't be hanging around in this shit..."

Nicole's rod bent into a crescent and she lurched forward against the aft parapet. What ensued was a thirty-minute battle captivating everyone's attention. When the blue marlin broke the surface in a tail dance, it was met with a bevy of 'oohs' and 'ah's', it's beauty was so striking.

Immediately, Stuart began defending his number one ranking. "Unless you get it alongside in the next twelve minutes, time's up."

The billfish was not trophy-sized by a long shot, but being immature meant youthful vigor and lighting fast speed. Nicole refused offers of relief; she wanted the personal gratification she would keep within herself of having displaced Captain Asshole as honorary angler extraordinaire.

As well as she fought the good fight, she did not have the advantage of sports fishermen cradled in a chair and an expert captain working in tandem. *Slipfinger* plowed ahead, no stopping or reverse engines. Twenty feet from the stern the marlin, looking to be one-fifty to two-hundred pounds, shook its head violently on the surface then, in a last-chance power dive, went deep. Eighty-pound test reached the breaking point and Nicole jerked backwards so many steps.

"Too bad, but I would have won anyways, times already up."

"You're such a gracious winner. You must get tired stroking yourself."

Rick was not about to see his brilliant idea, that did in fact while away the monotonous hours, end in a tit-for-tat between his brother and Nicole. He knew any continuance would only get ugly; issues that had nothing to do with fishing. "Alright that's it. Show's over, bets are off."

The consensus among the crew was the epic battle and near catch far surpassed Stuart's haul that was now being prepared. So they would eat in his honor, but Nicole's titanic struggle would be the topic of discussion.

Pan-fried dolphin steaks. The honorary victor was actually Roger, who pulled off a culinary feat. The only one not offering kudos was Stuart. He remained stolid, biting his tongue while eating his fish, and enduring the lavish praises heaped on the woman he still envisaged as the ultimate catch.

Admiral Connor strode the wharf, a bounce in his heavy step as he reviewed a rare sight: all four WPBs in port. *Tarpon* had returned from patrol last and was anchored in the channel tributary. The trio being outfitted for an extended tour moored dockside nose-to-tail, occupying every linear foot of the quay. Salutes were acknowledged from *Tailfin,* then *Amberjack,* and decorum greeted him dockside at *Sword.* The boatswain's call whistled 'flag-rank' officer about to board.

"Welcome aboard, Admiral." Chief Petty Nelson met him half-way on the plank. "Got your sea legs?"

"Chief, I'd appreciate it if you'd shit-can the admiral crap while we're at sea. Captain or Skipper will suffice."

"Ah, yes sir."

"Are the captains here?"

"Just waiting on *Tarpon's.* Nelson looked over his shoulder, the rubber raft was just now pulling away. "He's coming, sir. Let's go below, I got coffee and the chart set up, as requested."

Evening time and the crew was back on normal shifts. A moonlit night, steady drone of the diesel, and rock-a-bye swaying of the ship made for ideal sleeping conditions. The only duty that required attentiveness was steering clear of the expansive clumps of algae-laced seaweed. No one relished the idea of a midnight swim to untangle a seized propeller.

"Well, if we're lucky, we'll be free of this shit before the fuel runs out. By my calculations, we're only a hundred miles inside the southern semicircle. If we were dead center another 300 miles north, I doubt we'd make it out."

"When do you think that will be?," asked Nicole.

"Through the night, into the day...by high noon, I hope. Might be running on fumes by then."

Passing time at the wheel, the crew of three hunkered down with nothing to do but listen, as Rick spoke of this otherworldly place they hoped to soon escape:

A legendary sea of lost ships and unexplained phenomena. Columbus had even made note it was a place to be circumvented at all cost. Derelict vessels, shipshape but deserted, were found by more fortunate trespassers. On one occasion, a slave ship was sighted with nothing but skeletons aboard. In 1840, the *Rosalie* sailed into these waters...then vanished. Some forty years later, the schooner *Ellen Austin* reportedly came upon a deserted ship that matched records of the *Rosalie*. Placing a crew aboard, the two sailed in tandem for port. Two days later the schooner, lagging far behind, was sighted sailing erratically. When boarded again, the ship's crew had vanished.

In 1857, the baroque *James B. Chester* was found deserted in the Sargasso Sea, chairs kicked over and a stale -

meal on the mess table. Countless other bizarre cases, more contemporary: 1945, the Lost Squadron. Five Avengers on a routine training exercise vanished into thin air...still not found. Then, there was a large tanker, gone without a trace. Countless smaller craft, but what was spooky: many last transmissions, reported sights on radar, compasses gone haywire.

"At least we're not solely dependent on the wind. In the old days, men would go stark raving mad, languishing in vacuous despair."

"Jeez, Rick, thanks!" Smitty requested the plank be extended so he could walk it and be done with it.

Dawn's earliest light surfaced a hair-raising wake up call. A well-rested crew scurried topside to the hollering of "thar she blows." What was thought to be the hump of a rising whale, a couple hundred yards off the port bow, grew to immense proportions. The slate black behemoth kept rising, coming into full view. Heads peered out from the conning tower and salutations were exchanged; the encounter lasted long enough for the submarine to replenish with fresh air before submerging back to the deep. Almost two days of solitude sharing the vast watery expanse with no one, the ephemeral engagement left the crew contemplative that they had just witnessed an apparition.

"Wow, that was freaky."

"No Kaz, what's freaky is we've burned two-thirds our fuel." Artimus wiped his hands with an oily cloth, having added quarts of oil. He looked to Stuart and Rick. "We better find some wind in the next eight hours or we'll all be galley slaves rowing our way out of this fucked-up place."

"Yeah, well, all we can do is press on and hope for the best." Will tugged at his sling, clearly agitated with the painful inconvenience. "In the meantime, we make the best of doing nothing and get cracking on all that ganja piled up in the hold. I can at least man the scales and inventory."

Stuart was visibly perturbed. He had already decided that would be job number one, but Will's suggestion beat him to it. Anyone but **him** and it probably would not have been an affront.

Exasperated by the overt animosity, Rick butted in, preempting his brother from starting the day off on a wrong foot. He could tell by his scowl there was a caustic remark about to be hurled at Will.

"Kaz. How's 'bout some grub?" He turned to his brother who was stewing, "we're going below, and since there's nothing to do up here besides pull your pud, Doc and Jason can join in the production line."

Art had exempted himself, monitoring the engine that was running a bit hot and using an inordinate amount of oil.

Rick handed over the wheel to Stu. "Steer clear the gulfweed. First indication of a breeze, or any vessel that looks like it's coming our way, holler."

Zeppelin led to *The Who*, who rocked and rolled into the *Stones*. Doc had cued up the reel-to-reel, insisting tunes would make assembly line work more productive. It did.

Denuded stalks and twigs were compiled and then hauled topside to be ditched overboard and meld with the floating clumps of seaweed. Compressing, weighing, shrink wrapping, and documenting; the twenty-pound bricks were stacked proportionately against both sides of the ship's hull. One hundred two-foot square blocks and the cargo hold took on the appearance of a mini-warehouse, each cube representing a ton.

It was a non-stop process of asses and elbows. Dank and dark, stuffy and sticky, the band sweated to *The Band* commiserating the shape they were in: inadvertently stoned. Close confines, air permeated with a distinctive scent, resin soaking skin...by osmosis work became numbing, yet everyone managed to smile through the arduous task. 'Be happy in your work' need not be decreed.

Every hour, Arti came topside to inform Stuart of the fuel situation and the engine's heated strain.

"Just drained the last of the barrel. Full tank, that'll buy us two hours and minutes before we shut down"

"It's gonna' be close, but I think we're nearing the devil's asshole. I've just started seeing negligible ripples, sporadic, but a vestige of air movement nonetheless."

"So we run her dry. We're going to need some from somewhere unless you plan on sailing big mamma right into port. That I'd like to see."

"Already thought of it. I'm sure one of our 'connections' would be happy to accommodate, barter a couple of kilos for petrol. We near the Bahamas, make contact, and tell our client to bring along reserves."

Stu had been waiting, wondering if and when his fancy would be making an appearance. Another load of unmarketable refuse was ready to be hauled up and it was Nicole who insisted fresh air from the toxic quarters. Arti talked on about the idea of negotiating fuel for fodder; he conversed with himself.

The lilt in her 'hello' and impish smile, self-conscious from being high, made her appear approachable or, rather, vulnerable. It was a complete misread. Blinded by obsession and unfounded assumption, the parley was misconstrued for something it was not. Nicole sashayed away in her lighthearted mood, oblivious to the scrutiny as she cast upon the water the leftovers of labor. The cordial greeting festered in Stuart a fantasy completely void of sagacity. Like a junkie hooked, he was powerless against his fixation.

Celebrations were in order once the cache was wrapped, stacked, and recorded. The official tabulation was beyond their wildest expectations. It was like the parable of Jesus doling out the basket of fish. The more they processed, the more the stockpile quantified.

"And the official tabulation is..." Will penciled the numbers. "Two rows of six stacks, times one hundred packages per stack, times twenty pounds each...you ready for this...twenty-four THOUSAND pounds!"

"Holy shit! No wonder my back's killing me," exclaimed Doc. "I don't know about you guys, but that's the first time I've gotten stoned not lighting up." The silence around him was stupefying. "What I'm trying to say is..." The pause betrayed effort in his speech as he continued: "...this weed can command double what we're asking."

Will continued. "As it is, two million, four-hundred-thou'...split nine ways: twice the devil's mark."

"Man, you're as stoned as I am. How much is it per?" Smitty scratched his disheveled orange mop, more than one of the entire crew had the same thought: *crew cut or long enough for a ponytail, anything but the clown look.*

"*$266,666.66.* The sixes never end."

Arti was impressed with Will's mental math. "Hey, you some kind of savant?"

"Comes from working out batting averages and era's in my head while listening to the Sox on my radio. But let's just say we ask double after they sample our wares and we end up re-negotiating at one fifty...three mil, six hundred thousand divided by nine...four hundred grand apiece."

Stuart had enough of the show-off numbers-crunching. "WRONG! Divide that by eight equals four-fifty apiece."

And once again the gloves came off.

"What exactly are you implying?" Will knew, he just wanted it on the record and by doing so, earning the captain another feather in his cap for contemptible cad-of-the-year award.

Stu argued Nicole's FREE passage; that it came at a hefty price: a bunch of people got killed thanks to her and if-when it is discovered as to their culpability, the high stakes already in play would make smuggling the least of their worries. He also ranted that because of her, they had been pushed way off course and were soon to run out of gas.

Will did not dispute the allegations. Putting his arm around Nicole in a show of solidarity, the real purpose was cunning. Such a display was also a way of saying 'fuck you, eat your heart out', without actually uttering a word. He could tell by Stu's expression and body language the intended effect was achieved: he was livid and sidetracked, trying to keep his composure. This was evident in the effort he gave to keeping a straight face while trying to speak calmly and maintain a normal breathing pattern. Knowing it would only further infuriate, Will kept his good arm ready to block if it came to blows. "For someone born with a silver spoon in mouth, you've already said it wasn't about the money, but the kicks. So now you quibble over a mere fifty thousand? May I remind you that without Nicole's boat, that mother lode haul would not have been possible? She's held her own, and then some. Knows more about sailing than most of us. And let me just add that for someone who had not a clue as to what we were up to, has anyone heard her complain or show dread in the face of the consequences should we get busted?" Pausing for a rebuttal, yet receiving only silence, he closed in a serpentine manner meant to leave Stuart no recourse but to choke on his own self-righteous egotism. "But you know what, Captain? For the sake of keeping the peace, doing my best to respect your authority, you play it the way you see fit. In return, I expect you to respect HER and knock off the creepy advances. I don't own her, she's her own woman, and if she says back off...then back the FUCK off."

As if on cue, a zephyr cleared the stagnant air of any further dispute. The welcome breeze came and went, lending promise that they were nearing salvation. A cheer went up, Arti went back down to check how close to SOL they really were. Will was itching for a change of dressing and excused himself. Nicole followed.

The rest of the crew passed the hour over a couple bottles of celebratory wine, keeping fingers crossed and eyes watching the weathervane's gauge. The needle quivered upward in increments. Only when it attained and held at five knots did Rick dare declare; "no sign of letting up. By God, I think we're good to go!"

Nicole had finished cleaning the wound that appeared to be healing with no sign of infection. As she prepared new bandages, each time a little less constrictive, she asked Will what it was like living up north and if it was truly was like a Christmas song she once heard, "walking in a winter wonderland."

Will's exposé drifted a snowy description of what life was like snowbound for months in New England's northern reaches as her fingers ran through his hair. He could tell she felt the hardened gash on his scalp, so instead of going the Robert Frost route, he switched gears to a matter-of-fact, dead-beat dialogue of childhood misadventures that had her in stitches while re-bandaging to his recounting of boys' ill-advised exploits.

"That happened when I was eight. Parents were in the process of getting smashed, a weekend ritual, the old man glued to the tube watching football. It was near zero outside, but cozier than the tense atmosphere brewing another stormy fight. So, I'm wandering, wondering in what you call the winter wonderland and see this massive icicle as big around as me hanging from a neighbor's roof corner. I wanted to knock it down and try and catch it intact, lug it home for an ice sculpture. Well, I knocked it down and for the life of me don't know why I lurched forward to hug it before it hit the ground. I caught it with my head pile driving me into the snow. If it weren't so cold, I would have had a gusher of blood from my head, but the flow just froze. Instead, a stinging, searing that was like meat burning on a stove. I saw stars, but hardly any pain. I'm walking home, head tilted sideways, Pops sees me and thinks: *little shit, got snow down his back.* So I stand at the back door knocking, knocking, getting more light headed until finally he comes to the door and starts to light into me for interrupting his Packers game. I remember him cussing me out for the imposition, then a loud 'HOLY SHIT!'. Hair matted in blood, down my neck, I don't remember the ride to our family doctor for stitches."

"You poor thing, that's terrible."

"No, actually it was a good thing. It upset my mom so much, she forgot all about drinking and conjuring up issues to kick off another night of bitch fights with the old man."

Nicole bandaged, imagining just how ugly a child's home life could be to consider getting your skull split saving grace. She was silent.

Will did not mean for the story to be so melancholy, he followed immediately with stupidity. "Here's one that's heart-warming, but even colder. Ten below, we're sliding down this big hill behind our house. I had my sled standing up and not thinking, I licked the metal frame and got tongue-lashed to my sled. My friends had to lay me down gently and pull me home. Dad took one look at me laid out, tongue fused to the sled's frame. The prick just shrugged his shoulders, told the boys to park me in the garage to thaw out, and returned to his regular scheduled program I had pre-empted, this time hockey and Scotch on the rocks."

The visual did get her to laugh, but inside she could not help but empathize with a commonality: survivors of pasts they both were sailing from into unchartered futures hopefully offering a reset they could begin anew.

Will rambled on. He spoke to her of the time he was thirteen, he and his buddies took a short cut home from school, a mile walk across the frozen lake. White ice at least two feet thick, he lagged behind in the biting wind well below zero. Coming across an abandoned fishing hole there was blue ice. He could not resist trying to punch through. Books in both hands, stomping his foot, the ice was thicker than he thought. "All I wanted to do was start it cracking. Like an idiot I jumped with both feet."

"Why on earth did you do that?"

"I don't know. The old man said I proved his theory about teenagers. My mom actually thought I did it to get out of homework. Schoolbooks went straight to the bottom. I went in over my head, but somehow managed to retain handholds on each side of the hole where the ice was thick. Even with all the heavy clothing, the water was so frigid I shot out onto the ice like a hunted seal." He tried to imitate with both arms outstretched.

"Stop moving your arm, I'm almost finished."

"By the time my friends got me to shore and up the steep embankment, I was turning into a block of ice myself. Someone ran to get a sled and extra ropes for pulling. Dragged home by a human dogsled, and just like before, there's dad reeking of Scotch and shrugging it off with instructions: "well, we can't unzip zippers or unbutton buttons till he thaws out a bit. You boys remember the drill, park him."

"Did you love your father?"

"Yes, but to this day I can't stand the smell of Scotch."

"Not much of a winter wonderland."

"Oh, but it is. I can teach you how to snow ski, ice skate, dig snow caves. Snowshoe in three feet of fresh powder; all you hear is the crunch of snow pack, maybe a distant crow, and you could walk right by a white rabbit unless you saw two beady black eyes. Muffled silence, a charcoal painting of barren trees against a white canvas landscape, only the dark green of conifers drooping under the snow's weight..."

"There, all fixed up." Nicole knotted the new-and-improved sling. Reposed, she listened intently to his winterscape depiction.

"...you can see your breath taken in the cold, crisp air..." *what am I talking about*? Sitting before him was a flawless, striking, natural beauty; her face launched him to describe a wondrous vision. "Best part? Warming by the fireplace, sharing a vintage red, the glow from the fire casting a light on the most beautiful sight I could lose myself in." Will leaned forward, whispered his love then kissed her.

Her fervent response caught him off guard. Lips never parted, her svelte body straddled his lap. She was an armful and Will had to come up from for air. "Whoa baby, you're going to start something I don't know if I'm ready to finish. Come tomorrow, let's see if I can do without the sling. Just take it easy on me."

On the other side of the partition, Captain Derange chewed his last bite of fish from what Kaz had prepared. *Tomorrow may never come, Romeo. Be a shame you got dizzy and fell overboard tonight.* He eased away, mindful of the welcomed winds, hopefully ever-increasing; *will mean a busy night on the sails, not to mention roll, pitch, and yaw. Might have to check and see if a certain someone needs a helping hand...it can be dangerous in the dark sometimes.*

CHAPTER TWENTY-NINE

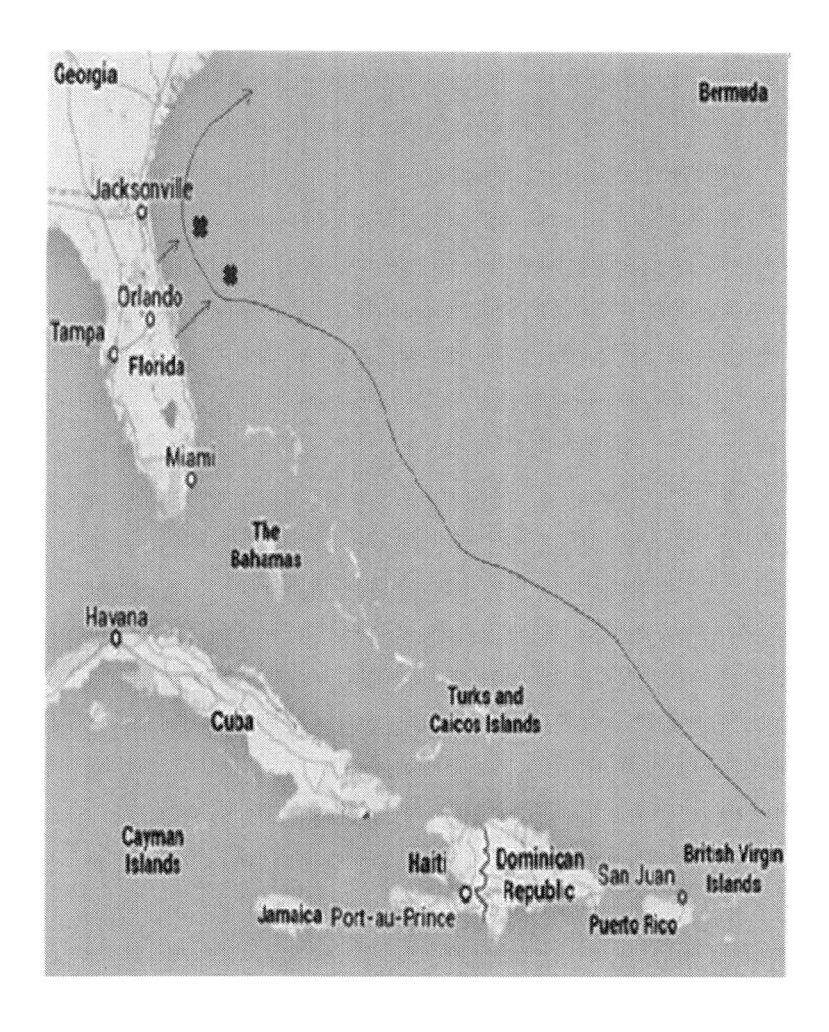

Night had passed perfect for sleeping: gentle winds and negligible swells. Stuart's dream of someone's misfortune was just that...a dream he slept straight through.

    North of the Turks and Caicos, approximated at 24.74 N / 72.06 W, course was altered north-northwest for a run up the Bahamas. Remaining well outside jurisdiction, they would parallel the island chain all the way up to Hope Town where a twenty degree turn to port would line them up for a straight shot to the Florida coast just south of Daytona.

    Attempts to raise their first contact began every hour on the hour. For now, the predetermined frequency offered only static, still too far out. Jason did listen in to other channels just to monitor who might be where and what weather lie ahead. Under no circumstances was there to be any conversing; how could there be with a ghost ship?

    Extra canvass fabricated two more sails: another jib to complement the existing one fore, and a modified spanker gaff-rigged and added to the aft mast. These combined to capture an additional two knots. *Slipfinger* was dressed out to gratefully receive every square inch of wind to augment their pace. All hands remained on deck until it was assured the configuration suited the conditions and what tweaking was required to maintain course, sailing a right angle to a starboard wind. The captains came to a consensus as to the precise position the spokes need be situated in order to equalize the broadside 'push.'

    Smitty deployed the topsails high above and added the finishing touch: a red pennant Nicole had fashioned out of her blood stained shirt. Instead of a triangle, it took

Slipfinger Nine

the form of a commemorative 'D', for David, with the insignia 'S-9'.

"Majestic. She's beautiful."

"She sure is," acknowledged Stuart, eyeing the awesome sight.

A wide stance, her taut leg muscles compensating for the ship's pitch and roll, Nicole shielded her eyes while looking skyward and admonishing caution.

Rick assumed they were on the same page...he should have known. "Yeah, just like now with every bit of sail. Father propped up in bed, headlong approach, then two passes so he can review her profile all around. What do you think, quite ceremonial huh?"

"What ceremony?"

A reinvented Frank Connor sat in his thinking chair, considering one more thing he had to do before going to sea. When he was down at the docks conducting the briefing, he had his adjutant follow up on the names, particularly the owner's sons. There was a phone number on his desk compelling him to dial. Strictly a courtesy call, tactful in that allegations not be impugned and thus upsetting the critically-ill owner. All he hoped to do was gain some insight on what made no sense at all. *Why in heaven's name would sons, heirs to a father's reportedly considerable wealth, risk a life paved in gold as pirating profiteers*?

He would tread lightly. No accusations. Under the guise of 'to serve and protect', he would assure the senior Blaine his sons' maiden voyage running solo, once nearing the east coast, would be monitored station-to-station safely home. *Well, here goes.*

The call was made. A slight British accent informed him he had reached the Blaine residence, but the master of the house was indisposed.

"This is Captain Frank Connor, United States Coast Guard Auxiliary. I apologize for the disturbance, but if it is at all possible, may I please speak with Mister Blaine concerning the commission he assigned his sons' to retrieve the schooner identified as *Slipfinger*?"

"Sir, is there a problem? The owner is quite ill, and if there is bad news, I recommend you speak directly to me, head of staff."

"No problems." Frank despised lying, but convinced himself there was a greater good which he was after. "I have been made aware of Mister Blaine's dire condition and thought a friendly call might assuage any concerns for his sons' safe return home."

A pause.

A female voice could be heard in the background asking if the patient felt up to talking. The nurse came online informing Connor that Mister Blaine was very weak and on oxygen. "Please make it brief, and understand his response will be limited. I will terminate this call if his vitals warrant it."

The frail, barely audible, voice made for awkward conversation. "Heh..lo?"

Feeble.

Frank introduced himself and apologized profusely for the disturbance, promising to make it brief and simple. Yes or no answers would suffice: Were they experienced sailors? Have they soloed before? Was the crew adequately staffed and qualified? Were they intent on any ports of call other than home? Could he vouch for the crew as all being legal citizens of the United States? Is *Slipfinger* REALLY her christened name?

No other ports of call intended, all other questions were answered with an affirmative. "Best of my knowledge", sounding taxing. Frank could tell by the waning tone that any moment the nurse would intervene. In a rush to conclude, he knew he screwed up the very second he asked, "Have your sons ever been in trouble with the law?"

Raspy, forced breathing, something uttered unintelligible...phone must have hit the floor, jolting the captain. "Hello? Is everything alright? I didn't mean..."

The commotion in the background was invaded by beeping alarms, and then the nurse's voice uttering words: "defibrillator...injection...STAT!"

A man's voice now commanded the phone, "how dare you! This call will be traced and I do not care WHO you say you are. Your superiors will be contacted regarding the extreme stress you have brought to a sick and dying man. You WILL be held accountable!"

The nurse called out for assistance while lambasting 'what's-his-name' with invectives. The last thing Frank thought he heard before the phone went dead was the British accent in the background: "His bloody heart's stopped!"

Jesus Christ! Frank lay to rest the receiver, fearing the worst for the ailing man on the other end. *Should never have made that call*.

He looked over his charts; a sighting from air recon out of Miami put the schooner in question less than a day out from the Bahamas. *That was twelve hours ago. Referring to the latest maritime weather forecast, which cited increased winds out of the east due to a low-pressure system, an assumption was made. Once clear of Bahamian waters, the suspect vessel should alter course due west, customary for ships under sail to utilize the Gulf Stream's conveyance. Winds forecasted at a steady ten to twelve, the prevailing Gulf Stream's current...Frank estimated flank speed maybe fifteen knots. Hmm, that could put our guests in the vicinity of the Florida-Georgia demarcation-line as early as twenty-one hundred hours the following evening, assuming no stops along the way. We set out tomorrow, sixteen hundred hours.*

Afternoon black clouds had sprung up; tumultuous energy from the looming storm cells enhancing stronger easterlies. *Slip* responded majestically.

"DAMN! Imagine what she'd do minus a payload?"

"Yeah, too bad America's Cup doesn't sponsor a regatta for big rigs! We'd be a shoe-in!" Rick had a tight grip on the wheel. He breathed in the moment: the sound of wind to sail, the crash of the ship's belly sinking into each trough and displacing a wall of ocean spray that drenched anyone near the bow.

"What a ride! Shit. Wonder if anyone's ever tried to water ski behind a sailboat before?" Gripping the stanchion, Will's feet left the deck after *Slip* crested a mountainous swell and dove headlong into another watery valley. The jarring impact when they bottomed out was a rude reminder of his injury. "Son-of-a-bitch!" Collecting himself, he considered his confining sling. "Tell you what, once we round the islands and get the wind to our back, I'm coming out of this thing."

"You might want to go below to ride this out!"

"Yeah, right, worse down there. Two hours' sleep before getting hurled out of our bunks! Move over, you got company." Will joined him at the helm. "How long before we change course?"

"At this rate, couple hours at least. In the meantime, looks like this squall line's gonna' overtake us. We get slammed broadside with gusts stronger than this, could heel over if we're not careful. Might have to douse some sail if the wind gets any stronger."

Stuart came to take over. "Well, one good thing. We're about to get a soaking and by the smell of everybody, a freshwater shower will do wonders the ocean baths haven't. Some, more than others, REALLY stink."

Will caught the insinuation and to his credit sloughed it off and excused himself. "I'll be back. Going below to get out of this sling."

Sure enough, within the hour two cloud formations had merged into one and overtook them. Anemometer registered gusts of thirty, testing the crew and schooner's limits. If it had been a major weather pattern, a front that had no end in sight, preemptive action would have been taken. But they could see clear skies to the east; all they had to do was endure a typical summer downpour that should pass or piss itself out. The crew at full staff, they battled the tempest in a refreshing downpour.

Will returned and began one-arming the lines, as his other hung limp by his side.

Nicole set a precedent that was admired by all. Bikini-clad and lathered in soap, even a shampoo...she tried to be discreet doing her thing far aft, but to no avail. Morale from battling the wind and rain was not the only thing being boosted.

"*Hello, I Love You*". Stuart could barely hear Morrison belting out the song from the radio room, but it was enough to send him on and on into spiral fantasy. He was lost.

A shiny razor glided over the wicked leg raised on the stern's balustrade like a ballerina's stretch exercise, and his daydream was rudely interrupted when Will came alongside to steady her.

Stu's attention faced forward, considering the ominous clouds which lie ahead. His focus should have remained there, but her silken laughter cut through all other thought and he just had to get one more look. There was Will, getting soaped up and washed down; a full-body sponge bath just short of what his shorts covered. *Playing it for all its worth. Damn his limp arm, or he'd be high up in the riggings...perfect weather for an untimely accident.* Grinding his teeth, and looking ahead into the driving rain, Stuart clenched the wheel spokes as if his hands were clamped around a certain someone's neck. An insatiable desire for her wrestled with his implacable loathing of him. If dark thoughts were tumorous, he would be a prime candidate for The Mayo Clinic.

The Doors segued into the highly apropos *Riders on the Storm* as the cloudburst's leading edge overtook them; with its passing, the wind eased considerably, but what had been a steady shower now came down in buckets.

It was an all-nighter seafaring up the Bahamian archipelago. Steady breeze, unwavering in direction, which had kindly shifted more to their backside coming out of the southeast, meant perfect sailing conditions. Excellent headway was achieved as minimal responsibilities were required. It was idyllic to the point of providing excess rest to the entire crew. Thus a routine was broken. Sometime after midnight it began; at different intervals those below would come and go. Not tired. No one could sleep due to the anticipation of the critical juncture soon to be reached where a change in course would put them on the final leg towards Daytona, and their first rendezvous. Stuart's reason for being an early-riser, who else? He tired from the all-night struggle with her in his shallow dreams.

The split shift operation was kaput. From here on out it was agreed by all that it would be catch-as-catch-can. Whomever required rest, whether it was forty winks or a dog-watch two-hour nap, no more than a third of the crew off duty at any one time. It was go-time, alertness and vigilance critical.

"25.83N, 74.55W"

"Mark."

Dawn's faintest light shed sanguinity; they had just reached the turning point east of Elbow Cay. With their heading changed to a more northerly direction, they would circumvent the Bahamas' northernmost outlying specks of land; it was a determined two hundred miles to payday.

Breakfast beat sunrise. Rather than beat a dead horse with his trepidations (now it was the actual dealing of contraband), Kaz whisked eggs, batter, and fried bacon to singe away the bad vibes that barred decent sleep.

Jason was already on the Ham, monitoring frequencies for any chatter from marine law enforcement along the Florida coast. It had been discussed, estimated, and decided that an averaging ten knots would have them in position sometime early a.m. the coming night. Jason had been told to wait till high noon before trying to raise their clientele; for security's sake, it was prudent that there be only one call to confirm.

The 'connection' was a close friend of both Rick and Stu, a graduate of Harvard last year. He had been all-in for the scheme from the get-go. Two years of discreet salesmanship, and Ted Funderburg had lined up all his eager buyers and the mother lode was already all but sold.

Well-versed in captaining his father's stately yacht, he had asked his unsuspecting old man for the keys under the pretense of a celebration cruise for alumni buds in town for the Fourth of July festivities. Timing could not have worked out better, his hardly-ever-home father was just that: on the West Coast as keynote speaker at a business convention. He did leave his son a parting admonition that upon his return he would conduct a thorough inspection and any damage to the cruiser...reparations would be imminent.

Ted's dark lie did have a smidgen of truth, or at least he told himself so. He was taking some buddies out for a cruise. Though not alumni in the traditional sense, they were, as Jimi Hendrix would say, "experienced" in the art of the deal as well as staunch herbal connoisseurs. As far as model citizens, well, they were cultured and of distinguished background, considering their profession. As far as holiday festivities, it was what they were buying that would provide widespread high-times for the vacationing throngs. A fertile market that was perfectly timed: July Fourth Happy Daze Sale.

    Tomato juice and vodka, the no-frills Bloody Mary's washed down breakfast in a toast to their soon-to-be-realized fortunes. It was an attempt at lightening the palpable anxiety, which everyone tried in vain to keep to themselves. The pall of David's demise still lingered, the death and destruction of Nicole's adversaries left questions: *would they, and when would they, be linked?* It was a superficial front displayed by all, that to be at this juncture, undetected, luck somehow was with them. Was it false bravado? Shifty eyes stole glances and betrayed the slightest flinches across painted smiles.

    Stuart's sideways stare at his affliction was a total misread. Nicole's arm found Will's waist, both of them staring out to sea; their expressions almost a peaceful indifference to his angst. *Love conquers all, my ass.* He rejected the maxim, only because of whom it concerned. Having no way of knowing, Stu was actually somewhat correct.

    Darkest secrets, which only the two of them shared, served as thin veils of pasts best left forgotten. Whatever it was that lie ahead beyond the horizon, the gamble was like playing with house money. Bankrupt of anything valued meant there was nothing left to lose. There was confidential serenity, indeed. Potluck had brought them together. The commonality of ugly circumstances fused a determination in that there really was a rainbow out there somewhere and at its end would be realized sanity and loving bliss...till now just a pipedream.

"...Hullo, anybody out there?"

Jason plunked in the chair, headset donned. He tasted what he had brewed and considered it superior to Kaz's coffee, which had been almost chewable. Squelching while dialing in the predetermined frequency, the tiny green light flickered as he fine-tuned in the narrow band. *Antiquated piece of shit. Might as well use Morse.* He was about to give-up...

"Sergeant Pepper's got a lonely heart, come in."

"'Bout time, Sarge. What's your twenty, over?"

"Dockside, waiting for a go. Is the show still on?, over."

"Affirmative. Billy Sheers currently south of Cocoa, appearing tonight for a one-time engagement; 29.36lat, 80.45long, over."

"Copy that, got front row tickets, over."

"Ten-four. A bit behind schedule, had problem with the roadies. Will update at twenty-two hundred when the main act's ready to go on. It's going to be a late night, over."

"Got it. We'll be in the parking lot waiting for the gates to open. Over and out."

Jason shook his head. The masquerade seemed a tad over-the-top. *Not doing THAT again. Anybody listening in hearing that nonsense is going to know something weird is going down.* He would have to have a word with the captains, and from now on just play it straight: call numbers, location, and time. Bullshit.

Perfect sailing conditions led to progress surpassing their projections; an unwavering sea breeze made for near hands-off deck duties while allowing everyone to cop between two and three hours of zees, as needed. Even Kaz, the resident worry-wart, was ordered to go get some.

"Man, go take a big swig of that rum if you have to. It may be a day or two before we get another chance. Once we settle up with our Daytona connection, it's on to Jacksonville for round two. Then it's haul ass out of there to Myrtle Beach. Barring any unforeseen screw-ups, we might be able to kill three birds in forty eight hours." Stu looked to Doc. "You got anything left to help him out?"

Doc rearranged Kaz's disheveled hair which oddly had grown twice the length of anyone else's. "Man, you worry too much. Come on, I might have a little something left to take the edge off."

The only development raising an eyebrow of concern was Jason's late-day weather update. A low pressure disturbance, not yet confirmed, had come up out of nowhere in the Florida straits just north of Cuba. Forecasted to spin itself up the eastern seaboard at a rapid clip, it was highly unlikely to attain tropical depression status.

"Probably won't develop into a well-formed storm", Jason queried the pipe-smoking Artimus, "so, likely won't be named."

"I know what I'd name her."

"What's that?" Jason followed Art's gaze to a resting sun worshipper laid out on the foredeck.

"Sure as hell been stormy seas ever since she crested our wake."

CHAPTER THIRTY

Jefferson Airplane announced the Volunteers' arrival much to the vexation of their drifting hosts.

Anonymity was not the issue; it had been hours since a lone vessel was spotted on the horizon. Three hundred sixty degrees as far as the binoculars could see, Doc reassured the coast was clear. "Good to go, we're in business!"

Rick hardened up, wheeling *Slip* into the wind. The schooner stalled, its sails luffing as the large yacht closed portside. Fenders being slung over the side, the rumbling inboard roared back in reverse for an impressive linkup. The engine died, along with Airplane, the grateful silence applauded by flapping canvas. Of the four scruffy long hairs, only the skipper was recognized: Stuart's college buddy who had graduated the previous year.

"Hey, wild man! Nice entrance!"

A dead ringer for Abbey Hoffman, Nathan Shoemaker flashed the peace sign and a wide grin. "How's it hanging, ya stiff prick? You ready to do this thing?"

"Let's get it on. Don't mean to be anti-social, but the sooner we part ways, the better for everyone."

Nate came aboard with the Moneyman, who was carrying two attaché cases. He was a shady character who was short on words, his shifty eyes long on scrutiny and quick to observe the precautions employed. Doc and Jason, posted bow and stern, had weapons brandished, standing sentinel.

"Friends, huh?"

Nate reassured his broker everything was cool.

Stuart did the same. "Look man, we've already had some unpleasant surprises. We're just a bunch of has-been boy scouts evoking a forgotten creed. Come on, let's sample what we got and deal."

The two remaining onboard the yacht kept lines taut, as did Kaz and Nicole. The vessels bobbed in unison, and the resulting view from below was pleasurable to say the least. The attentive duo's expressions were atypical. Their arm muscles strained to maintain a cohesive bond, while dreamy countenances plastered their stupid faces.

Will lent his only hand to assist Nicole. She saw the look on his face. "What's so funny?"

"Oh nothing, just thinking how lucky I am." *Might as well get used to it.*

The deal went down smoother than the snifter toasting the agreement. The only sales pitch needed was for Art to fire up a fat one and allow the smoke to speak for itself; customer satisfaction was achieved with two hits. Accolades were succinct amid coughing fits: "Wow, psycho-tropic, holy shit", summed up the critique.

The anonymous agent proffered the two briefcases. Released latches revealed Ben Franklins and Ulysses S. Grants, neatly bundled.

"One million, as agreed." He motioned for them to inventory the stash.

Art sat on the floor to perform a cursory accounting; Stuart shook hands with Nate and mister no-name, "deal. Let's get cracking."

Five thousand pounds, tightly wrapped in fifty-pound compressed bricks to reduce unnecessary air content, were transferred. One hundred handoffs were made, everyone-but-one forming an assembly line. Will kept tally of the process as each bundle went over the side. It was a humping workout that earned Nicole recognition, in more ways than one. Receiving from Art, who stood over the hatch, she relayed each square-yard block portside to Kaz and not once was she the hold up in the sequence. Nor did she bitch, unlike a number of the guys halfway through the exchange acting like kids on a long road trip. *Are we there yet?* A number of times, Will had to respond: "55....70....88". Her sweat-soaked tee and shorts clinging to curves was hard to discount, such a sight was reason for disruption in the routine and yes, worthy of respect.

With the conveyance complete, Stuart and Rick exchanged good-fortune with Nathan while a 'special' requisition was hastily performed: petrol bartered for one more package. Siphoned off into five-gallon chum buckets and relayed to fill a fifty-five gallon drum, the transaction topped off the business arrangement.

As the lines were relinquished, the vessels disengaged and the cabin cruiser's twin diesel roared to life, masking the distant reverberation.

"Smooth as silk." Stuart began offering to Rick and Art how the operation could have been further expedited, when a warning was yelled-out aft.

"I think we got company!" Will heard, and then felt, the thumping. As the yacht's din receded, the manifest chop of rotor blades grew undeniable. All eyes scanned the skies, Will advised Nicole she best go below and stay out of sight.

"I got a visual." Smitty had binoculars trained on the sound's origin. "Portside, nine o'clock, pretty high up."

Rick focused his spyglass in the direction and confirmed. "Got it. Damn!"

The helicopter descended from a mile-high to just above a thousand feet, approaching on line for the schooner before arcing east. They passed over a motor craft that was laying down a frothy wake, but it was the windjammer two miles ahead that was of interest. Their orders were explicit: confirm sighting of any large sailing vessels fitting the description and get the hell out of there. No hovering. No doubling back. A simple fly-by and report. It was imperative they not raise suspicion. A slight bank to the left, separation one mile, and the HH-3F moved on from its cursory surveillance.

The call went in to H.Q. with coordinates, present course, count of crew: "at least eight spotted on deck. Returning to base, low on fuel".

"Come back, I didn't copy." The spotter clamped down on his headset. "Negative, could not confirm a woman on board."

"I couldn't tell, slate-gray, no markings except for a tail number. Christ, I didn't know a whirlybird could go that fast! Whoever it was, didn't seem *too* interested." Stuart collapsed the spyglass. Both he and Rick watched the chopper minimize to gnat size then disappear over the western horizon.

"I don't like it." Rick was adamant that until they were divested completely of their consignment, they would venture no closer than double the international boundary. "Twenty four miles out, and if that's too much to ask, whatever's left goes overboard. Goddam it, Stuart, I'm not pushing our luck! We pulled it off and for me, the thrill is gone."

"Yeah, well, money may not be the issue to you and me, but to the rest of the guys..."

"Tough! I'm telling you, the next sign of trouble...I'm making the call."

"You're not going paranoid on me, are you?"

"You're damn right I am, and you should be too, but you can't see the light of day with your head up your ass."

"What? What are you talking about?"

"Your priorities have been all fucked up ever since she came onboard."

"What the hell brought this on?"

"I'm talking ACT like a captain. A fucking asset, not a liability!"

"Fuck you."

"Likewise."

Longtime mates, Doc and Arti, exchanged glances while overhearing the dust up. *Uh-oh* was silently conveyed between them, the last thing needed was bad blood between captains and brothers that would only serve to fracture the crew's allegiance. Both ceased working the ropes and diverged to their respective corners: Art joined Stu at the helm, Doc caught up with Rick, who was heading below in a huff.

Tactfully, Art changed the subject. "How's she feel?"

Stuart had a stranglehold on the wheel's spokes, clearly vexed. "How's who feel?"

"The ship, man. Two-plus tons less ballast, how's she handle?"

"Oh, yeah. Definite difference in handling...more responsive."

"I bet. Seems like we gained a couple knots also."

"I believe so. Problem is, she feels a little bow-heavy."

"We'll fix that next stop. Whatever the transaction is, it'll all come out of the forward stash."

It was nightfall, and the winds decreased to a gentle breath over the warm sea. Their forward progress up the Florida coast had to be powered mostly by the mighty Gulf Stream.

Contact had been made with their next prospect just north of Jacksonville: Art's college buddy, whose brilliance earned a full scholarship, was home for the summer working his father's shrimp trawler. A hard luck story: third consecutive season of marginal catches, business was teetering on bankruptcy...desperate dad caved in to the son's proposal. "I know it's illegal, pops, but it's a one-time deal. Lemme handle it, we'll be okay." Ten percent to play the mule meant emancipation from the bank's fifty thousand dollar lien...trawler paid off.

It was Art, not Jason, who would be on the radio to guide them through the process. Needless to say, both father and son required reassurance from a known entity to assuage their trepidation.

Light easterlies and an unvarying current lazed the crew through an interminable night. A zillion stars constellated the moonless firmament, etched by fleeting grains, the stark clarity ideal for celestial navigation. Sailing was a breeze. The only requirement was for the helmsman to keep the bow pointed toward the globular cluster M13, part of the western keystone of Hercules comprising three hundred thousand stars. Smitty nodded at the wheel. Rick was copping a few winks, laid out atop the stowage locker.

Glistening, not from the airy, mild evening, but rather from the frustration of passions checked, the couple emerged from behind the foremast. "Great, asleep at the wheel." Will caught the faint movement: head drooping perilously towards an eye-gouging wakeup on the twelve o'clock spoke. "Come on baby, we'll drive for awhile."

Groggy, Smitty willingly stepped aside while mumbling simple instructions and pointing to the whitish blur eleven o'clock high. "Juss keep er lined up to that cluster, 'kay?" Smitty passed off the small telescope to aid in the navigation. "Catch a few winks right over there, so don't rock the boat."

Sharing the wheel, they sailed by the lee in silence. Except for two sets of lights going nowhere on the far horizon, assumed to be commercial fishing vessels adrift, the world slept. Jowls in constant flex, the sound of grinding teeth elicited Nicole's concern.

"What is it, are you alright?"

Will winced as he rolled his shoulder, the dull throb a respite from needles and pins. "Arm feels like it's asleep. Bugging the hell out of me."

"Probably because it's healing, baby. Want me to massage it?"

"It?" The impish grin earned him no sympathy.

0400hrs.

Frank Connor reckoned the co-ordinates received from the dispatch, courtesy of air recon. Recalculating the possible position of sighted vessel in question, current estimate was at Lat 30.283, Long 81.145. Frank drew a line on the chart, which placed the rogue ship crossing over into Georgia waters possibly by mid-day, nullifying the original timetable for deployment. The Walrus limbered-up, reaching for the phone...*to the hunt.*

0800hrs.

Locals fishing the Brunswick River's inter-coastal waterway rocked in the Coast Guard's single file of wakes. Those with radios chatted-up conjecture: maneuvers, a hurricane brewing somewhere? Redeployment...was the base closing?

The waterway opened up into the expanse of St Simons Sound. Fanning out three abreast, the wide strait separating St Simons and Jekyll Islands loomed-ahead. As was his custom, Captain Connor left the bridge to stand attention at the bow. The crew respected the arcane tradition, a private moment of reflection; the skipper was not to be disturbed. It had never been divulged, but scuttlebutt amongst the crew surmised the ritual was in deference to his father.

In his mind's eye, Frank envisioned that fateful day long ago. Duty-bound through this very strait, onward into the tempest: swirling skies, dark waters roiling, they plowed headlong into the storm surge. The last of those with sense enough to get out of harm's way, hightailing it back into port, were in awe of a lone vessel and its intrepid crew defying nature's wrath.

Since that solemn moment now frozen in time, one recurring thought had haunted Frank Connor: did his father and crew even consider the possibility that they would never pass through this strait again? Was there ANY apprehension as they forged ahead into the maelstrom? Or was it duty and gutsy valor that superseded dire consequences...tempting fate and disregarding the distinct possibility they had embarked on a one-way trip into a watery netherworld.

An unblemished career was coming to an end and Frank's tour felt to be lacking that defining moment of truth where fortitude was measured and conviction was tested to the extreme. This would be his final deployment and, by God, it will be one for the books. *A fucking trifecta! Bust, possible murder solved, and a kidnapping, all in one.*

A mile into the Atlantic blue and Connor gave the signal. Flagship *Sword* held its course east to take up position along the twelve-mile territorial boundary. They were the backstop, the end of the road for the pirating scoundrels who would find themselves flanked in a pincer move and escorted directly into the trap. They also were in position to monitor any suspect traffic coming out of the sound for a clandestine rendezvous. *Tailfin* and *Amberjack* veered off to the south to their appointed positions. The waiting game was on, and patience was always paramount when fishing for big game.

CHAPTER THIRTY-ONE

"Smooth as silk, textbook." Art fist-pumped enthusiasm, the brothers waved farewell to the father-son company. The trawler veered-off with its catch: twenty five hundred pounds.

"Another half mil' in the bank, that's what I call a quick turn and a fast buck! Three more like this and it's home-free, boys."

In lieu of the previous clash, Rick refrained from raining on Stuart's exuberance. Yes, the transaction had been expedited without a hitch, which it should have been, considering the consignment was half that of the preceding deal. Of concern were the remaining contacts: anonymous, third-party connections, unknowns who had not been quite fully vetted...*the reason we're packing so much heat!* Rick shelved the caveat, bowing out to attend to a crew lax in directive.

The subsequent segment was expected to be a piece of cake. They were currently less than ten miles from the Florida-Georgia boundary line and, once crossed, it was the shortest distance between two points, north-northeast to their next engagement: Myrtle Beach, South Carolina. Now roughly twenty-four miles off the coast, doubling the insurance against jurisdiction, a straight shot would situate them much farther out to sea for a good portion of the journey. Due to the concavity of the southeastern coastline, east of Savannah would position them farthest from land nearly one hundred miles.

As well thought out their enterprise, precautions and contingencies taken into account, Murphy's Law can and will rear its ugly head. It has also been said that mishaps and disasters occur in triplicate. The haunting reality of David was becoming more surreal as time passed. An unexpected stowaway's presence gouged a deep rift between captain and a certain member of the crew, envied as one lucky son-of-a-bitch. Thirdly, and the only incident that was discussed unrestrained...the unsolicited melée that left everyone culpable for deaths, though collectively they agreed it was self-defense. Still, the residual effect of what went down had a collective impact...any vestige of youth's innocence had been blasted straight to hell. Try as they might, blithe veneer could not mask a lingering macabre atmosphere. It was as if they were sailing away from something best forgotten, but time and distance were insufficient: tethered to, enveloped by, a melancholic murk.

"It's weird, man. Last time I felt like this was when I lost my virginity. Like stepping through a porthole, passing a milestone from boyhood innocence into manhood."

Smitty looked at Doc, struggling to correlate the analogy. "That's a hell of a stretch, man. First time busting a nut, first time blowing someone away. Momentous moments never to be forgotten...for better AND for worse." Funny-man Karl's face turned dour, his tone's gravity capturing Doc's full attention. "You know, if this enterprise goes sour, we'd be looking at doing serious time and if they somehow tie Nicole's presence in with her husband's disappearance, we might never see the light of day. Doc, if we run into trouble there's no way I'm going to just give up.

We got to at least try and make a run for it...head for land, split up and haul ass."

"Jeez man, let's hope it don't come to that." Doc excused himself, feigning that the aft mast's cordage needed tending to. The habitual comedian's deadpan demeanor provoked considerations Doc rather not entertain. His medicinal stash had been severely and prematurely depleted, so Doc detoured below to roll up a joint. What was needed was something to take the edge off a growing anxiety so foreign to his typically laid back disposition.

Their odyssey would have been scrubbed right then and there if only they had the insightful services of an oracle. Cargo would have been jettisoned, a change of tack...an abrupt retreat far to the east and just shy of Bermuda's jurisdiction then from there a straight shot north to the Cape. A clean ship, culpable of nothing, a fabricated story rehearsed regarding David...they had anchored off the shallows of Bermuda so everyone could bathe, David was the last one in the water and it happened so fast. A scream, they tried to reach for him with a boat hook. Some kind of shark, a big mother, had him by the waist, it was over before they knew it; dragged under, they waited for something, anything to retrieve. They remained there until sundown, thought about calling in the tragedy, but there was nothing to be done, so why upset next of kin until they could get home and be there to offer support and share in the loss.

As far as Nicole was concerned, if they could not get her off the ship unnoticed when they docked, she would have to remain hidden onboard until darkness before they attempted extraction. She did not exist. With the disappearance of her VIP husband and his goon squad, the flotsam eventually correlated, hell, the investigation was probably well under way. If she was revealed, even the dumbest flatfoot conscript of the Keystone cops could put two and two together.

With the story of David agreed upon and the handling of their incriminating stowaway decided, they sailed onward towards an unforeseen snare, having no idea that, once tripped, it was designed to slowly, but surely, constrict its quarry into a suffocation stranglehold.

Captain Connor just slammed his Ensign with a twenty-point hand, chalking up another cribbage victory when the call came through. It was news of the shrimp boat's port arrival and a damning confirmation of the captain's hunch. *Tail* and *Amber* were raised, their orders were to move into position and wait.

DEA, Coast Guard, and local authorities were already standing by, watching from unmarked vehicles as the boat docked. The previous sighting of *Slipfinger*, a large vessel making haste to harbor, was enough to raise suspicion for a sting and initiate a shakedown. And the sighting, monitored from afar by helicopter, observed a sportsman's vessel's peculiar quick turnaround. Shrimping entails lengthy stints at sea, this jaunt clearly was not about dragging nets.

The bust was a slam-dunk. No sooner had the trawler been secured dockside, agents filed down the wharf and embarked. The father and son were detained, and when confirmation was hollered out from below, on went the cuffs along with their rights. Agents familiar with the recently raided government crop readily identified the superb uniqueness of the contraband: Red Bud, Columbian Gold, Jamaican, nothing grown in this hemisphere was comparable.

The son adhered to his silent right, but could not reel in his dad, who was more than willing to divulge anything and everything in exchange for whatever leniency might be negotiated. Not only did authorities now know the disposition of the culprits who perpetrated such a bold heist in the islands, it was the information about a female onboard that raised the other eyebrow. The missing persons report on one Alaine Moreau and crew, their wreckage spotted adrift north of the Turks, and a wife unable to be located…something smelled fishy and it was not because they were on a shrimp boat. The correlation of events with a presumed course positioned the scoundrels in the right place at the right time to incriminate on multiple counts: drug running, theft of government property, kidnapping, and possible murder charges. An additional charge was accompanied by a cautious warning to the Georgian auxiliary. Courtesy of pop's detailed account, there was now a confirmation of small arms. Just how small, or otherwise, was heretofore unknown.

"Appreciate the head's up, Jax. We are in position to receive, intend to coax them, but with caution. Out." Frank Connor made sure both cutters received that last communiqué. *Amberjack* was to call in once visual contact was made. Plunked down in the captain's chair, Frank ordered his crew to perform a weapon's check: side arms, M-16s, and the persuasive fifty cal mounted mid ship. He envisioned the sister ships doing likewise, *strictly precautionary. These boys are in a world of shit, but from what's known, we're dealing with a bunch of piss and vinegar college punks in way over their head. When they realize they're in a vice, they'll fold. They should, they better...I hope.*

The plot developed, leaving the main character out of the loop, oblivious to external circumstances. The mid-afternoon offered only a frustrating light zephyr, and what slow progress was being made could be entirely attributed to the prevailing Gulf Stream.

"Fuck!" The twenty-four hour forecast called for variable light winds coming from the east, "wrong direction and not enough oomph to work with. Jesus could jog to Myrtle faster than this!" Frustrated, Stuart hollered to Jason. "Get on the horn and try to raise Mickey Finn. Tell them it'll be at least twenty-four hours, probably more like thirty-six, for the hook-up."

"Possibly predawn, day after tomorrow, at least this one will be under cover of darkness." Art fired up his pipe, contemplating the occasional luff of sail. "Cap. We've got the extra fuel. If we have to, we can motor our way up the coast and barter for more petrol like before."

"Might just do that if the wind diminishes anymore. Right now we're making just enough headway, it would be a waste to power up. Would gain us only marginally more speed. Problem is, the wind direction. And it's force marginal, not enough to tack with...so we continue due north with what wind we can jam. But even with the rudder aiming us to one o'clock, the right angle breeze starboard seems to be pushing us slightly closer to the coast. We're still almost triple-safe the twelve-mile limit, but come night time, we'll conduct celestial navigation every three hours to see how far west we get pushed. If we have to, that'll be when we motor our way back out to safety."

"Right. More wind, or at least a shift out of the southeast would be nice. Plus there's always the chance of hitching a ride with one of those late afternoon thunderstorms."

Jason called out from below, "can't raise 'em. Must be out of range."

Doc came up with a hodge-podge of grub from the galley: three ales, cheese, grapes and salami. His eyes were bloodshot.

"What, no bread?" Stuart's query was met with admonishment.

"Don't press your luck, cookie's 'bout had it. Somebody got into the supply and didn't re-seal it properly. He's trying to salvage what little isn't molded." Doc popped his bottle, "here's to a smooth run up the coast."

Bread was not the only thing growing stale. The overall spirit of the crew was dulled by the tedious routine and certain personnel conflicts that made the ship's confines shrink. There was also growing dissent about continuing their dangerous scheme. Proponents, Stu and Art, seemed to have the backing of Smitty and Doc whose need of money trumped all reason. Jason had become a loose cannon with an "I don't give a shit" attitude. The way he saw it, what could be worse than what had already had taken place? Maybe finishing what they started would somewhat mitigate the traumatic event that still hounded him. Will and Nicole preferred to quit while they were ahead, feeling the crew's luck had been pressed far enough. Secretively, they had discussed jumping ship upon the next rendezvous, but Will battled the thought of abandoning Smitty in particular. Kaz, the consummate worrier, had been ready to call it a wrap since the first foray back in the islands. Rick shared the same gut feeling as Will and Nicole, but could not bring himself about to discuss it. He may not have been an architect quite on the same level as his brother and Artimus, but he sure went all-in on the concept. *What the hell were you thinking...stupid son-of-a-bitch!*

Even if Nicole had a say in a vote, the decision to press on and finish what they started would have squeaked by. When shift change came about, Rick pulled Will aside before going topside.

"Hey, man. Whatya say we work on Smitty tonight?"

"What do you mean...'work' on him?"

"Unless I'm reading everyone wrong, there's four of us that think it wise we give up on this shit and split for home. Problem is, one of us is Nicole, and you know damn well any vote won't include her. So that makes it five to three. If we can get your pal to realize that fifty percent of something is a hell of a lot better than a hundred percent of nothing, it'll be deadlocked and then maybe we can get Doc to come around."

Will was taken-aback by the candid confessional. Here was the co-owner, co-conspirator, co-captain, expressing reservations to a subordinate whose trepidations mirrored what was just spoken. Oddly, the confirmation did not enhance concern, but rather gained Will's confidence and respect. The forthright admission of doubt, verbalizing what Will was trying so hard to renounce or play off as growing paranoia, spoke volumes as to his moral fiber. *Self-assured enough to bare true feelings, no bullshit, pragmatic. Such the antithesis of Stuart.* Will again speculated: *Kindred? No fucking way.*

"How long have you been thinking this?"

"What happened to David might have been an omen, but ever since that chopper fly-by the other day, I've not been able to shake the feeling we're sailing right into a trap..." Rick paused for a reaction.

"Yeah, the old saying...if something appears too good to be true, it usually is. Both connections went off without a hitch, smooth and easy."

"Maybe too smooth. I just have this gut feeling that it might be best we quit while we're ahead, know what I mean? We might be in the clear right now, but the farther we go up the coast, from Washington D.C. to Boston, traffic gets real heavy and the Coast Guard becomes a lot more prevalent. I don't know about you, but the idea of spending the rest of my life, or the part that matters, in the slammer is becoming more and more profound in my decision-making."

Will felt compelled to reciprocate with an apology. "Man, I'm so sorry for the fucked-up escapade. I know her being onboard further complicates matters. Hell, guess I deserve a shot in the arm for stupidity. Man, now that she's my responsibility, the whole game's changed. Before it was damn the torpedoes and full speed ahead, never gave a second thought about repercussions, what-ifs. But now...it's all I can do to keep from jumping ship the next rendezvous and get her the hell somewhere safe, just a little pocket money and...'sayonara'. If it wasn't guilt for bailing on my friends, we'd have already done so on the shrimp boat." Will offered a handshake. "I'll talk to Smitty, feel him out. But I'm with you about one more deal then we call it a wrap."

"Thanks, Will." On impulse, Rick patted the injured arm, "oh, uh, sorry 'bout that."

"Hurts a little, but I think a few more days and I'll be out of this damn sling." Will started to leave, and then turned back. "Just a friendly warning Cap'n. If your dickhead brother threatens one more time to kick us off the ship, you WILL have a seven-man crew when we make Myrtle."

Six-foot-five Chief Petty Larson, updates in hand, did not stand at attention. He could not, ceiling height prohibited such protocol. He took a seat across from the skipper, thankful that the porthole was open as smoke from the full-bent pipe mercifully funneled directly out. Aptly referred to as "The Tomb": there were two chairs, a small table, and a bunk unlikely to accommodate the walrus...just enough room left for claustrophobia.

"Should call it plugged nickel or thin dime instead of quarters."

"It's the Coast Guard, Chief, not a cruise ship." Frank looked up from the chart, too big for the table, "it's adequate. What you got?"

Beyond the horizon, forty miles east in Georgia waters, *Amberjack* lay in wait. They had received coordinates and course heading from a spotter plane flying high and distant, a mere speck unnoticed. Positioned strategically to thwart any attempt of making a run for refuge, *Amber's* radar monitored the slow progress of their unsuspecting guests.

With the backdoor guarded, *Tailfin* posted sentry twelve miles off the coast, due east of St. Andrews Sound separating Cumberland and Jekyll Islands. Like *Sword*, the comings-and-goings could be monitored while awaiting word from *Amber* that visual contact had been made and pursuit initiated. Of the crafts sighted, the vast majority could be seen on the western horizon adrift over a popular fishing-destination aptly called The Hole. A deep depression, haven for a variety of shark, more than once had the Brunswick auxiliary had to dispatch a boat to answer distress calls. Booze and pissed-off sharks being hauled on board was not a healthy combination. Legs, hands, arms lacerated...on at least one occasion, an angler's right forearm became a Bull Shark's last meal.

Killing time, high-powered field glasses were passed around to observe the closest boats: a thick rod bent downward, man versus beast. It was not so much the titanic struggle and questionable outcome that the crew found most entertaining, but the hilarity of watching utter chaos that often ensued. Conjecture aired over the fishing party's sobriety, their lack of coordination and the level of disarray emblematic as to the weekend anglers' sincerity and priorities. Was it sharking...or an opportune excuse to get knee-walking drunk?

Lieutenant Smalley sat in the captain's chair, thumbing through Playboy's April edition...its condition tattered. "Yeoman! Where the hell's May?"

Standing by, monitoring the radio's frequency dialed in to *Amber*, seaman Bass collared the headset. "MIA, Skip. She's probably being held in custody aboard one of the other boats."

"Some stiff prick raided our mail call. There WILL be an investigation! We get back to base, SAR WILL be conducted."

The tongue-in-cheek repartee was interrupted by the anticipated broadcast.

"*Amber* to *Sword*, *Tail*. We have visual contact. Will commence shadowing suspect vessel. Maintain current position until we see how they respond. Update coming on the half hour, out."

LT discarded worn-out April in the wastebasket. "Bosun! Inform the crew we are on standby alert. Bass, did they copy?"

"Affirmative."

The situation report wafted through the plume of smoke belching from the cherry wood pipe. The small porthole, opened for exhaust, provided marginal venting. Connor nodded, pointing his pipe stem at the Chief. "Make it clear no action is to be taken, just close in on their flanks. We don't know their temperament, so maintain separation out of harm's way. Only if they drop their sails and surrender are we to close in and board."

Larson stood, remembering to slouch with a salute.

"So, we wait to hear from *Amber*. I'm going to catch a little shut-eye, get me when we hear something."

"Aye-aye Skipper." The short-cropped gray beard could not mask a faint grin. Larson sensed something amusing. "Is that all, Captain?" The bunk creaked under the captain's stout frame, Chief Petty waited for whatever came first: dismissal or the bed's collapse.

"Today's the third, right?"

"Affirmative, sir."

"That's a coincidence."

"How's that, sir?"

Fourth of July fireworks. We might have a front row seat."

Larson bowed out, well aware of the door's low header. Twice he had whacked his head before getting it through his thick skull: head first and backing out. "Thirty winks and a wake-up."

Jason Douglass

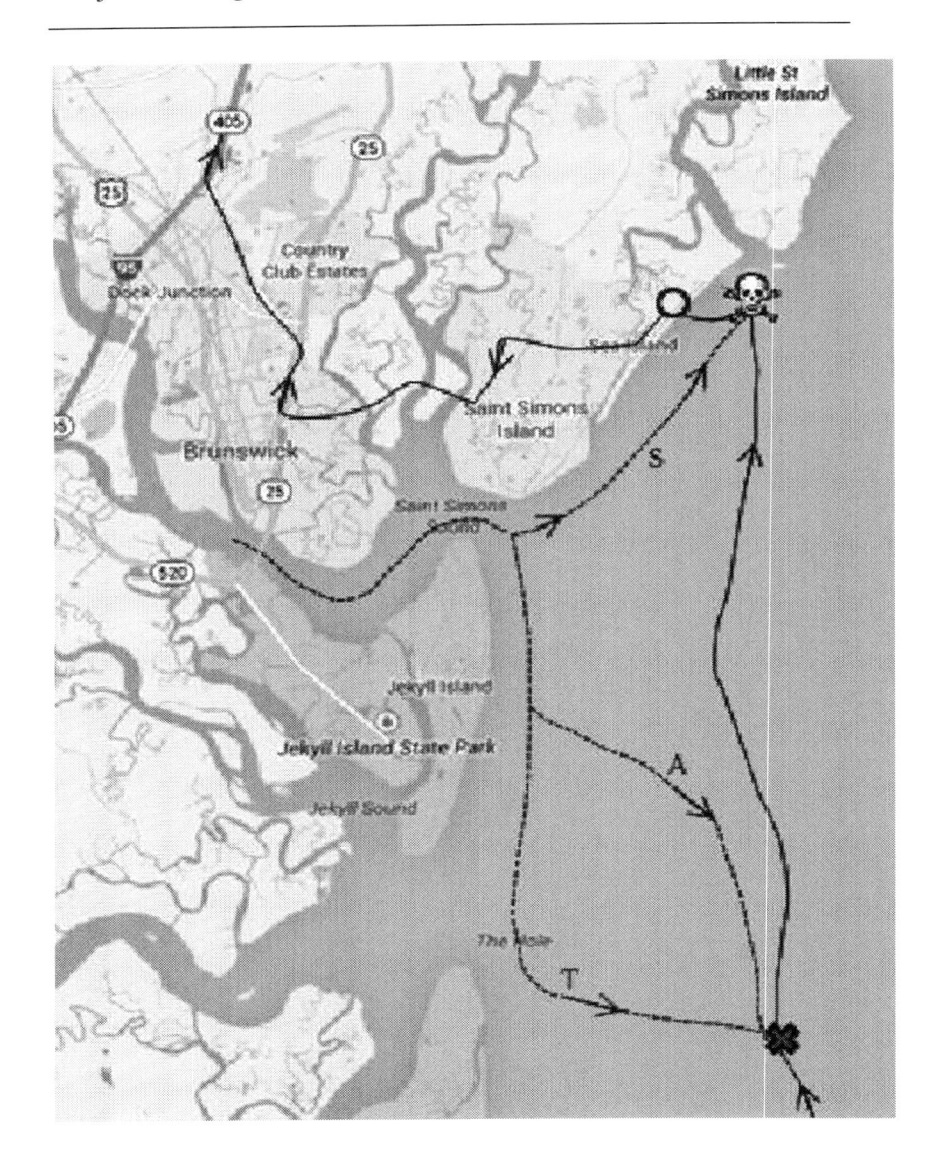

CHAPTER THIRTY- TWO

"Geez skipper, I don't think they realize they're being tailed."

Captain Miles dialed the field glasses to maximum magnification.

The majestic vessel with full complement of sail appeared as a ghost ship reincarnate from the nineteenth century. "That's one beautiful ship. Can't make out any of the crew, too far away. Come five more degrees to port, increase speed, five knots...and find out *Tailfin's* twenty!"

"Aye, Cap'n, Sheers has them on the horn as we speak. They intervening with a fishing party. Squabble between two boats gotten tangled up, large marlin caught in a tug-of-war. Tempers flared, neither angler agreeable to cutting their line, then some drunken fool with a rifle fired a warning shot...that's when *Tail* rushed to mediate."

"Oh, for Christ's sake! Tell them to get on with it and move out!"

Stuart, A.K.A. "Casey Jones", ceased his sing-along to chug a toast to the lady in the red bikini. Every time Nicole bent over to grab another parcel passed up through the hatch, it called for another belt of Captain Morgan. The Dead melody rose from below as the assembly line readied the next shipment topside. The dinghy's tarp had been removed to cover the staged pile. Like a Daytona pit crew, they would be ready.

Rick and Art were preoccupied tuning the sails. A little slack in the lines, the canvas accommodated the air current's modest augmentation, courtesy of mid-morning's warp up.

"Maybe two more knots." Art pulled the cordage taut through the boom vang. At the desired tension, Rick made fast the excess around the belaying pin.

"Two's better than zip, Art, maybe a harbinger of things to come."

"Yeah. Catch a ride on some afternoon tempests and we'll make up for lost..." CCR's warning of a bad moon rising was shattered.

"You fucking kidding me! Take the helm!"

Locked in a face-off, Will had removed the sling and was wrapping it around his left hand. Red-eyed and swaying with the undulation, Stuart had Captain Morgan by the neck, droplets dripping from jagged glass.

"That's the last time you talk to her like that, you son-of-a-bitch!" His unproven left arm readied to deflect, other fist clenched to counter with an abrupt right to the nose.

"I call it as I see it, asshole: cock-teaser, cut-and-dry."

If looks could kill, Nicole's would have already settled the issue. Smitty caught her from behind and pulled her away at the same time Stuart found himself in a chokehold and disarmed by a swift kick, weapon overboard.

"You're fucking drunk? What the hell's wrong with you, man?" Rick was furious, atypical of his usual mild-mannered disposition. Stuart submitted a few garbled profanities, constrained by the stranglehold.

Doc, Jason, and Kaz rushed topside in time to hear Will's announcement.

"That's it, we're done. I won't even quibble over Nicole's share."

"Get off of me." Stuart broke free. "You're not getting shit. The agreement was *if* and *when* we make it home safe. You get off at Myrtle, better hope your woman's got change for bus fare."

Will directed his comment to Rick, "Mister Christian, if I were you, I'd confine Bligh to quarters and take sole command. Your brother's fucking lost it."

"You and your bitch can go to hell!" Stuart made one step and was restrained immediately by Doc and Rick.

"And spend eternity with you? No thanks. Send me a postcard, dickhead."

"Hey, knock it off you guys! Starboard aft, four o'clock!" Max magnification, the craft kept bobbing in and out of view. Artimus tried to compensate, moving in concert with *Slip's* up-down motion. *Come on, dammit, where are you?* The rhythm was attained long enough to focus, orange and white depicted, worst-case scenario confirmed. "Wicked pissah, man. Looks like they're closing."

Rick yanked the glasses and acknowledged Art's assessment. "Get your ass up here, Stuart!"

Mutual 'fuck-yous' concluded the parley. Doc hollered they best make haste and get the stockpile out of sight.

"Negative! They probably have a good bead on us already, would look suspicious. Cover it up with the tarp and everyone spread out. Remember, we're yachtsmen working out the kinks." Inspecting the crew, it was Smitty who looked least the part: his wiry, orange hair was disheveled and twice the length of anyone else. "Damn, man! You look like shit. Take Nicole and stay out of sight."

Neither made eye contact, it was all Rick could do to maintain restraint. "You think you can drive and keep your mouth shut?"

Stuart relieved Art of the wheel, a surly grunt his only riposte. Cogent enough to realize he had no leg on which to stand...hell, even with two legs it required both hands full of wheel just to maintain equilibrium...the combative narcissist wisely acceded to his brother's command.

Nauseating vibes akin to looking in the rearview mirror and seeing a police car tailing and just itching for an excuse to ruin your day...the ship's on-deck company, with the exception of one, held steadfast their resolve to play it cool. Kaz was visibly shaken and more than once had to be reprimanded to get a grip.

Will was discreet, offering reassurance to Rick. "I got him, don't worry."

"They close on us and Kaz's still paranoid, get his ass below." Rick returned attention to his brother. Estimating they were at least thirty miles off the coast, he called for a subtle course change of five degrees port, "just shy the boundary limit."

It had been a narrow decision, but if push came to shove they would make a run for it. Ditch, split up, and haul ass. Even if just one were to get away, which everyone imagined it to be their fortune, it was worth the try.

The alternative: life, or at least the part that mattered, wasted away in lock up...inconceivable.

Anxiety increased, commensurate to the decrease in separation. Will kept reassuring Kaz that if they played it cool, there was nothing to get uptight about. "Neutral waters, man. We're untouchable."...*I hope.*

Tailfin had since disengaged from presiding over the intoxicated dispute. The winner: a twelve foot Tiger, cut loose from entangled lines. Any gratification from helping out the less fortunate was short-lived as the earful rolled in from their counterpart, *Amberjack*. Expletives seasoned the urgent call requesting their whereabouts and that the engagement was well under way.

"Captain, you might want to take this." The headset's handoff was brusque.

"Yes, yes, I'm well aware!" Co-ordinates were exchanged, the ETA reaffirmed, and the skipper terminated the chastisement with a simple 10-4 and assurance that a rendezvous would be ASAP.

Captain Connor had been called to the bridge to monitor the action. Penciling in the updated coordinates, he drew a line east-west to intersect with the northwest approach. "We're too far out, reposition eighteen miles west. Any deviation in their advance, I want to know immediately." *Keeping their options open, huh? Scallywags don't know whom they're dealing with.* New directive: cutters close and escort vessel to checkmate Lat 31.137, Long 81.321; twelve miles off the southern tip of St. Simons.

The captain's chair creaked as he leaned back, tamping his pipe. Match to bowl, the endgame played out on a smoky screen: *Like being driven into a box canyon. A contingent of my men boarded, rogues busted...stripped of sail under auxiliary power, in short order the procession returning up the Sound to base...a sight to behold.*

Frank mused on his delivery: the account articulated to reporters of a high seas drama played-out in textbook fashion. *Hell of a way to go out on top!* Brunswick's evening news, a captivated audience...the family dinner a mere prop, as with popcorn consumed perfunctorily, theater patrons riveted in the moment. Culminating the report, a segued forum: tribute to his father, a remembrance of heroic sacrifice, and an impromptu history lesson for the baby-boomers.

The reverie was just that. Four horizons to the south, *Amberjack* was in the process of royally screwing-up the Captain's pipe dream.

Amber had drawn to within a quarter-mile starboard when *Tailfin* materialized on the western horizon.

"A-jack, we have visual. On course, flank-speed to intersect." Timing the link-up was imperative to impose a non-negotiable escort.

Up till now, *Amber* and *Slip* had exchanged a cordial façade, both crews displaying innocuous gestures of greetings and kismet. The crew's apparent nonchalance perplexed Miles.

"Something's not right."

"How's that Captain?"

"For a bunch of smart-ass college boys in big trouble, they sure aren't acting like it. Either we got the wrong ship, or they're cock-sure of their indemnity under maritime law."

"You want me to bring us in closer, or wait on *Tailfin?*"

"Affirmative. Close enough to holler a few standard questions...assess deportment. Hell, I don't see any sign of weapons, a girl, nothing out of the ordinary except for a big lump aft covered with a tarp. Something's fishy."

The encroachment was a sphincter constrictor, but it was Doc's low-key warning of trouble coming hard-on out of the west that had the effect of a juiced cattle prod rudely introduced...minus lubricants.

Kaz was coming undone. "Check on her for me, make sure she's okay." The instruction was merely a ploy. Will knew the assignment would be a panacea. *If that don't keep him distracted, he's either dead or queer.*

If curiosity killed the cat, an over-zealous captain, incapable of adhering to protocol, will indubitably muck-up tactics. What happened next was unanticipated, altering all rules of engagement.

The starboard porthole was open, and the shotgun primed, his mind racing: *thirty years to life...no way. Bastards better back the hell off!* With his weapon in hand as if it just magically materialized, Smitty vacillated, caught in a dreamlike juncture.

Kaz lost it when he peered out the portside porthole. The second patrol boat was within a mile and closing fast. "We're fucking screwed!" The manic shout-out triggered an involuntary reflex, the recoil flashed Smitty to his senses only to realize what he had just done.

Miles' query as to point of origin and intended destination was violently answered, the response terminating any further feigned civilities. What followed was stupefying to both crews, shell-shocked by the salvo...absolutely nothing! *Slipfinger* forged ahead, no one hurt.

Unintended, the impulsive shot could not have been placed more strategic. In a desperate attempt to ward-off their worst nightmare, Smitty's intention was to fire one across the bow. Instead, the ill-timed shot caught its target at the apex of a large swell, blowing a gaping hole in the bow's hull just above the waterline. Upon decent into the trough, forward progress took on water. *Amberjack* was knocked out of commission, it's only course-of-action was an about-face in reverse.

May Day was radioed: "taking on water, immediate assistance required." *Tailfin* diverted from its headlong approach, *Slip's* crew stood stationary in comprehension of what had just transpired. They watched aft as the two boats conjoined, inverted, lines flung in preparation for a painstaking return to port.

"Hot damn! Talk about killing two birds with one grenade!" Art's jubilation was in stark contrast to Rick's realization that what just transpired quashed any need for debate.

"Well, that settles that! I garun-damn-tee you there's an APB being called in right now. Here to Maine, law enforcement will have us pegged number one on the hit parade." Rick snatched the map from underneath Captain Indignant. The obstinate antagonist's refusal to yield spoke as he pitched for a showdown; matters were made worse no doubt by the afternoon sun fermenting one heck of a hangover. "Don't say a fucking word, Stuart, at least until I'm finished...I mean it."

The mock golf-clap from Jason, Art, and Doc acknowledging Smitty's appearance was not for the grenadier's implausible feat as much as a diversion to temper the mounting animosity. Kaz, doing his rendition of a Jack in the Box, sprung from the hatch bemoaning their death sentence.

"Get a grip, man! Captain's got a plan." Will offered his hand to Nicole, the look on whose face told him they were of like mind...*if it wasn't decided the venture be terminated here and now, if it meant relinquishing their share in exchange for two paddles and the small inflatable raft...time to go.* Stuart seethed at the embrace, their approach hand-in-hand excruciating.

The chart was spread out on deck next to the helm, the crew gathered around. Rick proceeded to dictate what he knew to be their only option.

"You know damn well that as I speak all authorities here to Maine are being raised on high-alert, developing a hard-on for our ass..." Rick sketched, his calm delivery holding everyone attentive, barring one. Stuart may have lent an ear, but his focus was split between guiding *Slip* straight ahead, and staring holes into the couple conjoined as one.

The course of action was highlighted on the map: present direction had them nearing the coast off the southern tip of St Simons Island. If they were to alter slightly north some six miles, there was nothing but boondocks, wetlands and estuaries penetrating deep inland.

"Man! I remember years ago your old man telling us stories of pirates hiding out in these parts."

"Precisely what we're going to do. Look here." Rick pointed out to Doc another twenty miles north between Doboy and Sapelo Sounds: "Blackbeard National Wildlife Refuge."

Stuart exercised his waning authority. "Wait a minute." He knew Art and Jason would back up his sentiment…Doc teetered on the fence. "Some of us happen to differ. I say we haul ass into the wild blue yonder. The remaining clientele will just have to voyage farther out."

"You can take us in, drop us off, and have at it. Good luck manning the ship with less than half a crew…you also better hope the fish are biting and pray for rain minus a hurricane. What are you going to do, stay out there and die of old age?"

"Make a run for Canada after we unload the rest of the weed."

"Oh that's ripe, Captain Kidd. You know damn well Canada will be alerted. Besides, just because you THINK you're untouchable, doesn't mean the authorities won't know exactly where you are every minute of the day. And one more thing, any further transactions…just offer your sincere condolence once the deal's sealed."

"For what?"

Rick squinted into the sun directly behind his brother's faceless head, "they'd never make it back, and you know it." The cold-hearted fact that profit was valued over the welfare of others brought him to his feet. He dismissed his brother as no longer recognized from the wheel. "It's my call, we're headed in. Once we ditch, you can do whatever the hell you want."

Stuart's endeavor to protest was squelched by the commanding directive: "all hands man the riggings, we're making a run for it!"

Amberjack's crew had stuffed life jackets, cushions, whatever they could come up with to fill the bow's hole. A bilge pump was operating to remove what water still entered, in tandem the two patrol boats limped back to port. *Tailfin* had radioed ahead their situation to *Sword*, and now, as they witnessed the schooner's final sighting before it disappeared over the horizon, a final call was made.

Connor was in disbelief at what had transpired, but what he now heard could not have presented a more fitting conclusion: he and his crew would play vanquisher. *Numbskulls are headed right for us!* Order was given: weapons check, lock and load the fifty, and hold position. Radar locked on the blip, its approach was being monitored, and *Sword* was suspended inanimate as all eyes focused on the horizon.

CHAPTER THIRTY-THREE

"Visual contact off port bow, eleven o'clock!" Ensign Prescott collapsed the Captain's vintage spyglass, a keepsake handed down father-to-son. "Top mast just broke the horizon, it's her."

Frank Connor ordered a slow retreat in reverse. At such a distance, they would maintain a visual of the schooner's mastheads while remaining invisible due to the patrol boat's lower profile. The plan: withdraw from their current position and halve the distance to the coast. With the afternoon sun behind them and a low haze, the result of surface evaporation, visual limit in their direction at sea level was six miles at best. Once their objective crossed over the twelve-mile demarcation...there would be no dispute, fair game. *Sword* receded. Minor course adjustments mirrored that of the schooner, its topmast fixed dead ahead off the bow.

"By my calculations, 15 miles due east of St Simon's." Artimus reveled in proving his prowess with the sextant.

Stuart's ego was still smarting, and he was in no mood to stroke someone else's. Marking an "X" on the chart, he put down a straight edge and dotted a line northwest to the mouth of an unnamed watercourse. Pivoting the compass twice, from the "X" to the inlet's entry point, marked twenty miles.

Both studied the topography, Art had to concede to Stuart that Rick was on to something. "Might not want to admit it, but your brother's put some thought into this." Art traced the surprisingly wide river system from entrance to exit. "Plenty wide enough, question is its depth."

The map showed a maze of tributaries branching-off into nothingness...inaccessible marshland, except for a dotted line denoting a primitive access road dead-ending into nowhere. What was enticing was that the waterway that sliced all the way through the wetlands and spilled out into a backwater Sound named "Buttermilk", its water source derived from the primary Sound, Altamaha, demarcating St Simons from Wolf Island and the vast uninhabited wildlife preserve.

"Shit, we could lose ourselves in this morass! Look at this other river shooting off Buttermilk, goes all the way inland past I-95! Talk about a backwoods escape route!"

Stuart had to acknowledge it did offer cover and the potential for a clean get away. Not one to commit without caveat, he rolled the chart and rose from the deck. "He's right. But if high tide's not with us, we're screwed."

Oblivious to what loomed, they sailed ahead of mounting storm cells, augmented by onshore winds. What was perceived as a Godsend in actuality was hastening their appointment with catastrophe.

Once it was calculated that the point of no return had been crossed, an aura of anticipation enveloped the crew. Vibes implicit of a bygone era of both fact and fiction: Columbus longing to see the New World, debunking once and for all the absurdity of sailing off an edge. The other analogy: Herman Melville's inspiration of a great white whale. To who first witnessed Ahab's nemesis, the gold coin spiked to the mast would be pried.

In the midst of duties performed, all eyes maintained perfunctory vigilance.

"When we disembark and split up, you coming with us, right?"

Smitty eyed the couple embraced as one, conveying mock indecision. "Oh, I don't know. I've heard threesomes can get a little complicated."

"Only thing complicated, besides figuring out how full of shit you are, is this stupid adventure we got ourselves into. Not fiddle-fucking around, Karl. The instant we make land I'm getting her out of this god-awful mess and you're welcome to come along." Will drew Nicole closer and kissed a whisper in her ear..."I love you."

An awkward conference, more like eating crow while having your teeth pulled, was taking place at the helm. Humble pie gagged Stuart as he forced himself to swallow admittance that his brother's plan was the way to go. In the midst of offering snake-oil contrition over conduct unbecoming a captain, Nicole's impassioned response halted the charade in mid-sentence. Stuart was a millisecond away from uttering contempt when above and beyond the affectionate display something caught his eye. Snatching the spyglass stashed below the wheel, he focused on the anomaly interrupting a straight-edged horizon.

Will stiff-armed a middle finger, saluting his antagonist in what was assumed mock voyeurism. Denied even a cursory response caused him an identity crisis...*what am I, invisible?* Turning in the direction of whatever was so absorbing, Nicole and Smitty did likewise.

To the naked eye, all that could be ascertained was what was to be expected. It was ludicrous to think they were sole proprietors of an endless water world, in fact, it had become a trifle unsettling to have come this far, closing in on the coast and yet not a soul to be seen. While solitude was welcomed for a furtive approach, their fortune had taken on an eeriness best described by the purveyor of gloom and doom, Kaz: "...it's like world war three and we're the only ones left."

The only one with glass vision still could not determine the ship's characteristics. "Can't tell if it's coming, going, or just sitting there." Stuart relayed what little he could ascertain at such distance, "no outriggers, not a shrimp boat. Too big for pleasure craft though."

Slip stayed its course. After all, a collegiate yachting team had nothing to hide, right? At two-o'clock off the starboard bow the object of concern appeared stationary, but *Slip's* unswerving approach...twenty degrees shy of a headlong game of chicken...at last revealed its true-colors.

"Moby-fucking-Dick!" Stuart hurled the spyglass to seize the attention of the consortium gathered at the bow. In actuality, the intent was a parting shot barely missing Will's head.

"Range, three miles."

The affirmation was what Captain Connor had been waiting for: at such distance, there was no way a schooner could pull an about-face and outrun them another three miles back to immunity. "That's it, take 'em down."

For the moment, no one spoke. From idle to full throttle until they planed off, the roar rendered communication not worth the holler. Besides, all the while they had been lying in wait; the plan of attack had been rehearsed ad-nauseam. All hands knew their duty inside and out and it was a foregone conclusion the scoundrels' exploits would inevitably be scotched.

The oncoming juggernaut made further pretense futile, and frenzied activity ensued. Rick veered twenty degrees to port, the angled approach for the coast now a dead run. What canvass had not yet been deployed, was. Turnbuckles were turned, ropes were relaxed or tightened in order to tune close-hauled sails and accommodate the onshore winds.

Fifty-eight years since its inaugural voyage, and *Slipfinger* never looked or performed so regal. *Damn, if only father could see her…barring the circumstances.* Gripping the helm with a white-knuckle resolve, there was no looking back. Anger beset desperation…*how could we have been so stupid! What were we thinking?* Mind racing, heart thumping, maintaining a steady course was oddly comforting; not so much the concentration required, but the steady feel of holding firm the wheel. It served to keep him from doing a rendition of a condemned con's rude acquaintance with two thousand volts…*can't unravel, get a grip.* There was no relief in correlating con to prison time. *Life, or the best part of it…no fucking way!*

Desperate times called for desperate measures. Stu and Art had gone on the offensive, knowing it was their only defense. Weapons were broken out with the understanding the intent was not to inflict bodily harm, but to keep their adversaries at bay long enough to reach land and haul ass. To a man, incarceration was not an option.

Kaz wanted no part of it, backing away as if the allocation was signing a death warrant.

Rick declined, insisting someone had to drive. Fortified with a white hand towel to signal he was unarmed, he hoped such a display would grant him immunity if, god forbid, the situation turned ugly.

Five hundred yards starboard aft *Sword* eased back, matching speed. "Captain, got visual of two taking up positions fore, another two aft. They ARE armed. Two more at the helm appear to be unarmed. Bastards still won't answer the radio."

"That leaves three unaccounted for and we sure as hell aren't going to replicate *Amberjack's* miscalculation. Circle three times no closer than one hundred yards then ease off, flanking their starboard."

"Aye, Captain."

Bullhorn in hand, Connor exited the wheelhouse to monitor the tactic's effect, two-fold in purpose: a three hundred sixty degree assessment and psychological intimidation...*end of the line, boys.*

Late afternoon and the light of day was prematurely fading behind a cloudbank brewing inland, the dark underbelly of mushrooming thunderheads. It was a gloomy backdrop befitting a seemingly hopeless situation. Fight or flight; capitulation or continuance? The moment of truth suspended all animation, perpetuity lingered as the patrol boat circumnavigated with impunity.

Just as Kaz was about to come unglued, the futility of escape a foregone conclusion, Rick grabbed him by the neck forcing his awareness forefront. "God damn it, Kaz, we're closer than we thought!"

Diffused sunlight had cast a pall melding sea and sky into oneness, but out of the blue-gray...an uneven periphery demarcating water and air made manifest a metaphoric silver lining: an unbroken tree line of Georgia pines.

On the third go-around, the captain was already rehearsing his introduction and diktat to board when he sensed a subtle change in the crew's deportment. Having outmaneuvered their adversary, and with the fifty-cal trained at the ready, they expected any minute to see the proverbial white flag of surrender. Yet the call from the bridge that they had visual of the coast coincided with the transformation from sedentary bewilderment to one of defensive comportment spoiling for a fight.

"Another one, aft hatch, captain."

All he could see was a rifle barrel and the top of what looked like a wide brimmed Stetson. *Son of a bitch!* Raised binoculars revealed one under or in the dingy, another taking cover behind the aft mast, cowboy aft hatch, two assumed unarmed at the helm, and one of the two using what was undoubtedly a mountain of contraband as cover had scurried to reposition in the fore hatch. *Enough!* Time was of the essence. An obscured sun hastened pseudo-dusk. There would be no sunset to witness, no afterglow. Transition to darkness would be as if the Big Cheese flipped a circuit breaker.

Will could not shake the unmistakable hoodoo, challenging his credence in the perilous getaway he insisted would not only work, but was the only viable option. He sat perched on the next to last riser, his attention focused on the rest of the crew more than the patrol boat slowing to match their speed off starboard. Of prime concern was Stuart, who had taken position in the forward hatch. Will whistled attention to draw a thumbs-up of readiness, but what he really wanted was Stuart's awareness of his whereabouts. They were about to bring on enough hurt as it was, no need to take on friendly fire as well. Hence the reason for Karl's fedora and a broom wedged upside down, deck level.

Frank Connor looked to his ace marksman, seaman Dobbs, and told him to keep his sight trained on the porthole. "If it opens, shoot." They were now about four miles from land and light was fading as fast as he had reckoned, Captain was in no mood for discourse. Horn cued, he bellowed; "Douse your sails, disarm and desist, and prepare for boarding."

Kaz snatched the white towel and waved. Rick released the wheel waving like a gridiron line judge calling for an official timeout.

Stall tactics. "Mister Blaine, whichever one you are, this is an order not a request! If you don't comply, your father's prized possession will suffer the consequences...and I doubt such a tragedy would bode well his frail condition. You have thirty seconds." The nod was given, and the fifty's sight was leveled on its first objective.

There was nothing Rick or Stuart could say in response. Identified by name...*and how the hell do they know of father's ill health*...continuance of the charade was rendered pointless. It was no longer a matter of "if" they knew, but rather what and how much. The Man held the upper hand. Bluffing was off the table and if they were not already all in, the smart play would have been to fold. But they had to hold; passively resisting, stalling, and drawing ever closer to a perceived sanctuary...yes, the odds were as probable as being dealt that one card to fill inside a royal straight flush.

"Five, four, three..."

Their weaponry was never intended to take on the law. The penalties for smuggling STOLEN contraband of such quantity had a severity undoubtedly earning life...include murder of an officer, and might as well throw away the key, or better yet, throw the switch.

"ONE!" Nothing. It was as if they were chasing a boatload of deaf mutes. *Insolent little bastards.*

The gunner expected the command to open fire. His assistant stood alongside, ammo at the ready.

Yet the aficionado of vintage classics hesitated, the captain appreciating a magnificence seldom seen anymore...*stubborn bastards, surrender!* A stay of execution achieved nothing except to delay the inevitable. *A goddamn, crying shame!* "Ah hell, get on with it." His etched grimace faced what he hoped would not come to pass, and the command to commence firing was given.

Unless directly fired upon, the fifty's function was demolition, literally taking the wind out of their sails. Tracers every tenth round zeroed in on the foremast, the gunner's mate hand-signaling they close to within seventy-five yards. The fusillade splintered the mast, spraying the deck with wooden shards. Closest was Stuart, the barrage forcing him to cower just below deck, gingerly extracting a piece of wood that had impaled his cheek.

For the embattled schooner crew, lethal fire was not an option. There was one key objective imperative it gets taken out: three antennas clustered atop the pilothouse. If fortune was on their side, if somehow they could hold out and make it to shore, communications had to be knocked out pronto. Were local authorities to be given a heads up, the feat of making landfall would be for naught. They were headed for unfamiliar territory in a labyrinth of marshland, and no matter how far inland they could navigate before running aground, having to abandon ship and split up on foot, essentially blind in foreign surroundings...capture would be inevitable.

All ordnance concentrated on the skinny targets. A skilled marksman would be truly tested firing from a moving platform, trying to hit wagging rods. With five amateurs expending copious rounds, eventually one would find its mark, although it was anyone's guess as to who had made the lucky shot.

Their wetsuits were donned, and fins at the ready for when it was time. Nicole double-checked the tanks and regulators while Karl loaded two grenades into his trusty friend. The din of gunfire and holler topside made conversation difficult, but not knowing exactly what was going down was what made it all so unnerving. Nicole's suit was a perfect fit, albeit a tad tight...in places a teenage boy of the same height lacked extra padding, and dangerous curves. The neoprene second skin left nothing to imagine as to form and figure. Karl just stood there watching her cram ten thousand dollar stacks of hundreds into the only belt pack available. Two hundred grand was a tight fit.

"Don't just stand there, Karl...help me zip this closed."

Karl snapped out of it, knelt to assist, and noticed a single tear streaking her face. "It's gonna be okay...I know it. We'll get out of this mess and Will too." Her belt adjusted and clipped around the hourglass waist, pack to the front so as not to interfere with the air tank, Smitty stood and asked she help stash his cash. With his wiry frame, it was an ill fit for a suit that was one size too big, but left ample room for storage. A stack was wedged up each sleeve, two more down the waistband, and the rest around the torso with some slipping around to the backside. Karl looked like a deformed seal, garnering the slightest smirk from Nicole.

"Okay, Lumpy?"

Grinning at the name, while biting his vulgar tongue from referring to a lump not artificial, he pulled tight the jacket so she could zip him up.

Kaboom! A resounding thud quaked the ship. Instantaneous, a gruesome wraithlike shriek jolted Nicole into an embrace. Shattering reverberation, Nicole in his arms, Smitty was electrified. "Hold on."

The rumble of horsepower filled a momentary break in the action.

Rick throttled up and threw up. What had just gone down, besides the foremast felled, threw the rules of engagement overboard. Even with the wind at their back, the fifty's chainsaw precision had hacked away the backside of the trunk and caused the mast to fracture such that it appeared the worst place to be was at the helm. Kaz abandoned Rick, who maintained the wheel in a death grip. Watching the collapse accelerate toward him, an unconscious catholic ritual was exercised for the first time since doubt crept inside his thirteen-year-old noggin. The wind shift, or maybe it was the pitch-roll, inexplicably yanked the imminent crush to port. Kaz was Protestant, and now crushed underneath a tangled mess of shrouds, cordage, and mast.

    The last thing Will witnessed before taking cover was Kaz's wide-eyes as he sprinted and stumbled his way for the stern. The upper section of the mast had karate-chopped into the aft mast's topsail: riggings snapped, spars shattered, the felled mast was split in two...the severed section tumbling end over end in the midst of wires, ropes and crosstrees. The loud crash and macabre sound shuddered the imagination as debris kept him hunkered down.

    "Are you alright?" Nicole's far away inquiry quelled the onset of sickly bitter bile rising.

    "Stay where you are! Just be ready!" Reloaded, Will re-emerged into the fray that was about to turn deadly. Stealing a look, immediately wishing he had not, the mangled body immediately burning an indelible image. Kaz's horrific end spurned a reaction throughout the crew, beginning with Doc who lost it seeing red spewed onto his sweat-soaked tee shirt. A knee-jerk vengeance opened up with lethal intent that drew return fire in-kind. An all-out firefight ensued, with passions blurring reason. Except for Will, who stayed on task: one antenna still remained.

    Two ricochets off the fifty's protective armor kept the gunner crouched, now working over what was left of the aft mast's sails. The sharpshooter and another guardsman each squared off two against one, fore and aft. Two marksmen shielded by a bulwark of thick steel versus four weekend warriors firing helter-skelter from behind wood and a pile of weed...tactical advantage: Coast Guard.

Foremast gone, aft mast mangled, what few sails remained were rendered useless. Riggings were shot to hell; flapping canvas was riddled with holes. Progress had been reduced to a few knots of auxiliary power.

The shoreline was enticing, and the onset of dusk a welcome cover, as delusion trumped rationale and incarceration was inconceivable.

"Skipper! We just lost communications!"

That does it! Signaling a halt, Captain barked new orders: anyone unarmed leave be, if possible shoot to wound and above all, abstain from punching holes in the hull. It was imperative the schooner remain afloat, its cargo evidence validating search and seizure.

Will tipped his hat, and then placed it over the broom's brush, brim level with the deck. All but one round expended, he propped the rifle against the top riser, and aimed. One last look around, everyone still situated, it was time to split.

His bad arm was aching from the awkward firing position, as he hurried an exit leaping half way down...a jolting reminder of why their escape had been devised so.

At the ready, Nicole's abject expression required soft-spoken assurance that was not possible. "Baby, it's gonna be..." one hell of a racket. Lull shattered, Will hurried to quell her quivering and be heard. "It's gotta be this way, I'll be right behind you." He looked to Smitty, who handed over the shotgun, "Don't wait for me, just get her to shore." His lame arm wrapped her waist and he landed a long kiss he hoped did not construe a farewell. Before she could voice misgivings, he backed away and warned they both take cover.

The assistant gunner called out 'Jesus Christ', his index finger having been manicured to the knuckle. Assuming the culprit to be the one who had popped out from behind the tarp-covered mound and let loose a salvo, the fifty cal swung around. There was a brief interlude adjusting to a one-handed feed of ammo.

Sitting with his back up against the pile of hemp, Artimus changed out magazines.

Stuart hoped to draw attention as he fired a couple of rounds and then took cover just as the fifty opened up.

The density was insufficient to withstand the munitions' penetrating force…the loaded gun suddenly weighed a ton. Head dropped chin to chest, seeing his shirt tie dying a far-out burgundy…the last thing Art sensed was the onset of serious heartburn.

Stuart re-emerged to face a sight his brother at the helm was still hollering at, while getting no reply. Blood oozed from the mouth, onto a shirt once white. "Payback, mother fuckers!" Drawing a bead on the gunner whose attention was now turned on the two firing from the stern, the trigger finger a twitch from discharging a head-shot…and *Slip* quavered.

The explosion blasted a gaping five-by-five hole in the transom and decked Jason, who was kneeling behind the lazarette aft end. It also hacked-off Connor, screaming expletives that one of his crew had disobeyed direct orders. Someone had to have fired low into the side and inadvertently hit the fuel tank. The mêlée momentarily suspended, Doc was seen struggling to get out of the suspended dinghy. His leg bloodied, he fell to the deck and crawled for shelter. He was done.

Stuart yelled to his brother, "Can you see Bradford?"

Rick looked: gun unmanned, broom tilted back, hat lying feet away on the deck. He was not about to reveal what was obviously wily subterfuge. The explosive development suddenly occurred to him that it was no accident. He feigned a curt response, "I think he's dead!"

"Hurry!" One last kiss, one last admonition that they go all-out for shore and NOT wait for him, a promise was reiterated that his injured arm might slow him up, but the distance doable.

Both guys hoisted Nicole up, her back splashed by a waterfall of sea water…"I love you." Regulator mouthed, her fins last to be seen.

"Man. Fucked-up trip, huh?" Karl shook Will's hand, "God dammit, you better be right behind us."

Clad only in leggings, his injured arm unable to wrestle into the tight wetsuit's torso portion, no extra fins to be had, a mask and half tank of air off to the side, as soon as his good buddy was shoved out, maybe thirty seconds and ready to go. "I'm not leaving her with you, you nuts?"

A vigorous shoulder slap and Will interlocked his hands. "Come on, Smithers, let's get outta here!"

Face-first into the cascade, Smitty grabbed the jagged beam. On three, Will thrust upwards, the last number fed him a mouthful of water.

There was no time to adjust, the force of water so strong, Smitty had to immediately lunge through the hole. Headfirst, right away he realized why divers always fell backwards. Mask filled with water, tank clunked him in the base of his skull, and the regulator ripped from his mouth. He had to surface hoping no one would see, especially the Coast Guard. Hastily restored, he dove down. Twenty feet out of sight would be sufficient, and he began pursuit of the vague figure that was already well along. *JEEZUS! What the fuck?* Only then, alone with the sound of his breathing, did he become aware of the searing pain emanating from his left leg. Whatever the hell was wrong, the salty water made sure he was aware of it. *Oh well, can't do anything about it now, just get to shore and deal with it.* Unbeknownst to him now, when he had leapt over the transom, a serrated piece of lumber sliced a considerable gash in his calf. Smitty swam to catch up, without a second thought given to the stinging inconvenience. What he DID think about was...*how the hell is HE going to get out on his own? Shit!*

Will had his tank strapped on, mask donned on his forehead...*at least I'm not bogged down with clumsy fins.* Commensurate with the stern's list, gradually becoming more distinctive was the inflow's increase to a deluge. The sputtering sound of mechanical malfunction told him the engine compartment below was flooded. Contemplating his way out, and speculating that his chances of success were bleak at best, Will deliberated, waiting until the aft section was completely submerged. The decision was made for him.

"Hey, Cousteau! You're going down with the ship, asshole!" Rick's response of 'I THINK he's dead', had sounded disingenuous. It was the word "think" that spurred Stuart into investigating his hunch. He stood framed in the sleeping quarter's opening, gun brandished and leaving no doubts as to the implication. "Where is she?"

Will glanced left. Out of reach, the grenade launcher lay upon the reefer mound, maybe a foot above the rising waters.

"Tell me where she is or I'll blow your fucking head off!"

You're going to do that anyways. "It's hot down here, she went for a swim to cool off."

"With your buddy?"

"Before you do what you've been dying to do, tell me why, and don't even bring her into it, since day one you've had it in for me."

"I think you're a smart-ass nobody, not suitable to be my window-washer-lawn-boy. As far as your fantasy girl's concerned, that's all she was." Stuart began sloshing down the slope, weapon raised to drop dead his bane.

"And YOU are a conceited, insecure narcissist. Fuck you!" Response anticipated, Will lunged for the equalizer.

Slip was already dead in the water, its engine kaput. His shirt removed, Jason whirled it in surrender as he knelt by Doc, whose leg bled a rivulet running down the incline to the stern. Jason ripped Doc's jersey for a tourniquet and tied it off just above the wound. Rick also acquiesced, releasing the wheel, hands raised. The detonation knocked him off his feet.

"What the hell?" Captain ordered *Sword* to close in, but not moor. Without a doubt, the schooner was on its way down, all they could do was stand by and fish out the survivors from the water. "God damn!" Once rescue was achieved, at least they could salvage the payload stashed on the bow for evidence, provided it was buoyant.

One of his crew made an off-hand comment. "Well, Captain, it *is* the Fourth of July."

Frank Connor acknowledged the fireworks connotation, "the whole shebang, blown to hell! Prep for recovery."

Waist deep in water, Will leaned against the mound which was beginning to shift and break apart. Floating on his back, Stuart was barely recognizable, face up amidst the floating clumps of weed. A grenade between the eyes at close range had left little to resemble a face. No, it had not exploded until ricocheting up into the hold's overhead.

Crazy son-of-a-bitch, you asked for it. It was the only eulogy he could think of, time was of the essence. His mask pulled down and regulator mouthed, at least he did not have to negotiate a climb. *Where there's a fucking will...and that I am...*

Finless and bearing a cumbersome tank, an arm not worth a damn...making headway through the half submerged opening brought to mind the mighty struggle salmon endure. *No wonder they all die.*

Rick shouted to the Captain, who resembled a damned walrus, "four crew unaccounted for! I'm going below!"

Scurrying the gradient, then down the almost vertical fore stairwell, the sound of everything not nailed down was making a racket in the galley...and that was about as far as he was going. Looking aft, bedding floated in sleeping quarters that were soon to be completely flooded. If he did not turn around and evacuate immediately, he would be joining his brother and the others. Two captains going down with the ship seemed superfluous.

If *Slip* had been a steel-hulled vessel, she would already be gone. Rick pulled himself out of the hatch. He was the only one left onboard. Jason and Doc had slid down the deck and off the back end; the patrol boat was coming around to fish them out of the drink. The angle may have been fifty degrees, shy of perpendicular, but jumping made no sense. Why pinball his way down when the slow ride allowed a little more time of precious freedom? In the onset of twilight, Rick scanned the waters for the four missing. *Sorry dad.*

Repeated calls from the coast guard vessel went unanswered; Rick was lost in reflection. Everything: David. His brother's downward spiral of irrational behavior...from the beginning consumed in some power trip, but when Nicole made the scene...*like Humphrey Bogart in the Caine Mutiny.* Art's body caught in the tangled web of collapsed sail, *probably going down with the ship,* which begged the question...*did ANYONE make it out?*

Will broke the surface and liberated himself from the spent air tank. *Was there that little air left in the used tank?* Maybe three hundred yards, he could have sworn he swam at least half a mile. He was barely able to make out the schooner's bow. *Looks like the head of a whale going down in slow motion after a breaching.* He ducked to avoid the search lights scanning the surface, and wondered who was being plucked out. *Are they dead or alive?* Cloaked in what soon would be nothing but starlight...*last night, closer* *to midnight, before a half moon rising...*the last vestige of light a blessing and a curse. Negotiating the escape undetected, of concern now was blindly navigating a two-mile swim.

Shit, I got to get some kind of bearing! Will treaded water, raising just enough to glimpse the last of a fading coastline. The underwater swim had been entirely executed in a painful breaststroke, dictating he now commence a backstroke. So, lying on his back, it was crucial he pick out whatever early evening stars were visible...and focus. A foreboding washed over him with the waves: where he surfaced in relationship to the schooner was nowhere near where he had intended, having executed a wide arc to the right. *That's why I wasn't as far away as I thought! I'll have to alternate back and breaststrokes to compensate.* It was painfully obvious his bad arm was not up to the task.

There! Two bright stars. There'll be more, provided that inland cloudbank doesn't make it east overhead...just hold off till I can hear the breakers... Will looked one last time to where he had seen the coastline, now no longer visible, laid back and plotted a direction off the two stars. It would be a slow pace: slow enough for his strong arm not to overpower whatever he could get out of his left arm. *Dammit, I sure could use some fins!* He settled into machine mode and methodically chopped at the surface. If he could just separate his humanity from the exercise, then maybe the work would be complete, and the excruciating pain behind him, by the time his back skidded against rock and shells....

The Coast Guard's searchlights were focused on the immediate area where the schooner was no more. Searching for survivors, while slowly motoring through debris floating to the surface, they retrieved bundles of contraband jettisoning themselves upward. Waiting... waiting for bodies. Doc's leg was being attended to. Frank Connor was cordial, more like entertaining guests. Rick and Jason fielded some questions, only those the Captain proved he already KNEW the scoop on...requests, not demands, details if they would be so gracious to offer freely. Their story was truly enthralling, even if devoid mention of any names.

"Captain, he's stable, but going to need surgery. Main artery got nicked. How long are we planning to hang around?"

"One hour." Frank returned to his detainees, "You guys really complicated matters taking out our comm."

It would be a mad dash back to port. *If we had a radio, we could call Tailfin to return to sea ASAP and continue the search throughout the night. Come morning, comb the beach.*

"Damn it all!"

Nicole and Karl had shed their tanks when the first sound of breakers was heard, less evidence to hide. They were winded. Silence spoke volumes...he knew she was consumed with doubt. *Hell, if he even made it out!* By the sound of the distant waves they still had a ways to go. A slow, methodical stroke allowed him enough breath to distract her, so he decided to talk her through the last leg of the swim with another chronicle. Only this one was not meant to be funny, laughter would only make the swim more arduous. He just began with how he met Will, dissecting him over a pool table.

Describing a technical cross-corner bank shot was not having the intended effect. Nicole heard his voice, but was not listening. The increasing sound of surf more comforting, though insufficient; imagery of her lover altered between a lifeless body floating suspended inside a ship at rest on the sea floor and one of being lost at sea, unable to overcome the outgoing tide. *Or, did they pluck him out of the water. Is he dead or alive?*

The exclamation of 'Jesus!' included in a pool game was oddly out of place and served to momentarily disrupt her contemplative supposition. She looked back.

Karl was treading water, whites of his eyes the only distinct feature. The pain in his leg which he had grown accustomed to all of a sudden hurt like a mother-fucker, but what really alarmed him was the lightening fast tug that yanked him to a standstill. "Oh shit." A freaky sensation of something very big passed just below his finned feet, and swept sideways with the undercurrent. Great White, Tiger, Bull, whatever it was had been savoring the blood-scent trail emanating from the leg gash. *Didn't seawater cauterize?*

"What is it? Come on, we're almost there!"

Mustering all the poise he could while being quite helpless, expecting any second to be his last, he did his best not to panic Nicole. "Nik. You need to get to shore now. I just got a cramp, but I think we swam into some jellyfish. I'll be right behi..."

What she saw and heard was something of which recurring nightmares are made. Karl ascended briefly, and then uttered a guttural groan that was punctuated by the distinct snap of bone. His sudden and quick disappearance witnessed close up by Nicole equated to a lifetime of horror that was over before she could even catch her breath. The fact that such little splash was made and the attacker never even showed itself...only pulled its prey under...made it all the more harrowing. It only served to leave Nicole wondering if, when, she would be next.

Nicole was maybe the length of an Olympic swimming pool from terra firma; she may have set a new world record for fifty meters. She felt as though she held her breath the whole way, not intentionally, she simply could not bring herself to relax enough to draw in the air. The hideous sounds of anguish she never imagined a human could produce...pure shock made the swim never to be recalled. Literally swimming onto the beach, her hands clawing in the sand, feet still kicking wildly...like a sea turtle hell bent on nesting, she crawled the slant of cool wet sand until her fingers felt sugar. Saltwater that had been gulped in sheer panic was disgorged with a grotesque recall, her mind flipping to a sanctuary only shock could provide. *Got to find something to do. I know...*

As if in a dream, she drifted toward the dunes to bury her fins and mask, and extract the discomforting sheaves of bills underneath the wetsuit and cram the pack girding her waist. *Maybe by then, he'll come ashore.*

Will discarded his mask and even thought of ditching the four packets of hundred dollar bills tucked down each leg of the wetsuit. *Anything to streamline, too much drag.*

But the effort it would take to tread water while struggling with retrieval from skintight neoprene...*no way.*

The underwater escape had done-in what little use his injured shoulder had to offer. Now reduced to an off-kilter backstroke, or a half-assed sidestroke on his right side against an outgoing tide, progress was painfully slow and unintentionally skewed in a southward arc. Unable to anticipate dark swells...mouthfuls were ingested and vision was blurred from the brine. The onset of irrational thought flashed snippets of a wayward life yearned to be forgotten. Will began a mental argument with himself: contention over decisions made, opportunities pissed away. *Stupid son-of-a-bitch. You don't deserve to make it.*

A lonely whisper rustled marsh reeds and an isolated stand of Georgia pine, as Nicole shivered in the balmy waft. Alone and with nowhere to go, she watched the Coast Guard's running light fade south...*you promised me, Will Bradford.* Rising from the depths of her despair, forced recall beyond the image etched in her mind...*oh no, please, not him too.* She focused on the fuzzy end of the coastline, and set out in a jog north towards what she thought to be a channel. It was at least two miles of searching. She would go back and forth until...*until what...until forever.*

Her heart pounding, the sandy sprint was filled with 'what-ifs'. She had reached the beginning of the end. A stranger in a foreign land, alone, she would either find him...*please be alive...*or walk into her next life. Afraid.

Like the winds that whipped through the palms, her thoughts were random and fleeting as Nicole felt she would be swept away to god-knows-where. She silently screamed "Gimme Shelter", and imagined his lips anchoring her to... *HIM*.

Paralleling the beach just beyond the waves, the sidestroke was no longer sustainable as Will gave in to sleep. Rolling over face down, smothered in a liquid pillow, HER face appeared, only to blend into the creeping unconsciousness.

Nicole was now frantic: fast walk, sudden stops, and full out runs, only the rising moon splashing a glimmer of hope and keeping her from falling apart. *There's no way he could be this far.* She stopped to catch her breath and wipe her watery eyes. *O my god...there*! Not twenty feet from the shore, cresting on a curling breaker. Flinging the satchel, she dove headlong into the surf.

As if the sea was discarding a nuisance, the limp body tumbled into her arms. Refusing to think the unthinkable, afraid to speak and not get a response, a frenzied recovery crash-landed her on her back. Will's dead weight fell on top of her, the last wave body-slamming the wind out of her, it was all she could do to drag him up to level ground. She turned him around so his head tilted back slightly on the downward slope, and commenced resuscitation.

Chest pumps were followed by mouth-to-mouth...over and over. Nicole lost count, but refused to quit. "Come on, fight, damn you! Don't leave me!" She continued the routine through a flow of tears, denying a reality unimaginable. It was not awareness of being marooned; after all that had happened, she really could not give a damn about her plight, whether she lived or died was of no import. Exhausted, she paused to get her breath before resuming the lost cause. Overcome with grief and the sight of him absent his essential being, Nicole lost it. With hands raised to the heavens in damnation of a god she no longer cared to recognize, utter anguish brought her full weight crashing down with clenched fists slamming his chest: "NO GOD, NO!"

CHAPTER THIRTY-FOUR

Off in the dunes the Grateful Dead crooned "Till the Morning Comes". Billy 'Sky Pilot' Vaughn and his woman Millie 'Moon Shadow' Hines were laid back and mellowed in the van. The side door was open as they stared into the embers of a low fire, the joint passing time inconsequential. Garcia's melodic riffs glided across the salty air and guided them through their after-dinner high. Moon's special garden salad, sprinkled with diced mushrooms of a certain variety not found in stores, was accompanied by foraged clams and a few crabs not quick enough to dodge these diners. A hearty meal cooked to perfection...life was good.

The previous day on their quest to leave civilization for a while, during an early morning pit stop on a lonely country road just to stretch the legs, the drifters had trespassed onto a fenced-in cow pasture in need of one more strand of wire. Strolling through the morning dew, karmic blessings were easy pickings. A pocket full of fungi and they were back on the road.

Just before crossing over Manhead Sound, a roadside stand of fresh produce spoke to them it was their last chance to stock up. They were right on with their assumption. Crossing over the sound onto Saint Simons, the natural world took over. Soon the two-lane pavement gave way to a backwater dirt road and from there on the map was of no use. A myriad of sandy trails branched off into the tall rush. Sky piloted one such path so narrow, marsh grass chafing the van's sides; he tried not to get uptight. The artistic mural was so painstakingly wrought, imparting panache to an otherwise ordinary Econoline: *man, I hope the lacquer holds up!*

Somewhere between seventh heaven and Moon Shadow's impromptu swirl around the campfire, sky-high Pilot was digging wavy tracks flowing from the twirling gypsy skirt.

The groove abruptly crashed with the chilling intrusion, a scream undeniably NOT wildlife. "Hey babe, did you hear that?" Billy lunged into the cockpit to eject.

Flower child's spirit dance was halted in mid-stride, the unnatural sound had her hugging herself in cold comfort. "Oh man, what a bummer, whatever that was." The only response was footsteps. "Hey, where you goin'? Wait for me!"

"I think someone's in trouble, come on!" Billy was already on the move, his senses acute, even if somewhat skewed.

Nicole was all over Will. Ecstatic, crying, she did not care about the saltwater-vomit. So violent had been her anguish, his heart was jump-started by the blow. The result had been a hijacking of Will's passage to another realm.

He was still semi-unconscious. His throat and lungs burned from saltwater and bile. *What, how, where is this place? And who's this beautiful angel?* He rolled away from her, the ocean's nutrients clearly not suited for human consumption. Nicole straddled him, pushing his hands into the middle of his back and upwards.

"Whoa! Hold up." Billy stood just outside the tall marsh grass. Millie ran into his straight-arm. From their vantage point, and their mind state, what was seen looked like something upon which one should not be intruding.

"Weird." Millie tilted her head as if doing so would add perspective to the human art form oddly changing shape. "Is it some new kind of yoga?"

"Might be some kinky beach sex. Far out."

They stood in wonder, stoned enough not to feel shame in being voyeurs.

"Looks like freaking cat woman," muttered Billy.

Only when the person on top stood, dragging the unresponsive body and then falling to their knees and rolling it over, did their speculation entertain the macabre.

"Maybe we mind our own business and just go." Millie was sure they were witnesses to a murder scene.

"No, Moon, I don't feel it, not getting those vibes. Let's check it out and if it's not cool, then we'll split."

So occupied with reviving, then monitoring his vitals, Nicole did not even look up when approached. The offer of assistance was answered by a curt "yes", followed by a plea they help get her get him off the beach.

Whomever this mysterious woman, clad in black second skin, and the dude strangely outfitted only in leggings, something told the goodly stoned Samaritans to refrain from prying too much. Each woman took a leg and when Billy dead-lifted the top, only then was it confirmed they were rescuing and not burying. Will's moan solicited a caution from Nicole, "be careful with his left shoulder, please."

Clothed in a tie-dye tee shirt and ragged jeans, Will lay on the mattress, covered by a motley blanket. The loaned shirt would have been a perfect fit, but Will had lost ten to fifteen pounds since they had gone to sea. When Nicole peeled off his wetsuit bottoms, asking the couple to please back away under the guise of privacy, she deftly seized the eight wads of hundreds and transferred them to her bulging satchel. She was feeding him sips of water, keeping a bucket close at hand just in case, when Moon Shadow leaned in the van. "Here hon, change into these and there's tea brewing. I'll watch over him."

Nicole returned from the shadows, as Sky Pilot rose from the campfire and extended a cup of herbal tea. Flickering firelight danced across a face most beguiling, and a body accentuated in gypsy fashion as cruelly undersized. He was quite content just listening to the snap-crackle of tinder while stealing glances at the pensive woman, her engaging eyes fixed on the glowing embers.

In Nicole's mind, she précised all that had happened: so mind-boggling, a sudden fear settled over her as she grasped at the possibility she was about to wake up. *Oh my god, a dream?*

Billy saw her sway, catching her from getting burned. Millie's regard shifted away from the patient to her man - whose attentiveness roused a twinge of jealousy. She hurried to help get her into the van.

Pre-dawn, when whispers are enough to overwhelm the stillness, Moon and Sky were awoken in their shared bedroll just outside the van. Comfy warm, they lay there trying, but unable, to decipher what was being said.

Nicole assured Will the story she had concocted would sell. He insisted that ten thousand dollars would buy them a one-way trip, but it would have to be immediate, no bullshitting around. It was imperative that they be far from this place come daylight.

"Go baby, do your thing." Will was perspiring profusely, and shivering. A fever, dry heaves, glassy eyes; Nicole kissed his clammy forehead and whispered she had it all under control. "Try and rest."

Stoking the few embers, and snapping twigs to add so she could boil water, Nicole pretended to be quiet, but in essence hoped to rouse them. The pretenders startled her with a groggy "what time is it?"

Nicole tactfully conducted the ensuing conversation while tending the small fire, leading them to ask what happened. She told them a story:

There had been a fire in the galley of their sailboat...they were asleep topside. Land was barely seen on the horizon, and neither of them thought there was a chance, but they had no choice except to try. Spent tanks, masks and fins ditched the last mile; they got separated in the dark.

Nicole's story about their pleasure craft sinking and the long swim to shore was a hard sell. Her mellifluous accent had an edge of urgency to it as she sidestepped the issue of Will's shoulder wound. Ensuing queries were fended off either with outright lies, or evasion through feigned confusion and shock from the ordeal.

The couple was cool, even though they sensed her story was just that, a fabricated story. They too lived outside the law. Existing for the moment, mother earth their provider and sovereignty, they subscribed wholly to the dictate "turn on, tune in, and drop out."

The moment of truth came when Nicole popped the question. "You've been so kind, I hate to ask you this, but we really need another, significant favor." She paused.

The duo was still nestled in the bedroll. Billy replied, "Shoot."

"We need to get out of here now. New York city is where we're going."

The request bolted them both upright, Moon was unmindful that her breasts flashed Nicole an eyeful. "You've got to be kidding!"

Billy waited for confirmation that it was a joke. Nicole just stared at them with pleading eyes. "Jesus, lady, we just got down here from Ohio. We barely have enough money for gas, pretty much livin' off the land." Lured into doe-like eyes that were unflinching, he waited for her response, content to just consider her gorgeousness. Moon had to elbow a jab to snap him out of it. "Ah, miss, we'd sure like to help but we..."

Like a panther closing on its prey, Nicole crept on hands and knees to kneel before them. From underneath Moon's loaned dress that Bill never realized looked so good, she presented the two of them a little something to consider.

Professed anti-capitalists, immune to avarice or anything reeking of material gain, these nonconformist, anti-establishment, free spirits were prideful of their self-sustained existence. Billy leafed through the Ben Franklins like a deck of cards, only instead of fifty two, he was blown away. "A hundred...hundreds? Geez, miss, we don't even know your names!"

"That's because we have no names. No home, no past...only the present." Nicole sweetened the pot,

"Consider this compensation for the inconvenience imposed, and your kindness. You take this money and put it away for a rainy day, we'll cover the gas and any food you require for the trip."

"That's it? You're not going to tell us what this is all about? The story you gave us, while interesting, just doesn't come up smelling quite right to justify all this. And what, do we just call you 'man and woman'?"

"Trust me, you don't want or need to know anything. It's for your own good."

There was a fleeting glance, the small space in time that was afforded to consult one another. The silent exchange was mutual agreement: *after all, there was no shame in lending a helping hand to your fellow man in need, right?* Principles waived in order to accommodate their guests, Sky Pilot rose to the occasion. Clad only in his underwear, he proclaimed they pack up, abandon camp straight away, and venture north.

A reflective Moon beamed at their fortuitous gain, which she clutched tightly between her cupped hands. "Wherever we go, there we are. Let's split this scene."

Will was still sweating out the effects of an unhealthy overdose of saltwater. Nicole was just flat out exhausted. Their navigators had penciled out the route to New York...so simple a stoned monkey could find its way. Retreating the same way they came in, once on I-95 it would be a mind-numbing drive straight into the Big Apple. The Pilot's reassuring words to his passengers mimicked the Greyhound commercial: just relax and leave the driving to us."

The way out back to civilization was jostling, not conducive to rest. Will fumbled around and found a little something he tossed into the cockpit. Soon the van's aromatic incense was overwhelmed with smoke and both driver and shotgun Millie could not stop mumbling superlatives. "Trippy...far out...righteous, man...outta sight...where the fuck did you get this from?"

Offers to partake were declined; however, the back of the van was nonetheless permeated by the odiferous onslaught. Moon became entertainment director, filling the void with tunes.

By the time they accessed the interstate, their guides were wrecked speechless, and total concentration was required in order to maintain the speed limit in the slow lane. This gave Will and Nicole a marginal amount of comfort to check in with each other after all the intensity that had gone down.

Now they lay together, staring out a small, customized side-window to the world. First light revealed a passing countryside of misty meadows as the Moody Blues serenely spoke truth that "Dawning Is The Day". They were leaving behind a past full of turbulence and nightmares, having been found and welcomed into a bright, new day offering promise and hope. The scene before them held the stark resemblance of a crisp morning newness that follows an intense trip. The light was brighter, colors seemed so much more vivid, and the edges of things spoke out their own stories of what they defined. The result was a new appreciation, a liberating rebirth into a second chance.

As they held each other closely, eyelids became as heavy blankets and the light outside turned to lit dreams.

So deep the sleep, both Carolinas and Virginia would pass before awakening to new horizons.

Tailfin redeployed to the scene of a floating buoy that had been left behind to mark the spot where the schooner went down. A shore party dispatched and met with local authorities to comb the beach. What was found raised more questions than answers. One particular piece of evidence, revolting in that it was just that...a piece of some poor bastard washed ashore. The upper torso was missing an arm; the frozen expression on John Doe's face told the tale of what sheer terror had preceded his demise. The gross morbidity left the discoverer balled-up, speechless, and bathed in puke.

Up and down the beach it was an Easter egg hunt of scattered currency and an occasional clump of soggy cannabis. One diver's fin found retreating in the receding surf. Someone yelled out a find of diver's gear that was unearthed near the tall marsh grass. This led to a recon which followed tracks inland to a makeshift campsite: tire tracks, fire extinguished, but the slightest vestige of warmth remained. *Who, how many, where...*

Frank Connor had returned with the *Tailfin* crew. The realization that quite possibly someone somehow evaded capture; the whole incident went down NOT according to plan, he was beyond tired. Kicking the ashes instead of himself, he knew then and there his last duty before resigning his commission would be an extensive report filed culminating a lifetime of service on a dismal note. *Fuck it all. I'm going fishing.*

Only brief pit stops for fuel, restroom functions, and one serious case of the munchies, and the troubadours negotiated the fifteen-hour trip in great haste. Uneventful, as tedious as interstate travel is, the only wonders to be seen were unnatural ones: billboards, road signs, and so many different states' license plates picked out to pass the time. Sky Pilot and Moon Shadow always preferred secondary road travel, pure country. Only one time did the cockpit experience turbulence, bumming out a righteous high: a nerve-wracking visual at the state line between the two Carolinas. A billboard, the size of a drive-in movie screen, depicted a rider cloaked in a white sheet with fiery red eyes peering out from underneath a conical hood and sitting rigid on a pale horse. The caption: "Welcome to Klan Country."

Remembering what one of his fellow longhair Yanks told him prior to leaving Ohio, "Man, you better be careful down South. The only thing those redneck boys hate worse than a hippie is a black man. Remember Easy Rider?" Sky did not have to request, Moon immediately rummaged through their belongings piled behind the seats and found his old Cleveland Indians ball cap. She steered, and he twisted his mane into a tail and hid it all underneath the hat so that he was sporting whitewalls around the ears.

Twilight in Time Square gave way to neon lights, a sea of humanity hustling and bustling, a thousand aromas emanating from the eateries...the din of a city just beginning to unwind and crank up for Friday night revelry. Cabbies honked or were being hailed, street vendors pitched their trade; it was a veritable cornucopia of sensory overload.

"This is why I don't like the city!" Billy was stressed out, traffic was insane and not knowing where the hell he was going only made matters worse. "Shit!" He almost clipped a taxi, drawing welcoming hand gestures and unintelligible curses from the driver. "Alright, we're north on seventh-avenue, gonna pull up at the next block and that's the end of the road for us."

Will and Nicole were ready. Moon Shadow's hairbrush did what little it could for Nik. Even though she felt like a vagabond, she still could hold a candle to the public at-large. Will had recouped enough to assimilate their surroundings. He was already assessing their predicament.

Got to find a place to stay for the night. Get something to eat. Tomorrow we check the ads for a place to rent...and buy my baby some clothes! Man, she's gorgeous, even in this condition. I'm sure I look like the walking dead...thankfully it's New York City, and we'll blend right in with the freaks and street people...

The van pulled into the first slot available to off load their passengers. A bit weak-kneed, Will hopped out the rear doors, extending Nicole a hand. To say they were traveling light was an understatement. Only the clothes on their backs and a satchel, which Will slung over his good shoulder. The thought he did not want to worry her with was their precarious situation as strangers humping a shit load of money.

"Thanks, man." Will grasped Sky Pilot's hand.

Slipfinger Nine

"Nah, man. Thank you. You and your pretty woman take care."

"Sorry to screw up your expedition. Where to now?"

"Sure as hell not going back where we just came from. Guess we'll hit the Lincoln Tunnel and head north. I hear Maine's pretty far out in the summer time." Bill looked at Will. "Man, you look like shit. Cold Italian pizza?"

"Could use a lemon squeeza. We'll be all right, thanks again. Happy trails to you and your woman."

Moon and Nicole hugged goodbyes as the Grateful Dead played on for the umpteenth time. The rear door closed and the Pilot was back in the cockpit. Moon bid a peace sign as her man re-entered the hectic melee of honking traffic. So apropos the artwork displayed on the back, Will could not help but chuckle a response: "You got that right." Bearded Mister Natural strode across the double doors, leading foot oversized, a parting admonition bid the embraced couple: 'KEEP ON TRUCKIN.'

"What's right, sweetie?" Nicole was concerned he was still delirious.

"Everything, Nik. Come on, let's grab a cab."

Jason Douglass

CHAPTER THIRTY-FIVE

Love and priorities that come with starting a new life from scratch sustained them through those first few days. It filled the void of a drab, sparsely furnished shit hole they leased for a week. The temporary living quarters could be best described as the spitting image of The Honeymooner's bleak stage setting.

She took cabs from one end of Manhattan to the other, getting dropped off and taking long walks to scope out areas appealing to her, providing good vibes to both, and which made logistical sense. They targeted a reasonable distance to access NYU's school of law, Broadway, and the fashion district.

Finally, having worked their way down from Central Park's ridiculously expensive digs, they had run out of real estate. Sitting on a bench overlooking Battery Park, Will scanned the New York Times rental section. They had both come to agree the up and coming, albeit borderline illegal So-Ho district fit the bill: a youthful atmosphere, artsy, a collage of individualism and industrialism that logistically made sense.

"Oh my God!" Nicole had just set down the entertainment/living section, and grabbed the front page when a headline caught her eye:

```
Calamity on the High
Seas:
```

Slipfinger Nine

> **Modern Day pirates' bold scheme foiled, See A4.**

There it was, fourth page near the bottom. The article's account, disputable in part from what they had actually lived, caused a flashback they both had purposefully not broached. Only the part detailing the search and recovery of the rogue buccaneers caught their imagination. Who died, who was now in custody, and who besides they were unaccounted for? Information had been gleaned from the initial interrogation, but identities could not be revealed at this time until families were notified. "Four confirmed dead." Will's thoughts went to David and Kaz. The brief caption of a disturbing discovery washed up on the beach brought a shudder to Nicole, *who was the fourth?* "Three missing." Well, two were sitting on a park bench a thousand miles away and would soon cease to exist, and Will knew the third one. Except for uttering "Stuart," he spared her the details. *They'll find the bastard when they dive the wreck.*

Simple process of elimination left them pondering: *Rick, Jason, Doc, and Artimus...which one didn't make it?*

By the end of August, all that was needed, and wanted, had been accomplished. A quaint row-apartment, altered identities: names, social securities, places and dates of birth, appearances slightly modified, shopping for stylish new threads in New York...orgasmic for her. Important contacts were established, offers for modeling and even an audition for a minor role in a Broadway musical, her aura and poise opened doors before she knocked.

His full head of hair now grown out, yet stylish, the once long-haired hippie gave way to a new man with purpose, he bought his way into NYU. First semester was to start September 15th. He also got a job driving a cab. What better way to learn the ins and outs of New York City? There was only one thing that needed to be done to consummate a successful new beginning.

Stealth, ingenuity, and the greasing of a few palms, made the lies seem even whiter. During the few days he had disappeared, it was a necessary cover. The clandestine plan was so outlandish, yet fitting the circumstances in which they met, and all they endured to come to this juncture.

It was the second Saturday in September, the 11th being the only day those he had made a deal with could accommodate his request, a romantic evening was to kick off a series of surprises. White linen and red wine was the backdrop. Her eyes glimmered wide in the candle light when she was presented a substantial diamond ring; his proposal answered by the most beautiful expression and a passionate "yes, I will."

After a dinner filled with talk of future plans, dreams set firm as goals; they walked a perfect sundown two blocks to another surprise, a bridal boutique he paid extra to remain open. On arrival, her remark was spoken only in jest..."Sweetheart, we should have done this BEFORE I ate too much!"

Slipfinger Nine

The big day arrived. No one in their right mind would dare wake a bride-to-be at four in the morning, but the groom's wits were immersed in the moment. Everything had to come off without a hitch.

Staying true to form, from their unique encounter on a far away beach, all the way to the present, nothing in their newfound lives resembled a norm. Back-ass-wards, he carried her down the one flight of stairs to an idling yellow cab. The driver, already paid handsomely, had no problem playing limo chauffeur: a kind smile was offered and a "good happy morning to you, miss". Once situated, he closed the door and with no further words drove them to a destination that was as high as it was far.

"You look dashing, my love. You're not going to tell me where we're going?"

He looked at his stunning bride. Bouquet in hand, hair done up in a French twist, the delicate strands dangled around a face too pretty to veil. The dress, exquisite in simplicity and fit, lacked a train by design. Where they had to go and the fact that only two other people would be there to witness the union, *WHY?*

The route to their ambition was strategic in a roundabout way. It was all part of the plan, subterfuge. Navigating the side streets, even an alleyway, was a cinch considering the city had just begun to stir. Canyon walls of brownstone and mid-rise structure hid the soaring towers until arrival.

"Good luck you two."

The groom's hand extended, and she emerged speechless at the sky-scraping edifice. Looking up, dizzy with wonder, it appeared she was going to collapse backwards. The arm around her waist steadied her, and he

Jason Douglass

escorted her into the glassed-in lobby where two men stood waiting.

The burly man tipped his hard hat. "Well, young couple, are you ready to go to the top of the world?" It had cost a hefty backhander getting the building superintendent to usher them to heights still only allowed access by those in the construction trade with permits.

The other man, diminutive in comparison, introduced himself as Pastor Wiley. Smiling, partly due to the uniqueness of the ceremony he had been paid well to perform, affably stated: "Let us rise to greet a marvelous sunrise, bearing witness to this special day."

Though the ride up was nonstop, it was still a good while getting there. It was long enough for the superintendent to fill the void with facts: South Tower was structurally complete, but would not be occupied until the first of the year. The North Tower already was a third occupied. One hundred ten stories, they would be one thousand sixty two feet up and outside on the observation deck. "Hope you're not afraid of heights."

Two-thirds of the way up, the big man noticed a slight contortion in her beautiful face. "Miss, you might want to yawn or kind of snap your jaw."

"You okay, baby?"

She nodded yes, saying her ears just popped. Ten floors from the top, more as a distraction, he asked her if she still remembered the vows they had rehearsed. The soft smile told him she in fact did.

The venue was the ceremony. Music was substituted by a whispering, cool breeze. The break of dawn rising from the Atlantic provided a most divine light. The couple gathered hand-in-hand before the parson. The superintendent stood by, serving as witness and ring bearer.

"Do you, Ethan, take this woman to be your wife?"

"I do."

"Do you, Marissa, take this man to be your husband?"

"I do."

The ceremony was cut and dry on direct request. No benediction. Customary marriage instructions needed not be explained. Rings were exchanged in silence; the formality of "with this ring" would be replaced at the conclusion with their own, chosen vows."

"I now pronounce you husband and wife."

Marissa handed off the bouquet so that they could hold hands. The recitation had been chosen: excerpts from The Moody Blues' *The Dream*. Each line of verse was alternated, the final one said in unison. Ethan commenced with acknowledgement of the noble bird on high...

Each placed their hands, and at that same time their trust, into each other's...it was a journey committed to, and fully embraced. From hereinafter, they each would provide cover, standing solidly back to back. It was the best defensive position, they, and best way forward amidst a world of unknowns. How beautiful to not have to worry about just one front...when there are so many already.

And that very end was a new beginning, as they intently looked forward through each other's eyes and boldly stepped over the threshold, and into their dream...

Jason Douglass

About the Author:

There should have been a marker posted at the college entrance, along with a cast-iron Rod Serling sculpture, admonishing: " That's the signpost up ahead - your next stop, the Twilight Zone!" After that momentous period of personal growth, a brief stint at college that was abruptly cut short with a 'get out of jail free card' precipitating an arbitrary excommunication from New England, my REAL education began as a sojourner in search of The Lost Chord...a road full of potholes, twists, turns, and more than once a flip of the coin, all of which directed me through crossroads that have miraculously delivered me to this current juncture in life. A famous baseball player once said: "When you come to a fork in the road, take it!" Taking many more lefts than rights, I somehow am still here to testify that *life is good*.

I look back at a turbulent past and can only be thankful for all that -- who -- I have: married, finally to someone I don't deserve, and three unique lads at 42, 24, and 17. That ought to tell you something of a life unscripted and out of the ordinary.

Made in the USA
Lexington, KY
21 January 2015